HATTER M

THE

NATURE

OF

WONDER

VOLUME THREE

To the Earth
and her infinite wonders...

HATTER M

THE
NATURE
OF
WONDER

VOLUME THREE

Written by Frank Beddor & Liz Cavalier
Art by Sami Makkonen

AUTOMATIC
PICTURES
PUBLISHING

Hatter M: The Nature of Wonder

Volume 3

Writers
Frank Beddor
Liz Cavalier

Art
Sami Makkonen

Cover Art
Vance Kovacs

Letterer
Tom B. Long

Editor
C.J. Wrobel

Reconnaissance & Analysis
Nate Barlow

White Flower Raconteur
Miss Emily McGuiness

Guest Writer/Researcher
Christopher Monfette

Logo Designed by
Christina Craemer

Interiors Designed by
Vera Milosavich

Institute Artists
Brian Flora
Tae Young Choi
Catia Chien
Vance Kovacs

www.lookingglasswars.com

The Looking Glass Wars® is a trademark of Automatic Pictures, Inc.
Copyright © 2010 Automatic Pictures, Inc. All rights reserved.

"Prologue", from *ArchEnemy: The Looking Glass Wars*®, *Book Three* by Frank Beddor,
Copyright © 2009 by Frank Beddor. *The Looking Glass Wars*® is a trademark of
Automatic Pictures, Inc. Used by permission of Dial Books for Young Readers,
A Division of Penguin Young Readers Group, A Member of Penguin Group
(USA) Inc., 345 Hudson Street, New York, NY 10014. All rights reserved.

From *Princess Alyss of Wonderland* by Frank Beddor, illustrated by Catia Chien
and Vance Kovacs, Copyright © 2007 by Frank Beddor. Used by permission
of Dial Books for Young Readers, A Division of Penguin Young Readers Group,
A Member of Penguin Group (USA) Inc., 345 Hudson Street, New York, NY
10014. All rights reserved

Printed in Korea

1

978-0-9818737-5-6

This is not the story
of a Mad Hatter

Nature does not hurry, yet everything is accomplished. —Lao Tzu

Thank You

Scholars, Antiquarians,
Reasoners, Logicians, Rationalists,
and Knights Errant

Contents

The Quest

The Rest

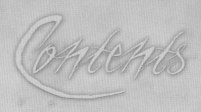

Who are we?

The Hatter M Institute for Paranormal Travel is a devout assemblage of radical historians, cartographers and geographic theorists pledged to uncovering and documenting through the medium of sequential art the full spectrum journey of Hatter Madigan as he traversed our world from 1859-1872 searching for Princess Alyss of Wonderland.

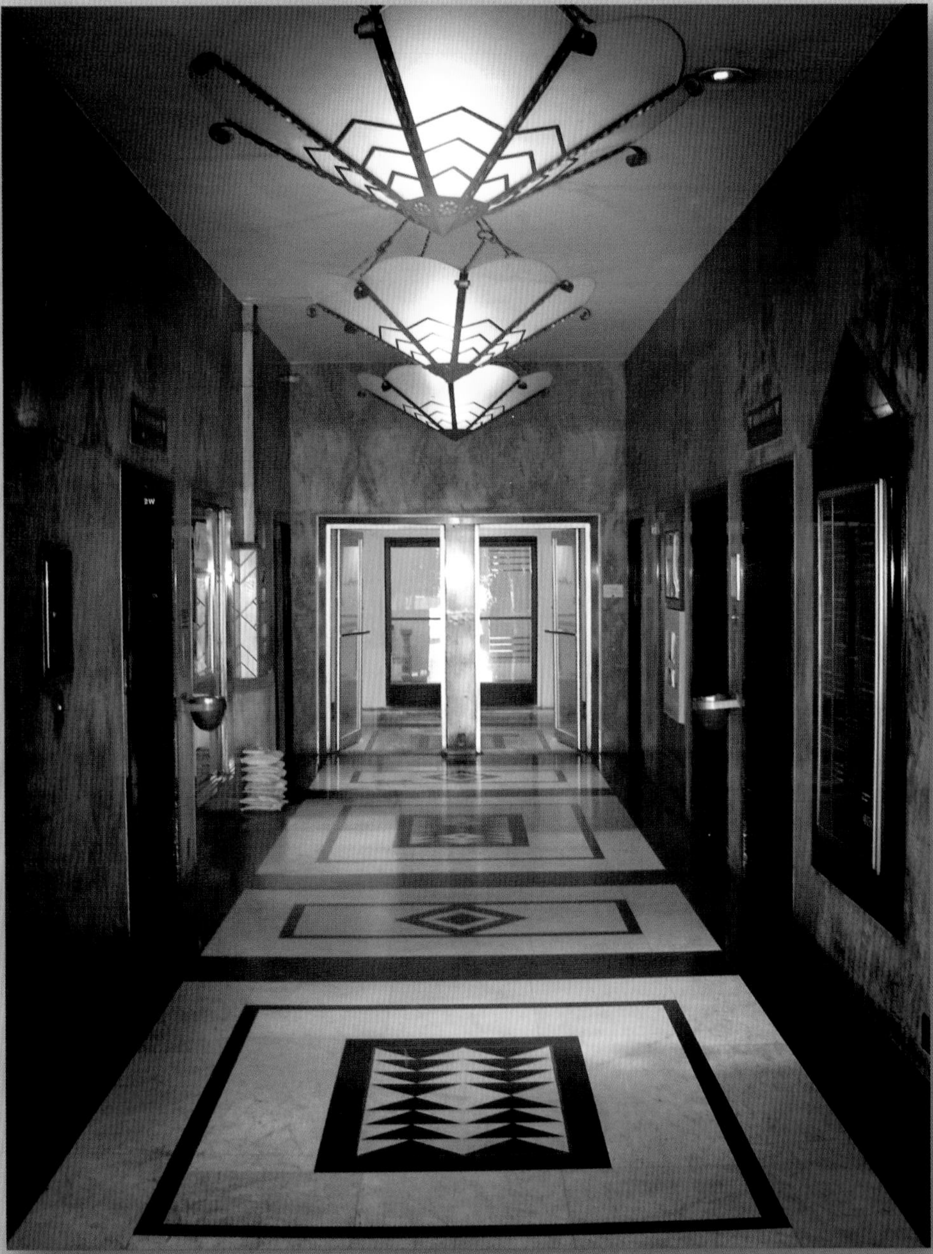

You have dared to cross the threshold and enter our realm.

Come...let us take you to drink from the well.

Introduction

Greetings fellow searchers and welcome to *Hatter M: The Nature of Wonder, Volume 3*, detailing and mapping the ongoing adventures of Royal Bodyguard Hatter Madigan, expert bladesman, and ranking High Cut of the Wonderland Millinery.

Pssst! Would you like to know a secret? Of course you would! We at the Institute believe few things in life are more satisfying than discovering a hidden history, cracking a code or knowing the specific knock that will open the door to illumination. Ahhhh the shiver of seeing a dusty, crumbling file authoritatively stamped TOP SECRET only to boldly open it and expose the truth for all to see. Imagine the volume you now hold in your hands is stamped TOP SECRET and that when you open it you find yourself travelling through 1865 America with Hatter Madigan in search of answers and finding secrets.

What hush hush 19th century 'X-Files' bureau invented the ray rifle and steampowered rollarskates? Which president's zeal for the unknown and passion for fine headwear launched the search for White Illumination? Where did the famous 1960's slogan 'Flower Power' originate and what in the world does it mean? What is hidden behind the locked door in Death Valley, California?

Now close your eyes and make a wish. If you wished for a secret map to guide you to the very nature of wonder then you are in luck. The map lies within. See you on the other side!

The Hatter M Institute for Paranormal Travel

What makes the desert beautiful is that somewhere it hides a well. —ANTOINE DE SAINT-EXUPERY

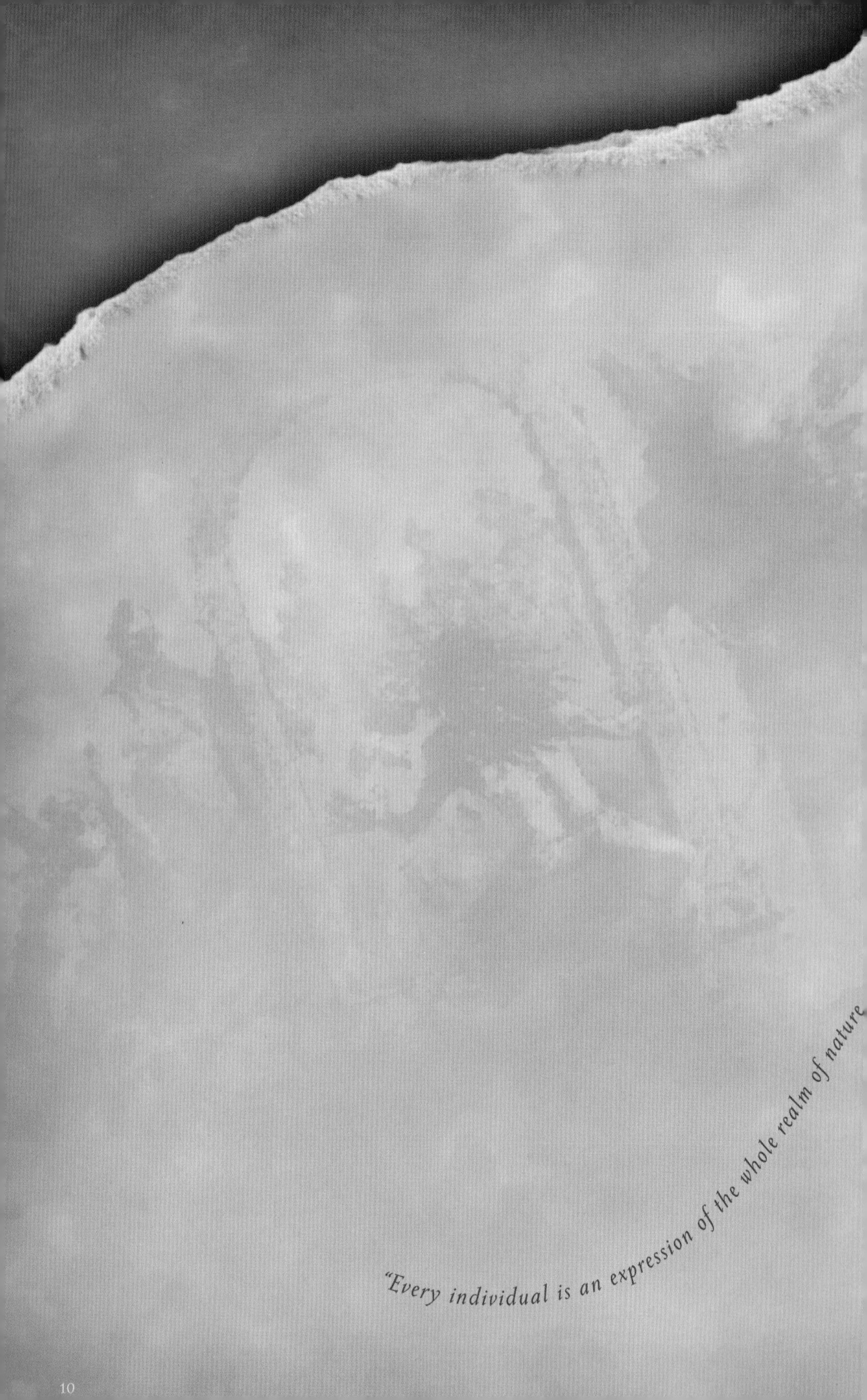

"Every individual is an expression of the whole realm of nature

"...a unique action of the total universe." —ALAN WATTS

Prologue

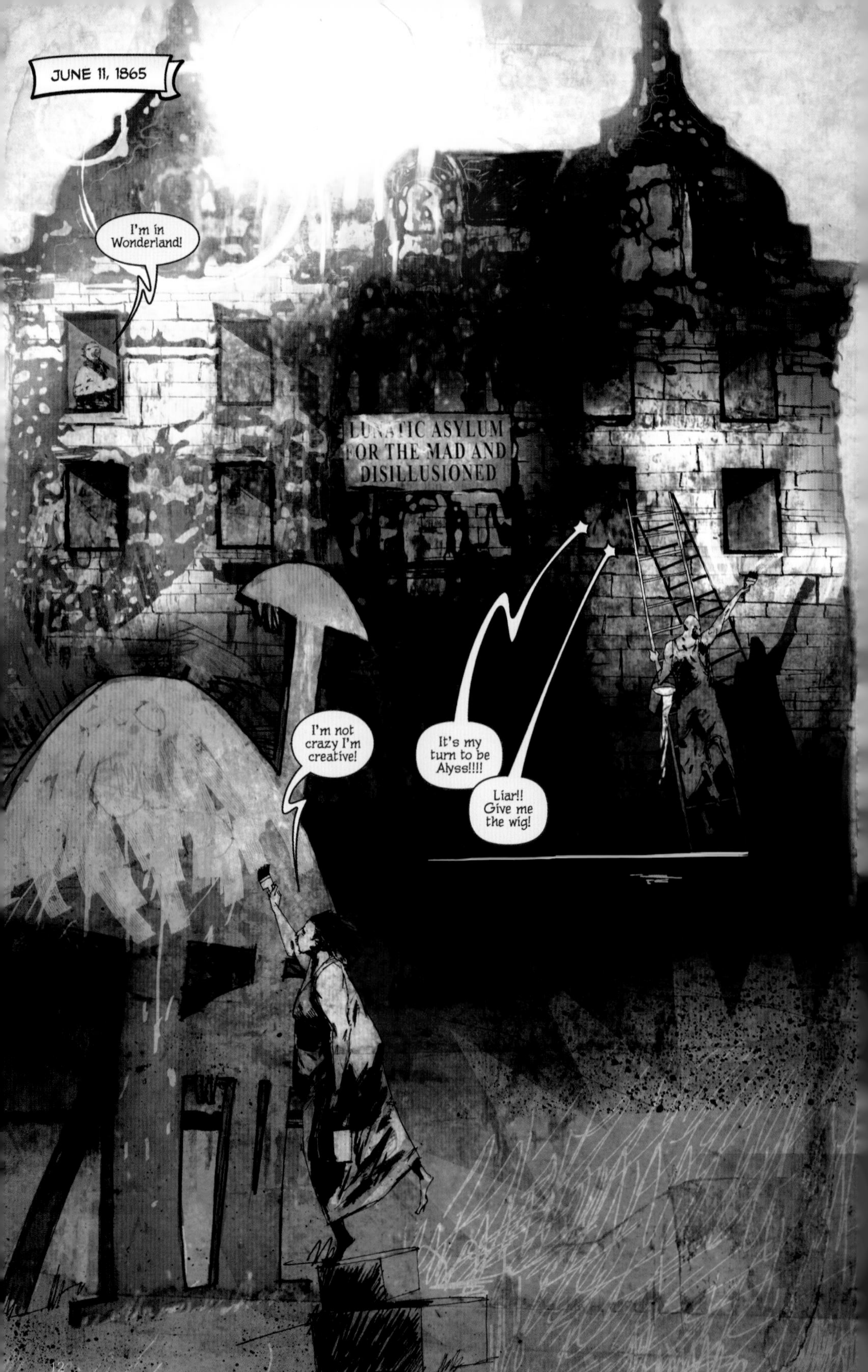
JUNE 11, 1865
I'm in Wonderland!
LUNATIC ASYLUM FOR THE MAD AND DISILLUSIONED
I'm not crazy I'm creative!
It's my turn to be Alyss!!!!
Liar!! Give me the wig!

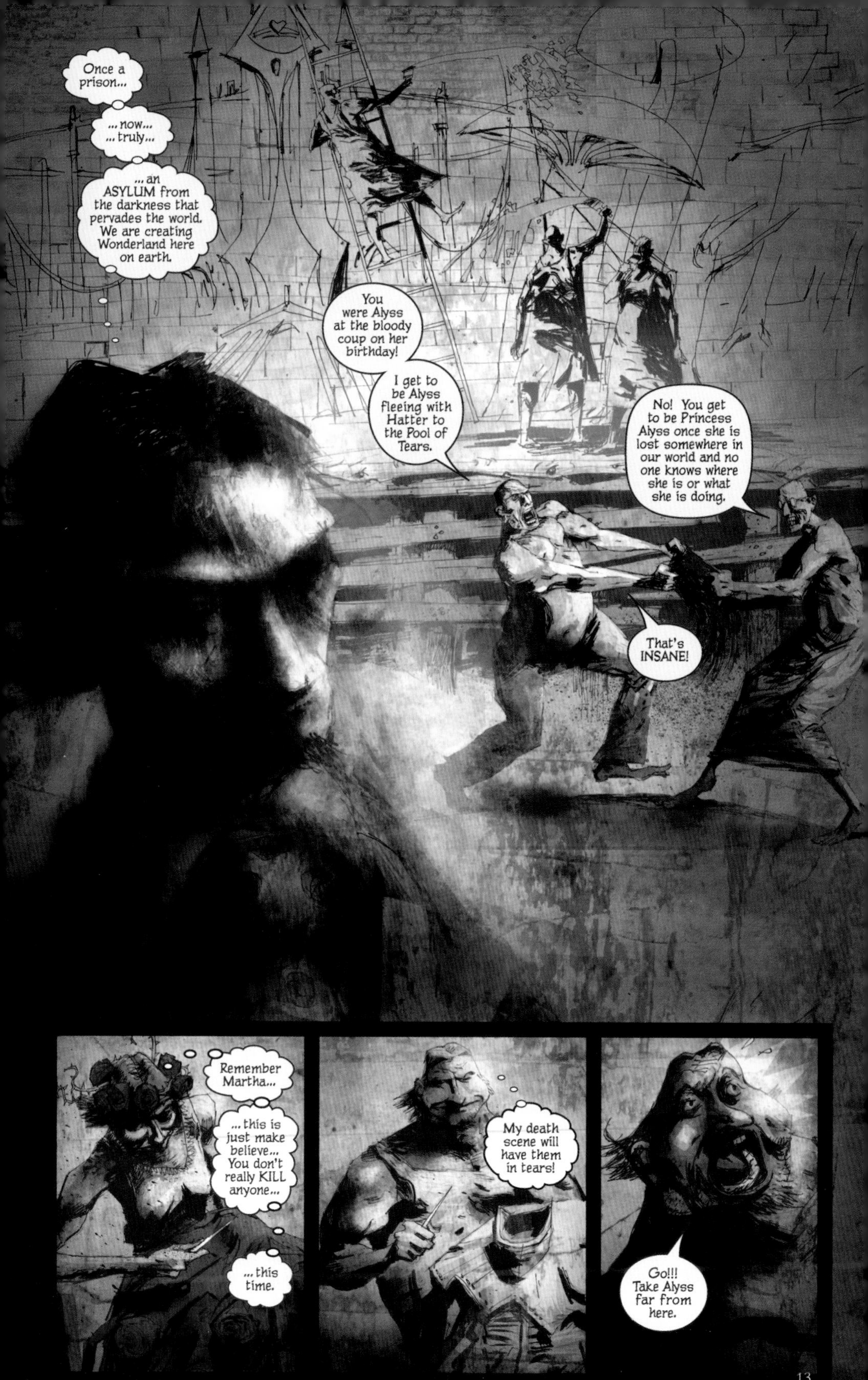
Once a prison...
...now... ...truly...
...an ASYLUM from the darkness that pervades the world. We are creating Wonderland here on earth.
You were Alyss at the bloody coup on her birthday!
I get to be Alyss fleeing with Hatter to the Pool of Tears.
No! You get to be Princess Alyss once she is lost somewhere in our world and no one knows where she is or what she is doing.
That's INSANE!
Remember Martha...
...this is just make believe... You don't really KILL anyone...
...this time.
My death scene will have them in tears!
Go!!! Take Alyss far from here.

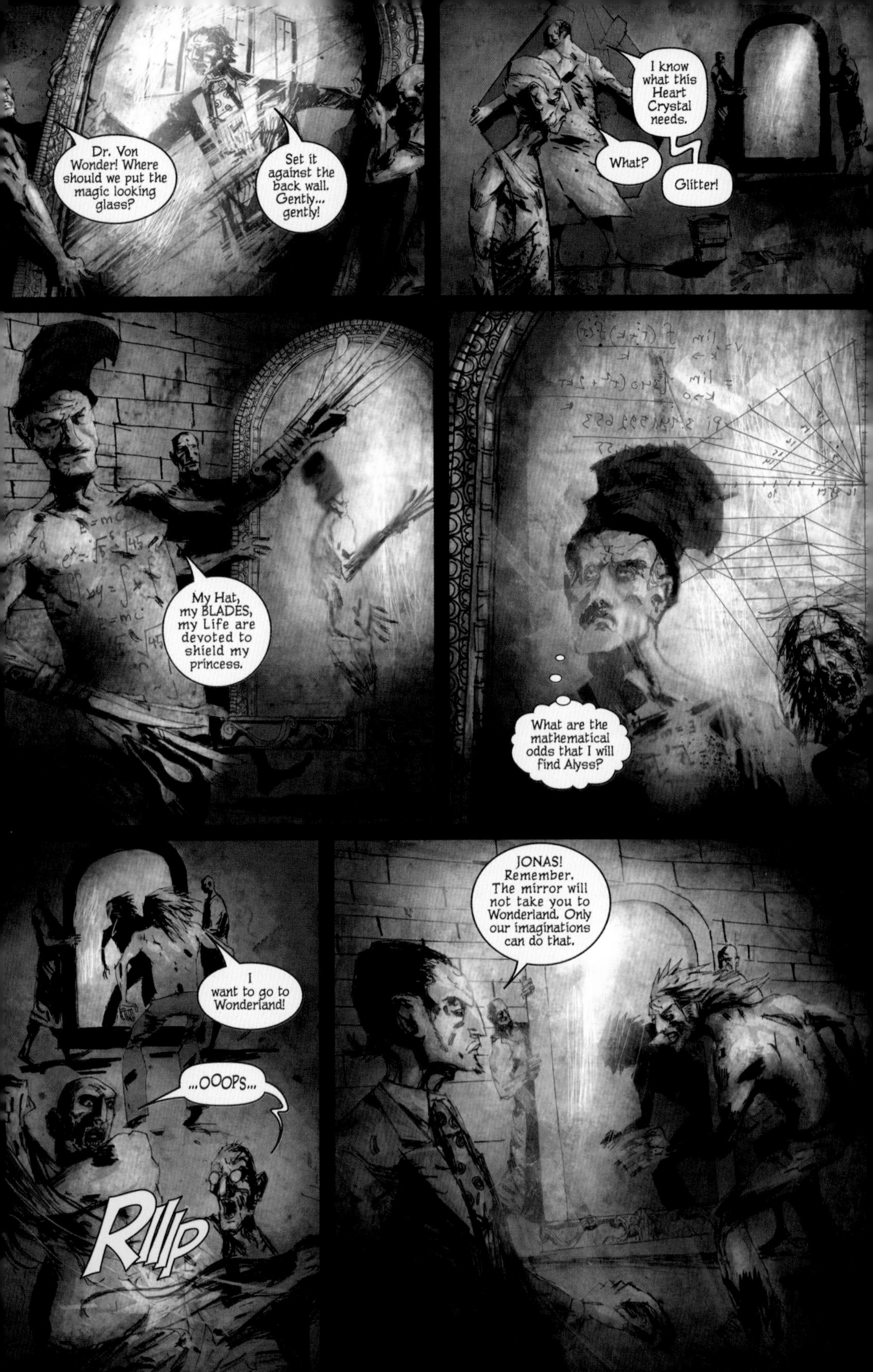

Dr. Von Wonder! Where should we put the magic looking glass?
Set it against the back wall. Gently... gently!
I know what this Heart Crystal needs.
What?
Glitter!
My Hat, my BLADES, my Life are devoted to shield my princess.
What are the mathematical odds that I will find Alyss?
I want to go to Wonderland!
...OOOPS...
RIIP
JONAS! Remember. The mirror will not take you to Wonderland. Only our imaginations can do that.

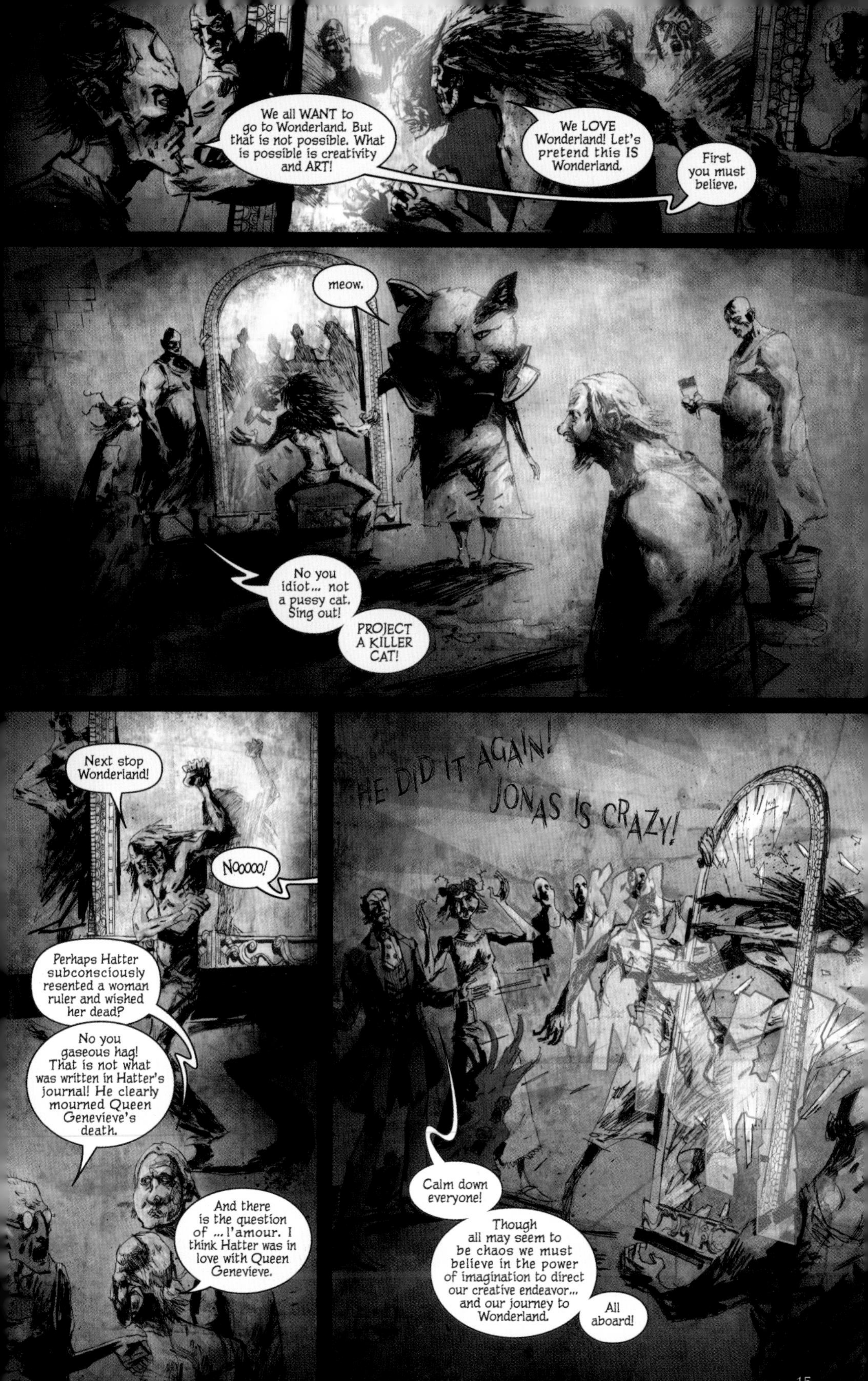
We all WANT to go to Wonderland. But that is not possible. What is possible is creativity and ART!
We LOVE Wonderland! Let's pretend this IS Wonderland.
First you must believe.
meow.
No you idiot... not a pussy cat. Sing out!
PROJECT A KILLER CAT!
Next stop Wonderland!
Nooooo!
Perhaps Hatter subconsciously resented a woman ruler and wished her dead?
No you gaseous hag! That is not what was written in Hatter's journal! He clearly mourned Queen Genevieve's death.
And there is the question of ... l'amour. I think Hatter was in love with Queen Genevieve.
HE DID IT AGAIN!
JONAS IS CRAZY!
Calm down everyone!
Though all may seem to be chaos we must believe in the power of imagination to direct our creative endeavor... and our journey to Wonderland.
All aboard!

Why am I here? I broke my own navigational directive and traveled east away from the Glow. And now as I tour this capitol city of unfinished monuments and muddy streets, fragments of my own city fly to mind in a rush of crystalline images and light. Could our worlds be more different? And yet, the potential for good and evil surely exists in both.

"To the dull mind nature is leaden.

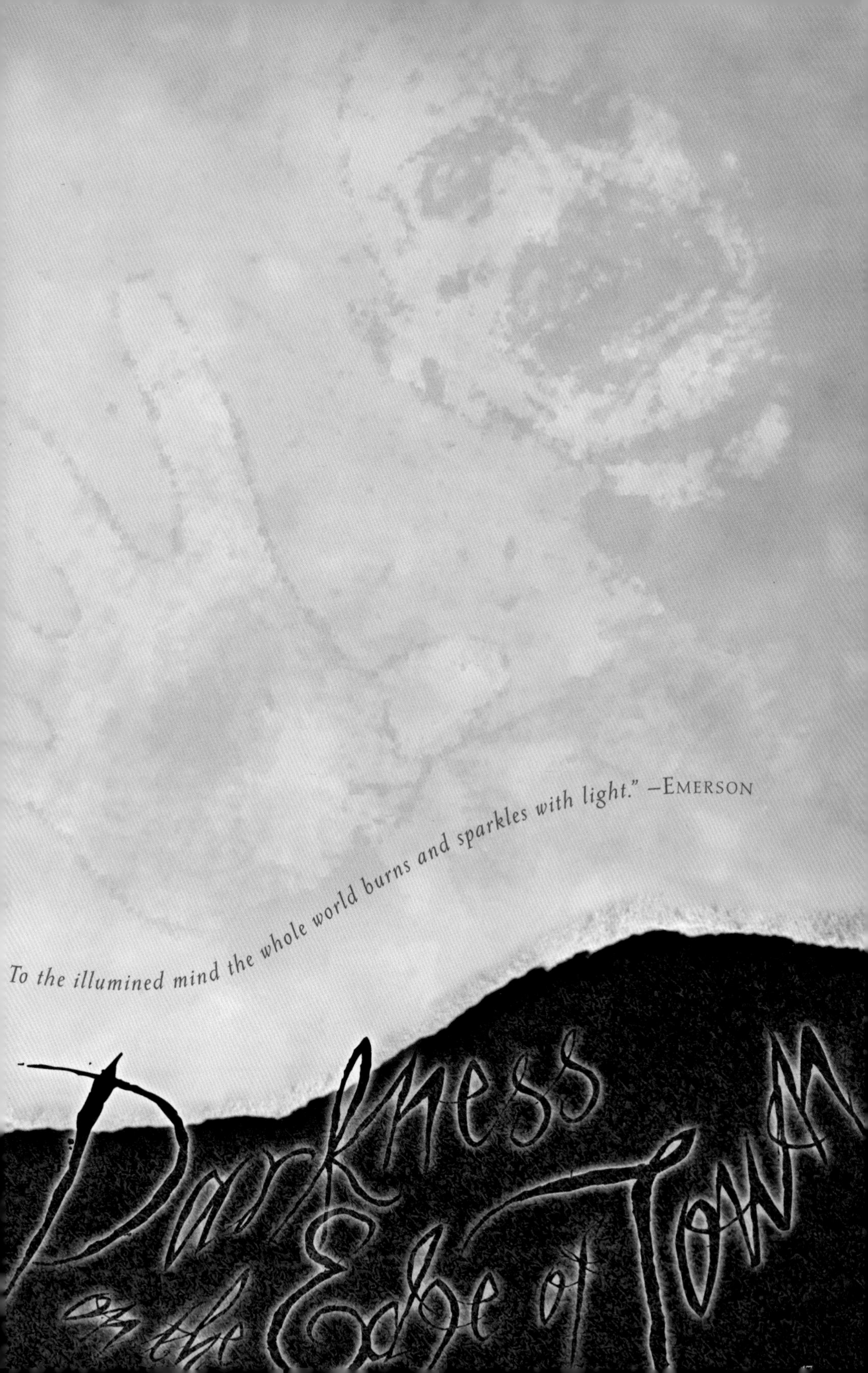

To the illumined mind the whole world burns and sparkles with light." –EMERSON
Darkness on the Edge of Town

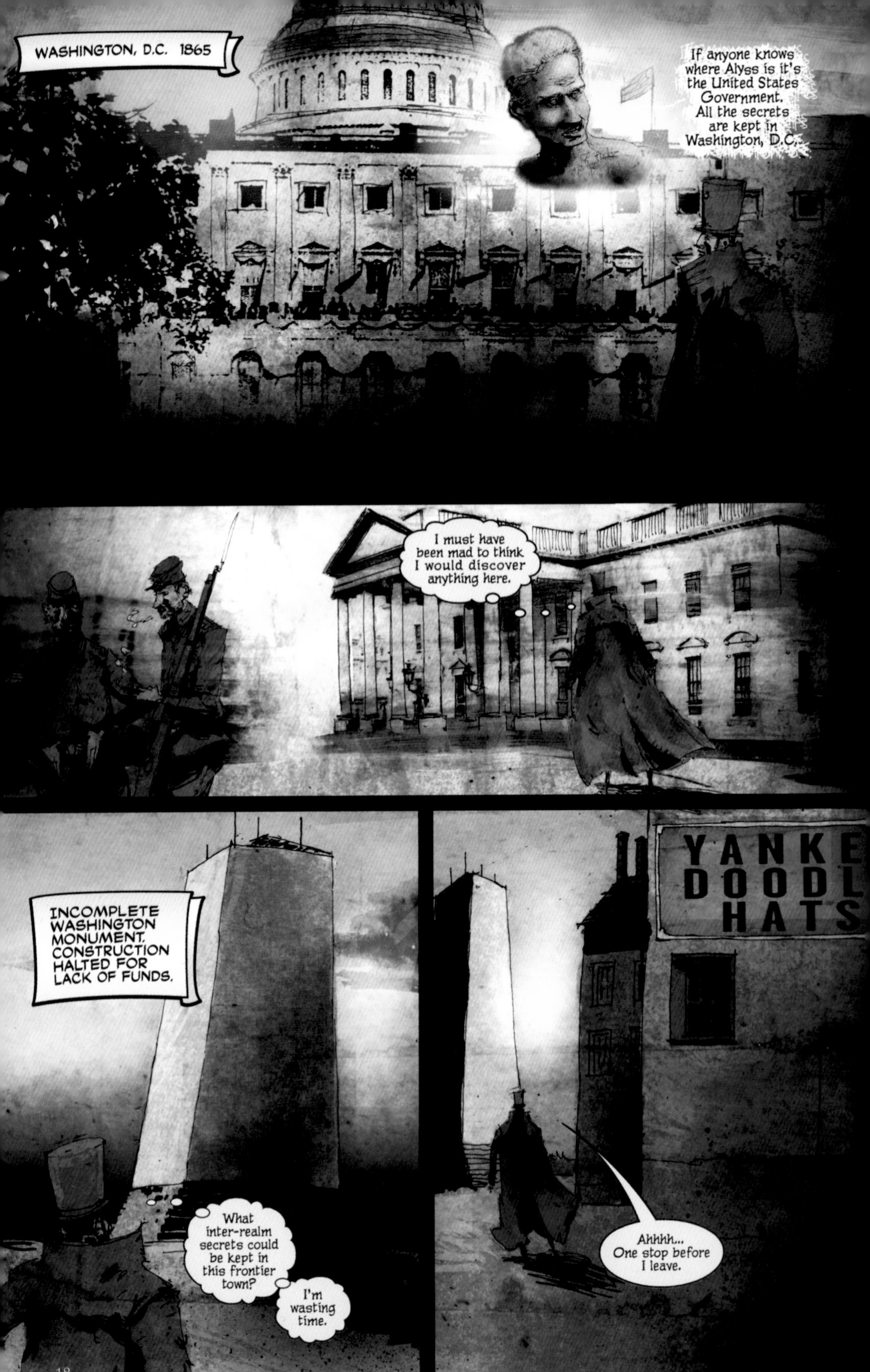
WASHINGTON, D.C. 1865
If anyone knows where Alyss is it's the United States Government. All the secrets are kept in Washington, D.C.
I must have been mad to think I would discover anything here.
INCOMPLETE WASHINGTON MONUMENT. CONSTRUCTION HALTED FOR LACK OF FUNDS.
What inter-realm secrets could be kept in this frontier town?
I'm wasting time.
YANKE DOODL HATS
Ahhhh... One stop before I leave.

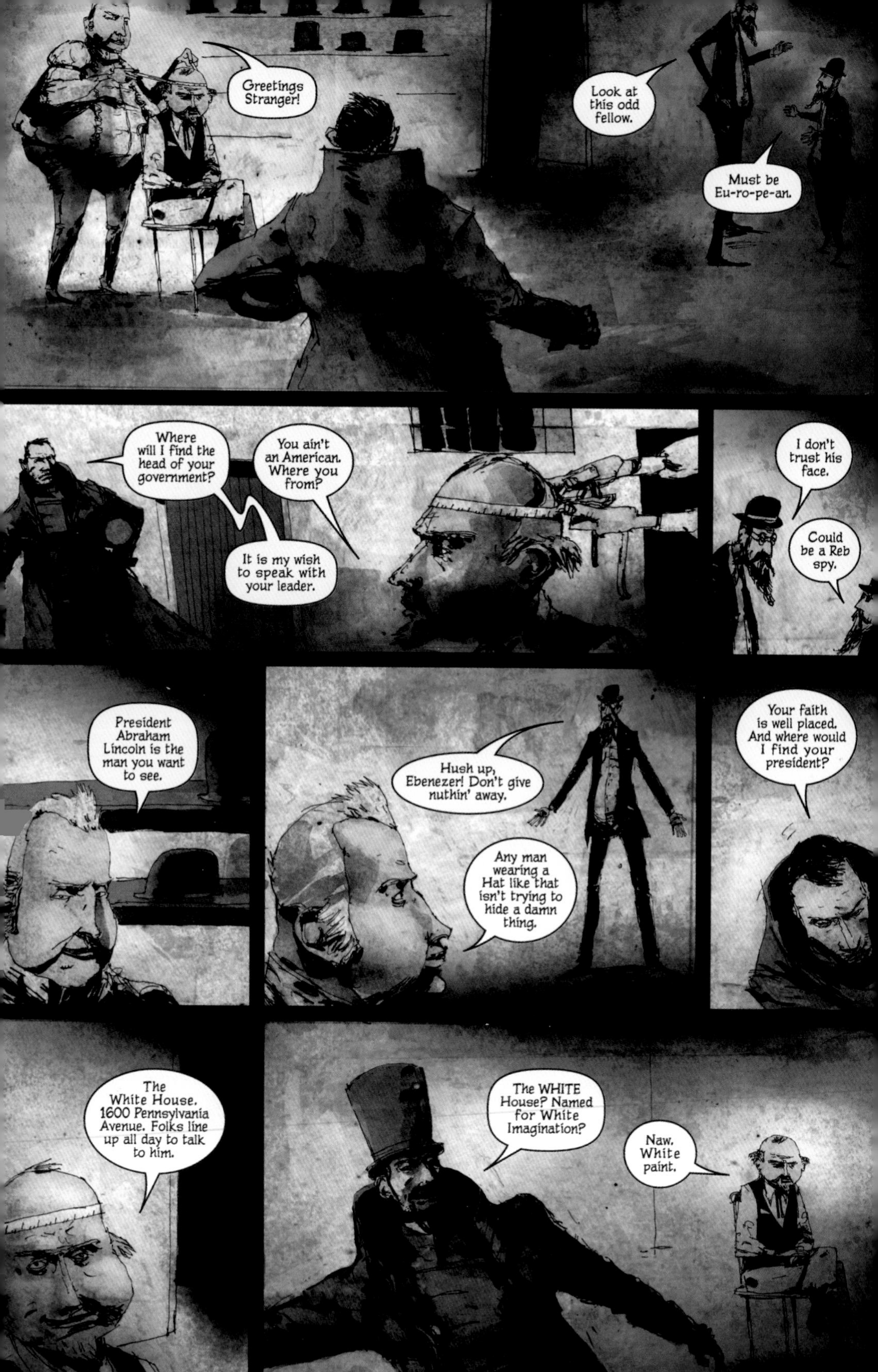
Greetings Stranger!
Look at this odd fellow.
Must be Eu-ro-pe-an.
Where will I find the head of your government?
You ain't an American. Where you from?
It is my wish to speak with your leader.
I don't trust his face.
Could be a Reb spy.
President Abraham Lincoln is the man you want to see.
Hush up, Ebenezer! Don't give nuthin' away.
Any man wearing a Hat like that isn't trying to hide a damn thing.
Your faith is well placed. And where would I find your president?
The White House. 1600 Pennsylvania Avenue. Folks line up all day to talk to him.
The WHITE House? Named for White Imagination?
Naw. White paint.

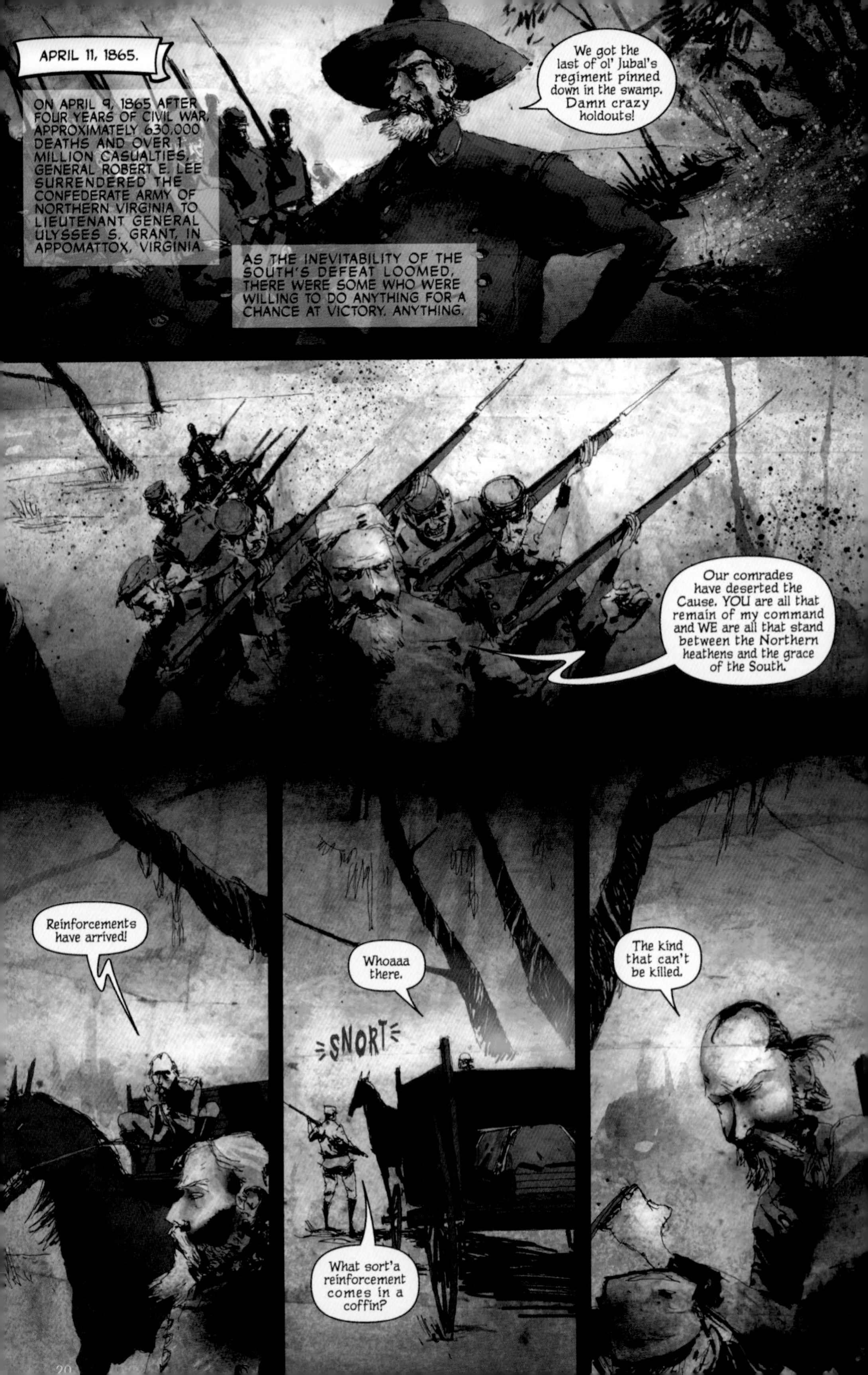

APRIL 11, 1865.
ON APRIL 9, 1865 AFTER FOUR YEARS OF CIVIL WAR, APPROXIMATELY 630,000 DEATHS AND OVER 1 MILLION CASUALTIES, GENERAL ROBERT E. LEE SURRENDERED THE CONFEDERATE ARMY OF NORTHERN VIRGINIA TO LIEUTENANT GENERAL ULYSSES S. GRANT, IN APPOMATTOX, VIRGINIA.
We got the last of ol' Jubal's regiment pinned down in the swamp. Damn crazy holdouts!
AS THE INEVITABILITY OF THE SOUTH'S DEFEAT LOOMED, THERE WERE SOME WHO WERE WILLING TO DO ANYTHING FOR A CHANCE AT VICTORY. ANYTHING.
Our comrades have deserted the Cause. YOU are all that remain of my command and WE are all that stand between the Northern heathens and the grace of the South.
Reinforcements have arrived!
Whoaaa there.
SNORT
What sort'a reinforcement comes in a coffin?
The kind that can't be killed.

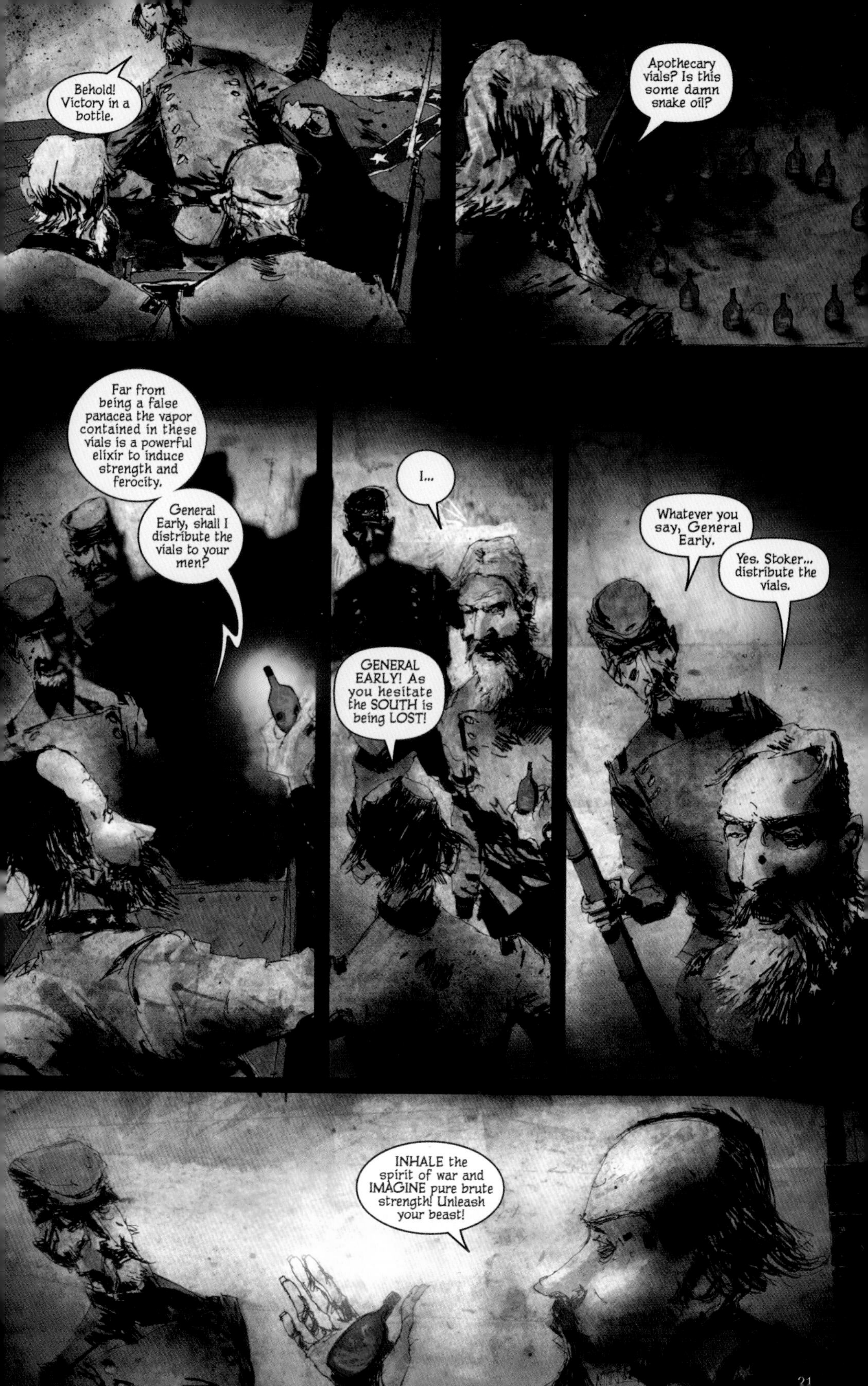
Behold! Victory in a bottle.
Apothecary vials? Is this some damn snake oil?
Far from being a false panacea the vapor contained in these vials is a powerful elixir to induce strength and ferocity.
General Early, shall I distribute the vials to your men?
I...
GENERAL EARLY! As you hesitate the SOUTH is being LOST!
Whatever you say, General Early.
Yes. Stoker... distribute the vials.
INHALE the spirit of war and IMAGINE pure brute strength! Unleash your beast!

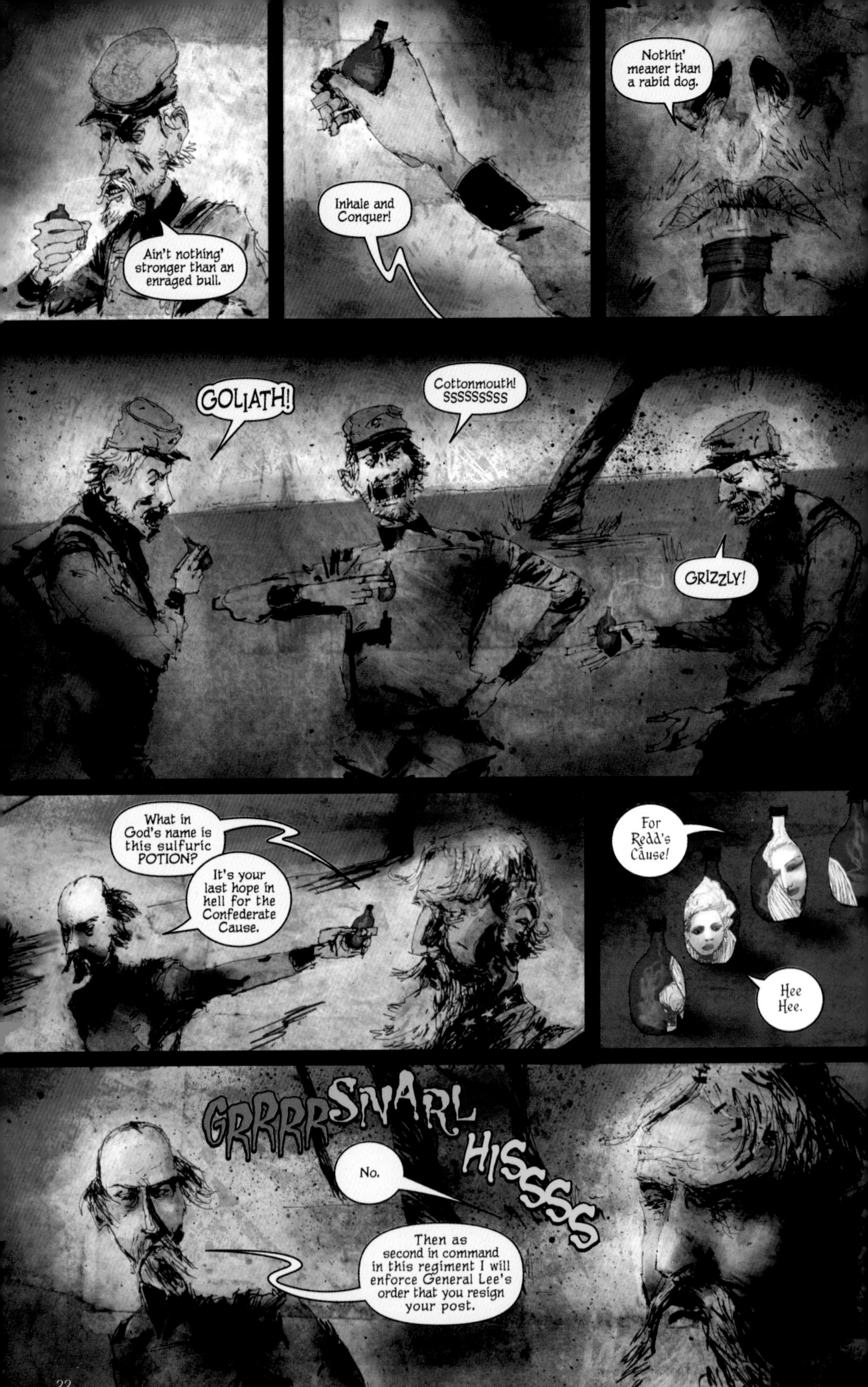
Ain't nothing' stronger than an enraged bull.
Inhale and Conquer!
Nothin' meaner than a rabid dog.
GOLIATH!
Cottonmouth! SSSSSSSSS
GRIZZLY!
What in God's name is this sulfuric POTION?
It's your last hope in hell for the Confederate Cause.
For Redd's Cause!
Hee Hee.
GRRRRSNARL
HISSSSS
No.
Then as second in command in this regiment I will enforce General Lee's order that you resign your post.

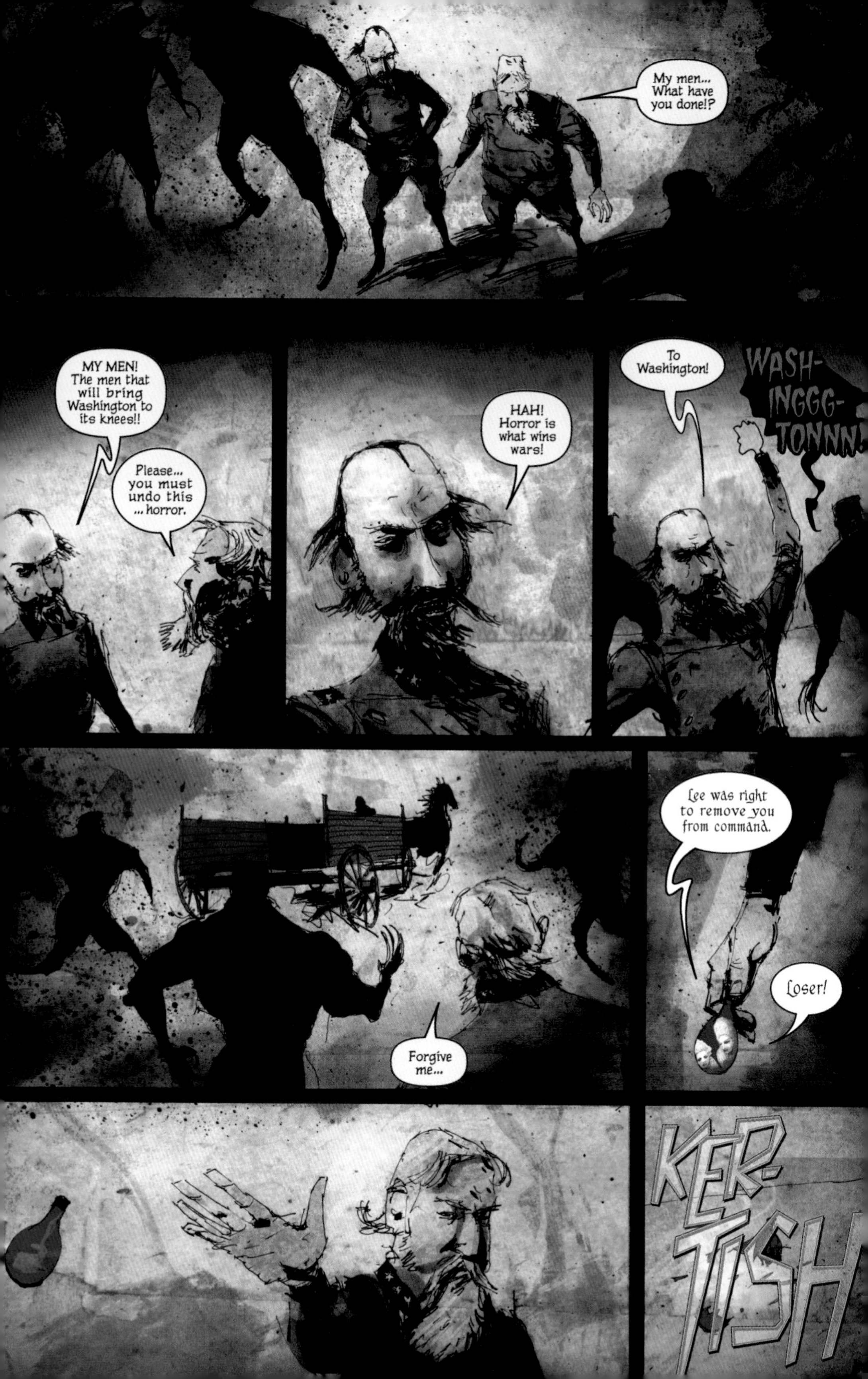
My men... What have you done!?
MY MEN! The men that will bring Washington to its knees!!
Please... you must undo this ...horror.
HAH! Horror is what wins wars!
To Washington!
WASH-INGGG-TONNN!
Forgive me...
Lee was right to remove you from command.
Loser!
KER-TISH

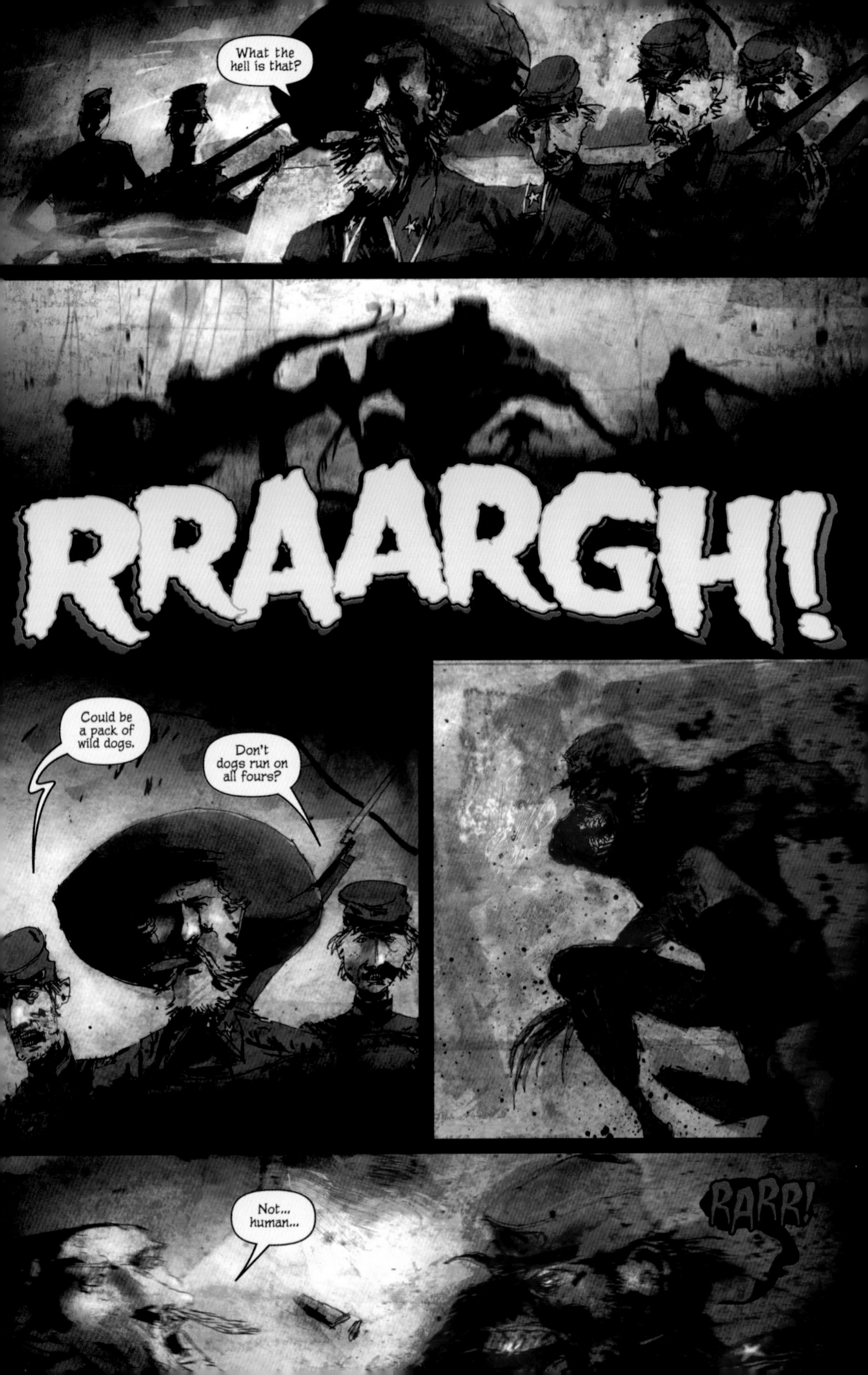
What the hell is that?
RRAARGH!
Could be a pack of wild dogs.
Don't dogs run on all fours?
Not... human...
RARR!

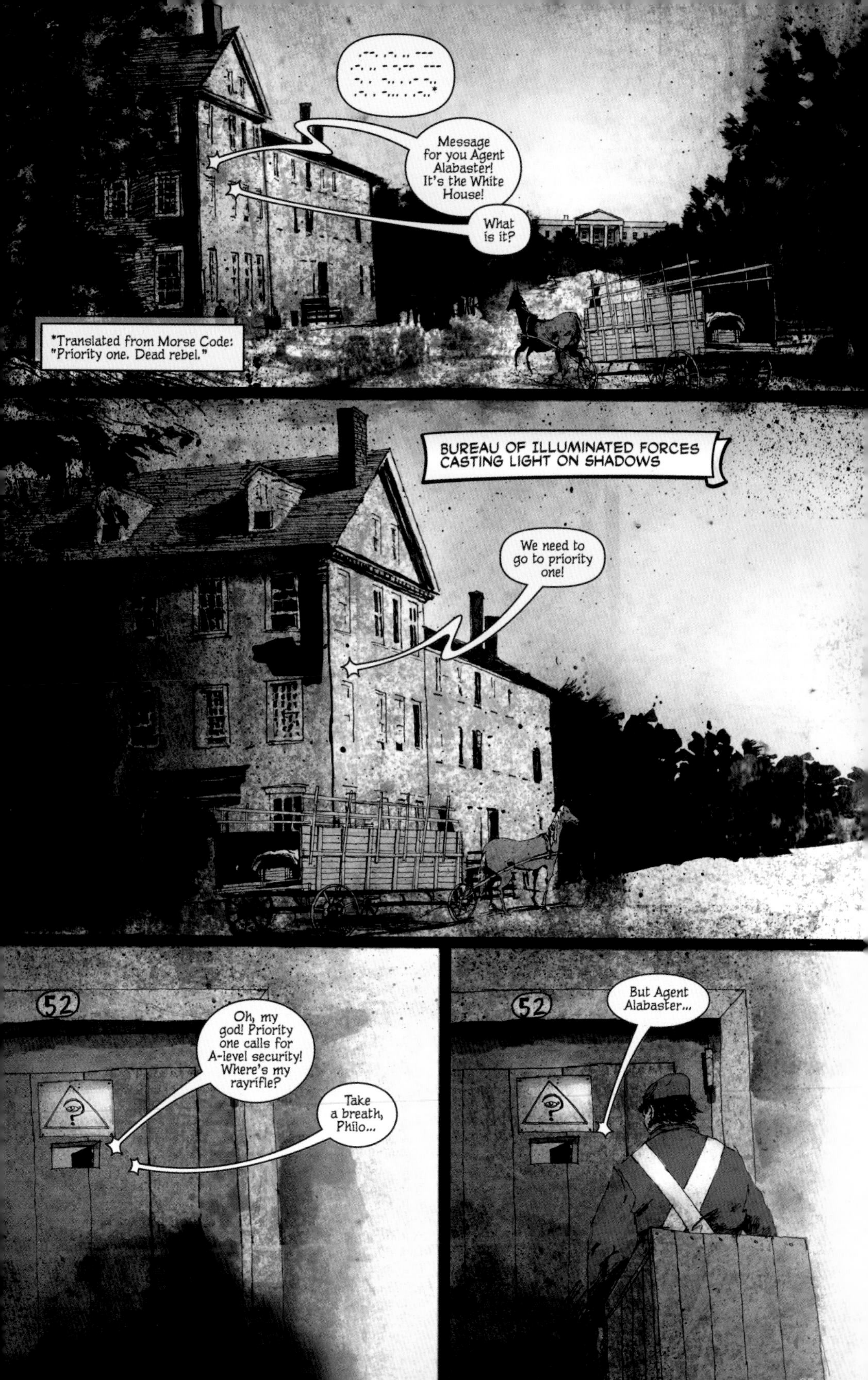
*Translated from Morse Code: "Priority one. Dead rebel."
Message for you Agent Alabaster! It's the White House!
What is it?
BUREAU OF ILLUMINATED FORCES CASTING LIGHT ON SHADOWS
We need to go to priority one!
52
Oh, my god! Priority one calls for A-level security! Where's my rayrifle?
Take a breath, Philo...
52
But Agent Alabaster...

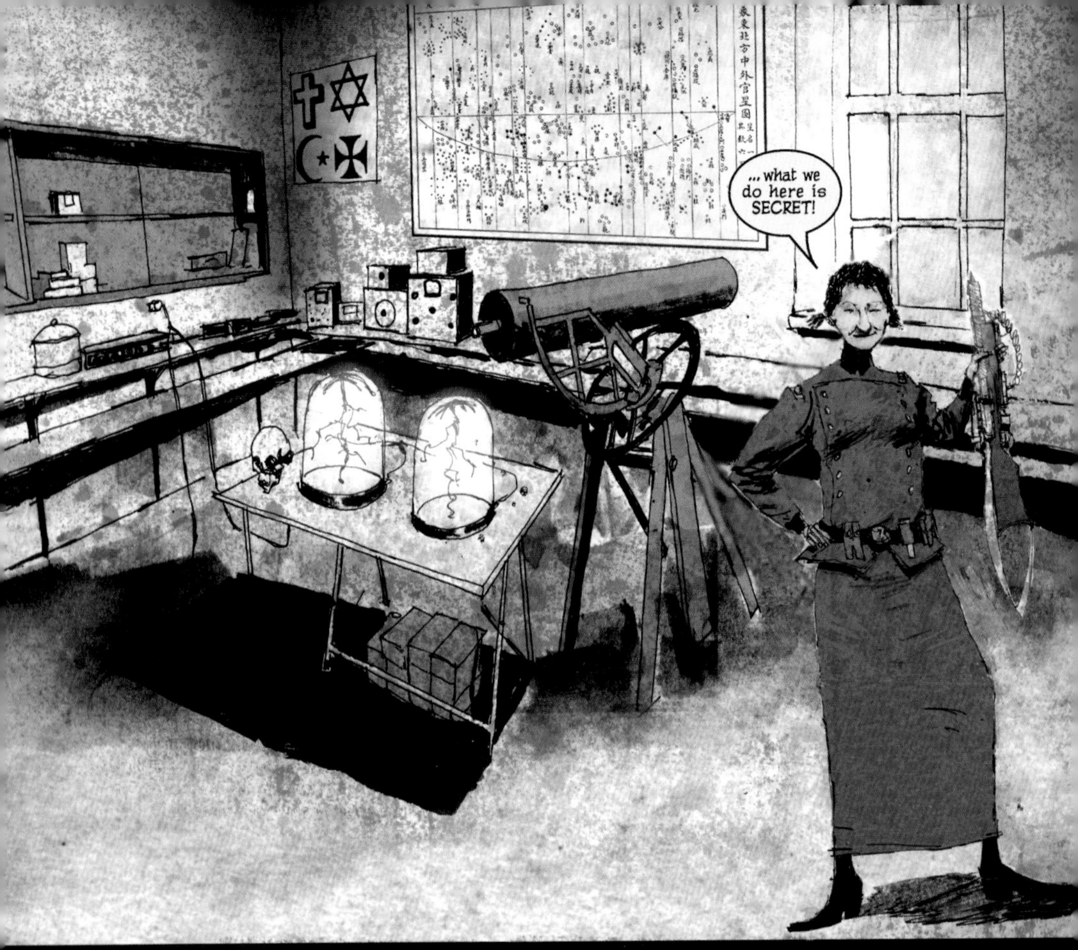
...what we do here is SECRET!

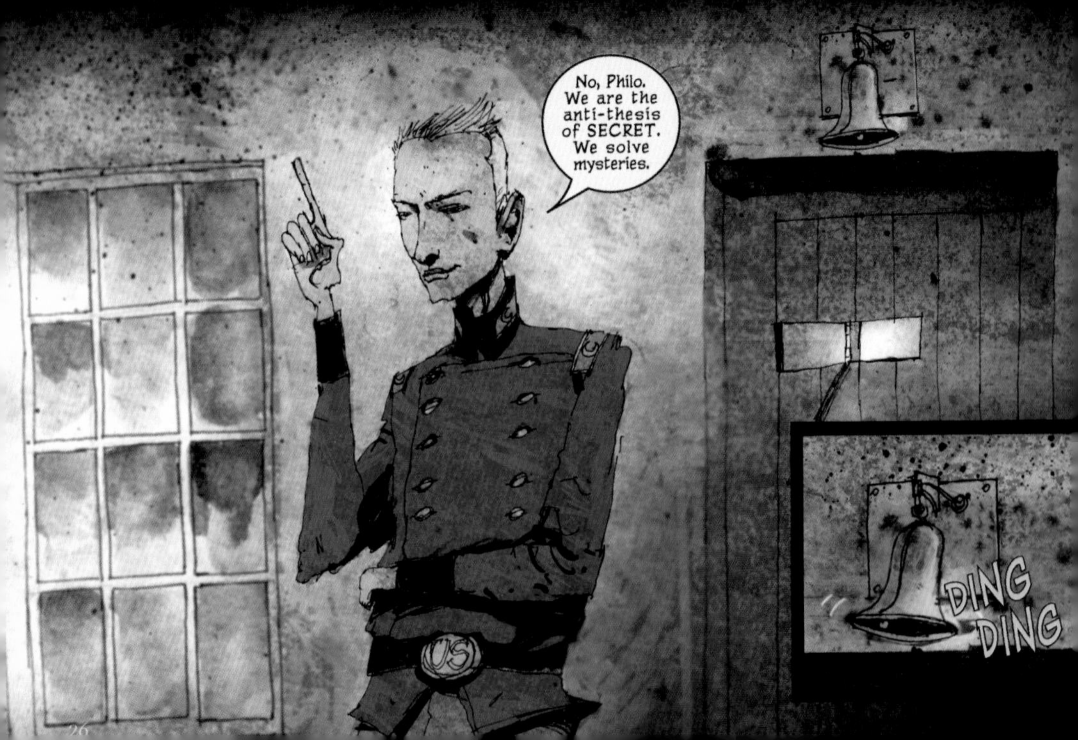
No, Philo. We are the anti-thesis of SECRET. We solve mysteries.
DING DING

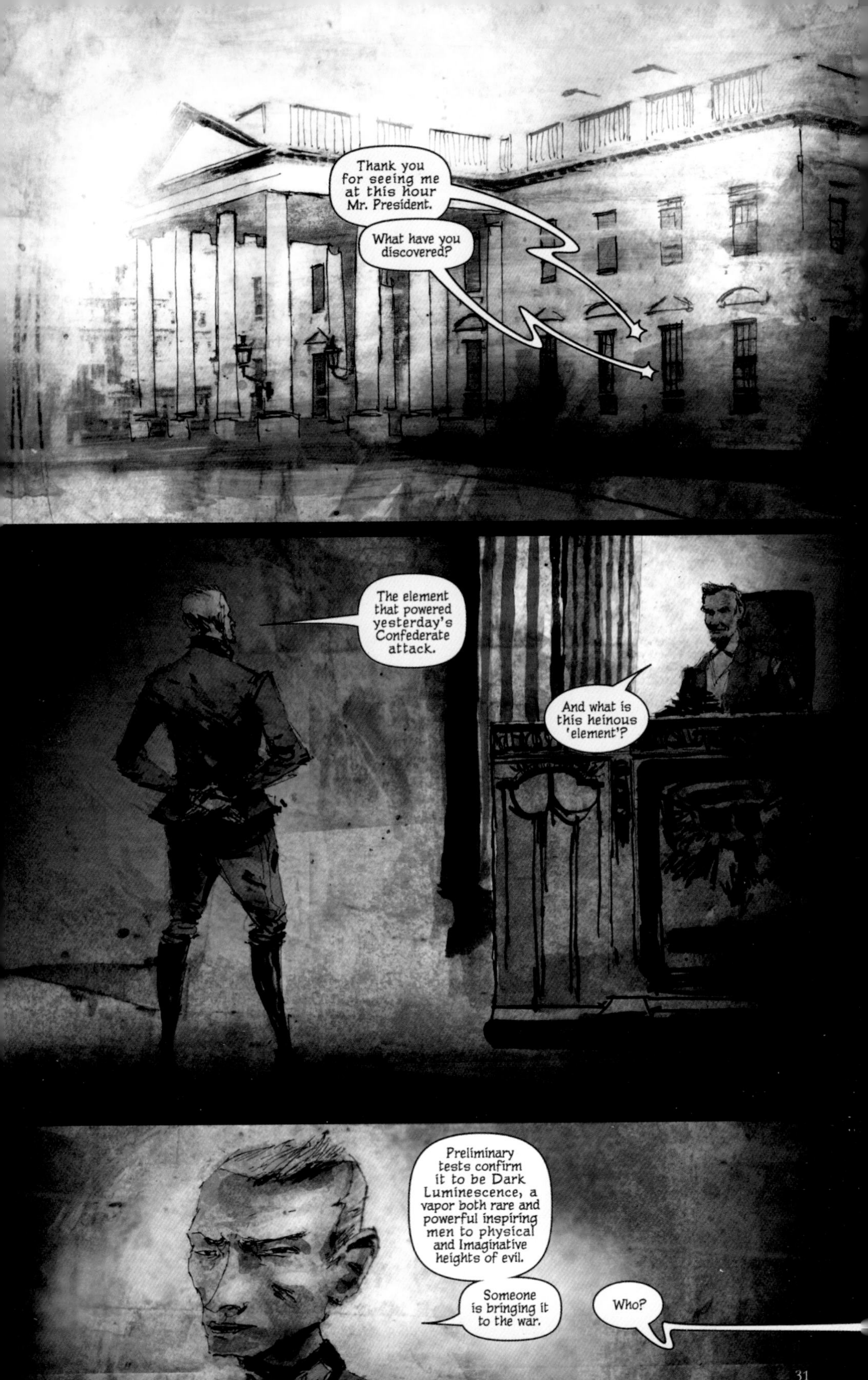
Thank you for seeing me at this hour Mr. President.
What have you discovered?
The element that powered yesterday's Confederate attack.
And what is this heinous 'element'?
Preliminary tests confirm it to be Dark Luminescence, a vapor both rare and powerful inspiring men to physical and Imaginative heights of evil.
Someone is bringing it to the war.
Who?

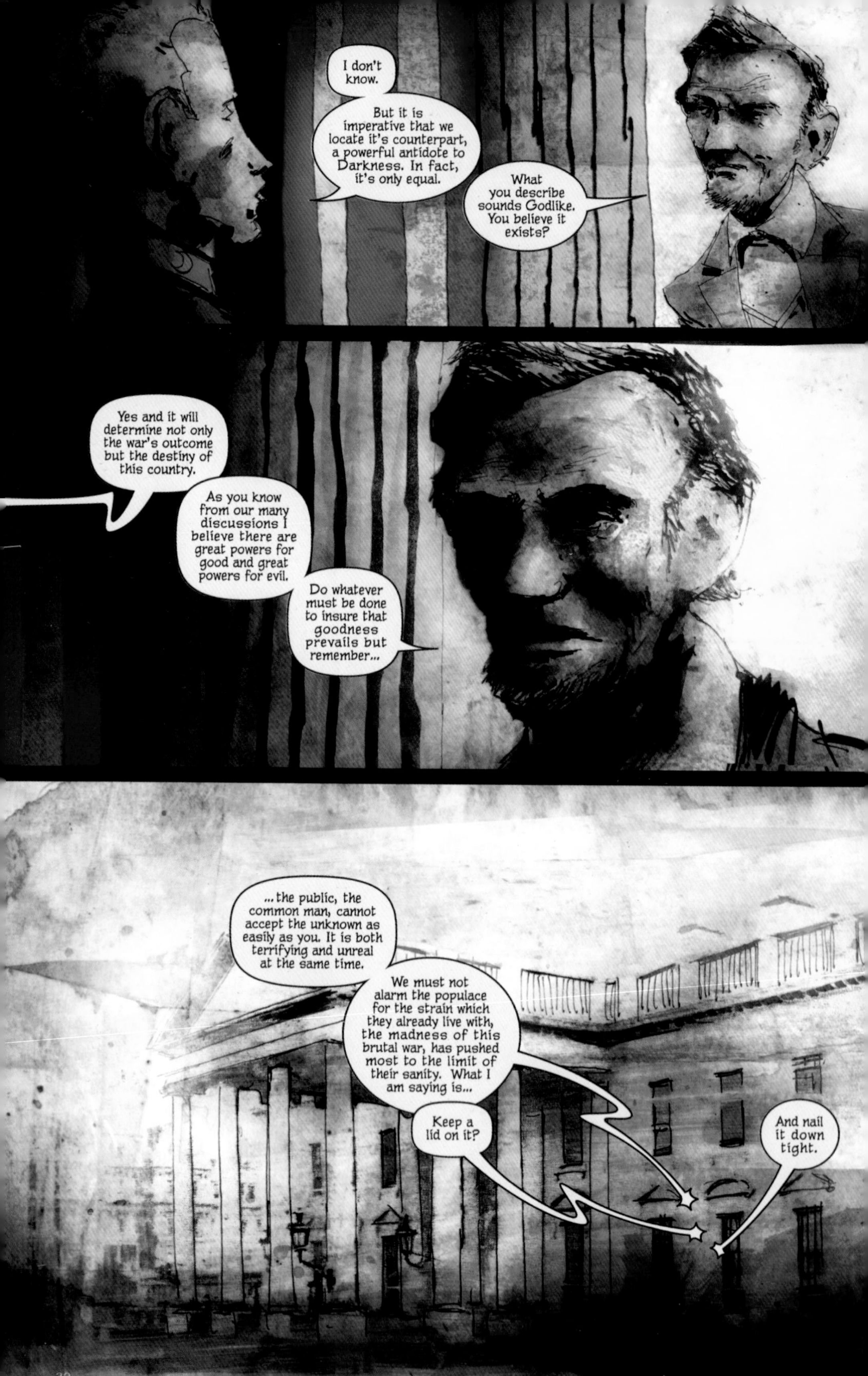
I don't know.
But it is imperative that we locate it's counterpart, a powerful antidote to Darkness. In fact, it's only equal.
What you describe sounds Godlike. You believe it exists?
Yes and it will determine not only the war's outcome but the destiny of this country.
As you know from our many discussions I believe there are great powers for good and great powers for evil.
Do whatever must be done to insure that goodness prevails but remember...
...the public, the common man, cannot accept the unknown as easily as you. It is both terrifying and unreal at the same time.
We must not alarm the populace for the strain which they already live with, the madness of this brutal war, has pushed most to the limit of their sanity. What I am saying is...
Keep a lid on it?
And nail it down tight.

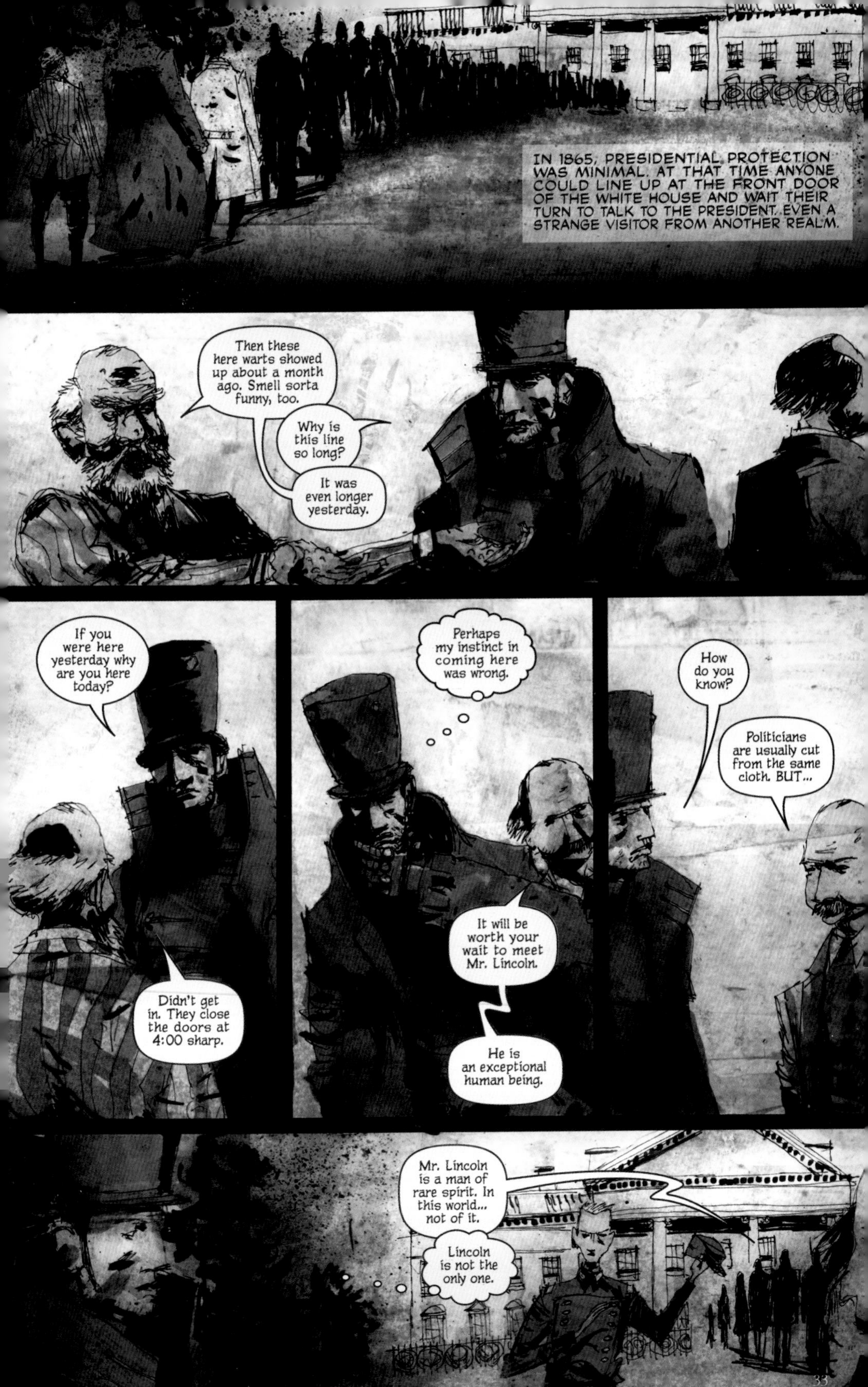
IN 1865, PRESIDENTIAL PROTECTION WAS MINIMAL. AT THAT TIME ANYONE COULD LINE UP AT THE FRONT DOOR OF THE WHITE HOUSE AND WAIT THEIR TURN TO TALK TO THE PRESIDENT. EVEN A STRANGE VISITOR FROM ANOTHER REALM.
Then these here warts showed up about a month ago. Smell sorta funny, too.
Why is this line so long?
It was even longer yesterday.
If you were here yesterday why are you here today?
Didn't get in. They close the doors at 4:00 sharp.
Perhaps my instinct in coming here was wrong.
It will be worth your wait to meet Mr. Lincoln.
He is an exceptional human being.
How do you know?
Politicians are usually cut from the same cloth. BUT...
Mr. Lincoln is a man of rare spirit. In this world... not of it.
Lincoln is not the only one.

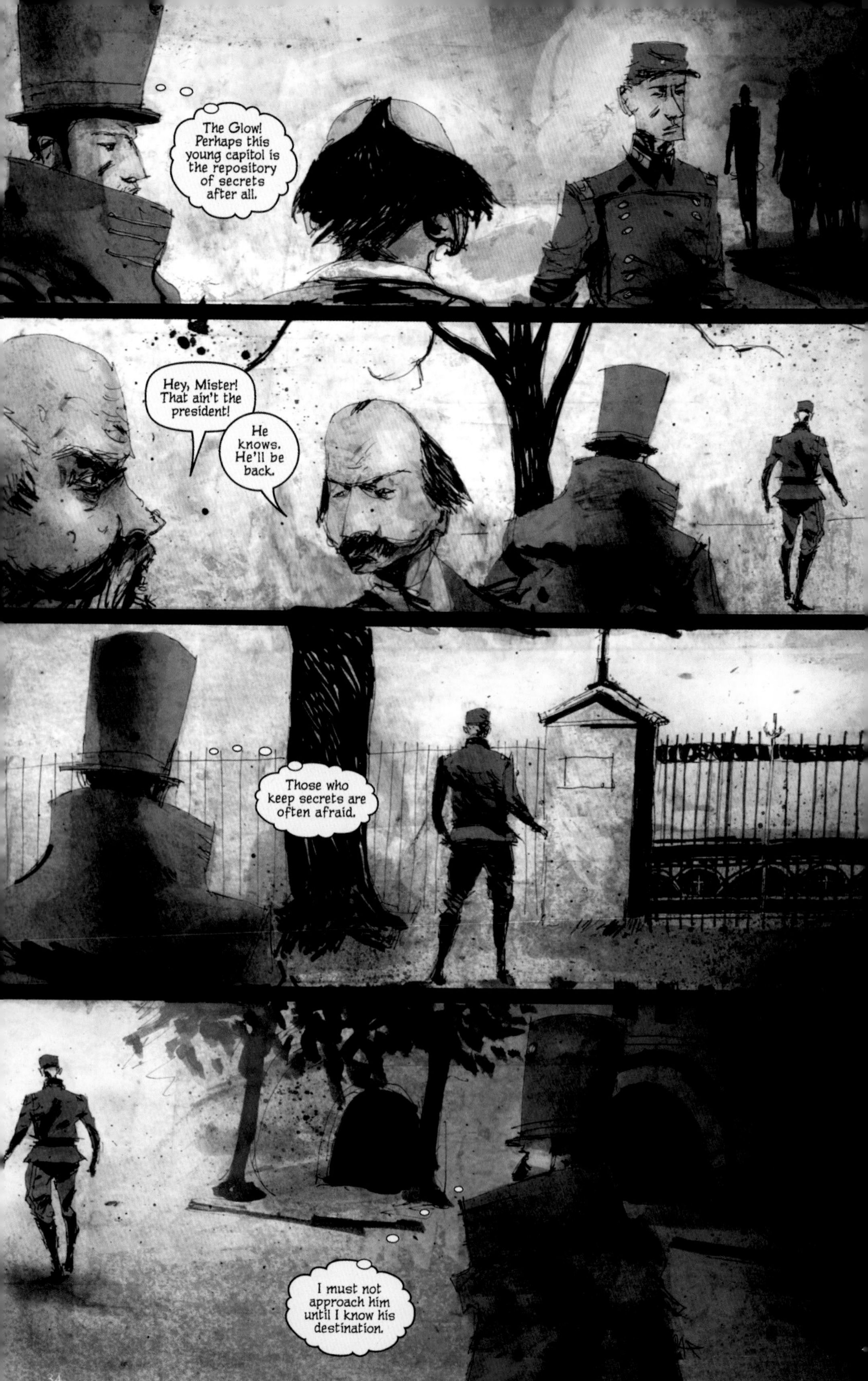
The Glow! Perhaps this young capitol is the repository of secrets after all.
Hey, Mister! That ain't the president!
He knows. He'll be back.
Those who keep secrets are often afraid.
I must not approach him until I know his destination.

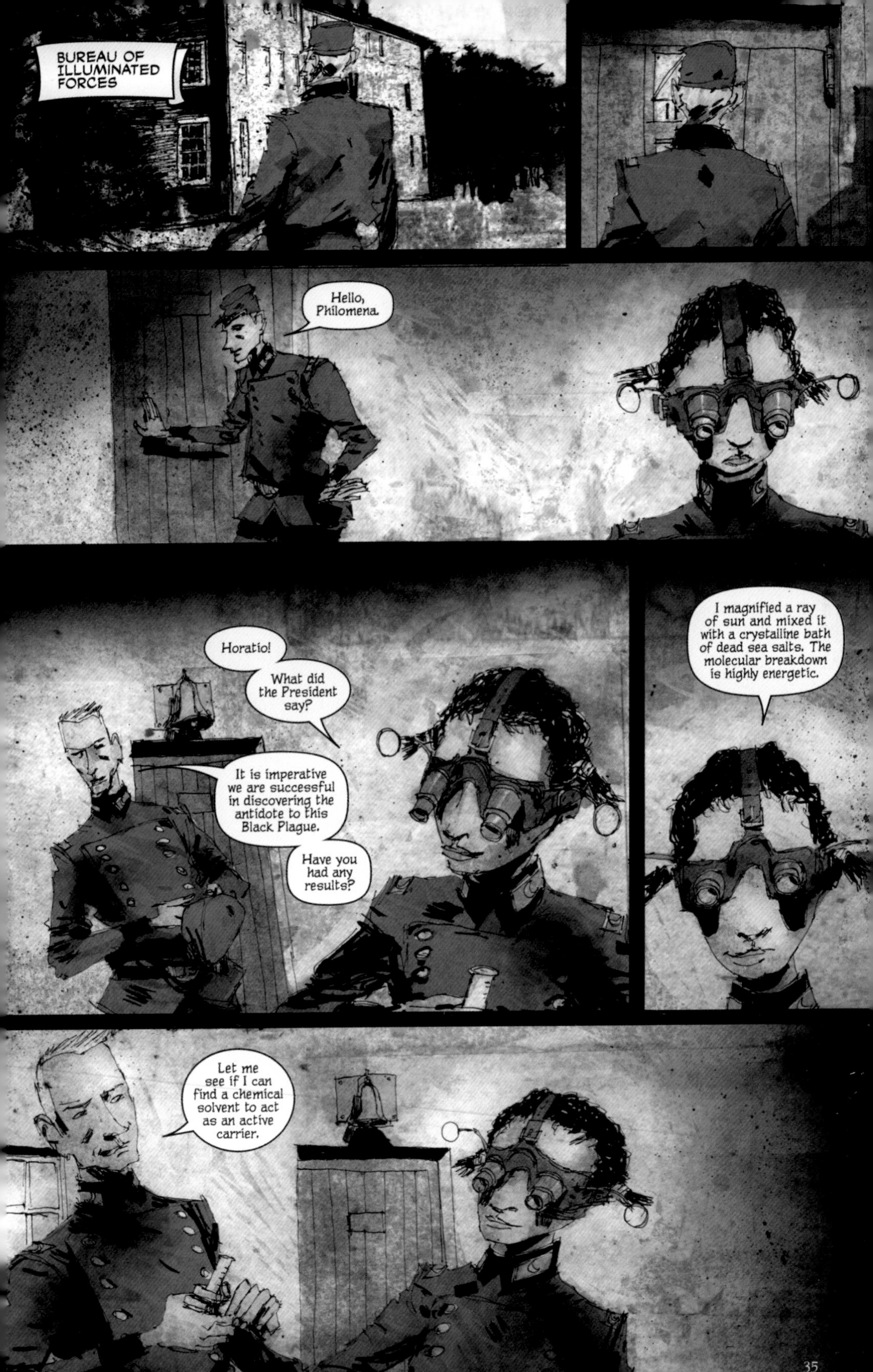
BUREAU OF ILLUMINATED FORCES
Hello, Philomena.
Horatio!
What did the President say?
It is imperative we are successful in discovering the antidote to this Black Plague.
Have you had any results?
I magnified a ray of sun and mixed it with a crystalline bath of dead sea salts. The molecular breakdown is highly energetic.
Let me see if I can find a chemical solvent to act as an active carrier.

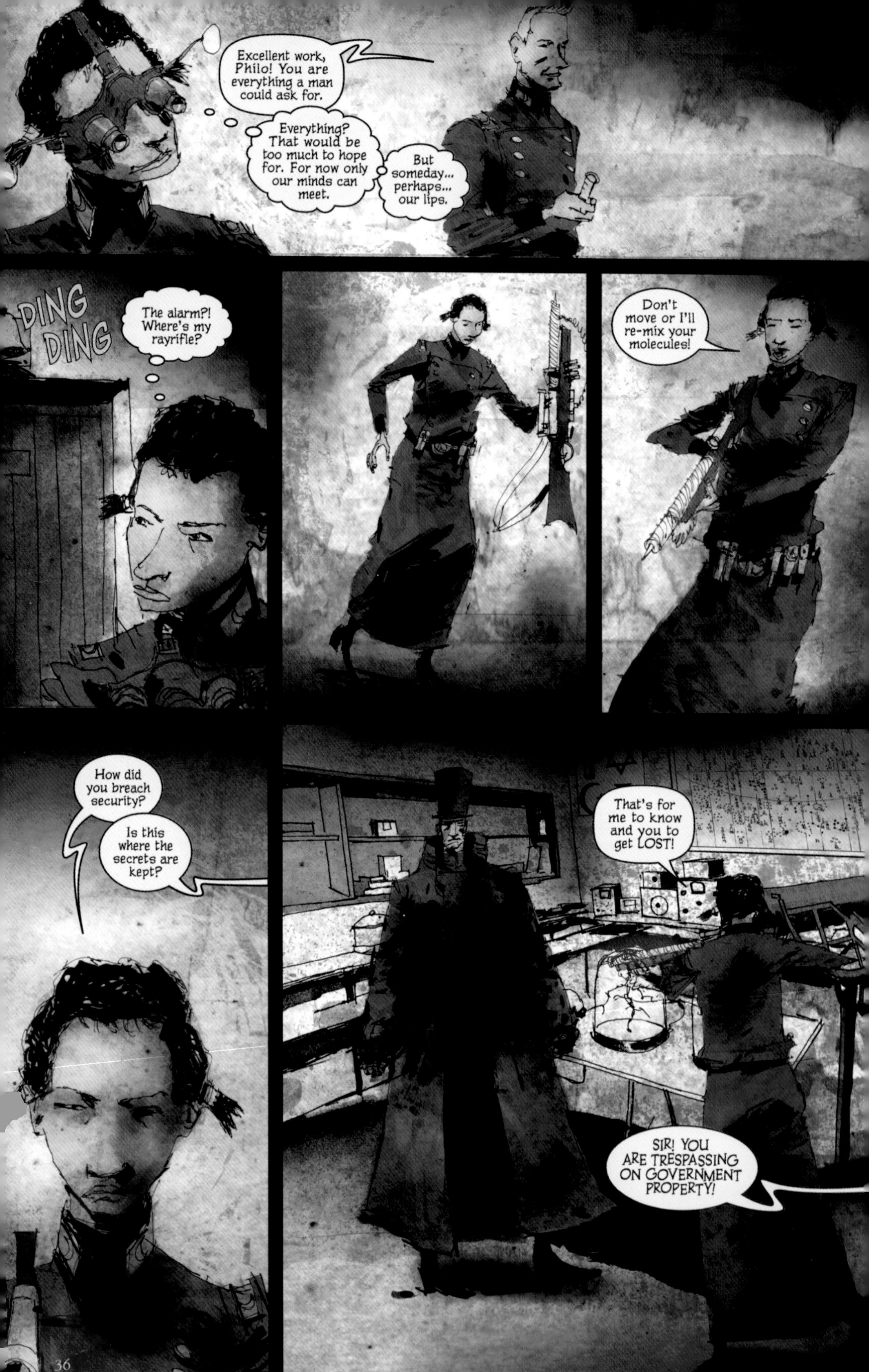
Excellent work, Philo! You are everything a man could ask for.
Everything? That would be too much to hope for. For now only our minds can meet.
But someday... perhaps... our lips.
DING DING
The alarm?! Where's my rayrifle?
Don't move or I'll re-mix your molecules!
How did you breach security?
Is this where the secrets are kept?
That's for me to know and you to get LOST!
SIR! YOU ARE TRESPASSING ON GOVERNMENT PROPERTY!

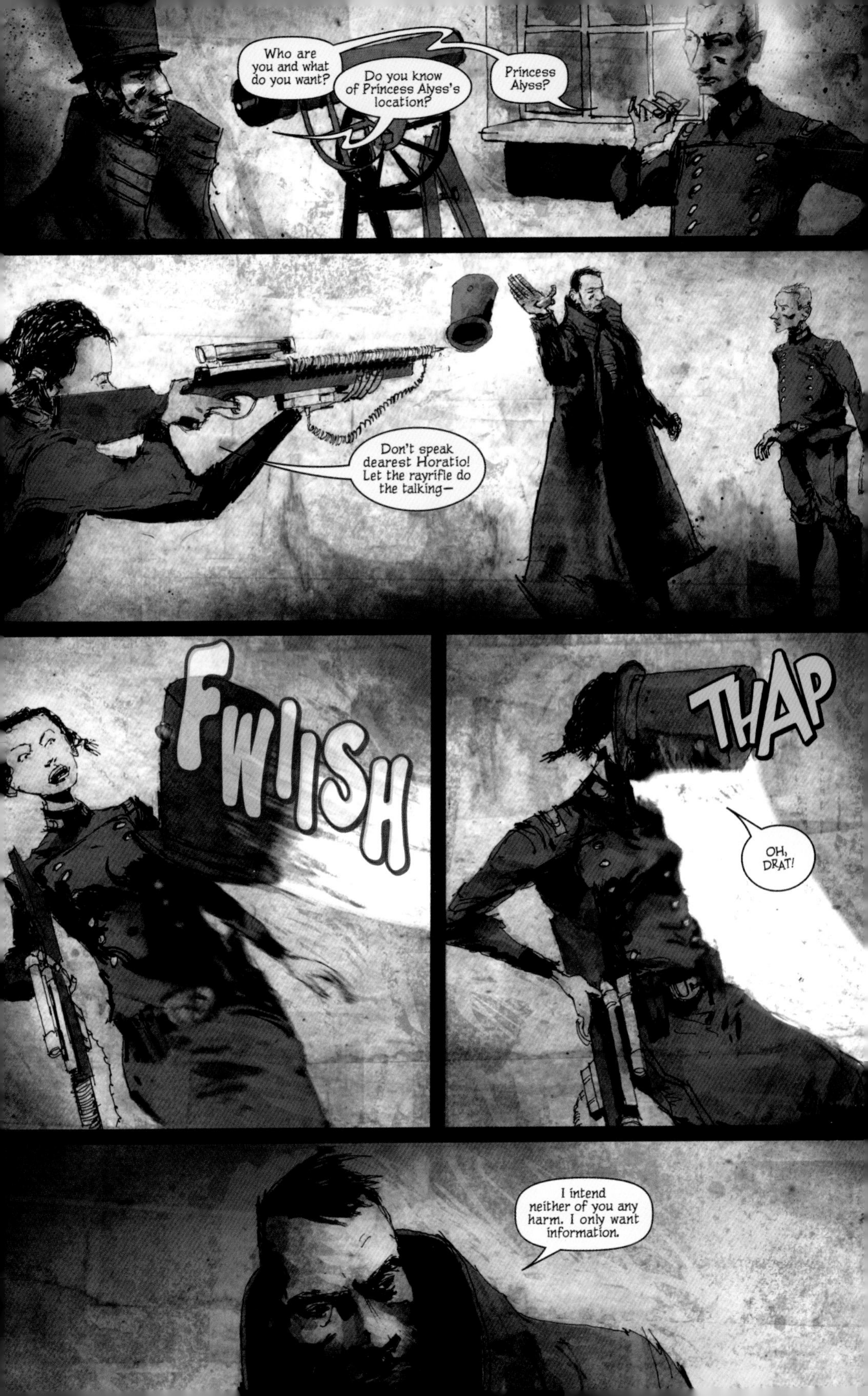
Who are you and what do you want?
Do you know of Princess Alyss's location?
Princess Alyss?
Don't speak dearest Horatio! Let the rayrifle do the talking—
FWISH
THAP
OH, DRAT!
I intend neither of you any harm. I only want information.

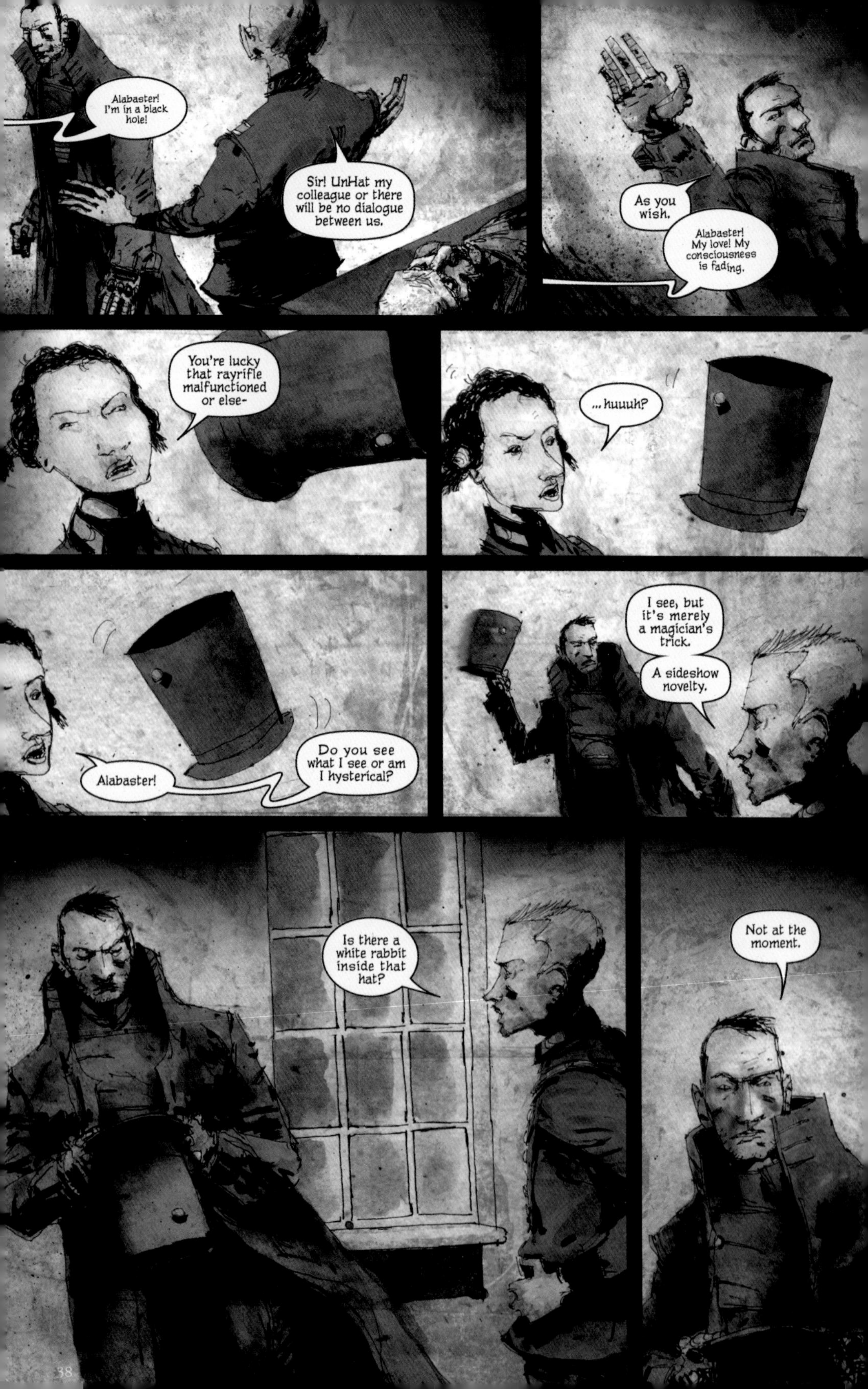
Alabaster! I'm in a black hole!
Sir! UnHat my colleague or there will be no dialogue between us.
As you wish.
Alabaster! My love! My consciousness is fading.
You're lucky that rayrifle malfunctioned or else-
...huuuh?
Alabaster!
Do you see what I see or am I hysterical?
I see, but it's merely a magician's trick.
A sideshow novelty.
Is there a white rabbit inside that hat?
Not at the moment.

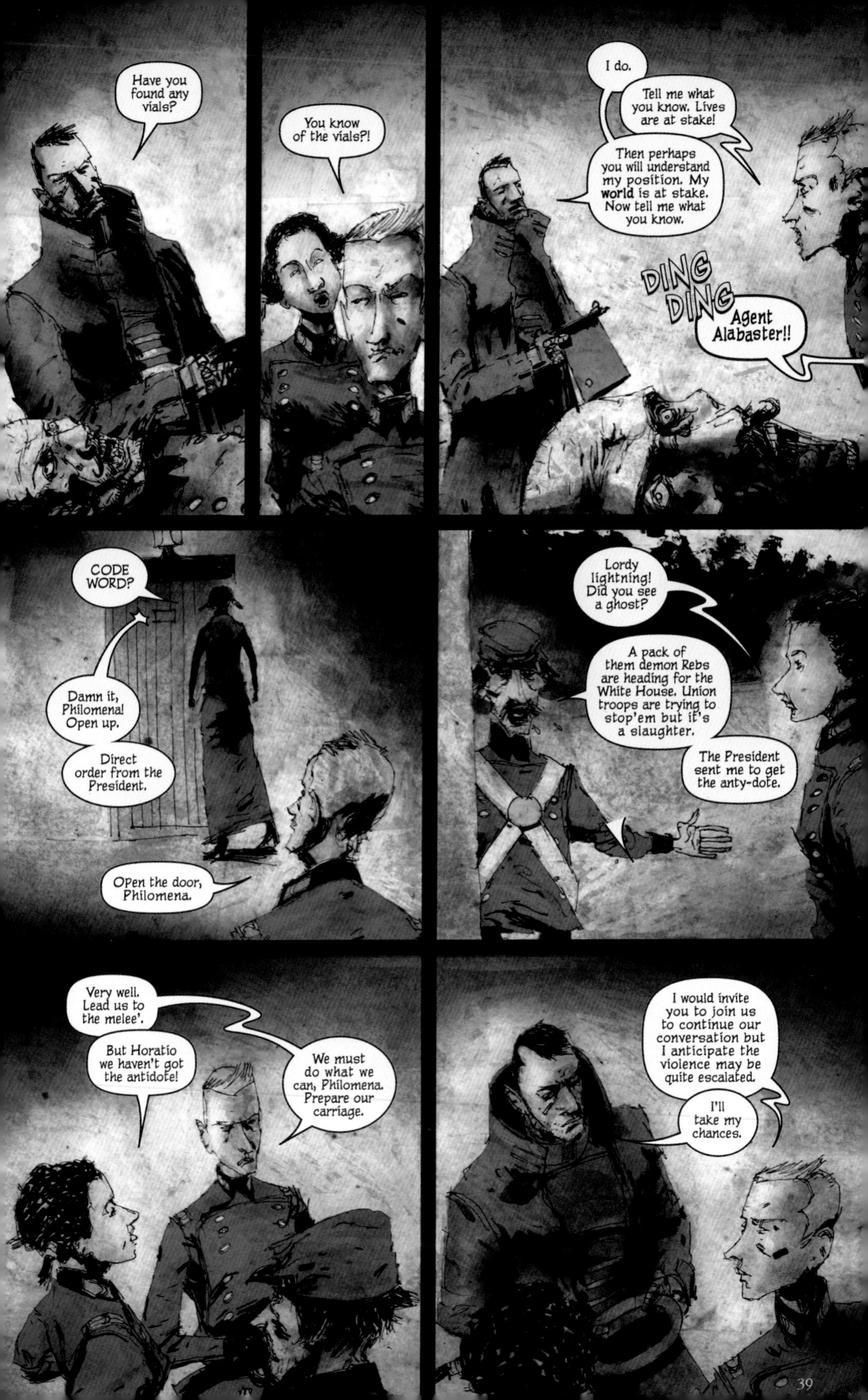
Have you found any vials?
You know of the vials?!
I do.
Tell me what you know. Lives are at stake!
Then perhaps you will understand my position. My world is at stake. Now tell me what you know.
DING DING
Agent Alabaster!!
CODE WORD?
Damn it, Philomena! Open up.
Direct order from the President.
Open the door, Philomena.
Lordy lightning! Did you see a ghost?
A pack of them demon Rebs are heading for the White House. Union troops are trying to stop'em but it's a slaughter.
The President sent me to get the anty-dote.
Very well. Lead us to the melee'.
But Horatio we haven't got the antidote!
We must do what we can, Philomena. Prepare our carriage.
I would invite you to join us to continue our conversation but I anticipate the violence may be quite escalated.
I'll take my chances.

YEEE-HAAAAA!!

CLEAR THE STREET!
THUDDA-THUMP THUDDA-THUMP THUDDA-THUMP

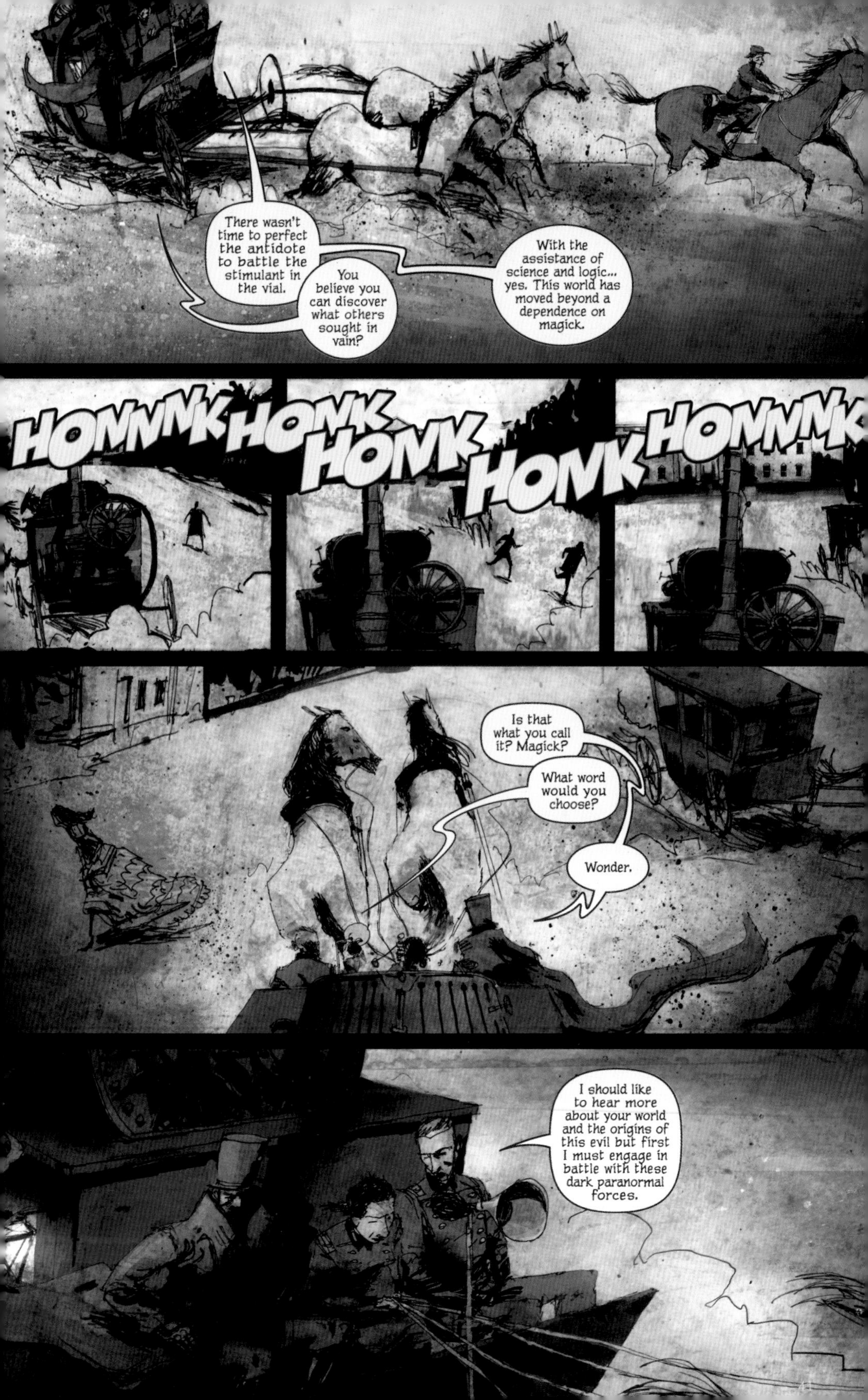
There wasn't time to perfect the antidote to battle the stimulant in the vial.
You believe you can discover what others sought in vain?
With the assistance of science and logic... yes. This world has moved beyond a dependence on magick.
HONNNK
HONK
HONK
HONK
HONNNK
Is that what you call it? Magick?
What word would you choose?
Wonder.
I should like to hear more about your world and the origins of this evil but first I must engage in battle with these dark paranormal forces.

GONNA GETCHA GETCHA GOOD!
MURDER!
MAYHEM!
WHEEEEE!
Halt Beelzebub!
Perhaps this darkness is the ANTI-GLOW which will lead me to Alyss via those that wish her dead.
Sir. I wish to offer my assistance in this battle.
NEEEIGH
Can you fight?

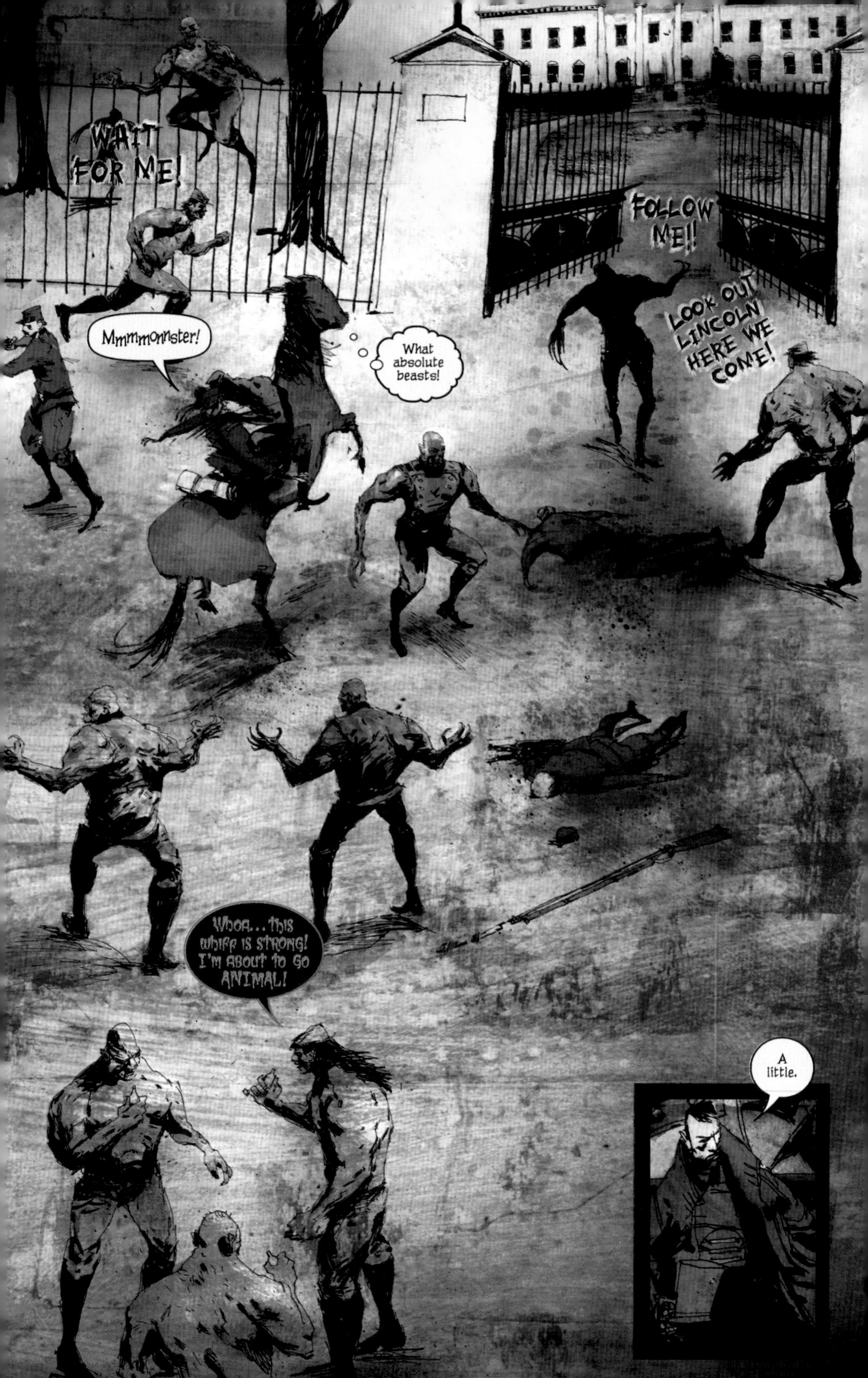
WAIT FOR ME!
FOLLOW ME!!
Mmmmonnster!
What absolute beasts!
LOOK OUT LINCOLN HERE WE COME!
Whoa... this whiff is strong! I'm about to go ANIMAL!
A little.

In this capitol I have discovered much more than secrets, I have found illuminated minds willing to search for and exalt the light of Imagination. From my experience, I now believe that the brilliant equations of that mad mathematician who directed me here were a numerical manifestation of the Glow...leading me as always. Surely a power as vast as Imagination is not limited to one form.

Did Wonderland honor our Queen as they honored their President? Not with a forbidden procession or parade. But silently, yes.

"The human spirit needs places where nature

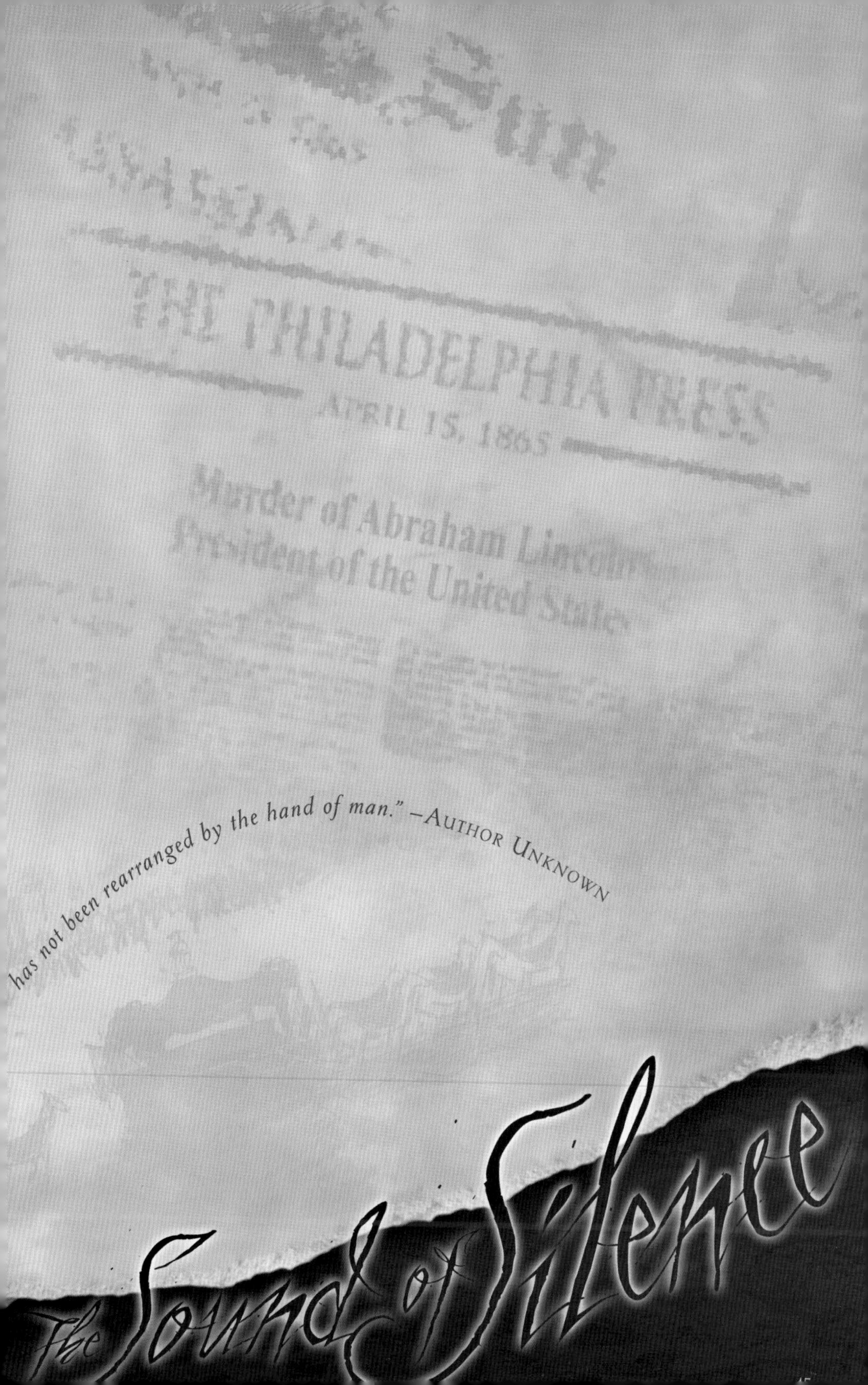
THE PHILADELPHIA PRESS
APRIL 15, 1865
Murder of Abraham Lincoln
President of the United States

has not been rearranged by the hand of man." —Author Unknown

The Sound of Silence

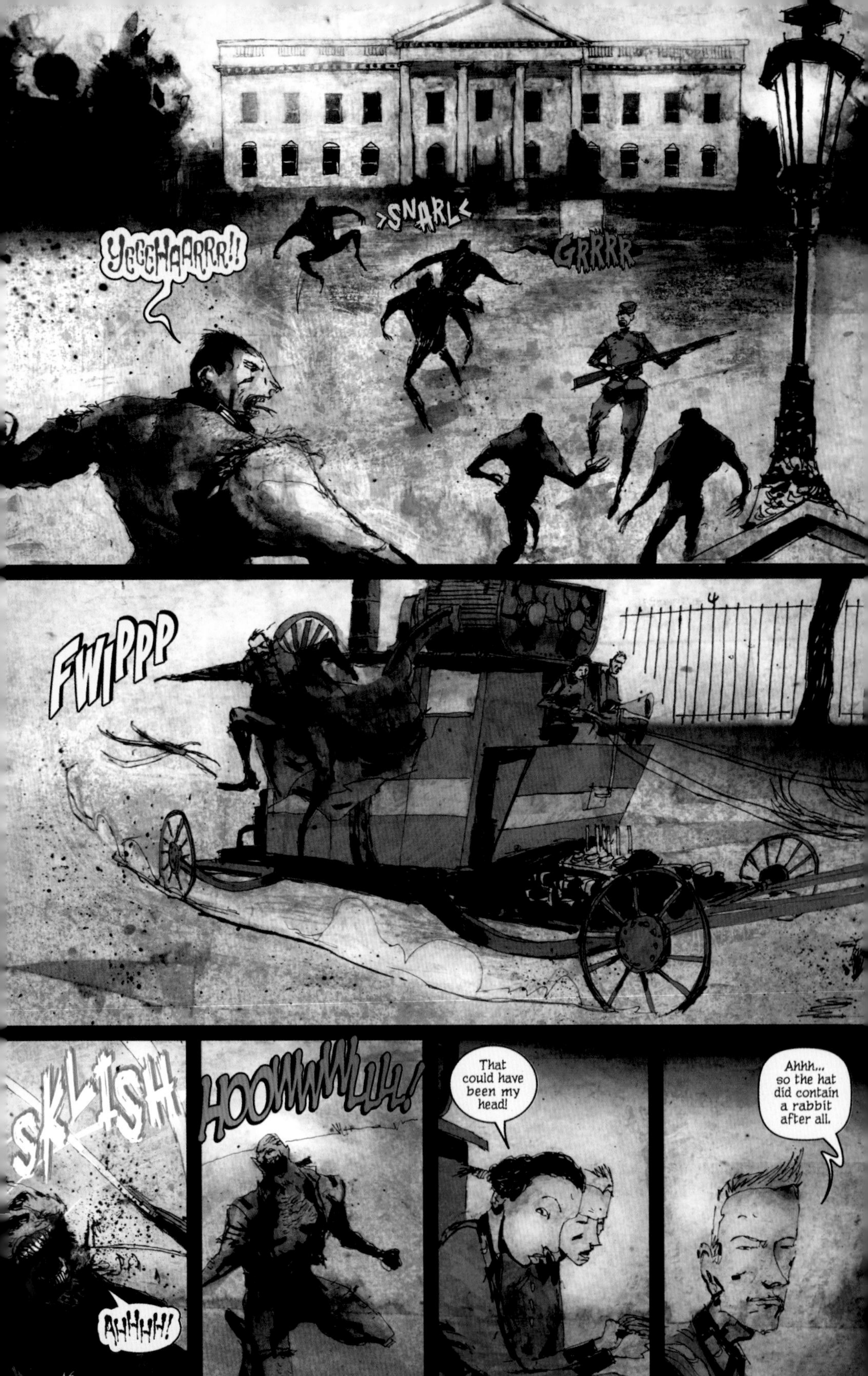
YECCHAARRR!!
>SNARL<
GRRRR
FWIPPP
SKLISH
AHHHH!
HOOMMLLL!
That could have been my head!
Ahhh... so the hat did contain a rabbit after all.

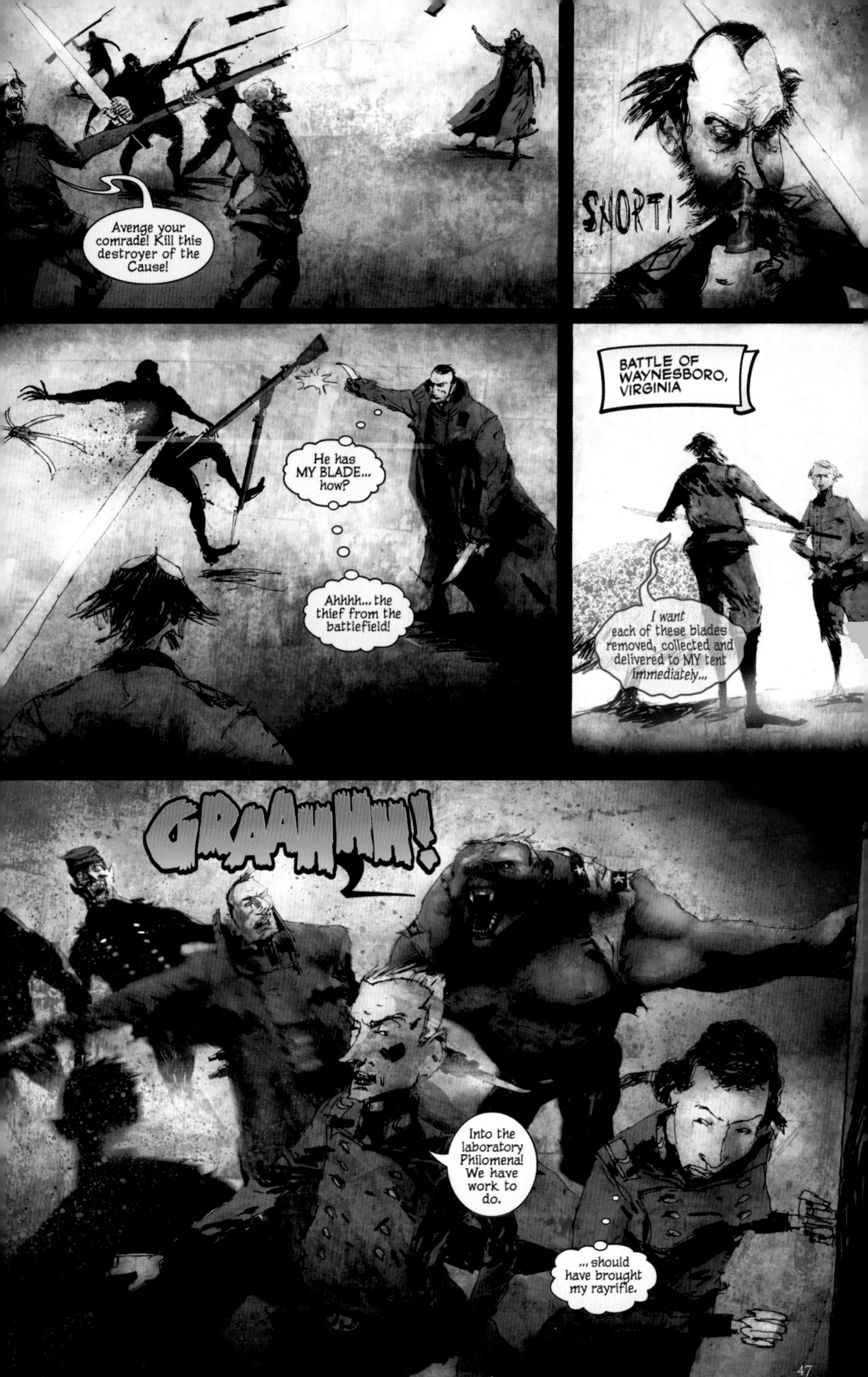
Avenge your comrade! Kill this destroyer of the Cause!
SNORT!
He has MY BLADE... how?
Ahhhh... the thief from the battlefield!
BATTLE OF WAYNESBORO, VIRGINIA
I want each of these blades removed, collected and delivered to MY tent immediately...
GRAAHHH!
Into the laboratory Philomena! We have work to do.
...should have brought my rayrifle.

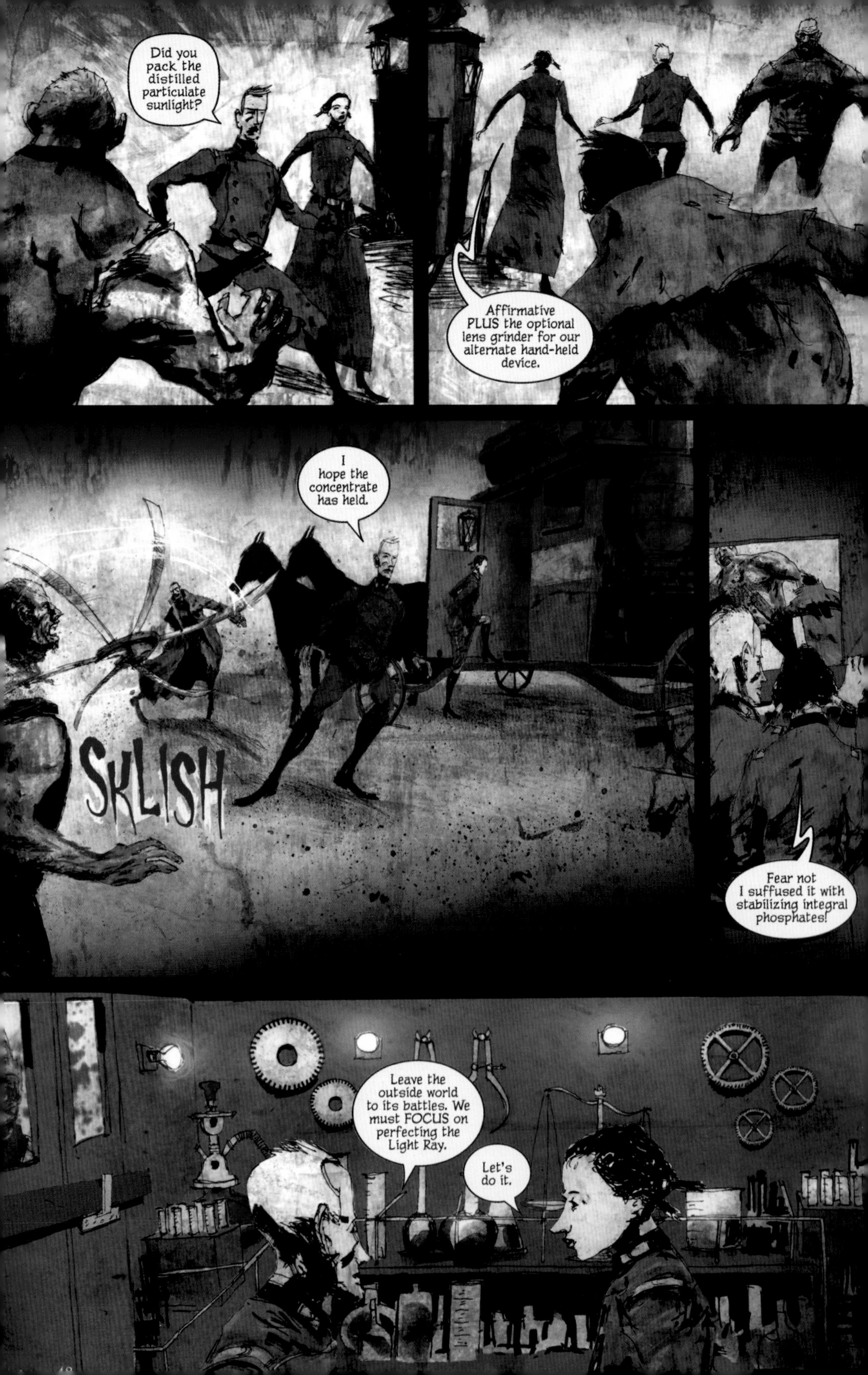

Did you pack the distilled particulate sunlight?
Affirmative PLUS the optional lens grinder for our alternate hand-held device.
I hope the concentrate has held.
SKLISH
Fear not I suffused it with stabilizing integral phosphates!
Leave the outside world to its battles. We must FOCUS on perfecting the Light Ray.
Let's do it.

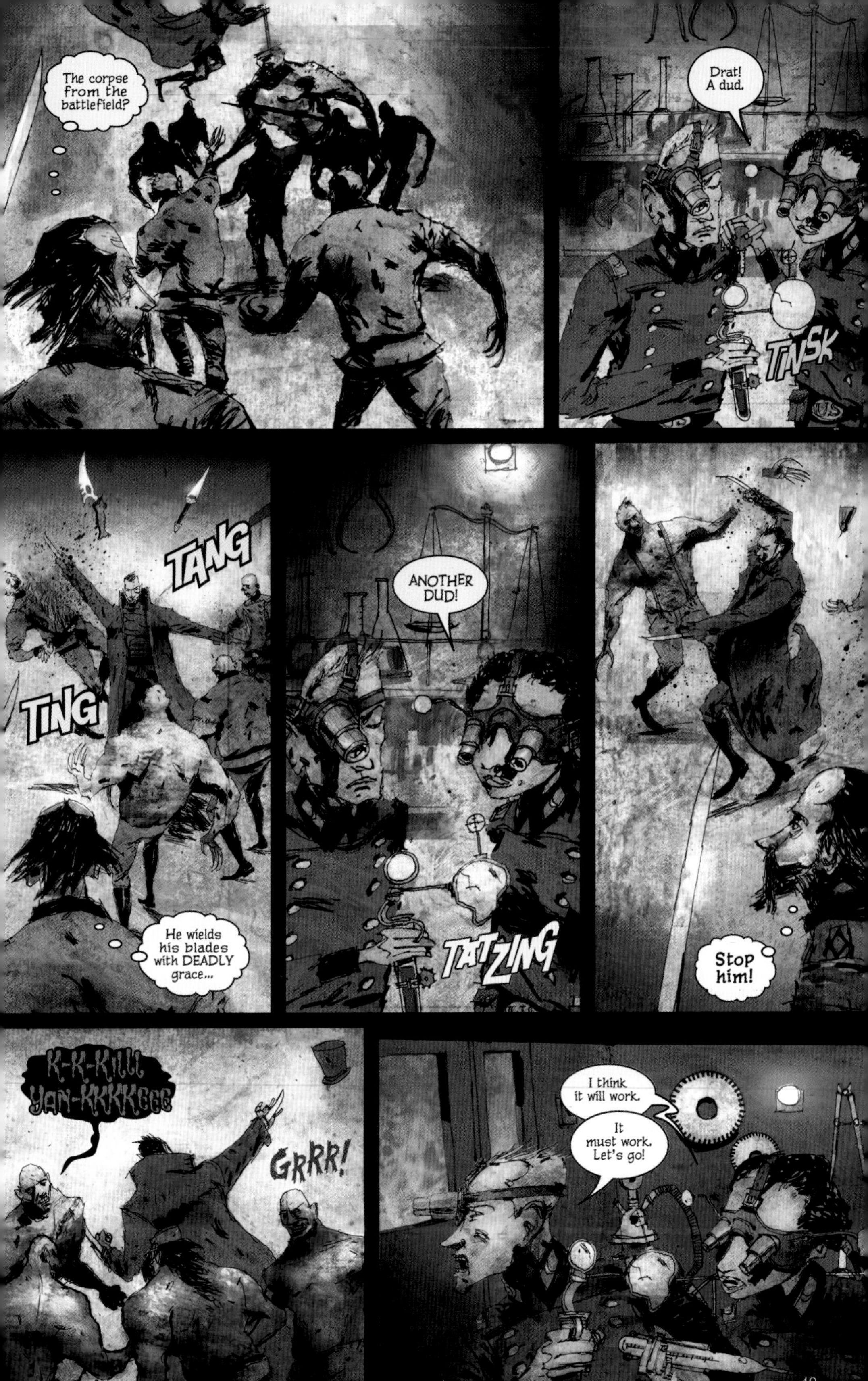
The corpse from the battlefield?
Drat! A dud.
TNSK
TANG
TING
He wields his blades with DEADLY grace...
ANOTHER DUD!
TATZING
Stop him!
K-K-Kill Yan-KKKKeee
GRRR!
I think it will work.
It must work. Let's go!

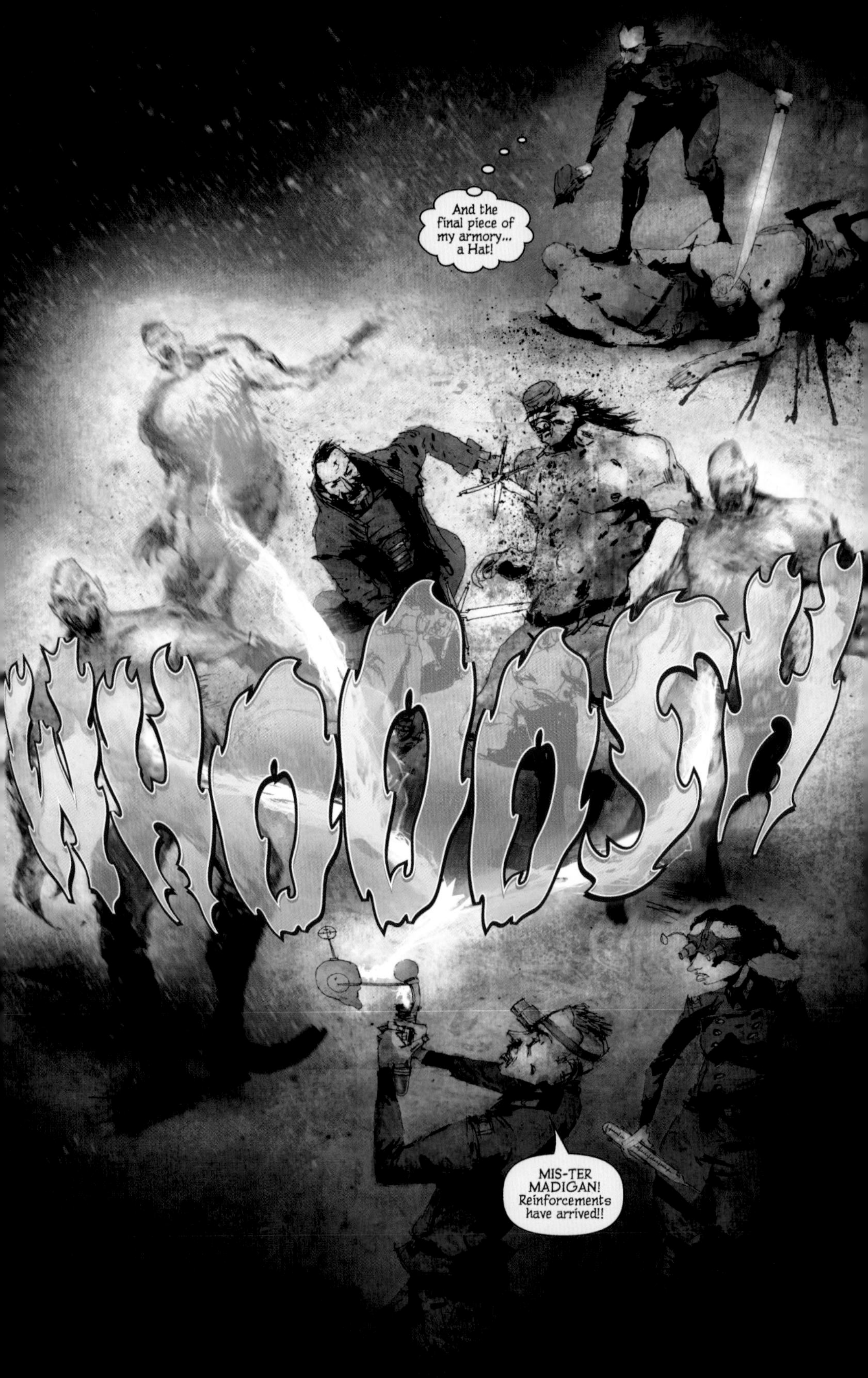
And the final piece of my armory... a Hat!
WHOOOSH
MIS-TER MADIGAN! Reinforcements have arrived!!

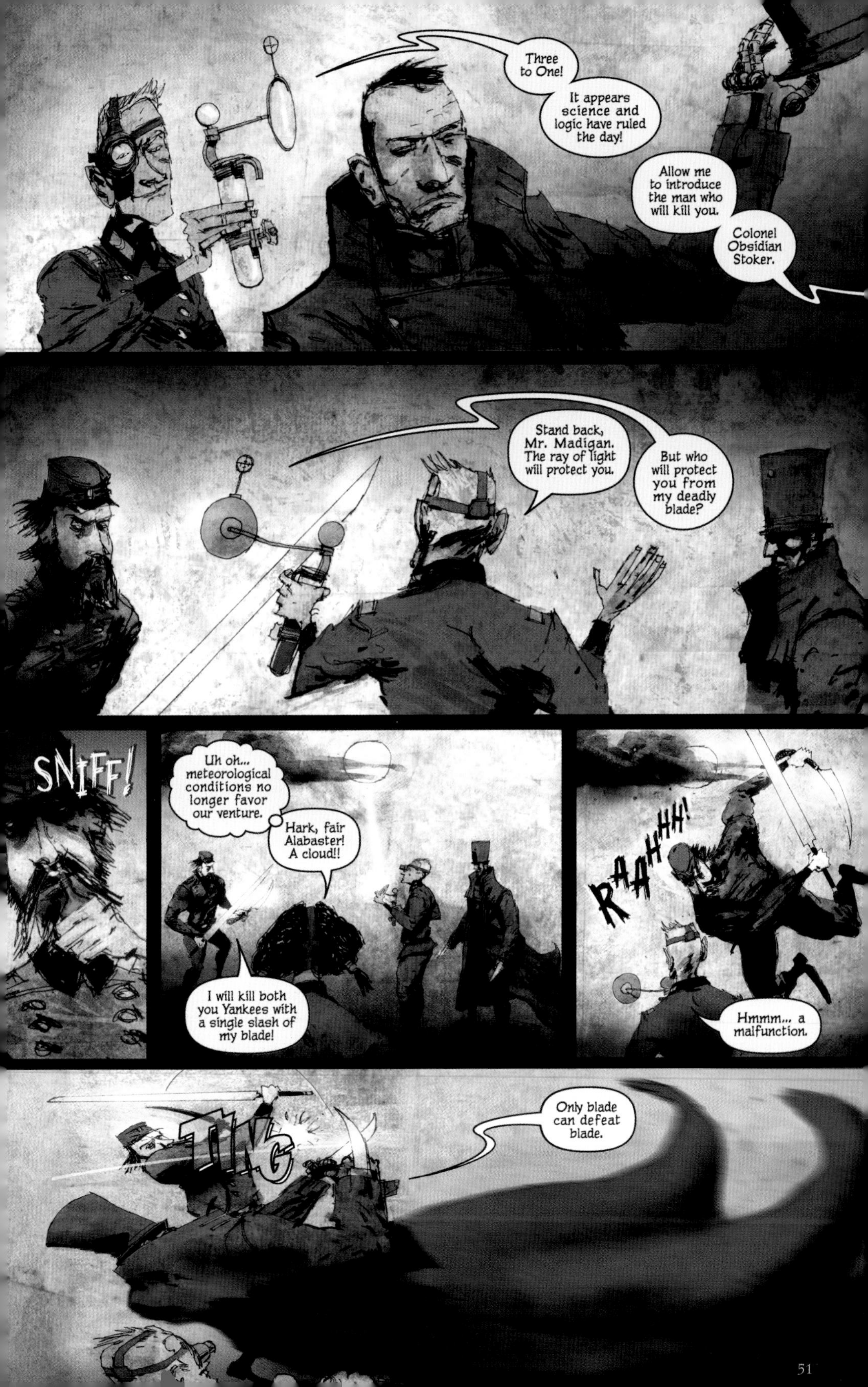
Three to One!
It appears science and logic have ruled the day!
Allow me to introduce the man who will kill you.
Colonel Obsidian Stoker.
Stand back, Mr. Madigan. The ray of light will protect you.
But who will protect you from my deadly blade?
SNIFF!
Uh oh... meteorological conditions no longer favor our venture.
Hark, fair Alabaster! A cloud!!
I will kill both you Yankees with a single slash of my blade!
RAAHHH!
Hmmm... a malfunction.
TING
Only blade can defeat blade.

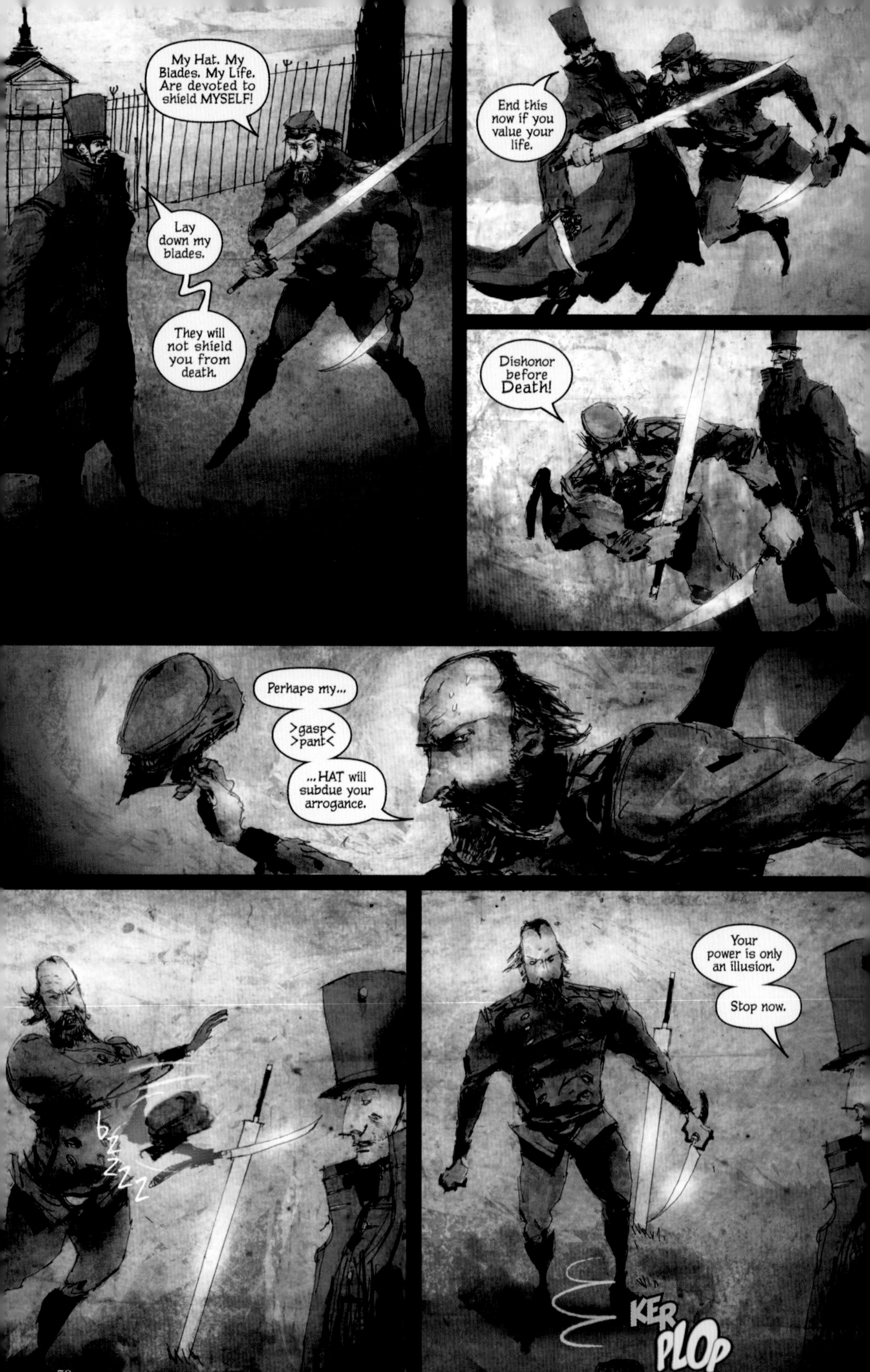
My Hat. My Blades. My Life. Are devoted to shield MYSELF!
Lay down my blades.
They will not shield you from death.
End this now if you value your life.
Dishonor before Death!
Perhaps my...
>gasp< >pant<
...HAT will subdue your arrogance.
bzzzz
Your power is only an illusion.
Stop now.
KERPLOP

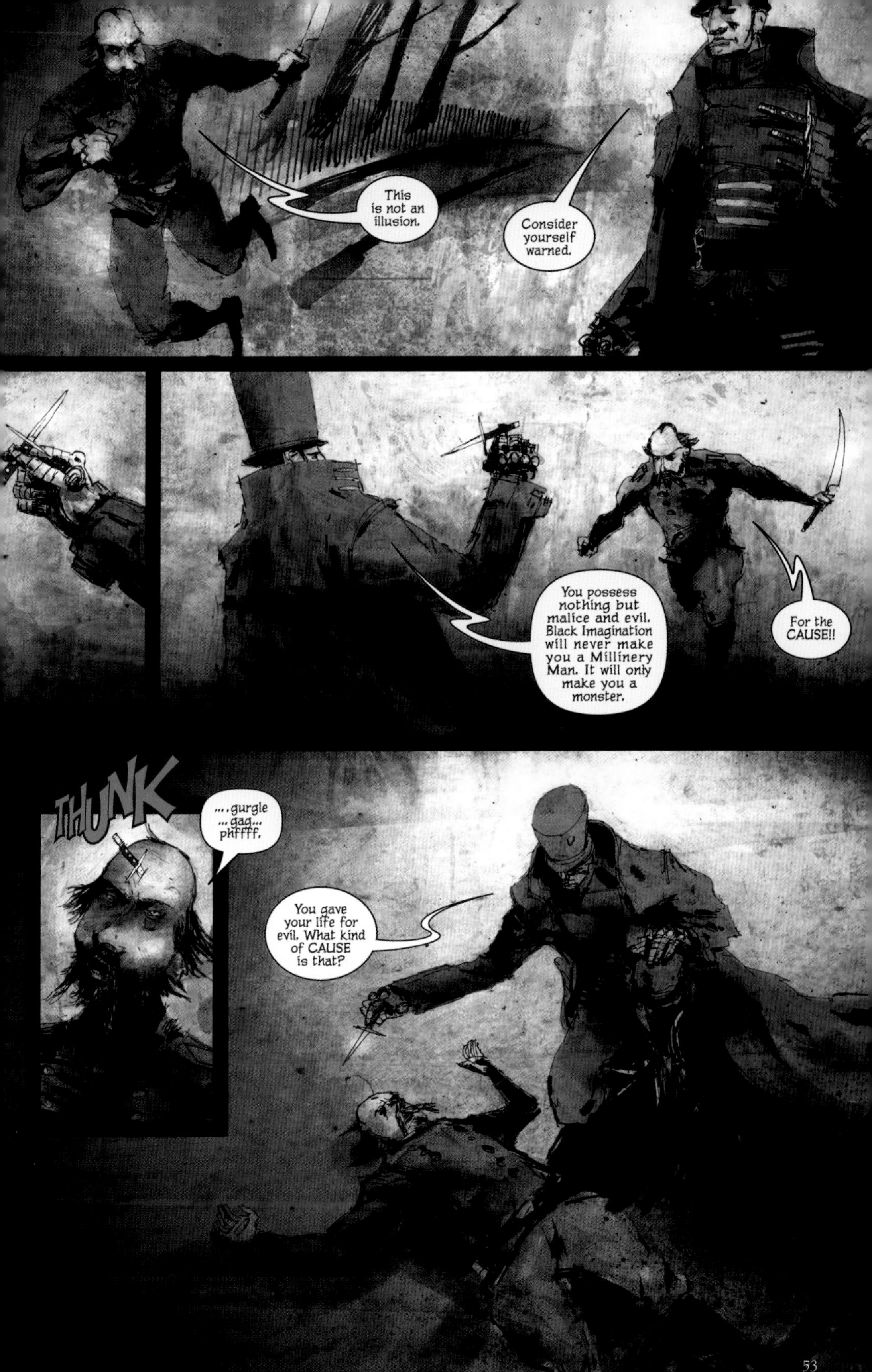

This is not an illusion.
Consider yourself warned.
You possess nothing but malice and evil. Black Imagination will never make you a Millinery Man. It will only make you a monster.
For the CAUSE!!
THUNK
...gurgle ...gag... phffff.
You gave your life for evil. What kind of CAUSE is that?

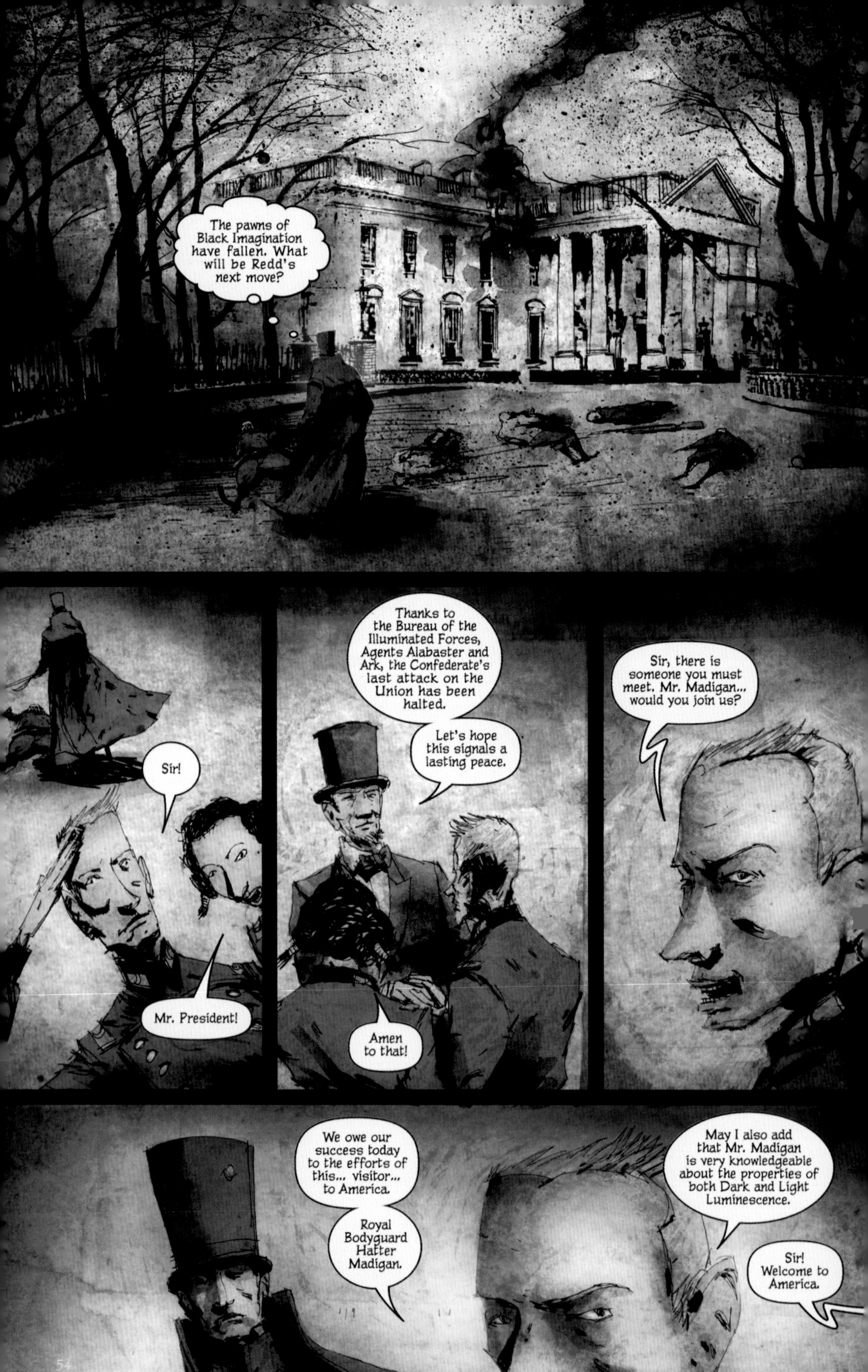
The pawns of Black Imagination have fallen. What will be Redd's next move?
Sir!
Mr. President!
Thanks to the Bureau of the Illuminated Forces, Agents Alabaster and Ark, the Confederate's last attack on the Union has been halted.
Let's hope this signals a lasting peace.
Amen to that!
Sir, there is someone you must meet. Mr. Madigan... would you join us?
We owe our success today to the efforts of this... visitor... to America.
Royal Bodyguard Hatter Madigan.
May I also add that Mr. Madigan is very knowledgeable about the properties of both Dark and Light Luminescence.
Sir! Welcome to America.

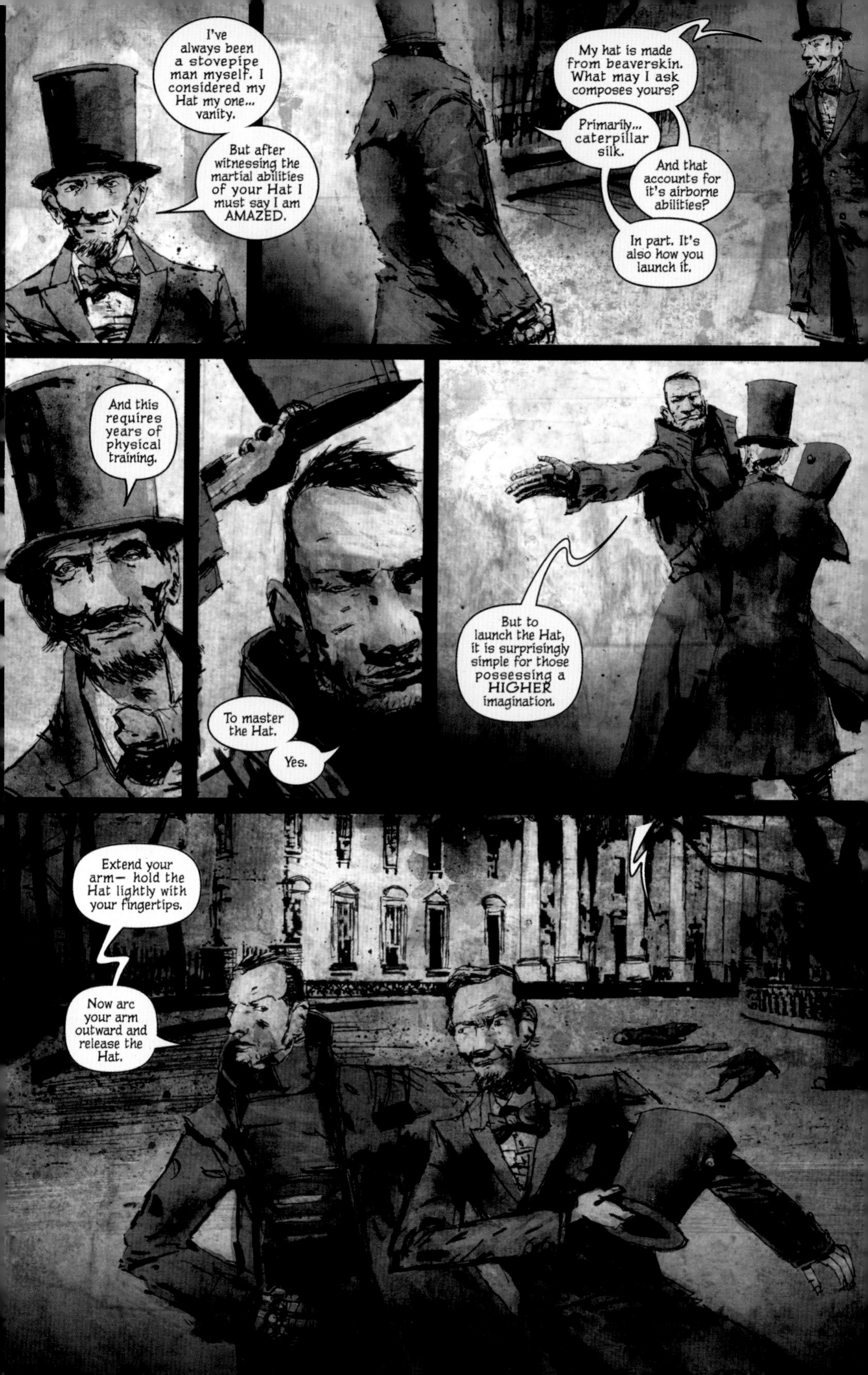
I've always been a stovepipe man myself. I considered my Hat my one... vanity.
But after witnessing the martial abilities of your Hat I must say I am AMAZED.
My hat is made from beaverskin. What may I ask composes yours?
Primarily... caterpillar silk.
And that accounts for it's airborne abilities?
In part. It's also how you launch it.
And this requires years of physical training.
To master the Hat.
Yes.
But to launch the Hat, it is surprisingly simple for those possessing a HIGHER imagination.
Extend your arm— hold the Hat lightly with your fingertips.
Now arc your arm outward and release the Hat.

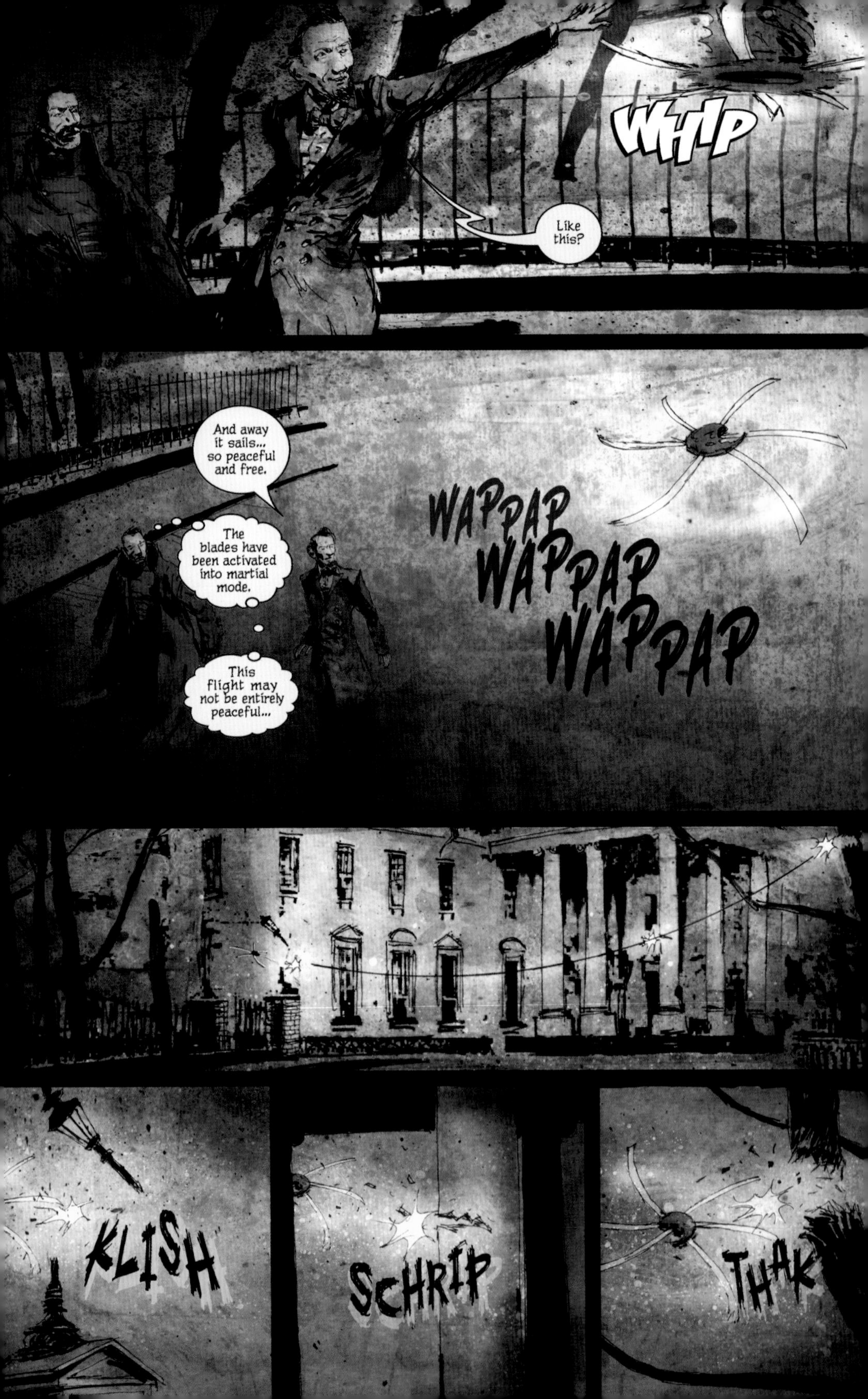
WHIP
Like this?
And away it sails... so peaceful and free.
The blades have been activated into martial mode.
This flight may not be entirely peaceful...
WAPPAP
WAPPAP
WAPPAP
KLISH
SCHRIP
THAK

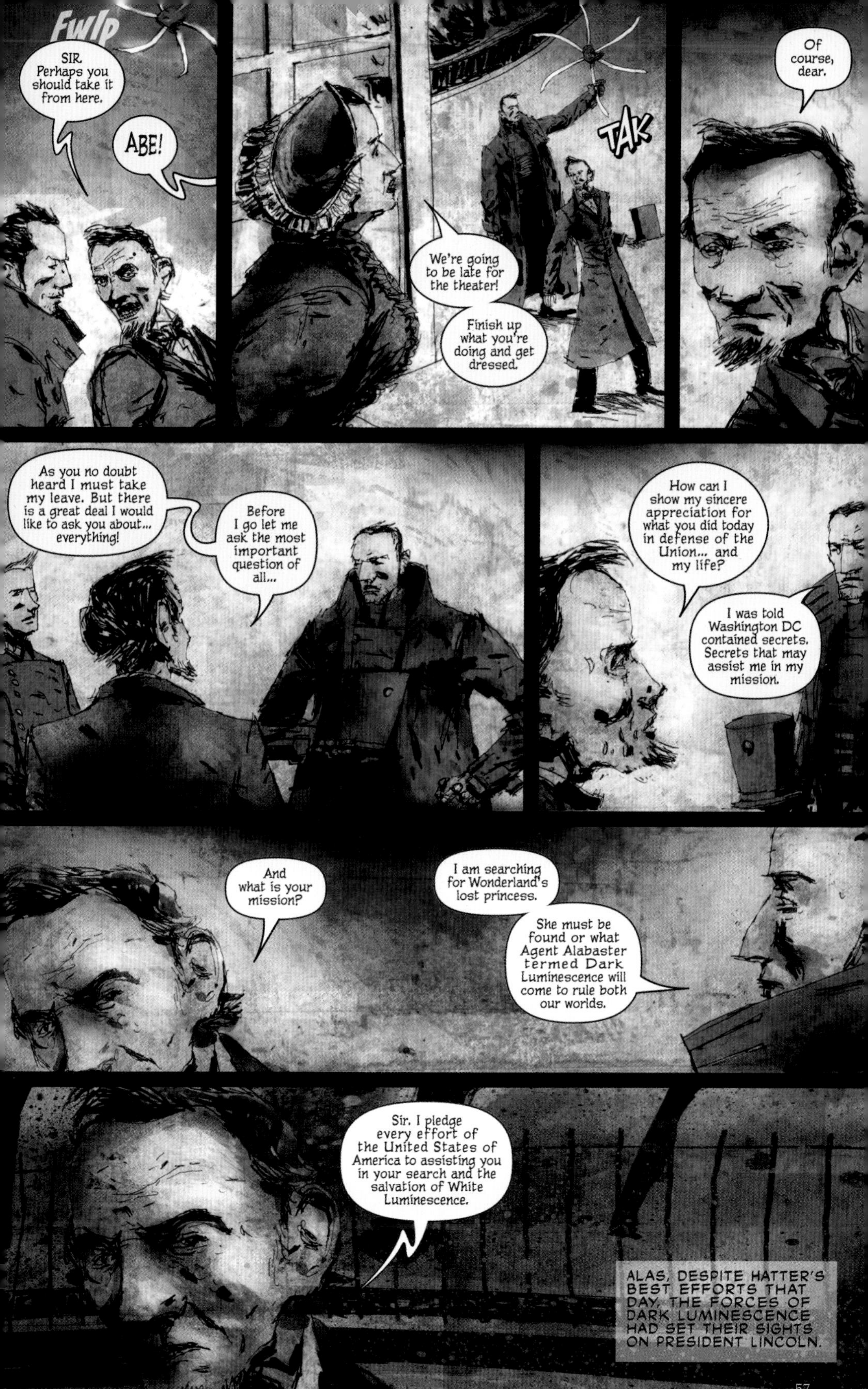
FWIP
SIR. Perhaps you should take it from here.
ABE!
We're going to be late for the theater!
Finish up what you're doing and get dressed.
TAK
Of course, dear.
As you no doubt heard I must take my leave. But there is a great deal I would like to ask you about... everything!
Before I go let me ask the most important question of all...
How can I show my sincere appreciation for what you did today in defense of the Union... and my life?
I was told Washington DC contained secrets. Secrets that may assist me in my mission.
And what is your mission?
I am searching for Wonderland's lost princess.
She must be found or what Agent Alabaster termed Dark Luminescence will come to rule both our worlds.
Sir. I pledge every effort of the United States of America to assisting you in your search and the salvation of White Luminescence.
ALAS, DESPITE HATTER'S BEST EFFORTS THAT DAY, THE FORCES OF DARK LUMINESCENCE HAD SET THEIR SIGHTS ON PRESIDENT LINCOLN.

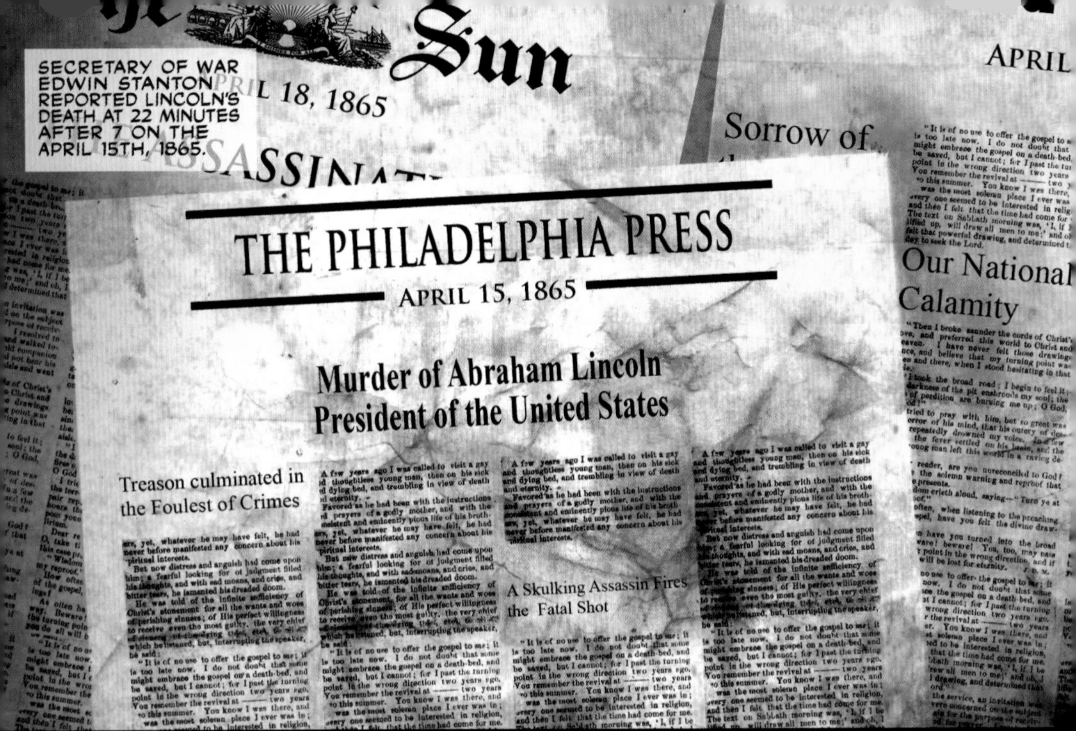
SECRETARY OF WAR EDWIN STANTON REPORTED LINCOLN'S DEATH AT 22 MINUTES AFTER 7 ON THE APRIL 15TH, 1865.
Sun
APRIL
L 18, 1865
Sorrow of
THE PHILADELPHIA PRESS
APRIL 15, 1865
Murder of Abraham Lincoln
President of the United States
Treason culminated in the Foulest of Crimes
A Skulking Assassin Fires the Fatal Shot
Our National Calamity

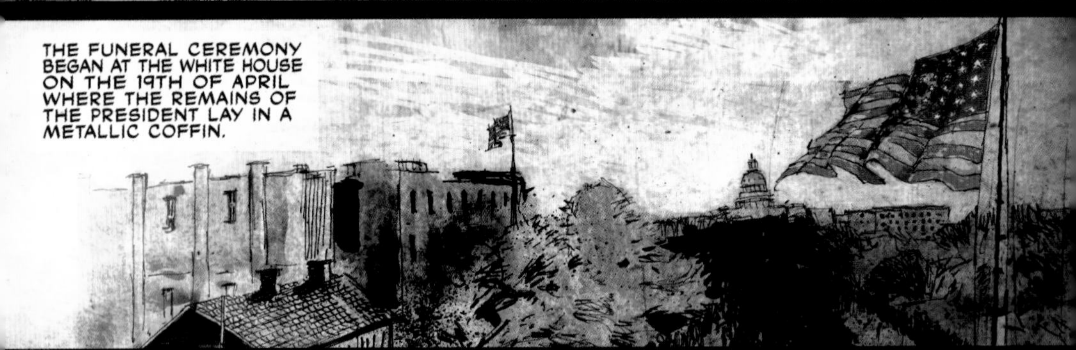
THE FUNERAL CEREMONY BEGAN AT THE WHITE HOUSE ON THE 19TH OF APRIL WHERE THE REMAINS OF THE PRESIDENT LAY IN A METALLIC COFFIN.

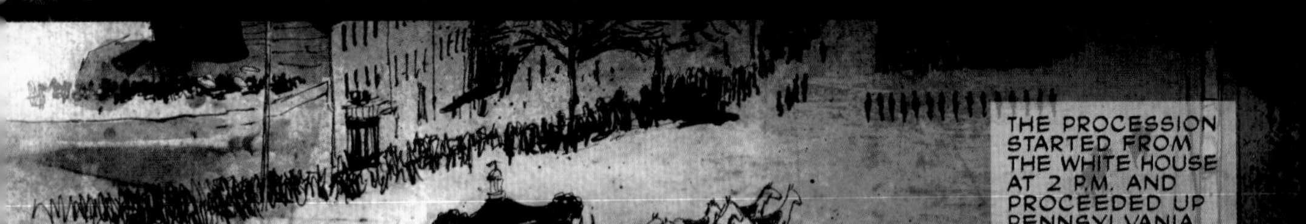
THE PROCESSION STARTED FROM THE WHITE HOUSE AT 2 P.M. AND PROCEEDED UP PENNSYLVANIA AVENUE TO THE CAPITOL AMIDST THE TOLLING OF BELLS AND THE FIRING OF MINUTE-GUNS.

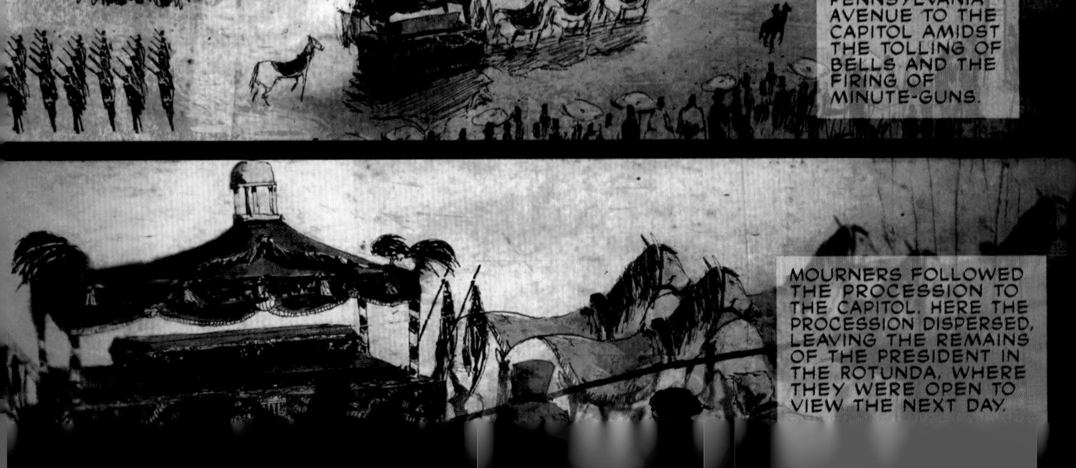
MOURNERS FOLLOWED THE PROCESSION TO THE CAPITOL. HERE THE PROCESSION DISPERSED, LEAVING THE REMAINS OF THE PRESIDENT IN THE ROTUNDA, WHERE THEY WERE OPEN TO VIEW THE NEXT DAY.

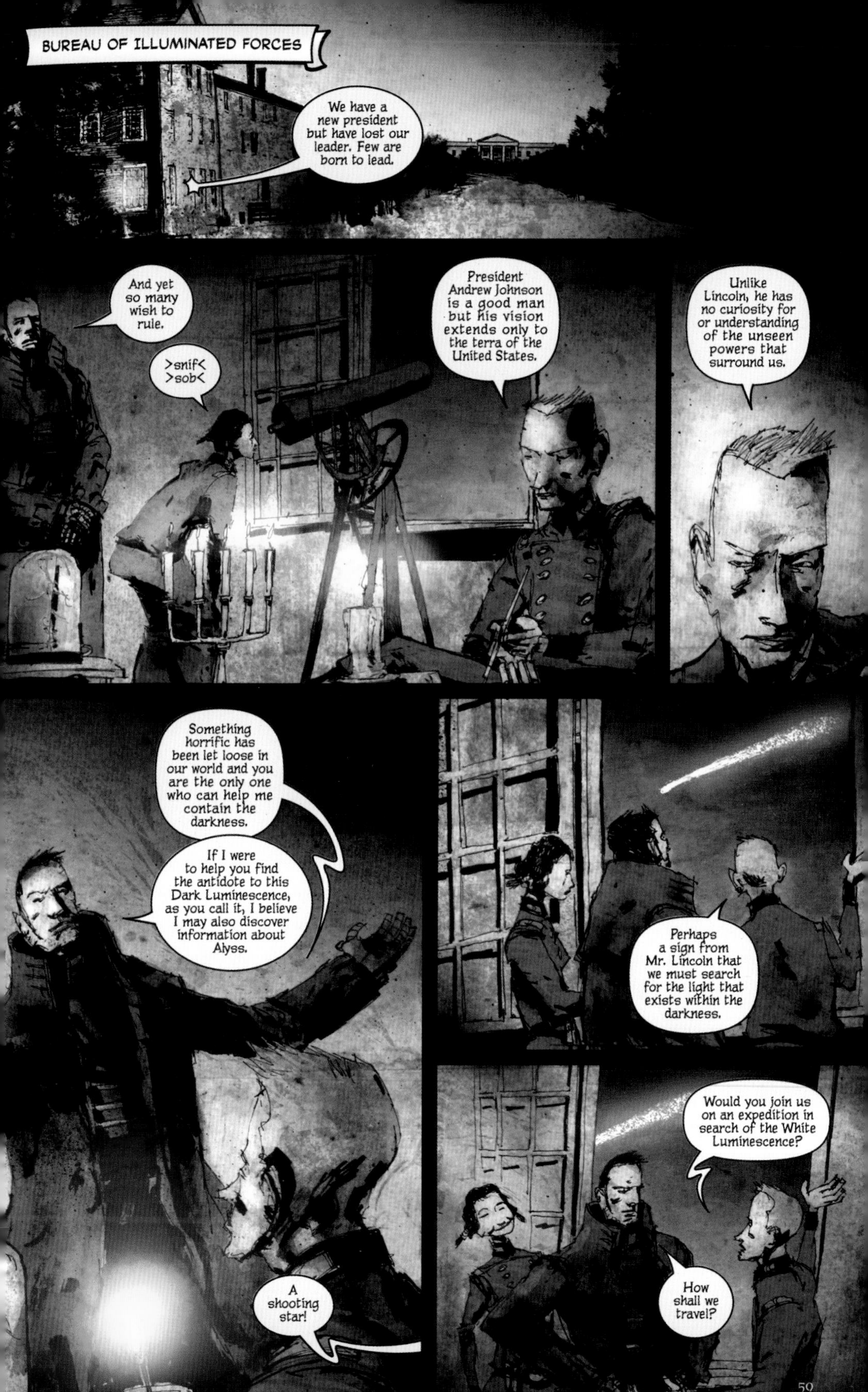
BUREAU OF ILLUMINATED FORCES
We have a new president but have lost our leader. Few are born to lead.
And yet so many wish to rule.
>snif<
>sob<
President Andrew Johnson is a good man but his vision extends only to the terra of the United States.
Unlike Lincoln, he has no curiosity for or understanding of the unseen powers that surround us.
Something horrific has been let loose in our world and you are the only one who can help me contain the darkness.
If I were to help you find the antidote to this Dark Luminescence, as you call it, I believe I may also discover information about Alyss.
A shooting star!
Perhaps a sign from Mr. Lincoln that we must search for the light that exists within the darkness.
Would you join us on an expedition in search of the White Luminescence?
How shall we travel?

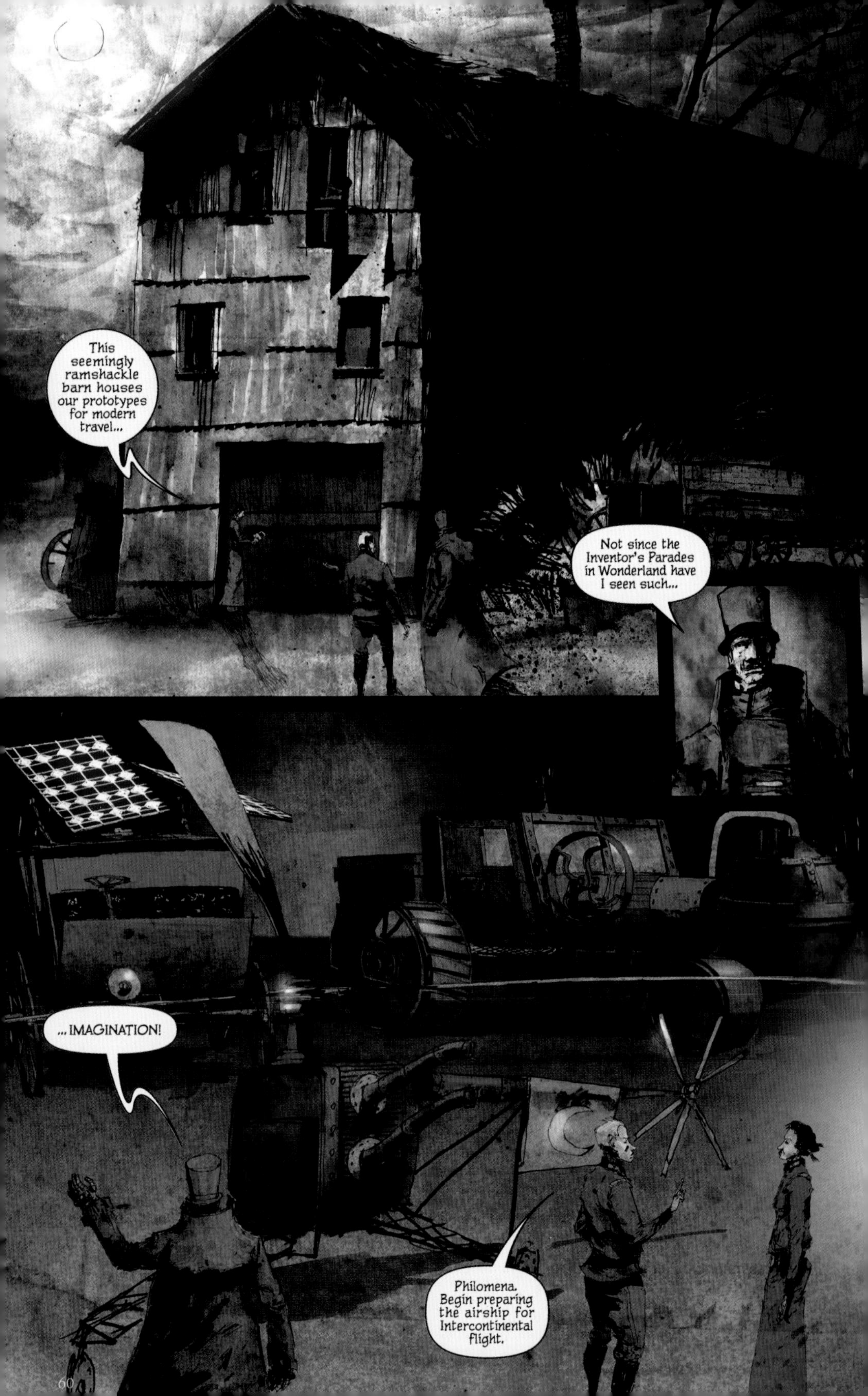
This seemingly ramshackle barn houses our prototypes for modern travel...
Not since the Inventor's Parades in Wonderland have I seen such...
...IMAGINATION!
Philomena. Begin preparing the airship for Intercontinental flight.

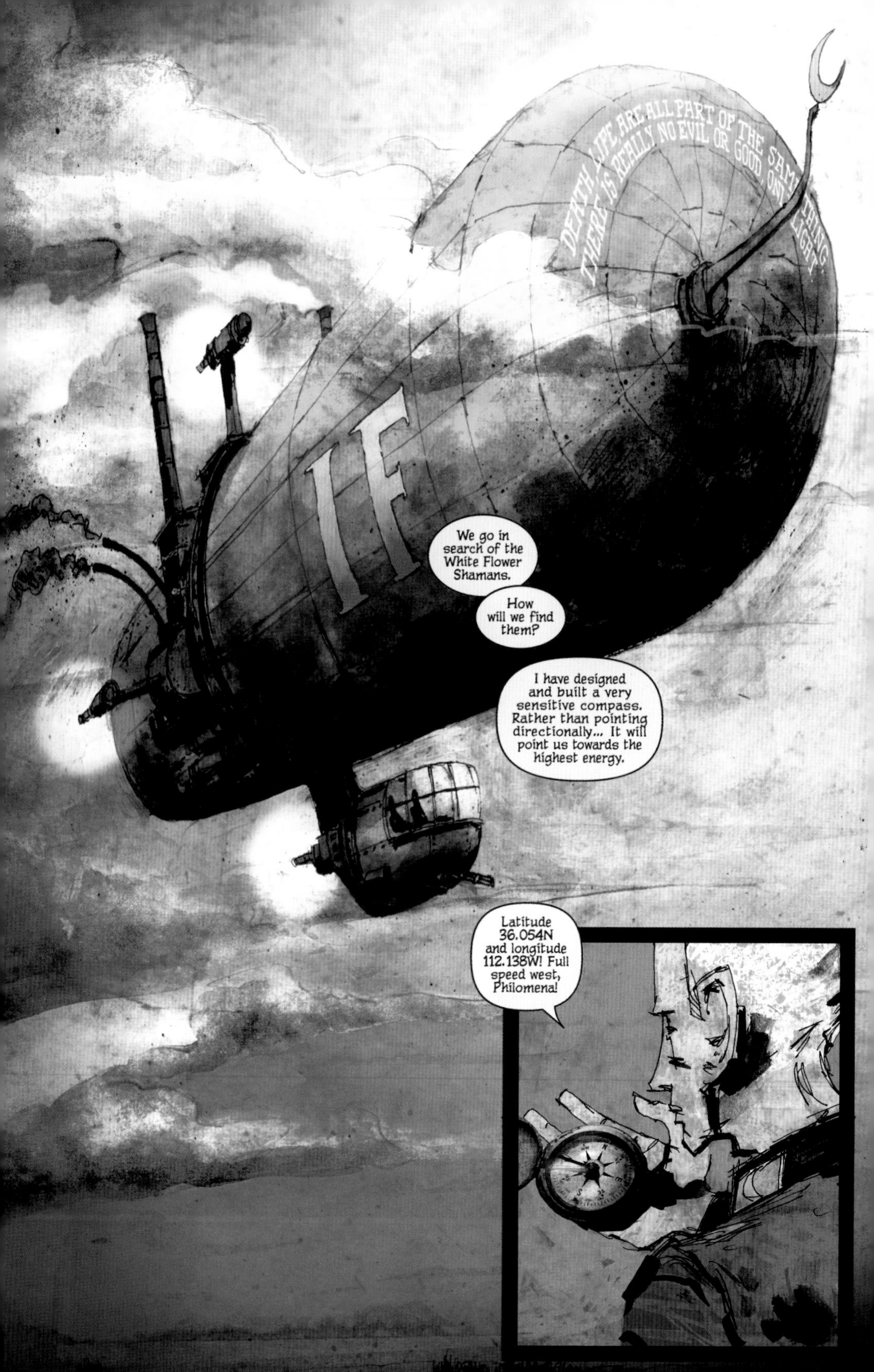

DEATH, LIFE, ARE ALL PART OF THE SAM THING.
THERE IS REALLY NO EVIL OR GOOD, ON LIGHT.
IF
We go in search of the White Flower Shamans.
How will we find them?
I have designed and built a very sensitive compass. Rather than pointing directionally... It will point us towards the highest energy.
Latitude 36.054N and longitude 112.138W! Full speed west, Philomena!

A spark, a shimmer, a radiance of luminescence explodes and suddenly I see past and present. I see a White Queen! And I see Imagination ruling a mindscape spanning both our worlds by the filament of Light. I must open my mind WIDE if I am to continue to be lead by such a force.

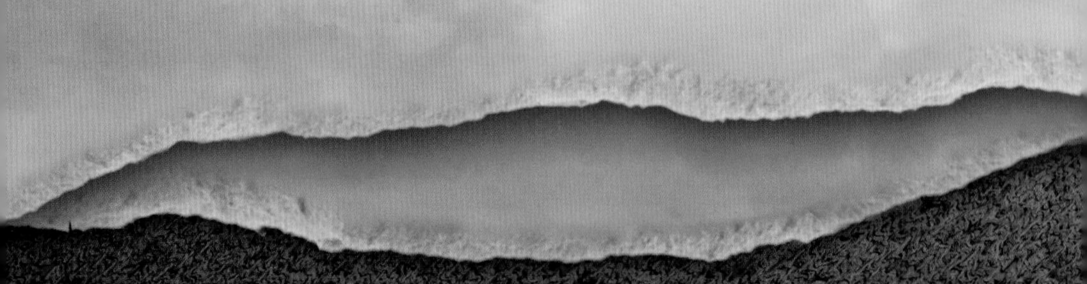

"I believe that there is a subtle magnetism in Nature, which, if we unconsciously yield to it, will direct us aright. —HENRY DAVID Thoreau

Blinded by the Light

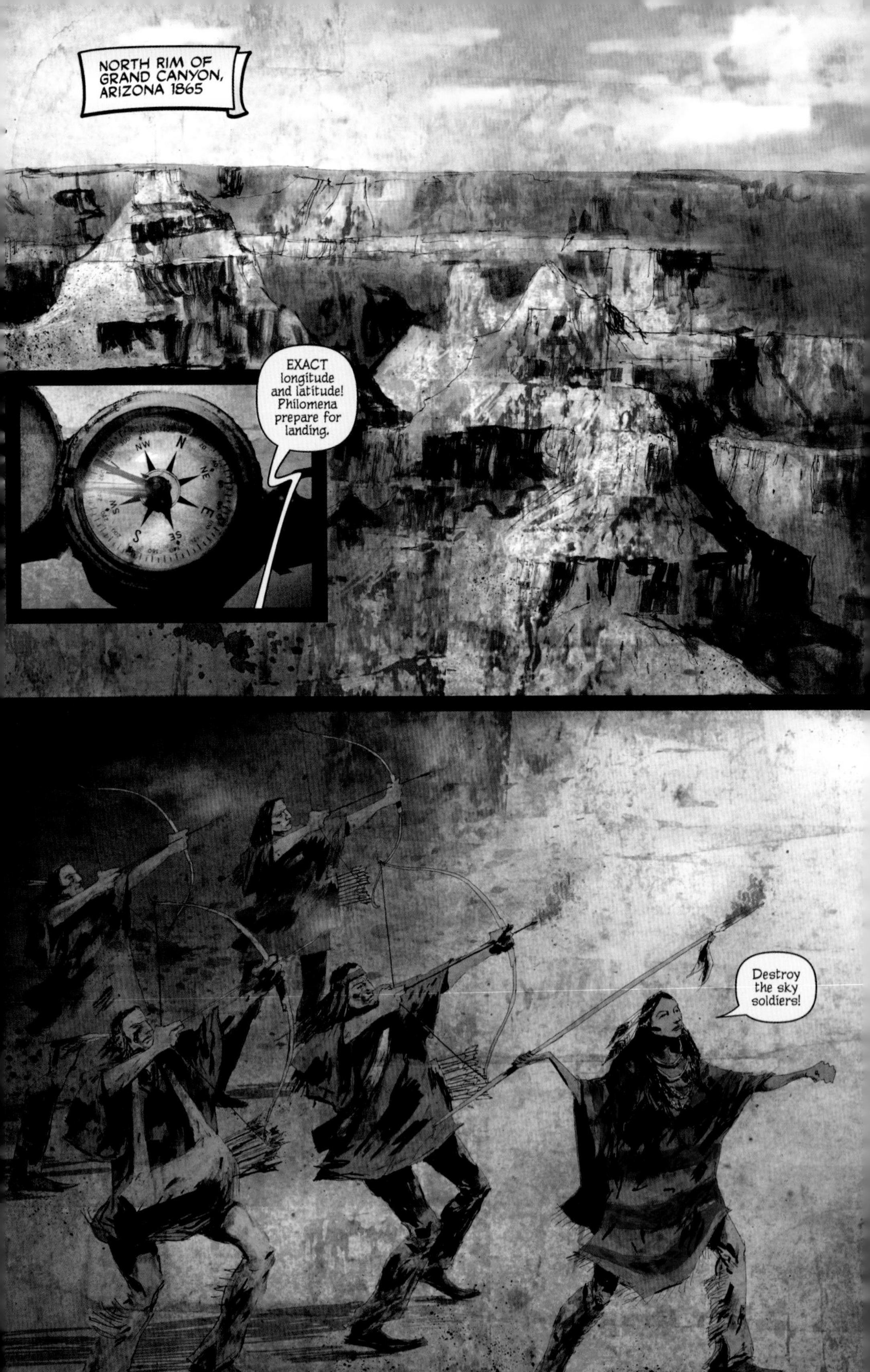
NORTH RIM OF GRAND CANYON, ARIZONA 1865
EXACT longitude and latitude! Philomena prepare for landing.
Destroy the sky soldiers!

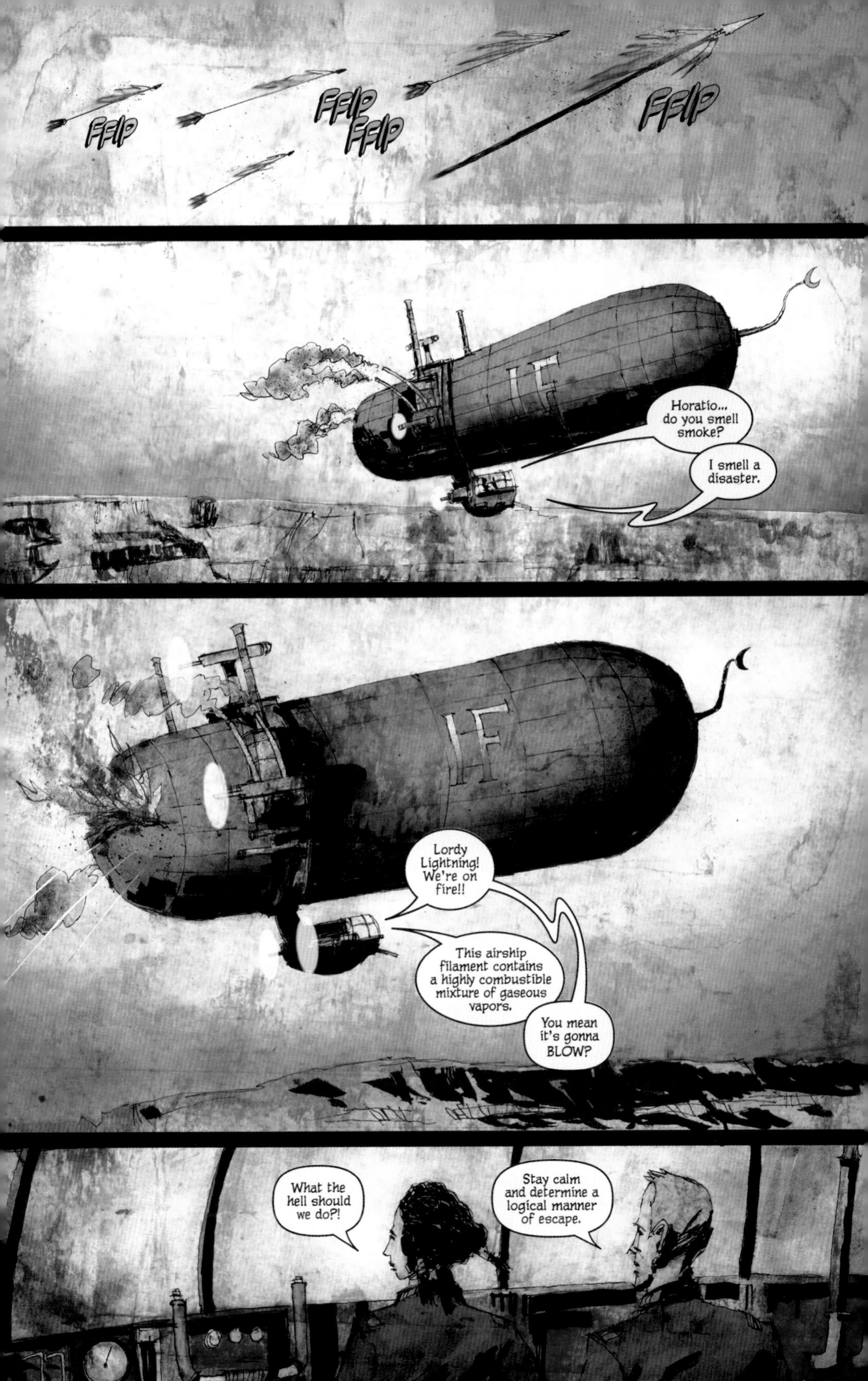
FFIP
FFIP
FFIP
FFIP
Horatio... do you smell smoke?
I smell a disaster.
Lordy Lightning! We're on fire!!
This airship filament contains a highly combustible mixture of gaseous vapors.
You mean it's gonna BLOW?
What the hell should we do?!
Stay calm and determine a logical manner of escape.

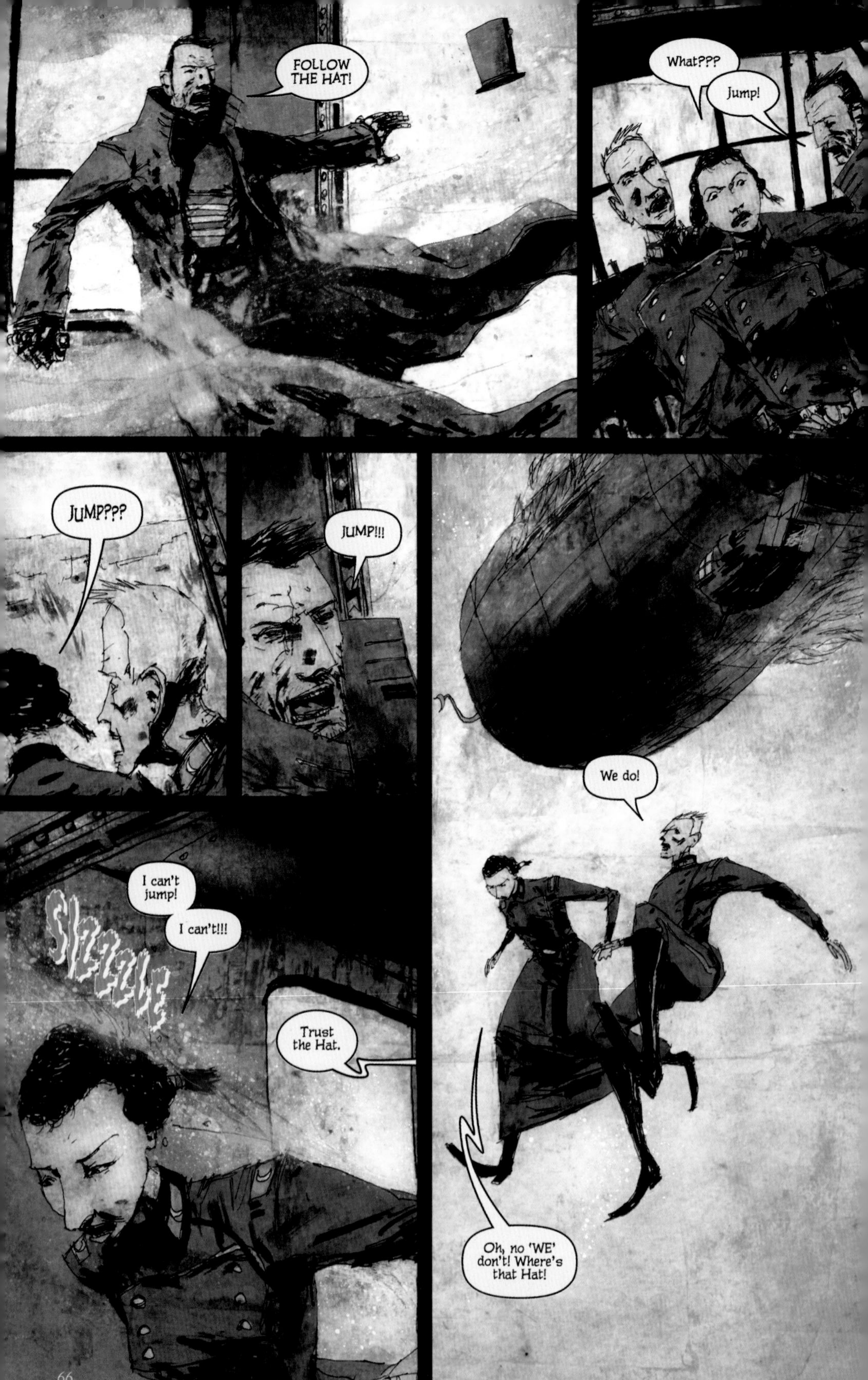
FOLLOW THE HAT!
What???
Jump!
JUMP???
JUMP!!!
We do!
I can't jump!
I can't!!!
SIZZZLE
Trust the Hat.
Oh, no 'WE' don't! Where's that Hat!

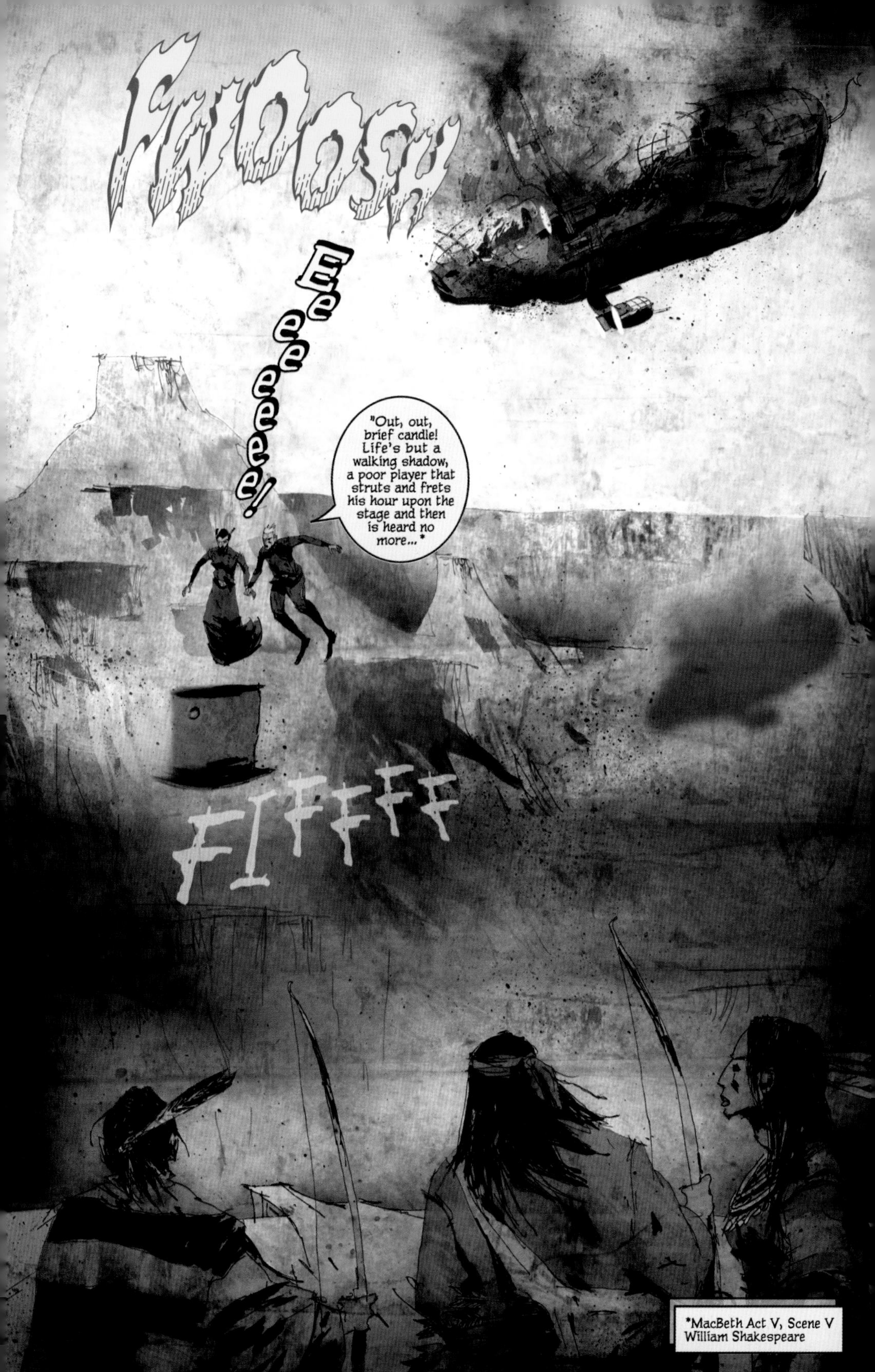
FWOOSH
Eeeeeeeeee!
"Out, out, brief candle! Life's but a walking shadow, a poor player that struts and frets his hour upon the stage and then is heard no more..."*
*MacBeth Act V, Scene V William Shakespeare

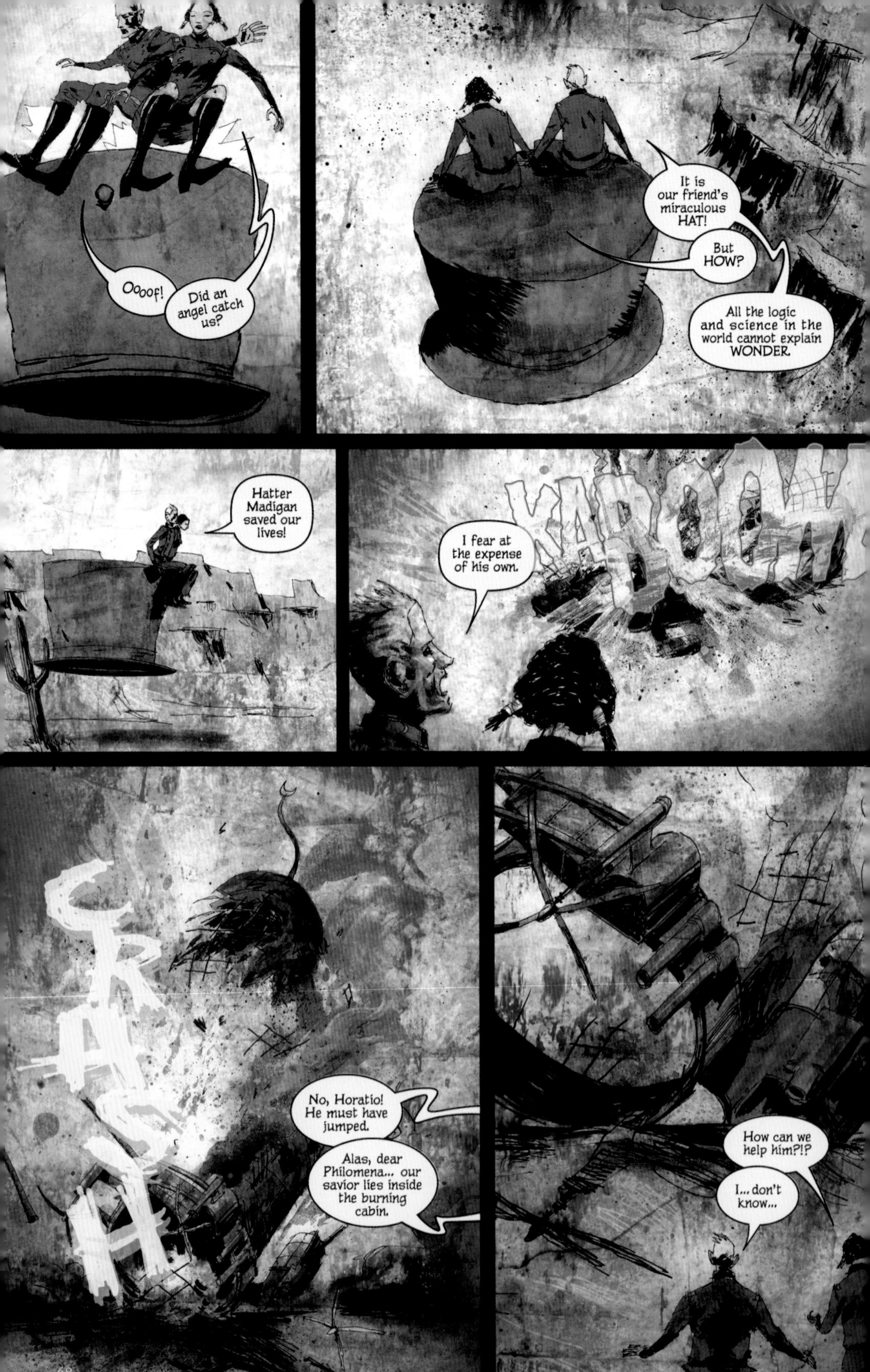
Oooof!
Did an angel catch us?
It is our friend's miraculous HAT!
But HOW?
All the logic and science in the world cannot explain WONDER.
Hatter Madigan saved our lives!
I fear at the expense of his own.
KABOOM!
CRASH
No, Horatio! He must have jumped.
Alas, dear Philomena... our savior lies inside the burning cabin.
How can we help him?!?
I... don't know...

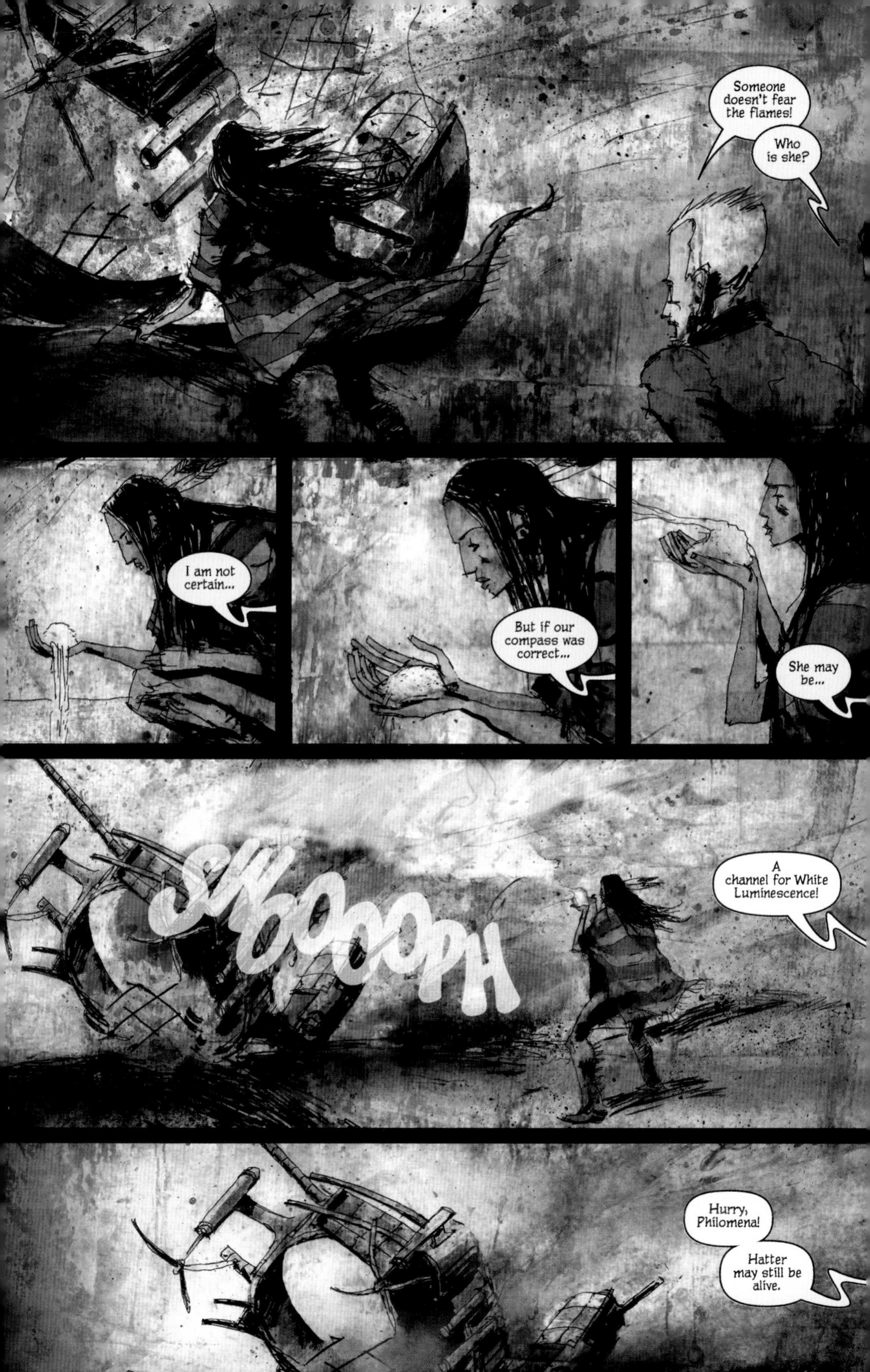
Someone doesn't fear the flames!
Who is she?
I am not certain...
But if our compass was correct...
She may be...
SHOOOOPH
A channel for White Luminescence!
Hurry, Philomena!
Hatter may still be alive.

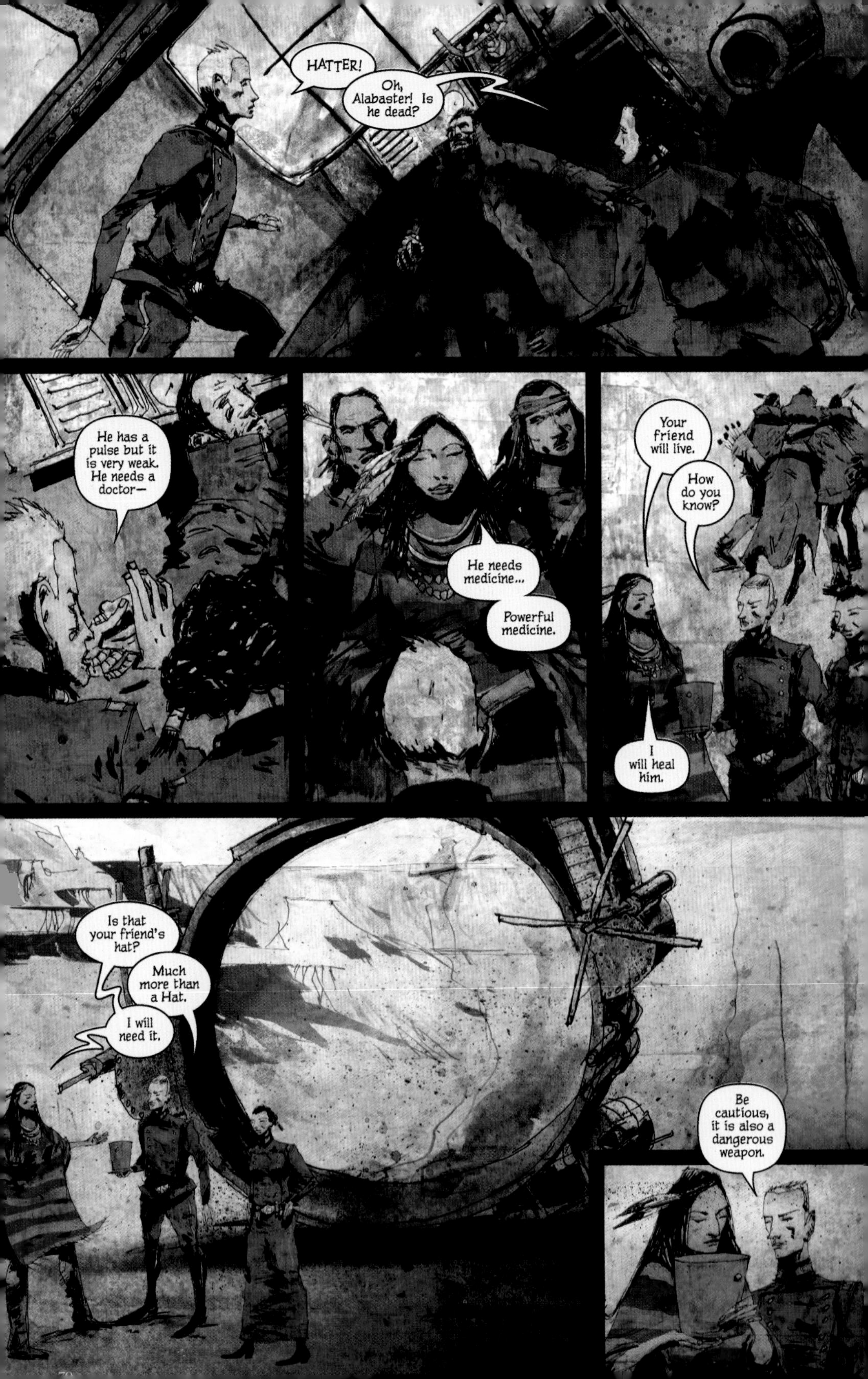
HATTER!
Oh, Alabaster! Is he dead?
He has a pulse but it is very weak. He needs a doctor—
He needs medicine...
Powerful medicine.
Your friend will live.
How do you know?
I will heal him.
Is that your friend's hat?
Much more than a Hat.
I will need it.
Be cautious, it is also a dangerous weapon.

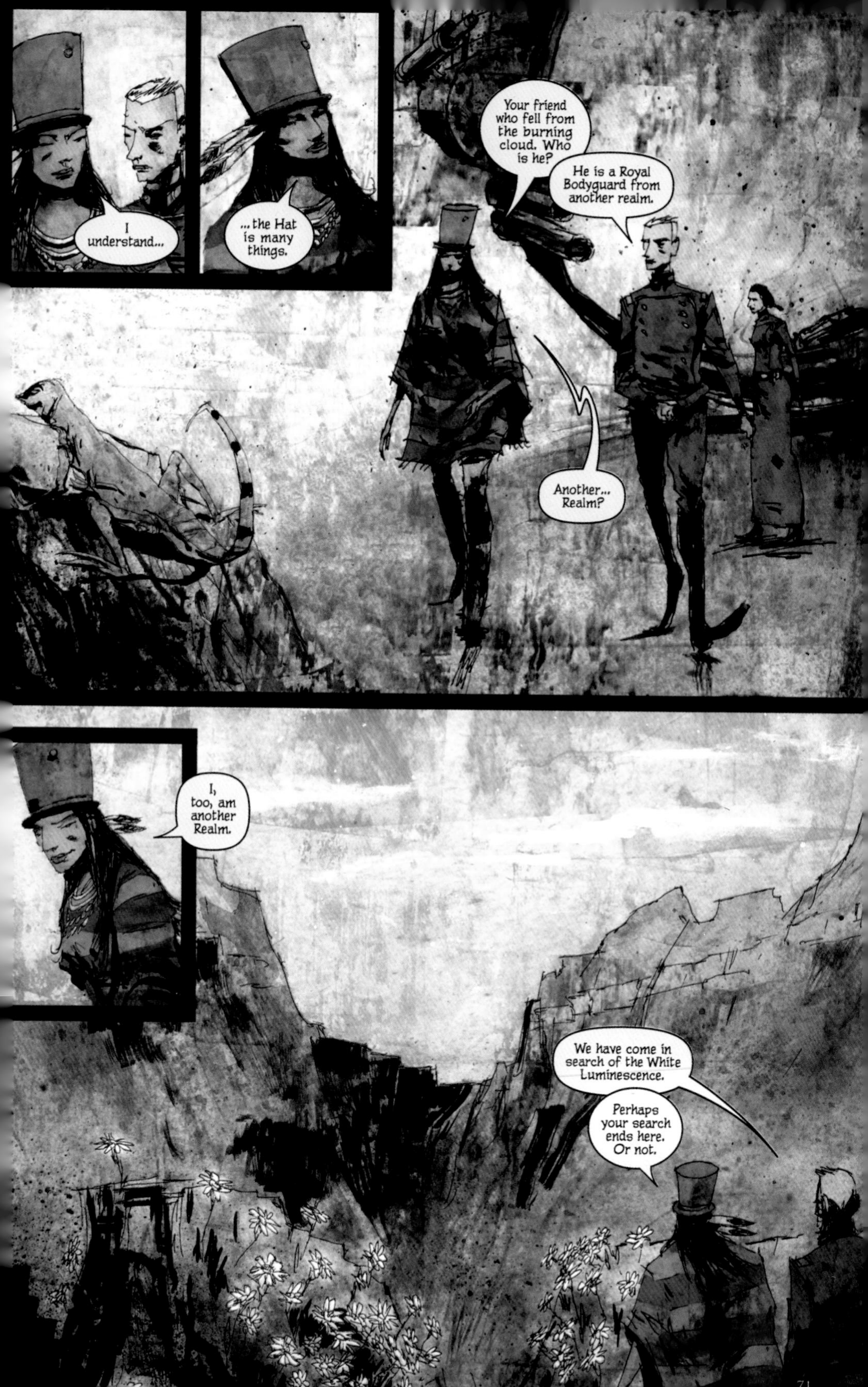
I understand...
...the Hat is many things.
Your friend who fell from the burning cloud. Who is he?
He is a Royal Bodyguard from another realm.
Another... Realm?
I, too, am another Realm.
We have come in search of the White Luminescence.
Perhaps your search ends here. Or not.

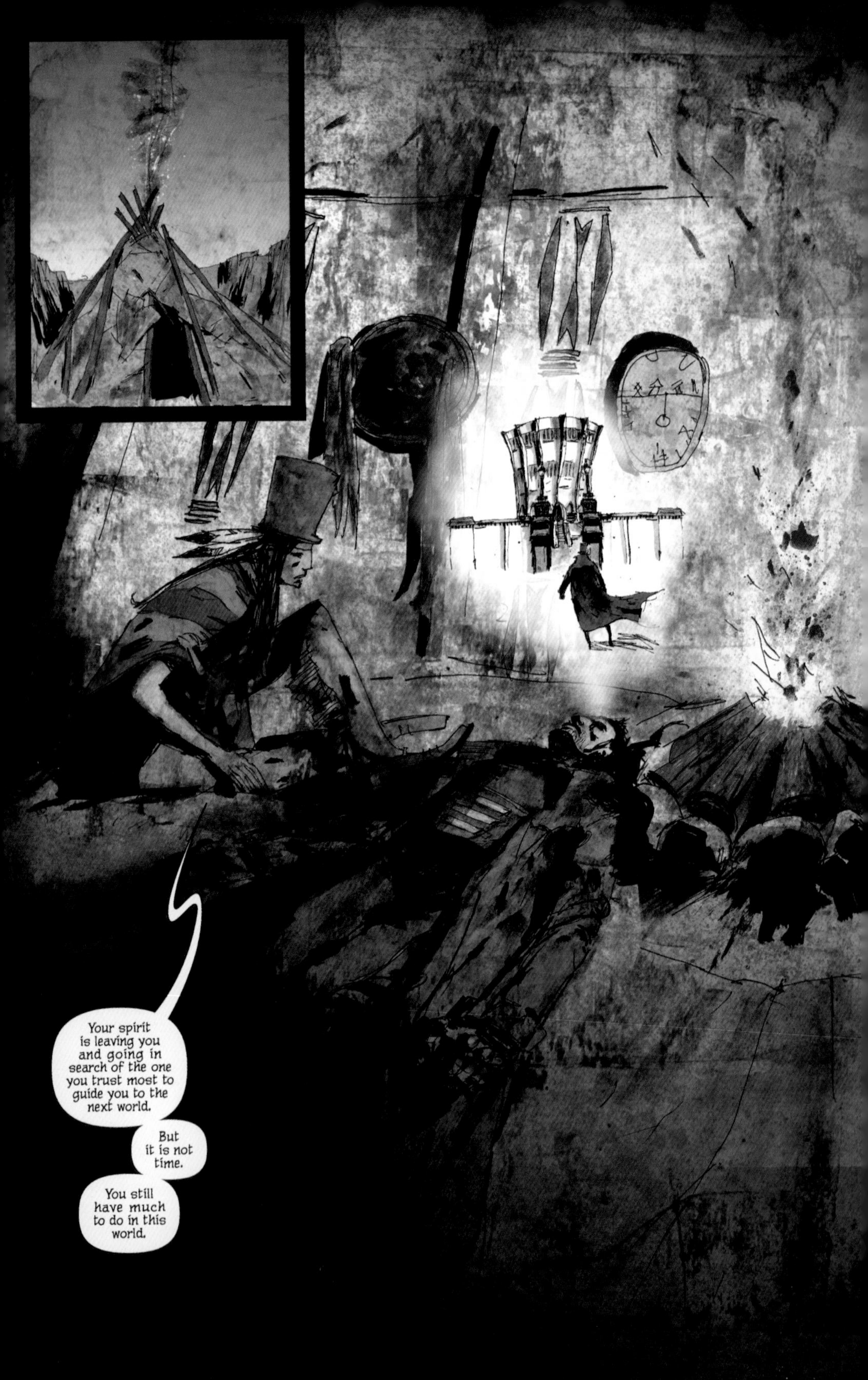
Your spirit is leaving you and going in search of the one you trust most to guide you to the next world.
But it is not time.
You still have much to do in this world.

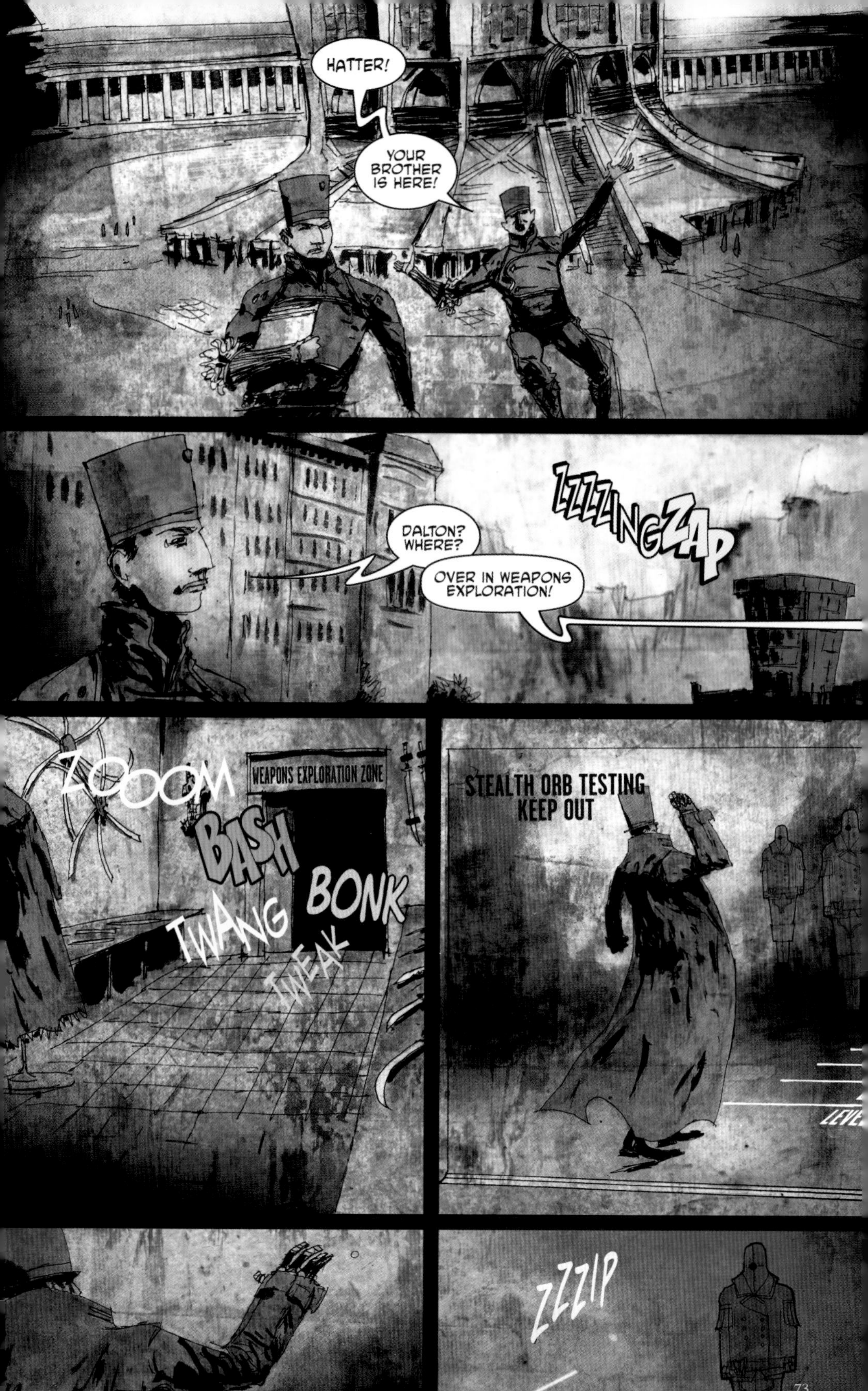
HATTER!
YOUR BROTHER IS HERE!
DALTON? WHERE?
OVER IN WEAPONS EXPLORATION!
ZZZZINGZAP
ZOOOM
WEAPONS EXPLORATION ZONE
BASH
TWANG
BONK
TWEAK
STEALTH ORB TESTING
KEEP OUT
ZZZIP

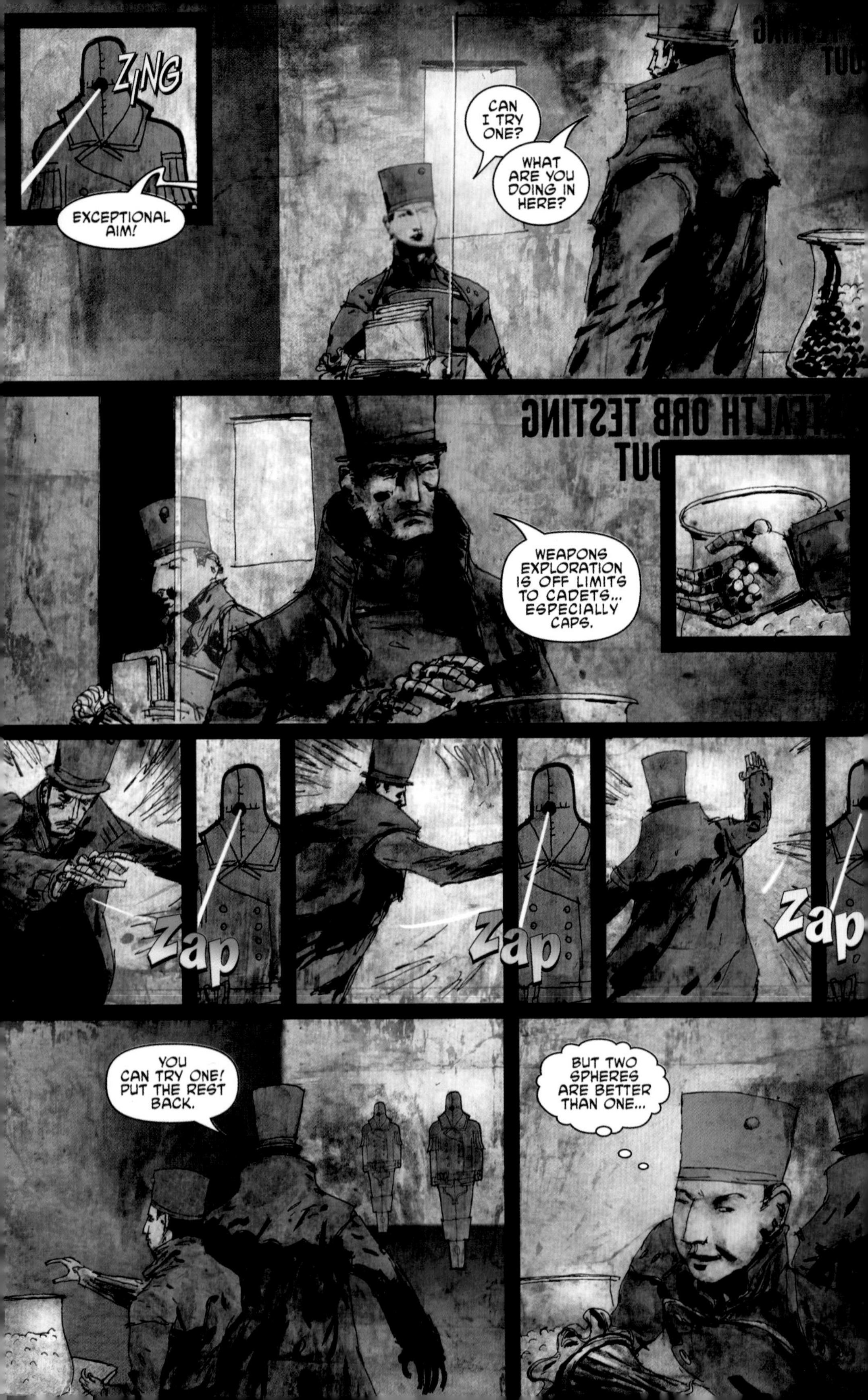
ZING
EXCEPTIONAL AIM!
CAN I TRY ONE?
WHAT ARE YOU DOING IN HERE?
WEAPONS EXPLORATION IS OFF LIMITS TO CADETS... ESPECIALLY CAPS.
Zap
Zap
Zap
YOU CAN TRY ONE! PUT THE REST BACK.
BUT TWO SPHERES ARE BETTER THAN ONE...

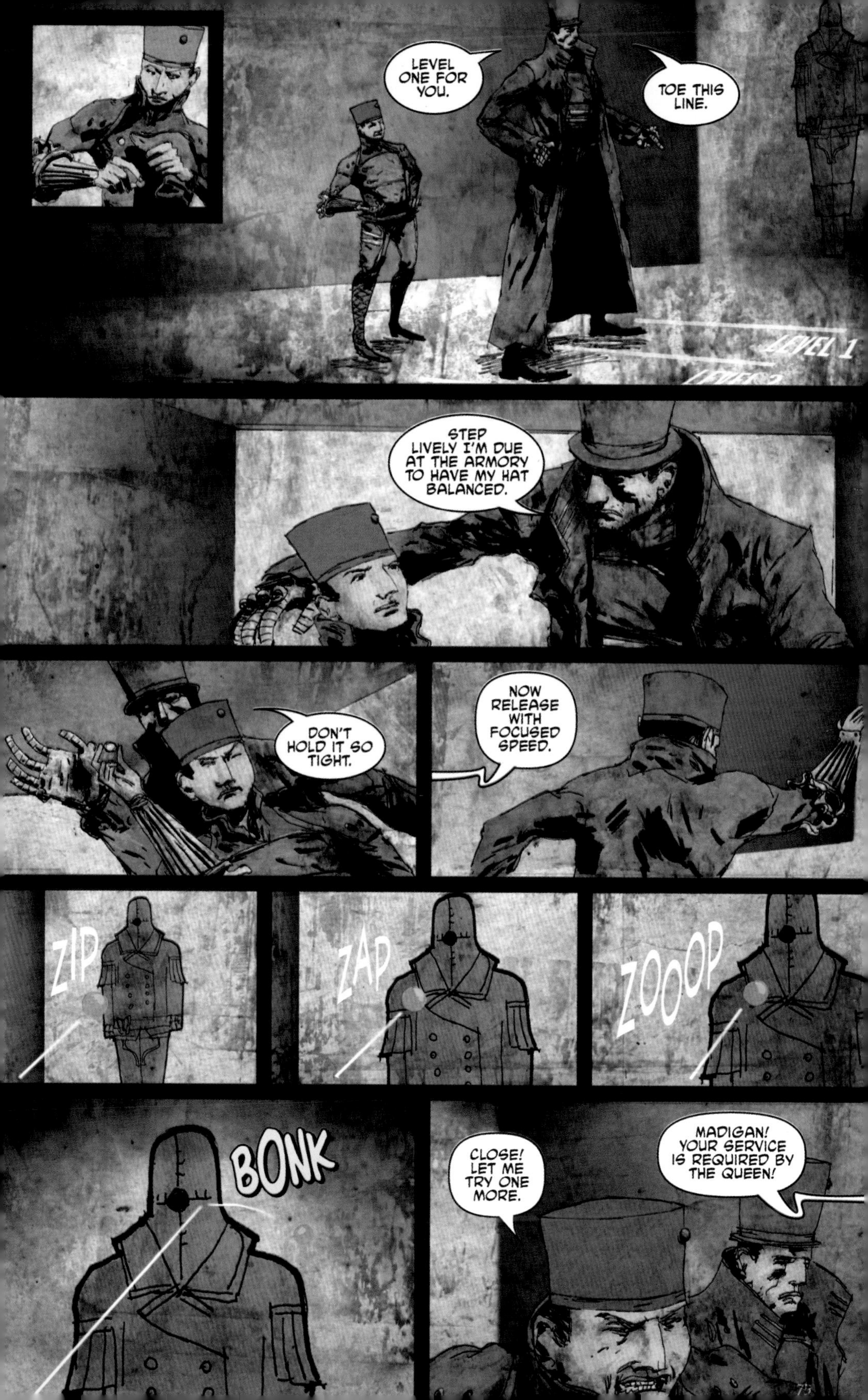
LEVEL ONE FOR YOU.
TOE THIS LINE.
LEVEL 1
STEP LIVELY I'M DUE AT THE ARMORY TO HAVE MY HAT BALANCED.
DON'T HOLD IT SO TIGHT.
NOW RELEASE WITH FOCUSED SPEED.
ZIP
ZAP
ZOOOP
BONK
CLOSE! LET ME TRY ONE MORE.
MADIGAN! YOUR SERVICE IS REQUIRED BY THE QUEEN!

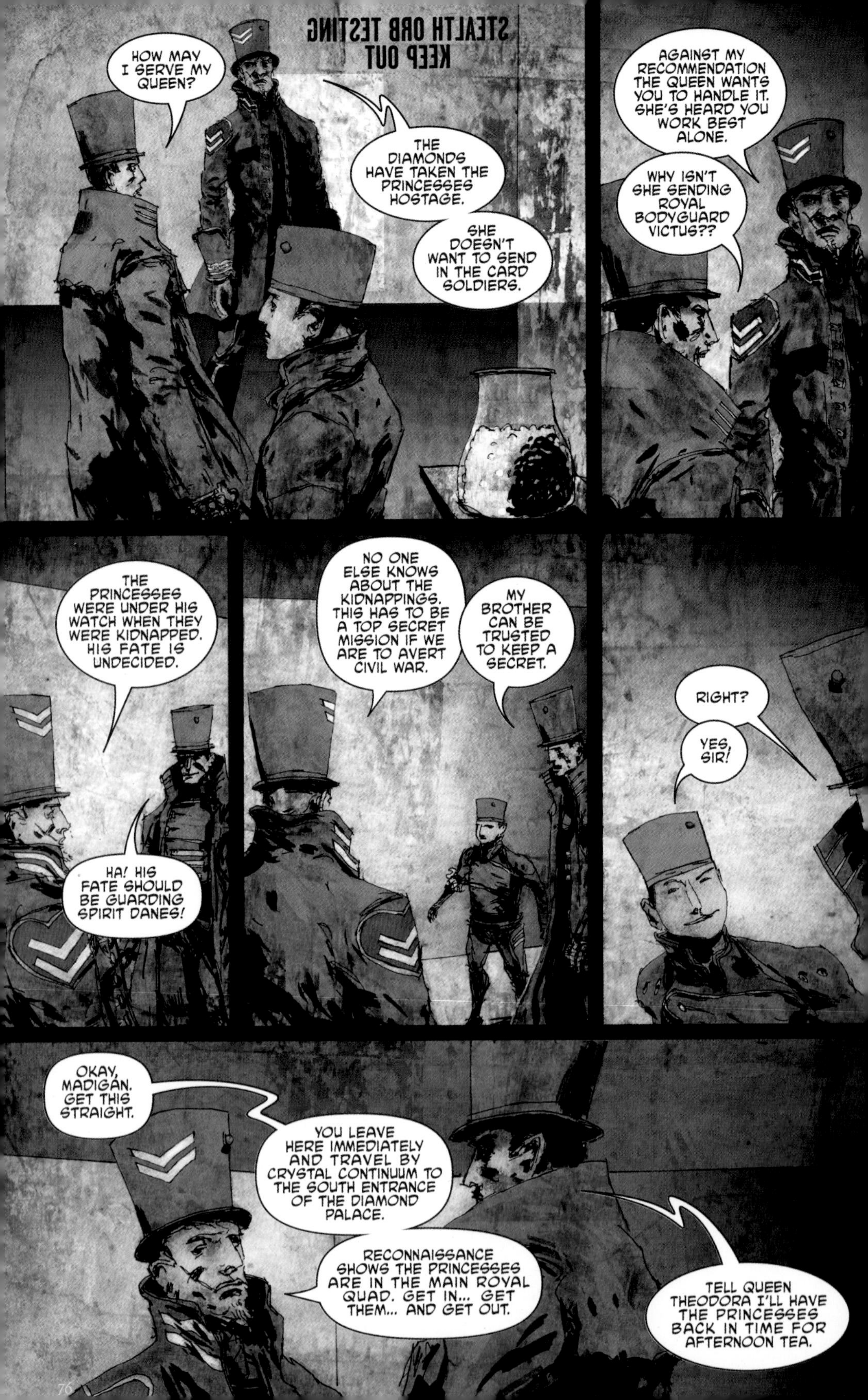
STEALTH ORB TESTING
KEEP OUT
HOW MAY I SERVE MY QUEEN?
THE DIAMONDS HAVE TAKEN THE PRINCESSES HOSTAGE.
SHE DOESN'T WANT TO SEND IN THE CARD SOLDIERS.
AGAINST MY RECOMMENDATION THE QUEEN WANTS YOU TO HANDLE IT. SHE'S HEARD YOU WORK BEST ALONE.
WHY ISN'T SHE SENDING ROYAL BODYGUARD VICTUS??
THE PRINCESSES WERE UNDER HIS WATCH WHEN THEY WERE KIDNAPPED. HIS FATE IS UNDECIDED.
HA! HIS FATE SHOULD BE GUARDING SPIRIT DANES!
NO ONE ELSE KNOWS ABOUT THE KIDNAPPINGS. THIS HAS TO BE A TOP SECRET MISSION IF WE ARE TO AVERT CIVIL WAR.
MY BROTHER CAN BE TRUSTED TO KEEP A SECRET.
RIGHT?
YES, SIR!
OKAY, MADIGAN. GET THIS STRAIGHT.
YOU LEAVE HERE IMMEDIATELY AND TRAVEL BY CRYSTAL CONTINUUM TO THE SOUTH ENTRANCE OF THE DIAMOND PALACE.
RECONNAISSANCE SHOWS THE PRINCESSES ARE IN THE MAIN ROYAL QUAD. GET IN... GET THEM... AND GET OUT.
TELL QUEEN THEODORA I'LL HAVE THE PRINCESSES BACK IN TIME FOR AFTERNOON TEA.

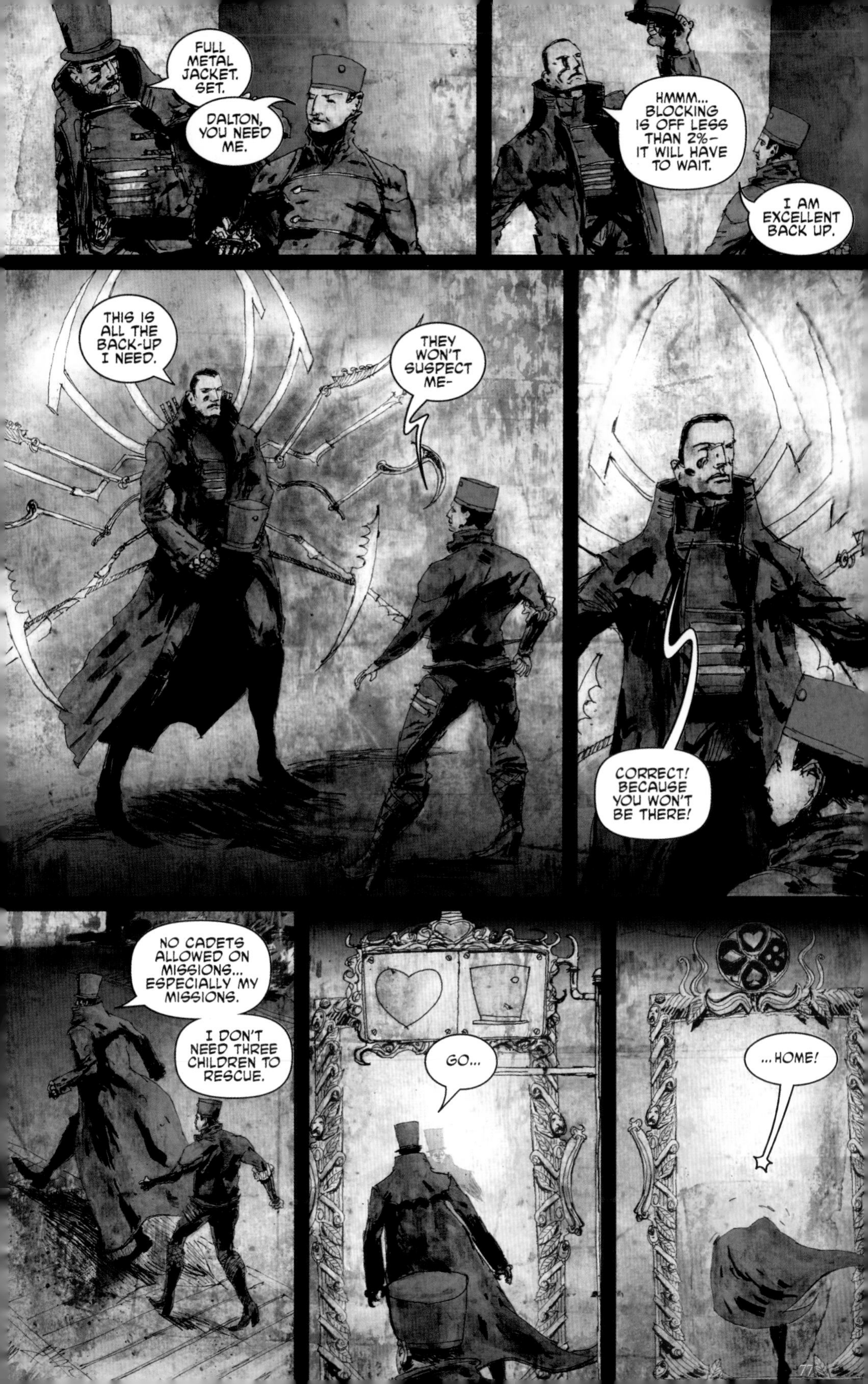
FULL METAL JACKET. SET.
DALTON, YOU NEED ME.
HMMM... BLOCKING IS OFF LESS THAN 2%– IT WILL HAVE TO WAIT.
I AM EXCELLENT BACK UP.
THIS IS ALL THE BACK-UP I NEED.
THEY WON'T SUSPECT ME-
CORRECT! BECAUSE YOU WON'T BE THERE!
NO CADETS ALLOWED ON MISSIONS... ESPECIALLY MY MISSIONS.
I DON'T NEED THREE CHILDREN TO RESCUE.
GO...
...HOME!

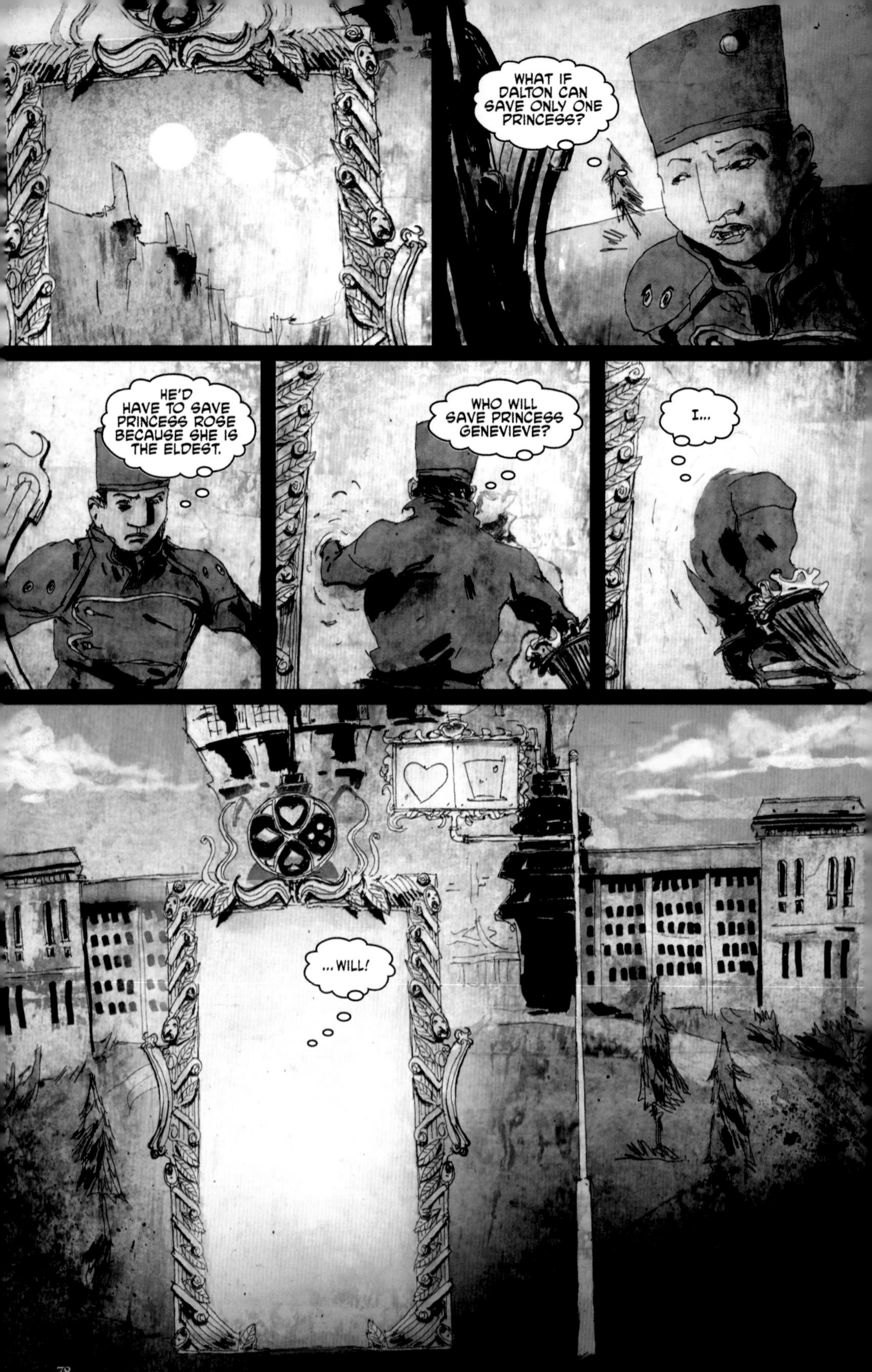
WHAT IF DALTON CAN SAVE ONLY ONE PRINCESS?
HE'D HAVE TO SAVE PRINCESS ROSE BECAUSE SHE IS THE ELDEST.
WHO WILL SAVE PRINCESS GENEVIEVE?
I...
...WILL!

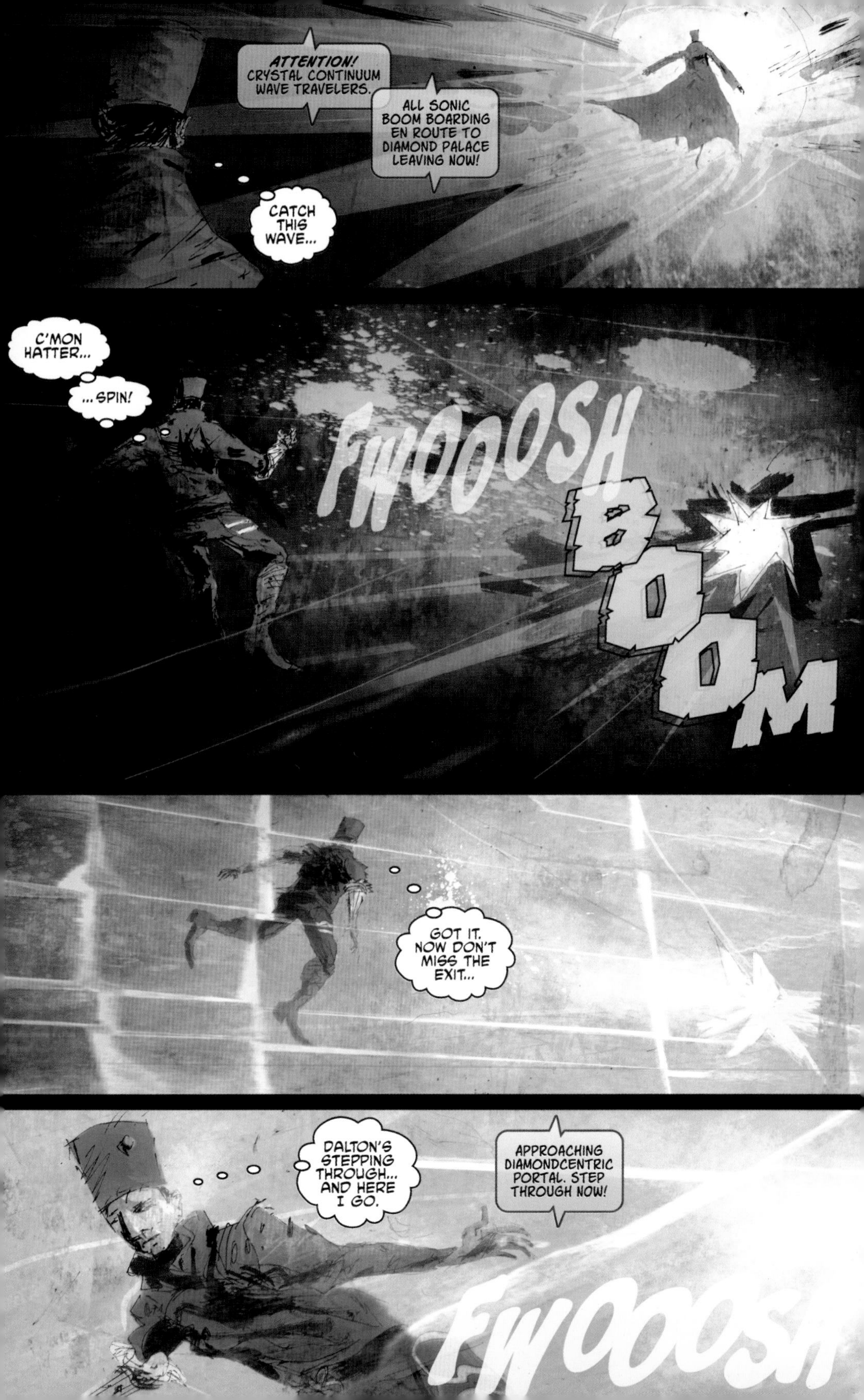
ATTENTION! CRYSTAL CONTINUUM WAVE TRAVELERS.
ALL SONIC BOOM BOARDING EN ROUTE TO DIAMOND PALACE LEAVING NOW!
CATCH THIS WAVE...
C'MON HATTER...
...SPIN!
FWOOOSH
BOOM
GOT IT. NOW DON'T MISS THE EXIT...
DALTON'S STEPPING THROUGH... AND HERE I GO.
APPROACHING DIAMONDCENTRIC PORTAL. STEP THROUGH NOW!
FWOOOSH

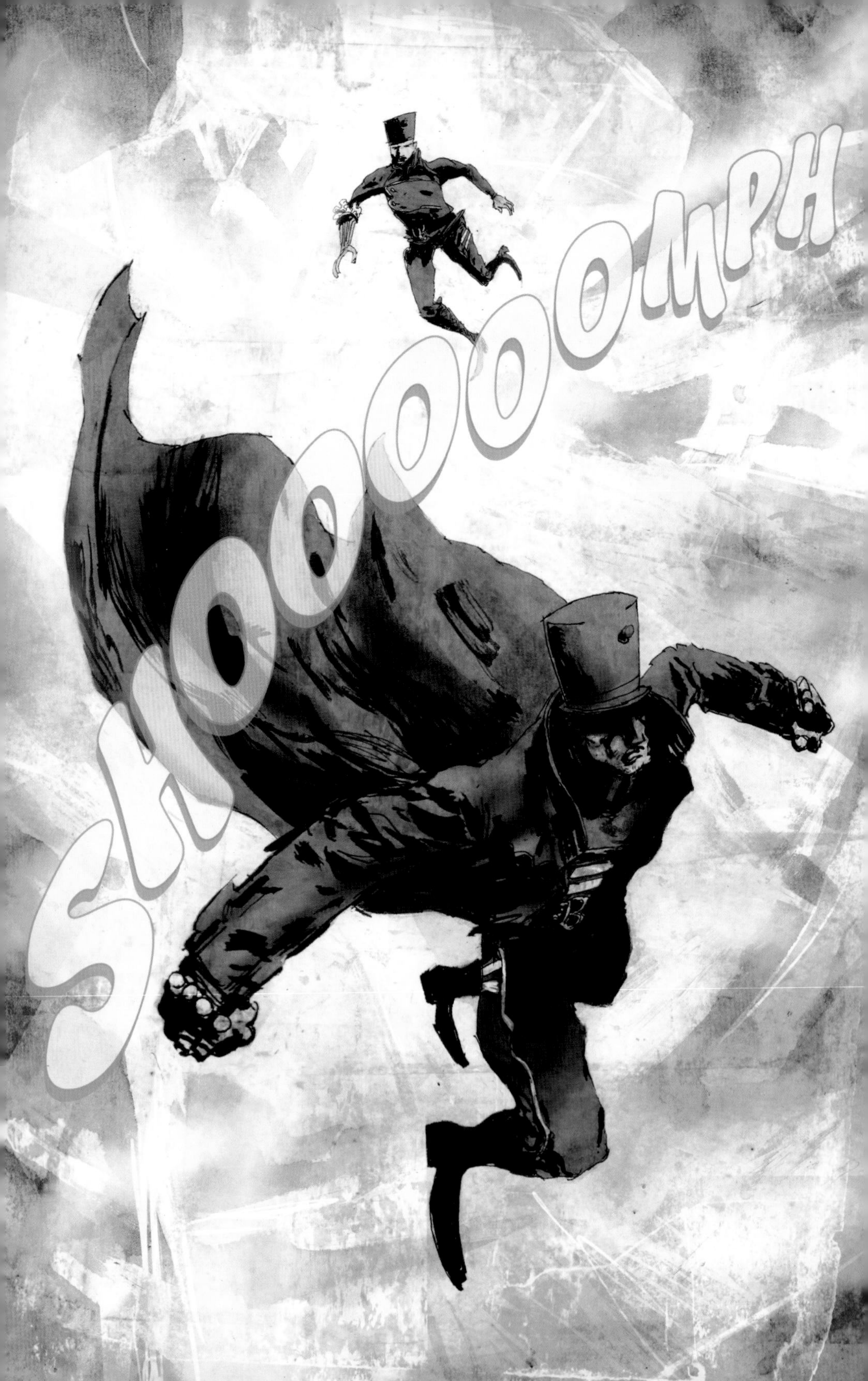
SHOOOOOOOMPH

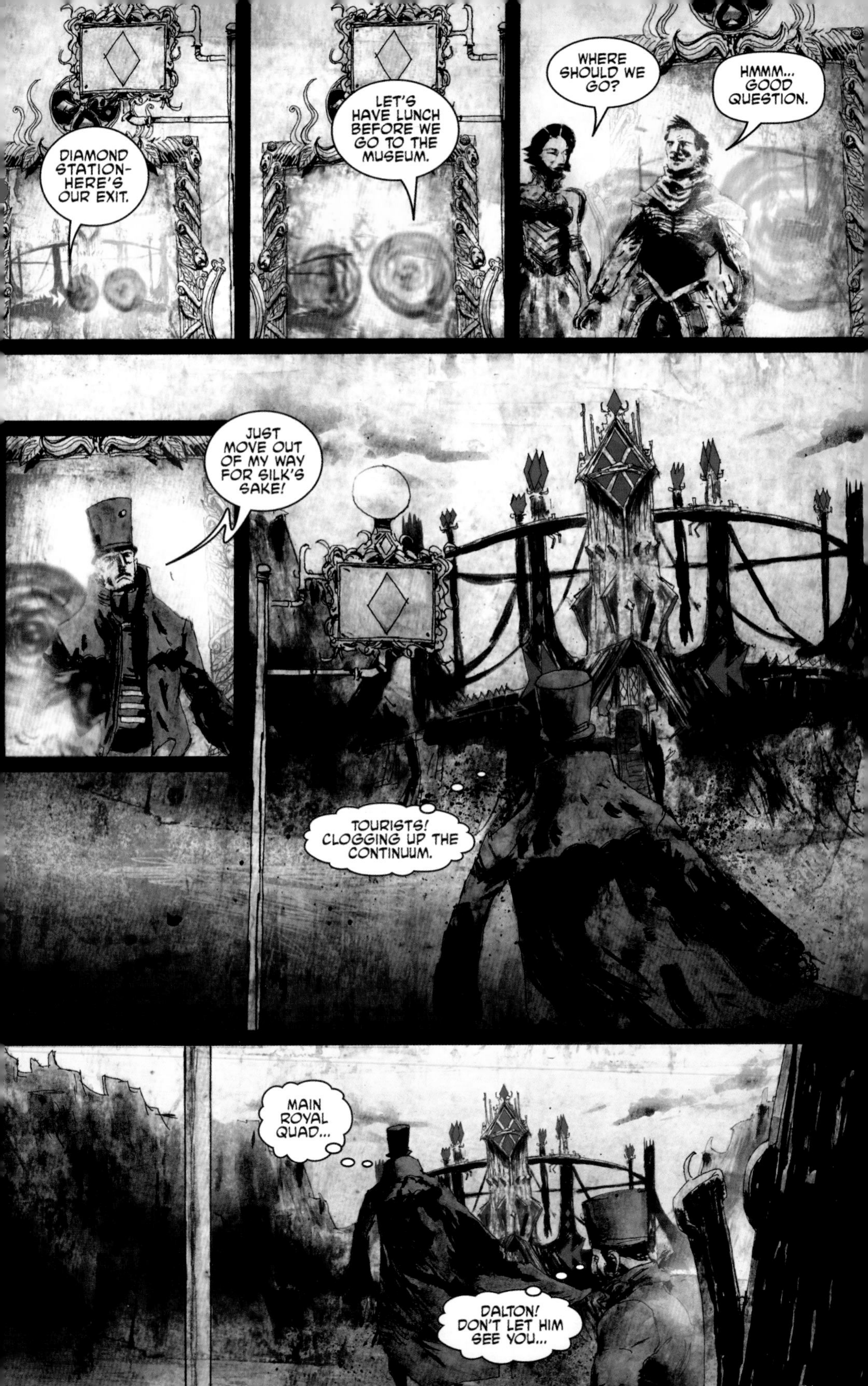
DIAMOND STATION- HERE'S OUR EXIT.
LET'S HAVE LUNCH BEFORE WE GO TO THE MUSEUM.
WHERE SHOULD WE GO?
HMMM... GOOD QUESTION.
JUST MOVE OUT OF MY WAY FOR SILK'S SAKE!
TOURISTS! CLOGGING UP THE CONTINUUM.
MAIN ROYAL QUAD...
DALTON! DON'T LET HIM SEE YOU...

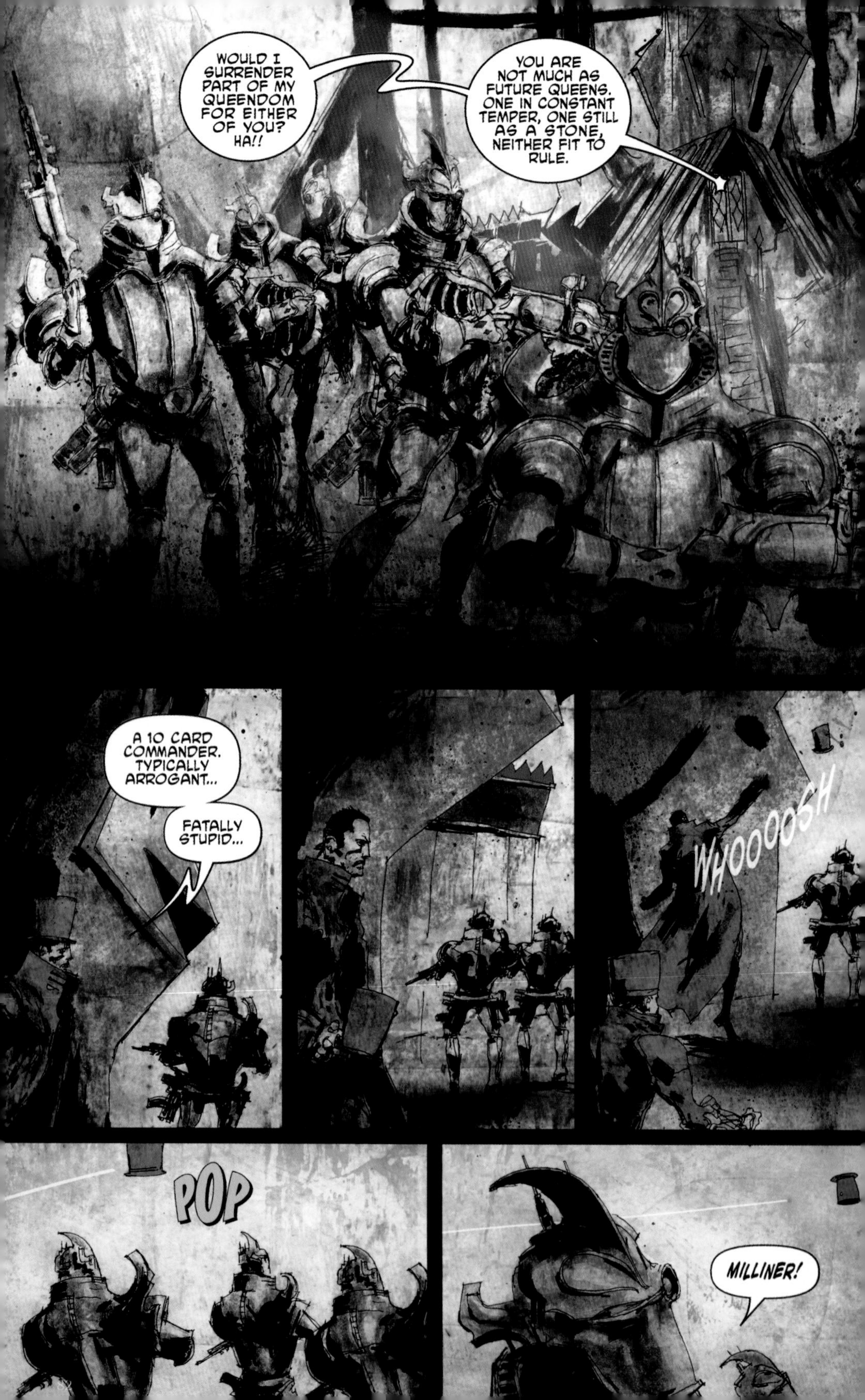
WOULD I SURRENDER PART OF MY QUEENDOM FOR EITHER OF YOU? HA!!
YOU ARE NOT MUCH AS FUTURE QUEENS. ONE IN CONSTANT TEMPER, ONE STILL AS A STONE, NEITHER FIT TO RULE.
A 10 CARD COMMANDER. TYPICALLY ARROGANT...
FATALLY STUPID...
WHOOOOSH
POP
MILLINER!

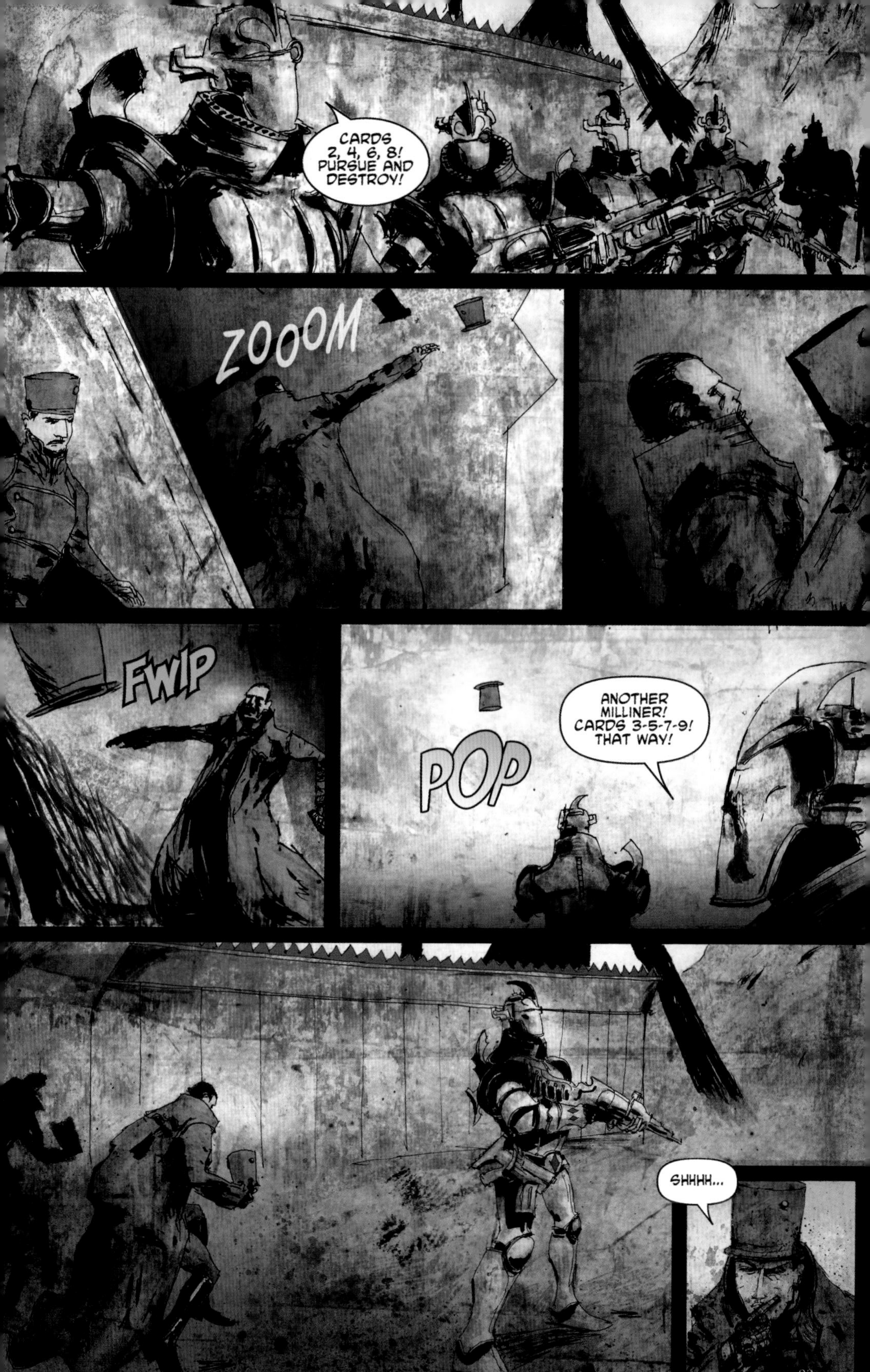
CARDS 2, 4, 6, 8! PURSUE AND DESTROY!
ZOOOM
FWIP
POP
ANOTHER MILLINER! CARDS 3-5-7-9! THAT WAY!
SHHHH...

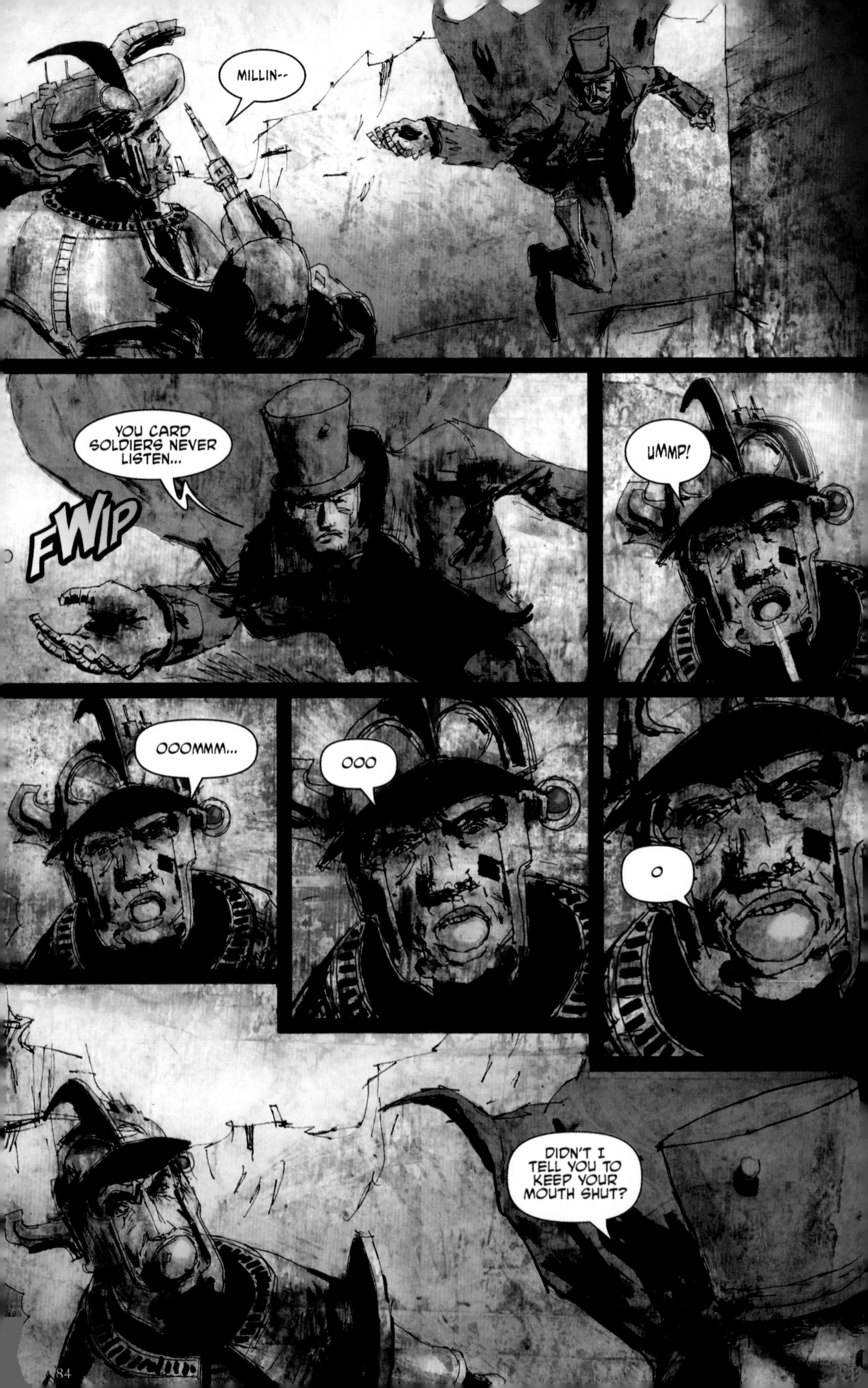
MILLIN--
YOU CARD SOLDIERS NEVER LISTEN...
FWIP
UMMP!
OOOMMM...
OOO
O
DIDN'T I TELL YOU TO KEEP YOUR MOUTH SHUT?

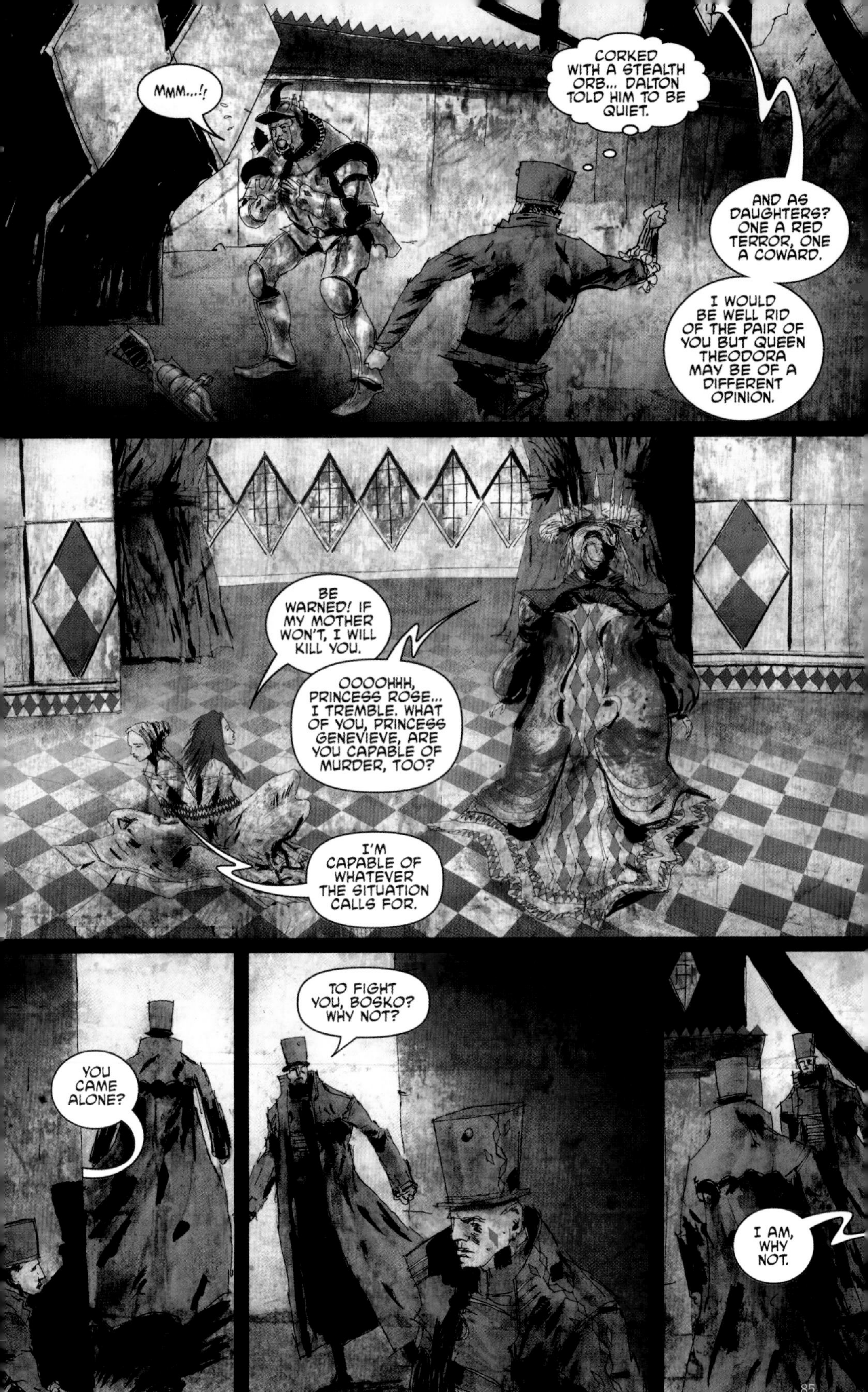
MMM...!!
CORKED WITH A STEALTH ORB... DALTON TOLD HIM TO BE QUIET.
AND AS DAUGHTERS? ONE A RED TERROR, ONE A COWARD.
I WOULD BE WELL RID OF THE PAIR OF YOU BUT QUEEN THEODORA MAY BE OF A DIFFERENT OPINION.
BE WARNED! IF MY MOTHER WON'T, I WILL KILL YOU.
OOOOHHH, PRINCESS ROSE... I TREMBLE. WHAT OF YOU, PRINCESS GENEVIEVE, ARE YOU CAPABLE OF MURDER, TOO?
I'M CAPABLE OF WHATEVER THE SITUATION CALLS FOR.
YOU CAME ALONE?
TO FIGHT YOU, BOSKO? WHY NOT?
I AM, WHY NOT.

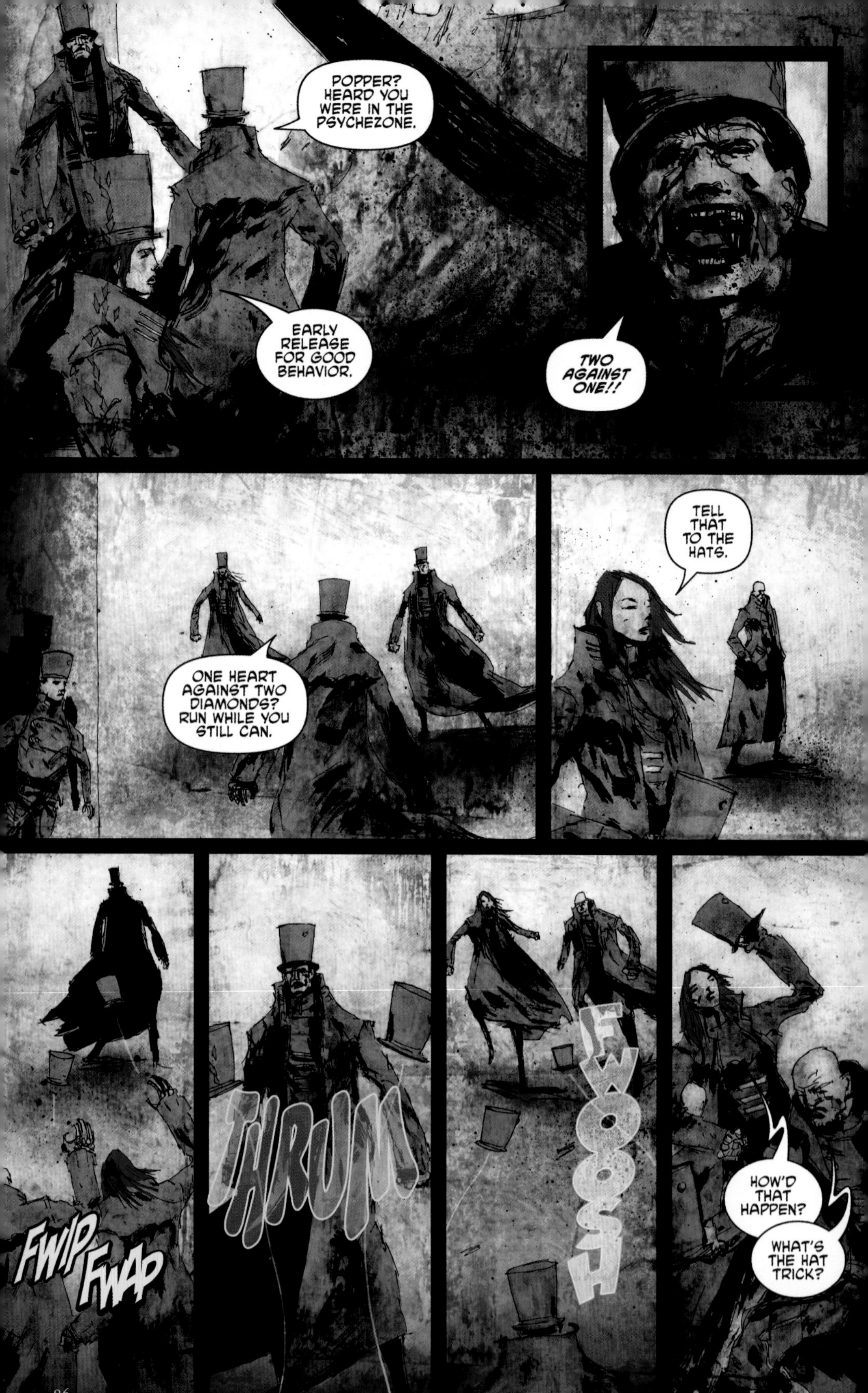
POPPER? HEARD YOU WERE IN THE PSYCHEZONE.
EARLY RELEASE FOR GOOD BEHAVIOR.
TWO AGAINST ONE!!
ONE HEART AGAINST TWO DIAMONDS? RUN WHILE YOU STILL CAN.
TELL THAT TO THE HATS.
FWIP FWAP
THRUM
FWOOSH
HOW'D THAT HAPPEN?
WHAT'S THE HAT TRICK?

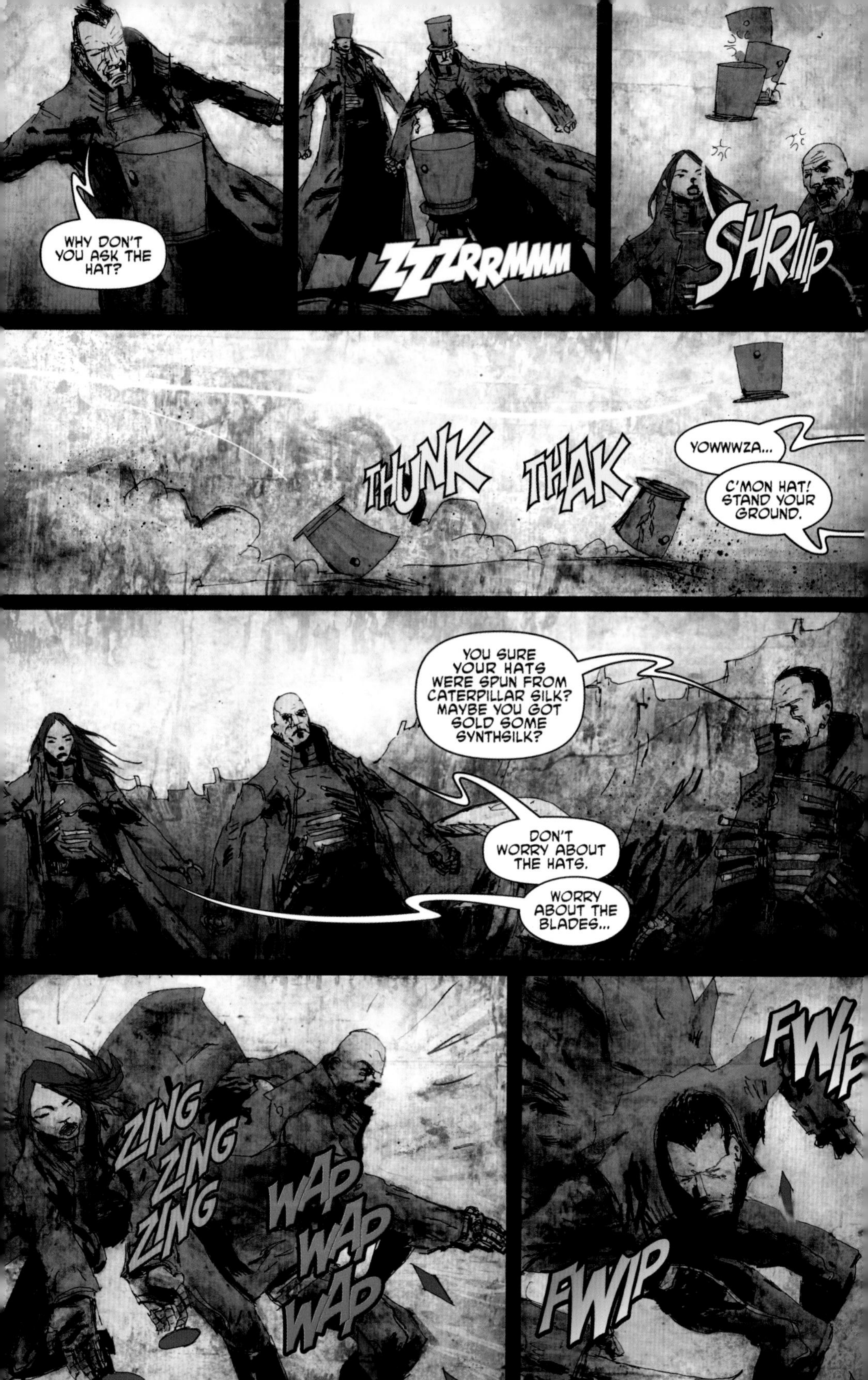
WHY DON'T YOU ASK THE HAT?
ZZZRRMMM
SHRIIP
THUNK
THAK
YOWWWZA...
C'MON HAT! STAND YOUR GROUND.
YOU SURE YOUR HATS WERE SPUN FROM CATERPILLAR SILK? MAYBE YOU GOT SOLD SOME SYNTHSILK?
DON'T WORRY ABOUT THE HATS.
WORRY ABOUT THE BLADES...
ZING ZING ZING
WAP WAP WAP
FWIP
FWIP

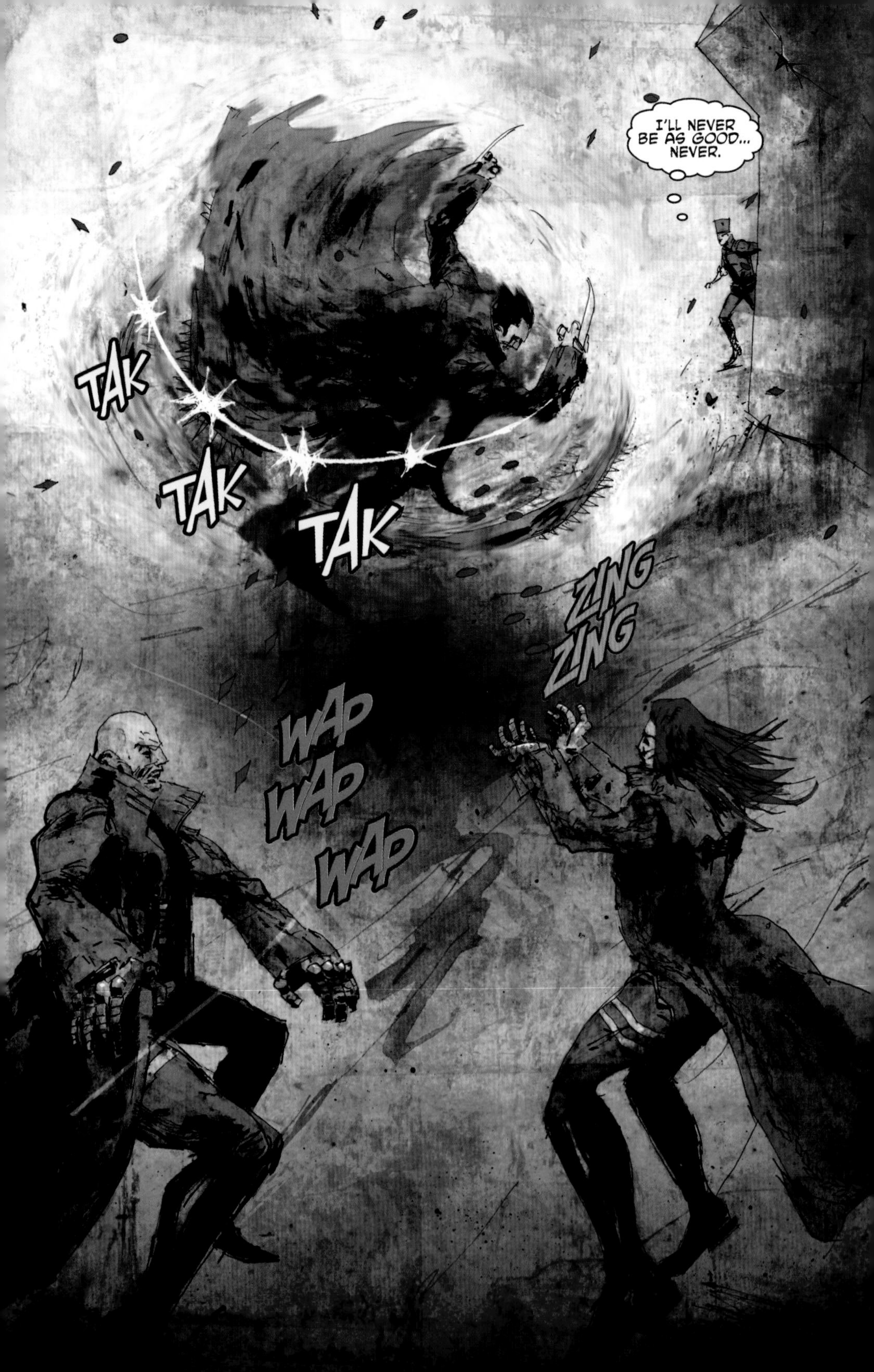
I'LL NEVER BE AS GOOD... NEVER.
TAK
TAK
TAK
ZING
ZING
WAP
WAP
WAP

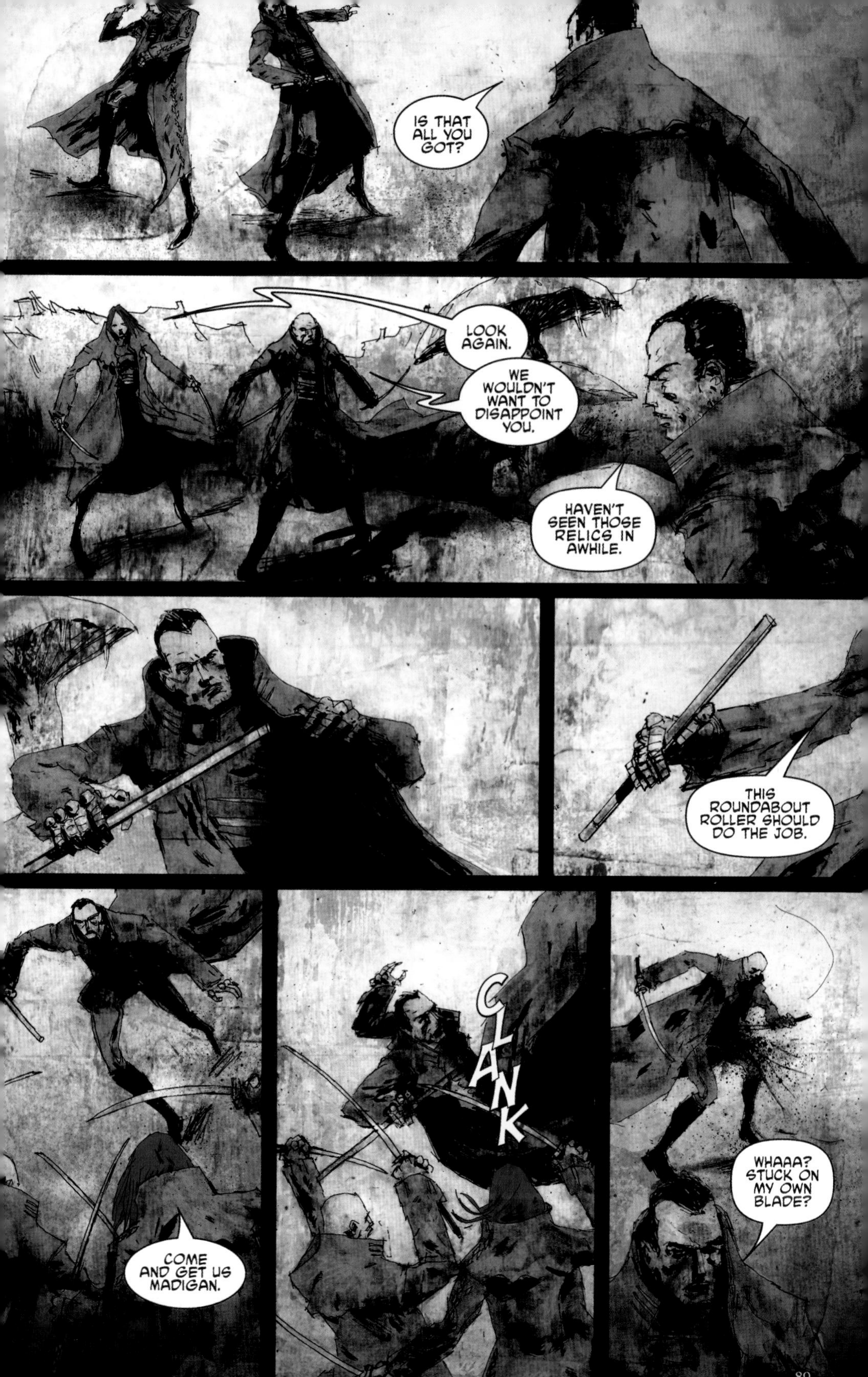
IS THAT ALL YOU GOT?
LOOK AGAIN.
WE WOULDN'T WANT TO DISAPPOINT YOU.
HAVEN'T SEEN THOSE RELICS IN AWHILE.
THIS ROUNDABOUT ROLLER SHOULD DO THE JOB.
COME AND GET US MADIGAN.
CLANK
WHAAA? STUCK ON MY OWN BLADE?

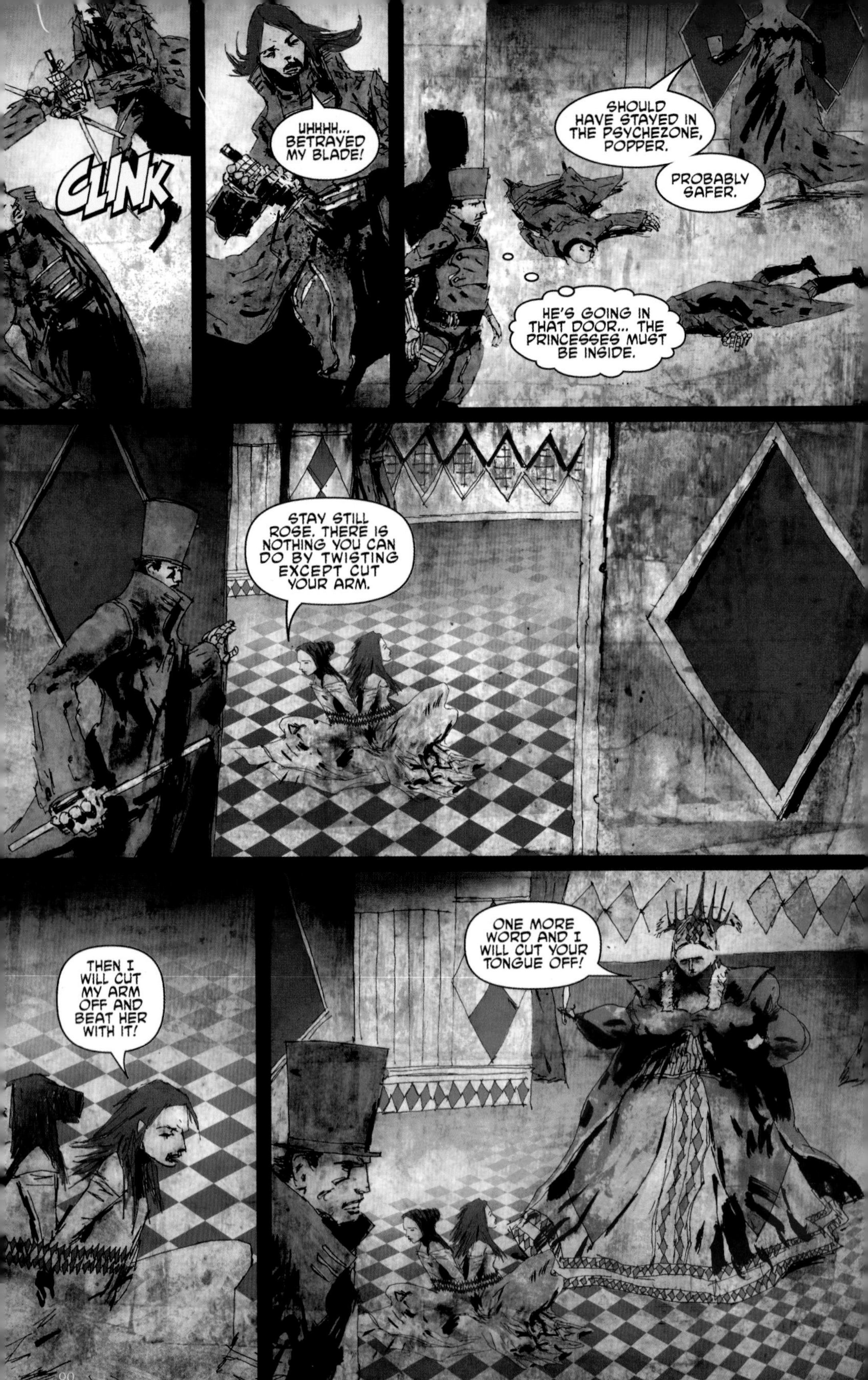
CLINK
UHHHH... BETRAYED MY BLADE!
SHOULD HAVE STAYED IN THE PSYCHEZONE, POPPER.
PROBABLY SAFER.
HE'S GOING IN THAT DOOR... THE PRINCESSES MUST BE INSIDE.
STAY STILL ROSE. THERE IS NOTHING YOU CAN DO BY TWISTING EXCEPT CUT YOUR ARM.
THEN I WILL CUT MY ARM OFF AND BEAT HER WITH IT!
ONE MORE WORD AND I WILL CUT YOUR TONGUE OFF!

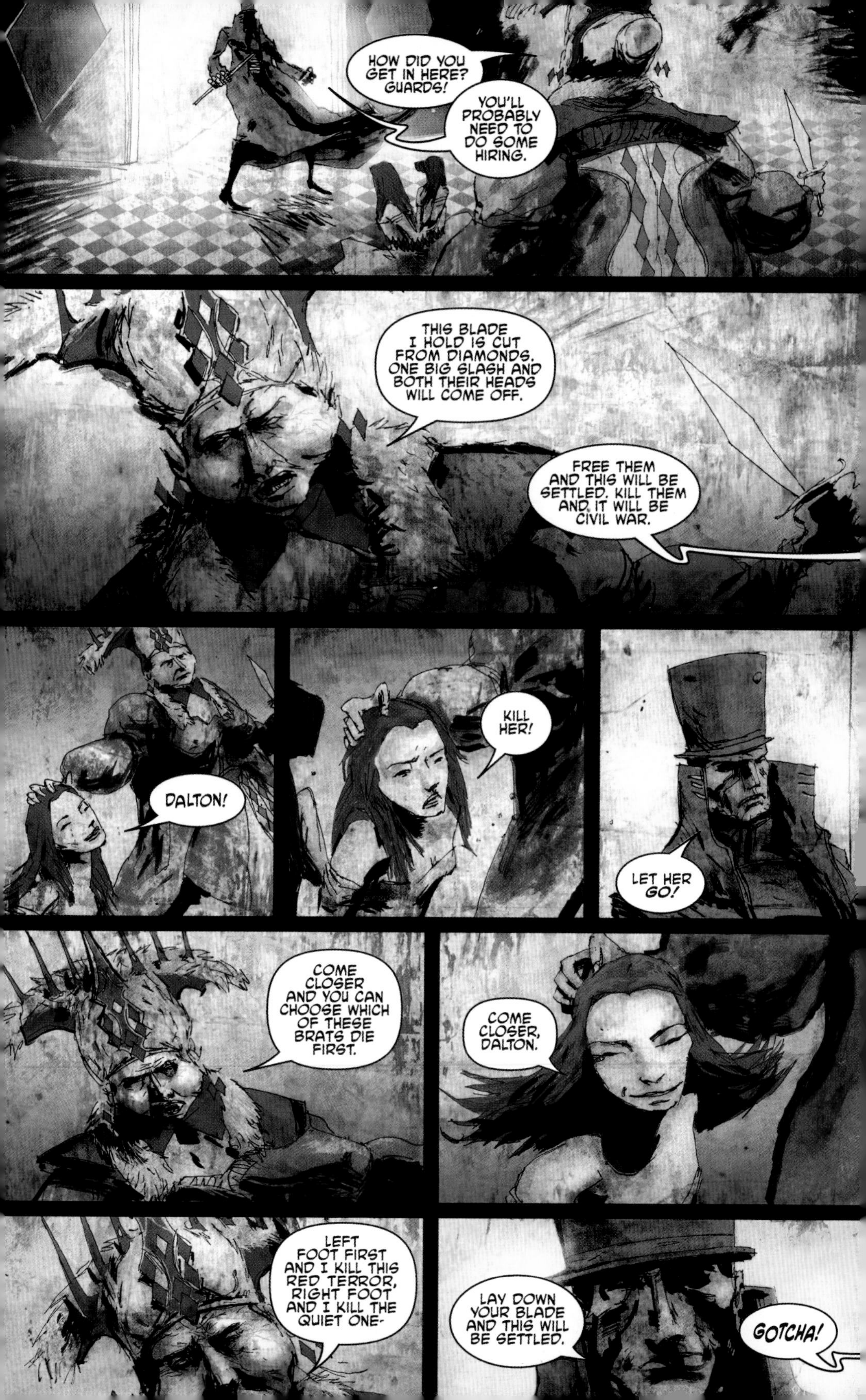
HOW DID YOU GET IN HERE? GUARDS!
YOU'LL PROBABLY NEED TO DO SOME HIRING.
THIS BLADE I HOLD IS CUT FROM DIAMONDS. ONE BIG SLASH AND BOTH THEIR HEADS WILL COME OFF.
FREE THEM AND THIS WILL BE SETTLED. KILL THEM AND IT WILL BE CIVIL WAR.
DALTON!
KILL HER!
LET HER GO!
COME CLOSER AND YOU CAN CHOOSE WHICH OF THESE BRATS DIE FIRST.
COME CLOSER, DALTON.
LEFT FOOT FIRST AND I KILL THIS RED TERROR, RIGHT FOOT AND I KILL THE QUIET ONE-
LAY DOWN YOUR BLADE AND THIS WILL BE SETTLED.
GOTCHA!

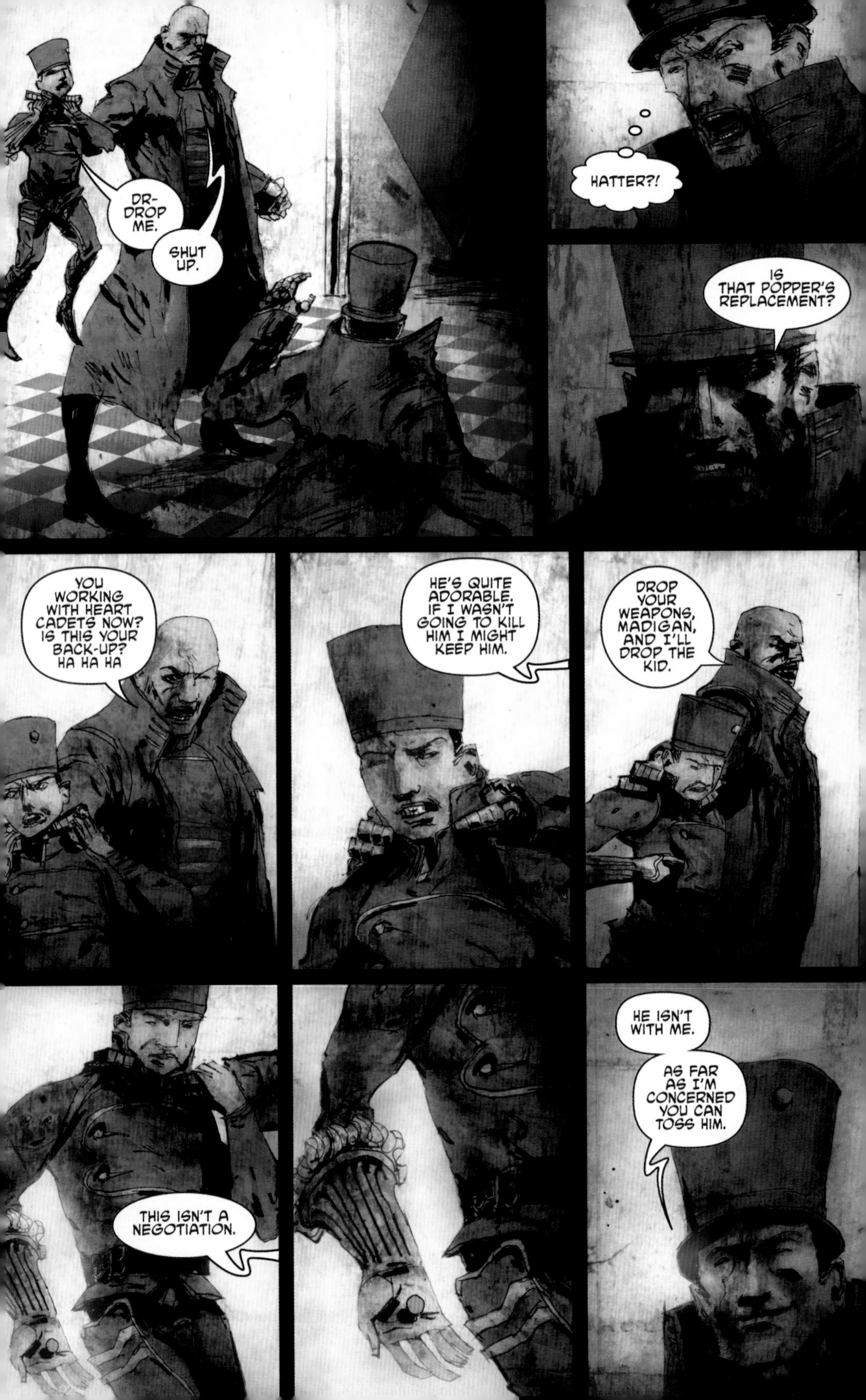
DR-DROP ME.
SHUT UP.
HATTER?!
IS THAT POPPER'S REPLACEMENT?
YOU WORKING WITH HEART CADETS NOW? IS THIS YOUR BACK-UP? HA HA HA
HE'S QUITE ADORABLE. IF I WASN'T GOING TO KILL HIM I MIGHT KEEP HIM.
DROP YOUR WEAPONS, MADIGAN, AND I'LL DROP THE KID.
THIS ISN'T A NEGOTIATION.
HE ISN'T WITH ME.
AS FAR AS I'M CONCERNED YOU CAN TOSS HIM.

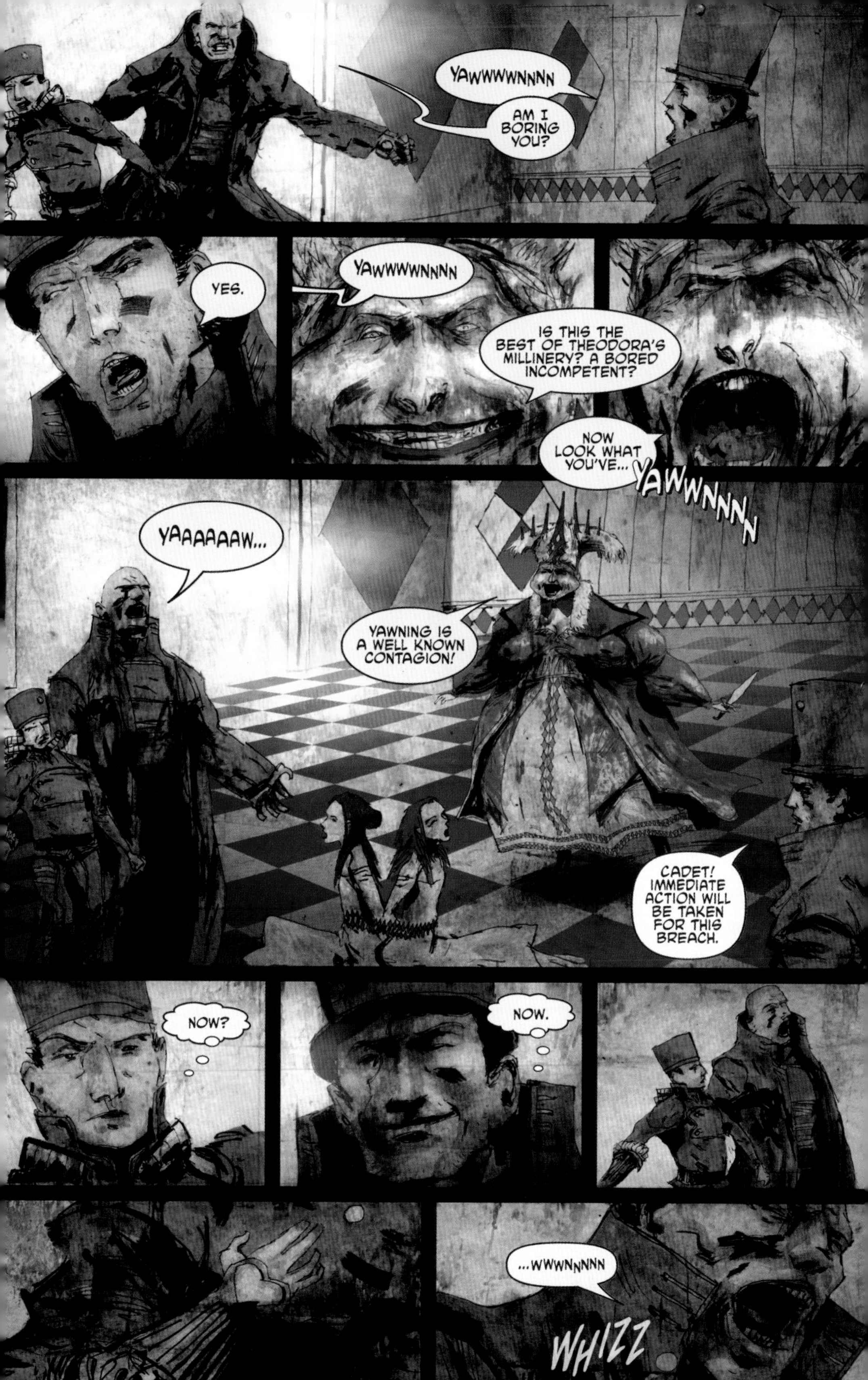
YAWWWWNNNN
AM I BORING YOU?
YES.
YAWWWWNNNN
IS THIS THE BEST OF THEODORA'S MILLINERY? A BORED INCOMPETENT?
NOW LOOK WHAT YOU'VE...
YAWWNNNN
YAAAAAAW...
YAWNING IS A WELL KNOWN CONTAGION!
CADET! IMMEDIATE ACTION WILL BE TAKEN FOR THIS BREACH.
NOW?
NOW.
...WWWNNNNN
WHIZZ

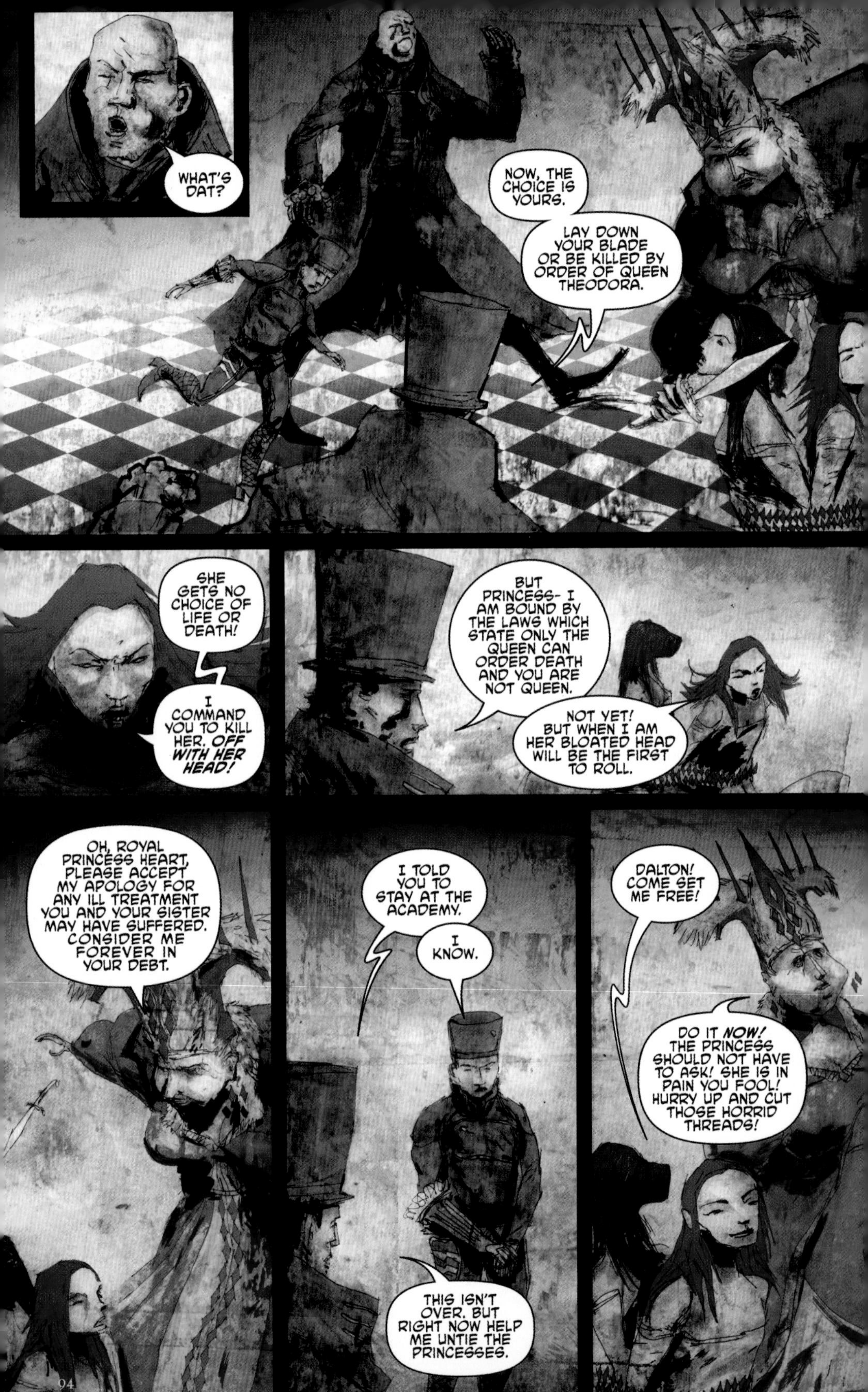
WHAT'S DAT?
NOW, THE CHOICE IS YOURS.
LAY DOWN YOUR BLADE OR BE KILLED BY ORDER OF QUEEN THEODORA.
SHE GETS NO CHOICE OF LIFE OR DEATH!
I COMMAND YOU TO KILL HER. *OFF WITH HER HEAD!*
BUT PRINCESS- I AM BOUND BY THE LAWS WHICH STATE ONLY THE QUEEN CAN ORDER DEATH AND YOU ARE NOT QUEEN.
NOT YET! BUT WHEN I AM HER BLOATED HEAD WILL BE THE FIRST TO ROLL.
OH, ROYAL PRINCESS HEART, PLEASE ACCEPT MY APOLOGY FOR ANY ILL TREATMENT YOU AND YOUR SISTER MAY HAVE SUFFERED. CONSIDER ME FOREVER IN YOUR DEBT.
I TOLD YOU TO STAY AT THE ACADEMY.
I KNOW.
THIS ISN'T OVER. BUT RIGHT NOW HELP ME UNTIE THE PRINCESSES.
DALTON! COME SET ME FREE!
DO IT *NOW!* THE PRINCESS SHOULD NOT HAVE TO ASK! SHE IS IN PAIN YOU FOOL! HURRY UP AND CUT THOSE HORRID THREADS!

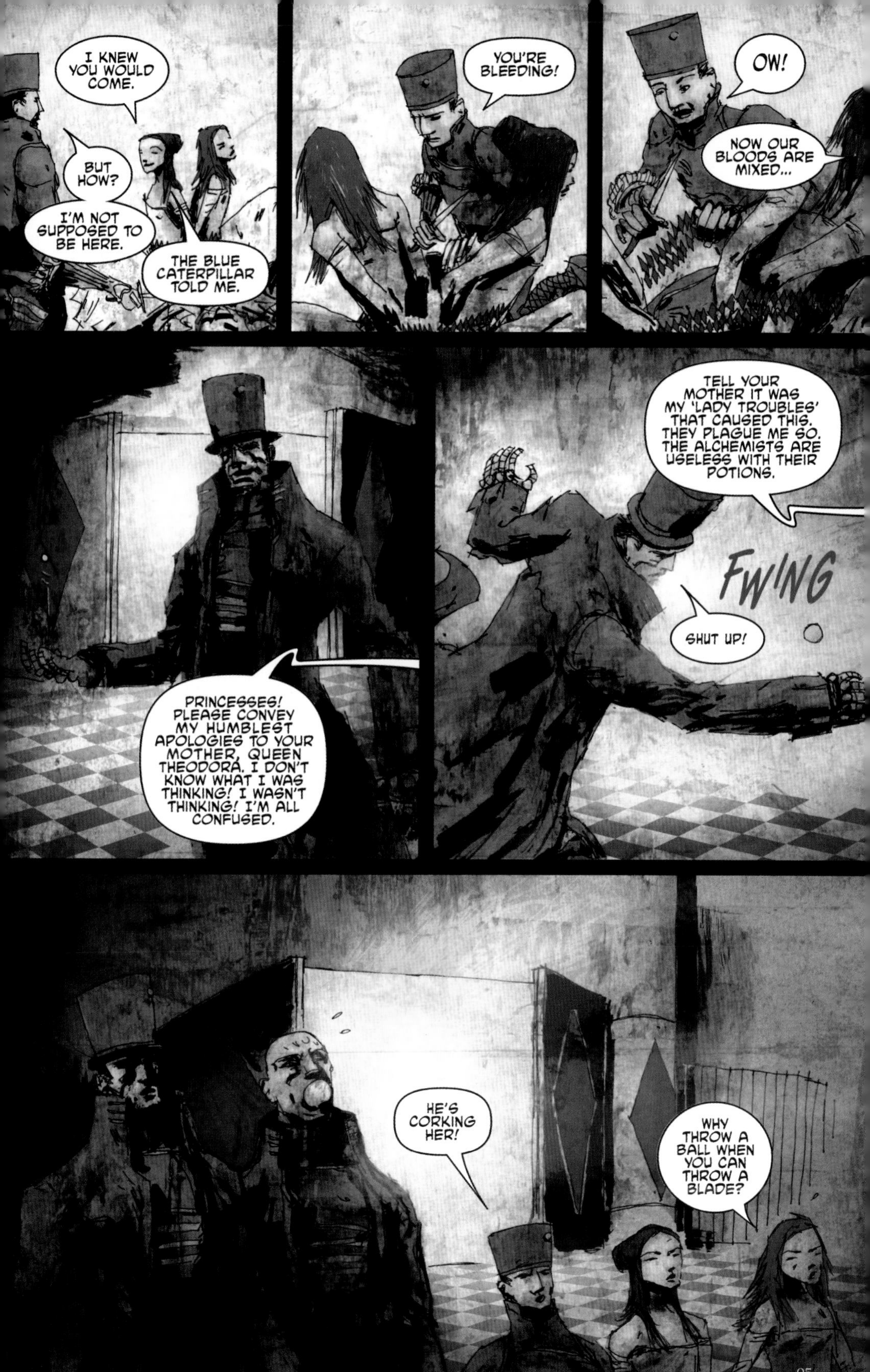
I KNEW YOU WOULD COME.
BUT HOW?
I'M NOT SUPPOSED TO BE HERE.
THE BLUE CATERPILLAR TOLD ME.
YOU'RE BLEEDING!
OW!
NOW OUR BLOODS ARE MIXED...
PRINCESSES! PLEASE CONVEY MY HUMBLEST APOLOGIES TO YOUR MOTHER, QUEEN THEODORA. I DON'T KNOW WHAT I WAS THINKING! I WASN'T THINKING! I'M ALL CONFUSED.
TELL YOUR MOTHER IT WAS MY 'LADY TROUBLES' THAT CAUSED THIS. THEY PLAGUE ME SO. THE ALCHEMISTS ARE USELESS WITH THEIR POTIONS.
FWING
SHUT UP!
HE'S CORKING HER!
WHY THROW A BALL WHEN YOU CAN THROW A BLADE?

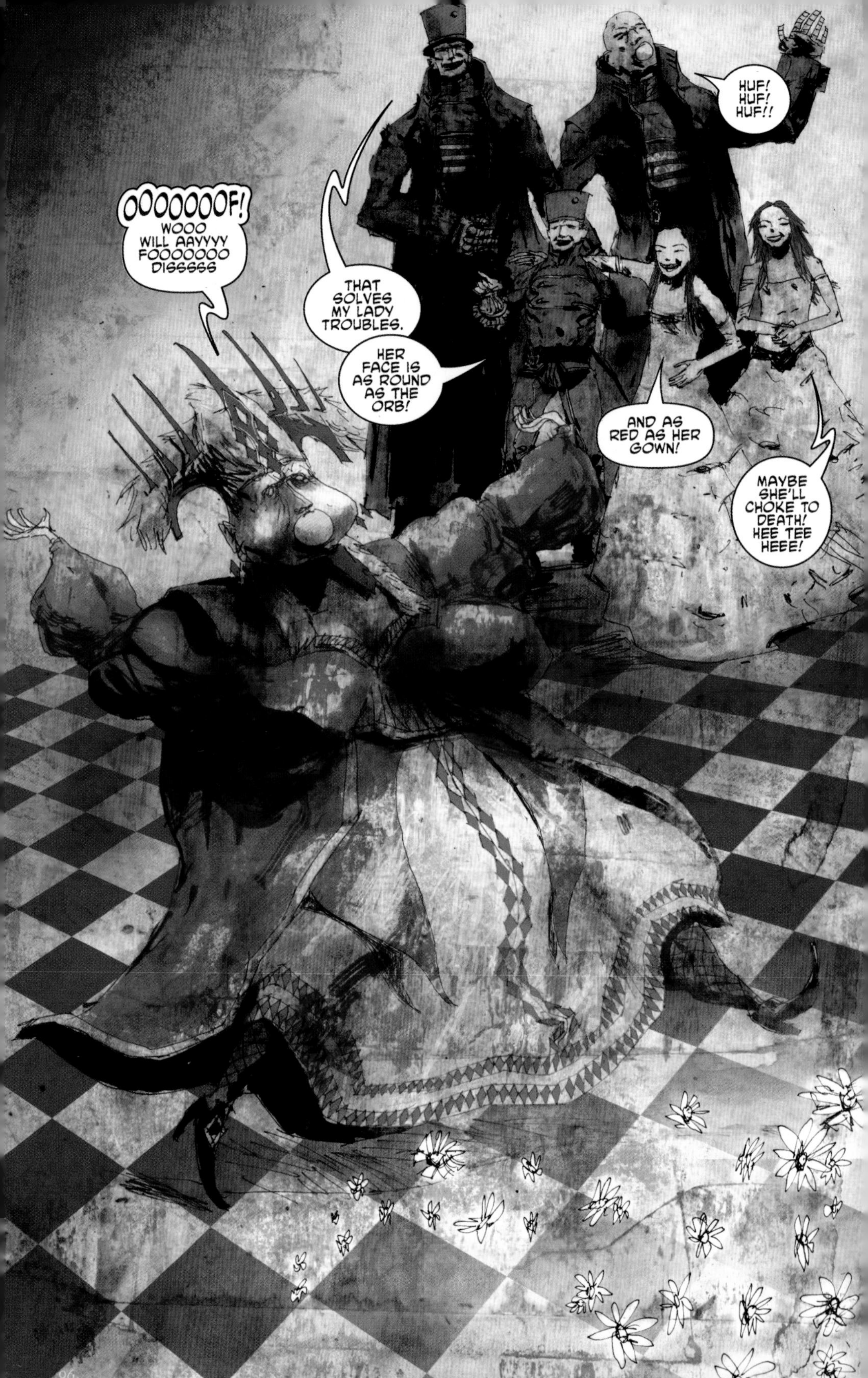
OOOOOOOF! WOOO WILL AAYYYY FOOOOOOO DISSSSS
THAT SOLVES MY LADY TROUBLES.
HER FACE IS AS ROUND AS THE ORB!
HUF! HUF! HUF!!
AND AS RED AS HER GOWN!
MAYBE SHE'LL CHOKE TO DEATH! HEE TEE HEEE!

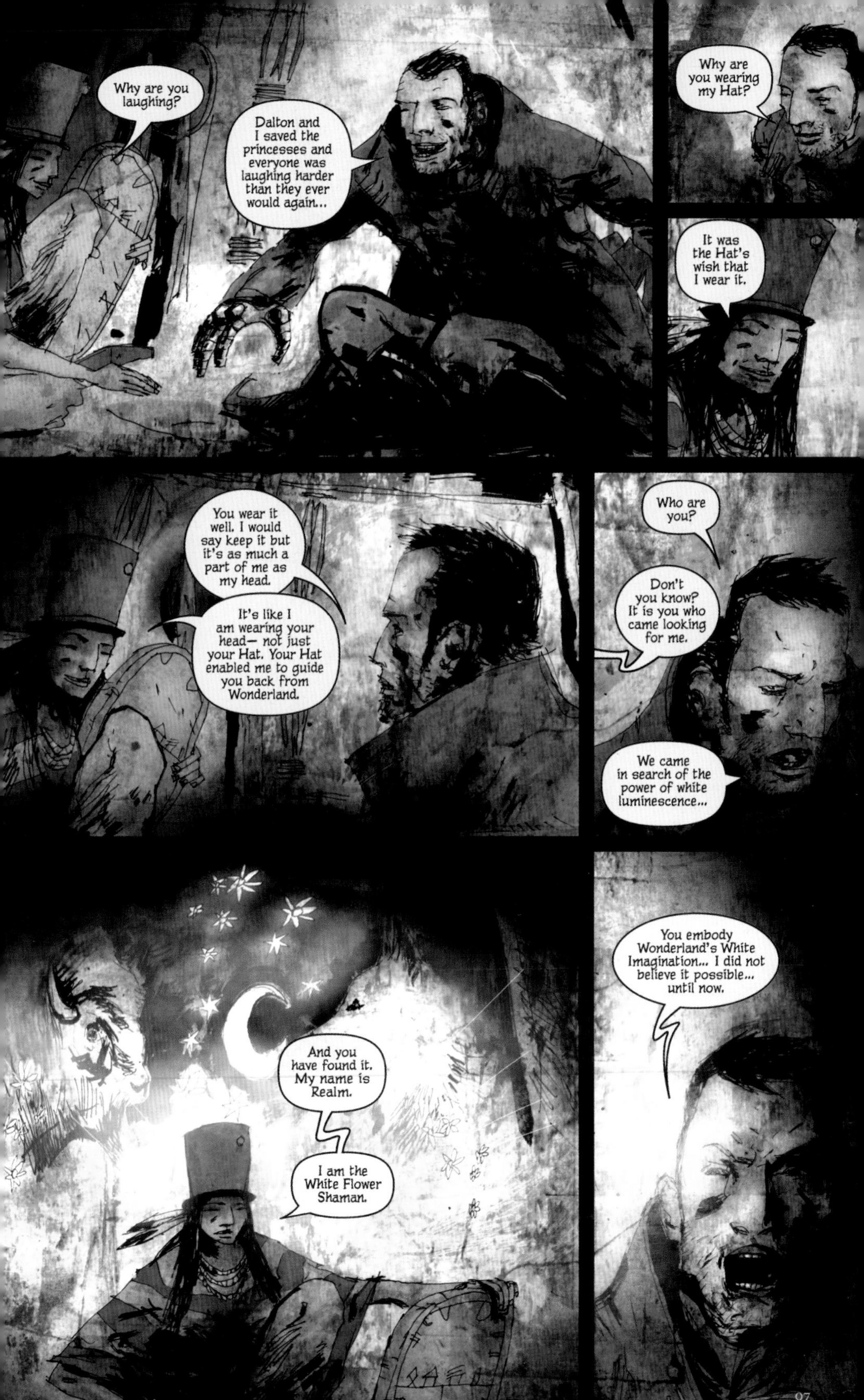
Why are you laughing?
Dalton and I saved the princesses and everyone was laughing harder than they ever would again...
Why are you wearing my Hat?
It was the Hat's wish that I wear it.
You wear it well. I would say keep it but it's as much a part of me as my head.
It's like I am wearing your head— not just your Hat. Your Hat enabled me to guide you back from Wonderland.
Who are you?
Don't you know? It is you who came looking for me.
We came in search of the power of white luminescence...
And you have found it. My name is Realm.
I am the White Flower Shaman.
You embody Wonderland's White Imagination... I did not believe it possible... until now.

We have located the caretakers of the source of White Luminescence but rather than appealing for their help, we must join with them in their battle against the dark forces intent on destruction. I have long contemplated that there was more meaning to my travels in this world than simply the return of Princess Alyss to Wonderland. While that is the primary motive of my quest, there is little doubt that the war waged in this world between White and Black Imagination is as powerful and critical as that waged in Wonderland. Is it the same war? Is it the same world?

My mission here is now clear. Every Queen needs a Bodyguard.

"Speak to the earth, and it shall teach thee." —JOB, 12:8

Have All the Flowers Gone

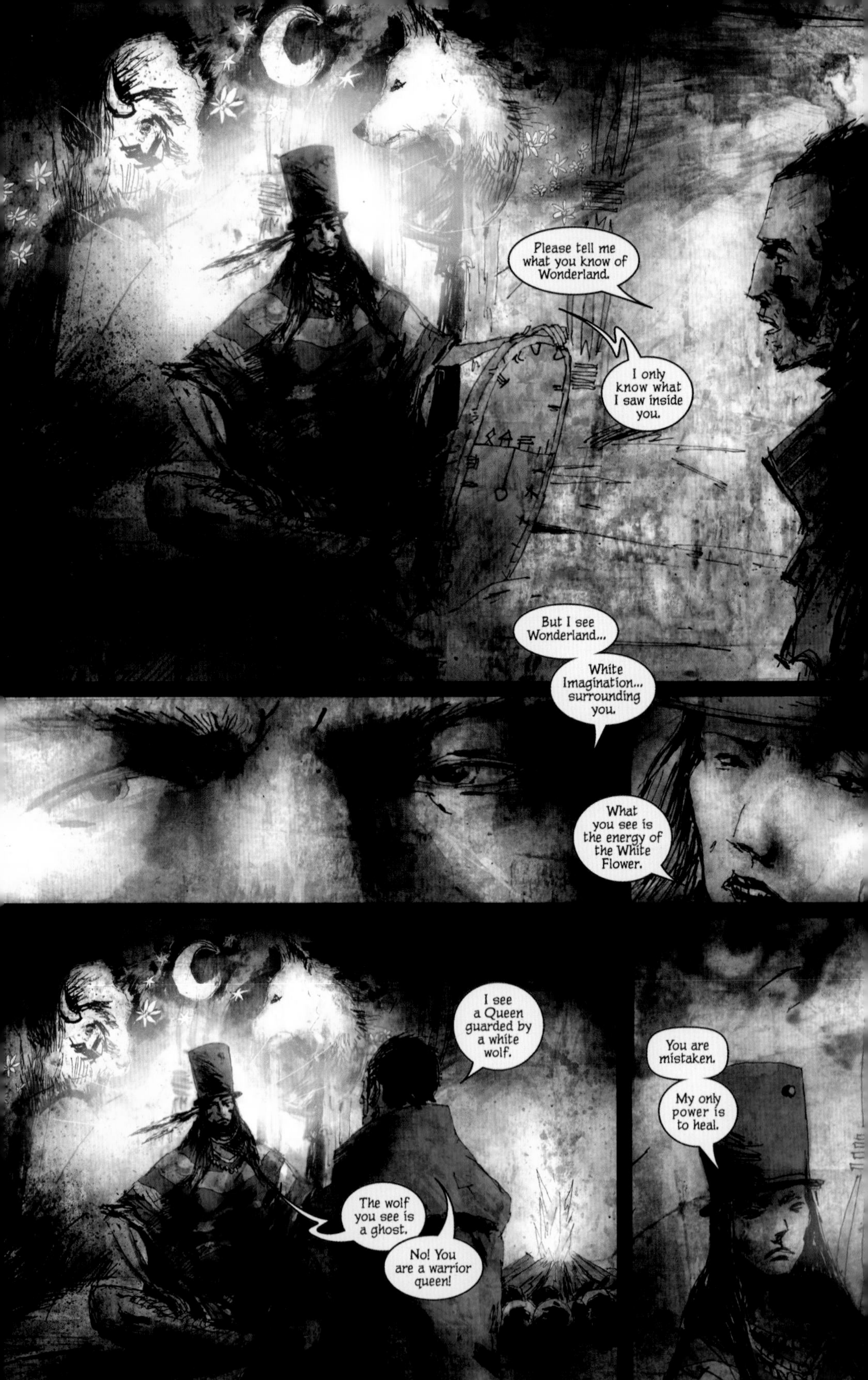
Please tell me what you know of Wonderland.
I only know what I saw inside you.
But I see Wonderland...
White Imagination... surrounding you.
What you see is the energy of the White Flower.
I see a Queen guarded by a white wolf.
The wolf you see is a ghost.
No! You are a warrior queen!
You are mistaken.
My only power is to heal.

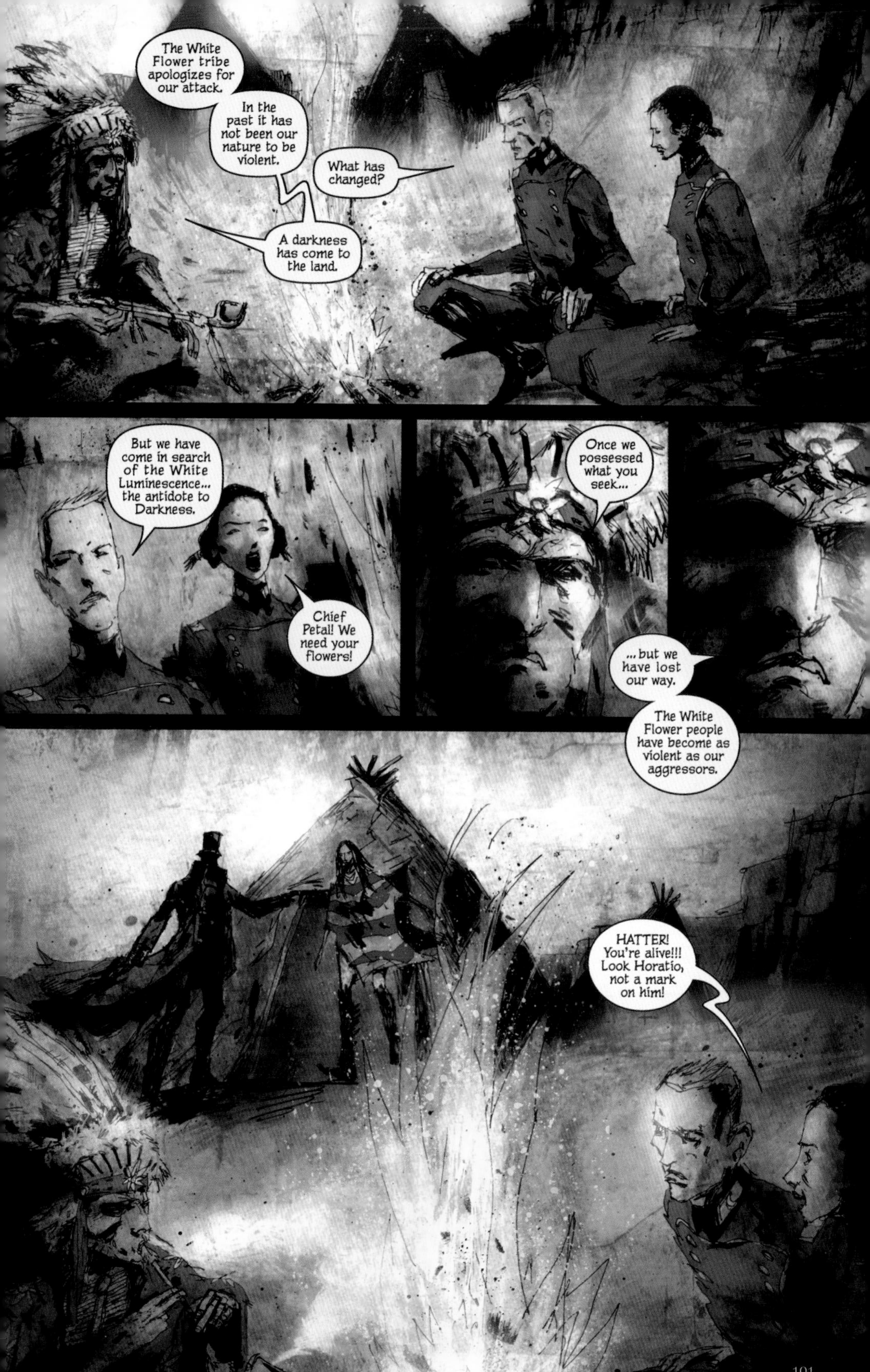

The White Flower tribe apologizes for our attack.
In the past it has not been our nature to be violent.
What has changed?
A darkness has come to the land.
But we have come in search of the White Luminescence... the antidote to Darkness.
Chief Petal! We need your flowers!
Once we possessed what you seek...
...but we have lost our way.
The White Flower people have become as violent as our aggressors.
HATTER! You're alive!!! Look Horatio, not a mark on him!

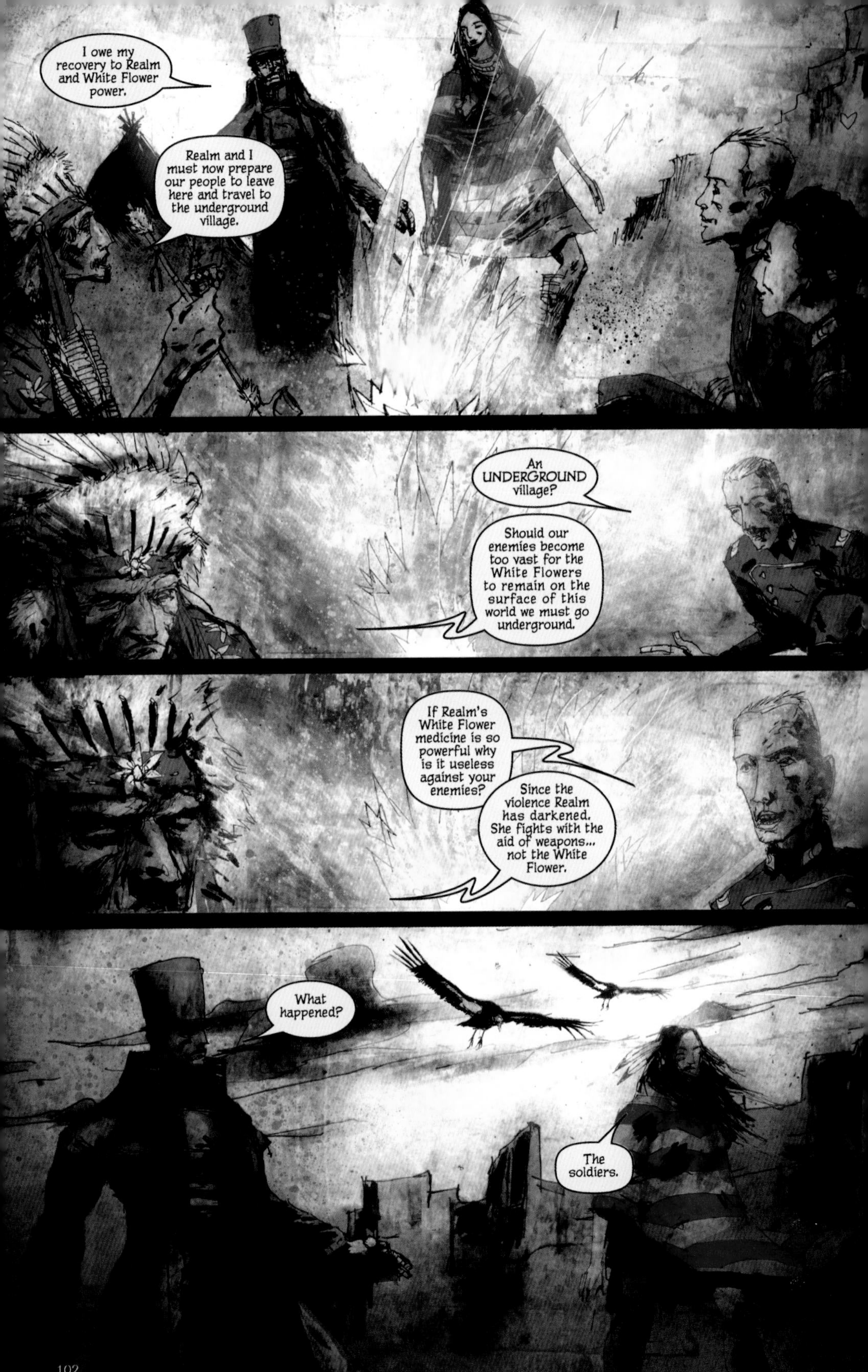
I owe my recovery to Realm and White Flower power.
Realm and I must now prepare our people to leave here and travel to the underground village.
An UNDERGROUND village?
Should our enemies become too vast for the White Flowers to remain on the surface of this world we must go underground.
If Realm's White Flower medicine is so powerful why is it useless against your enemies?
Since the violence Realm has darkened. She fights with the aid of weapons... not the White Flower.
What happened?
The soldiers.

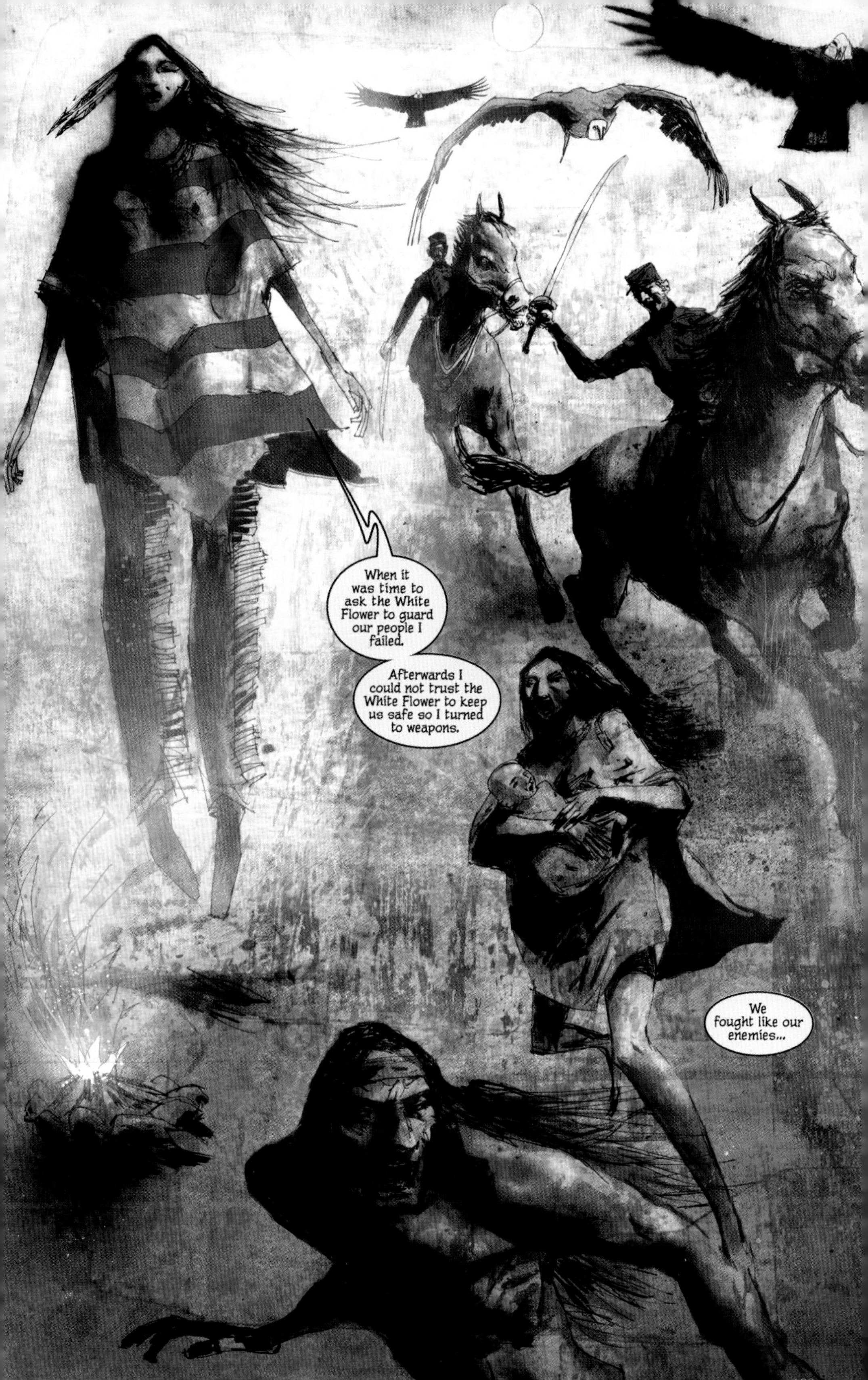
When it was time to ask the White Flower to guard our people I failed.
Afterwards I could not trust the White Flower to keep us safe so I turned to weapons.
We fought like our enemies...

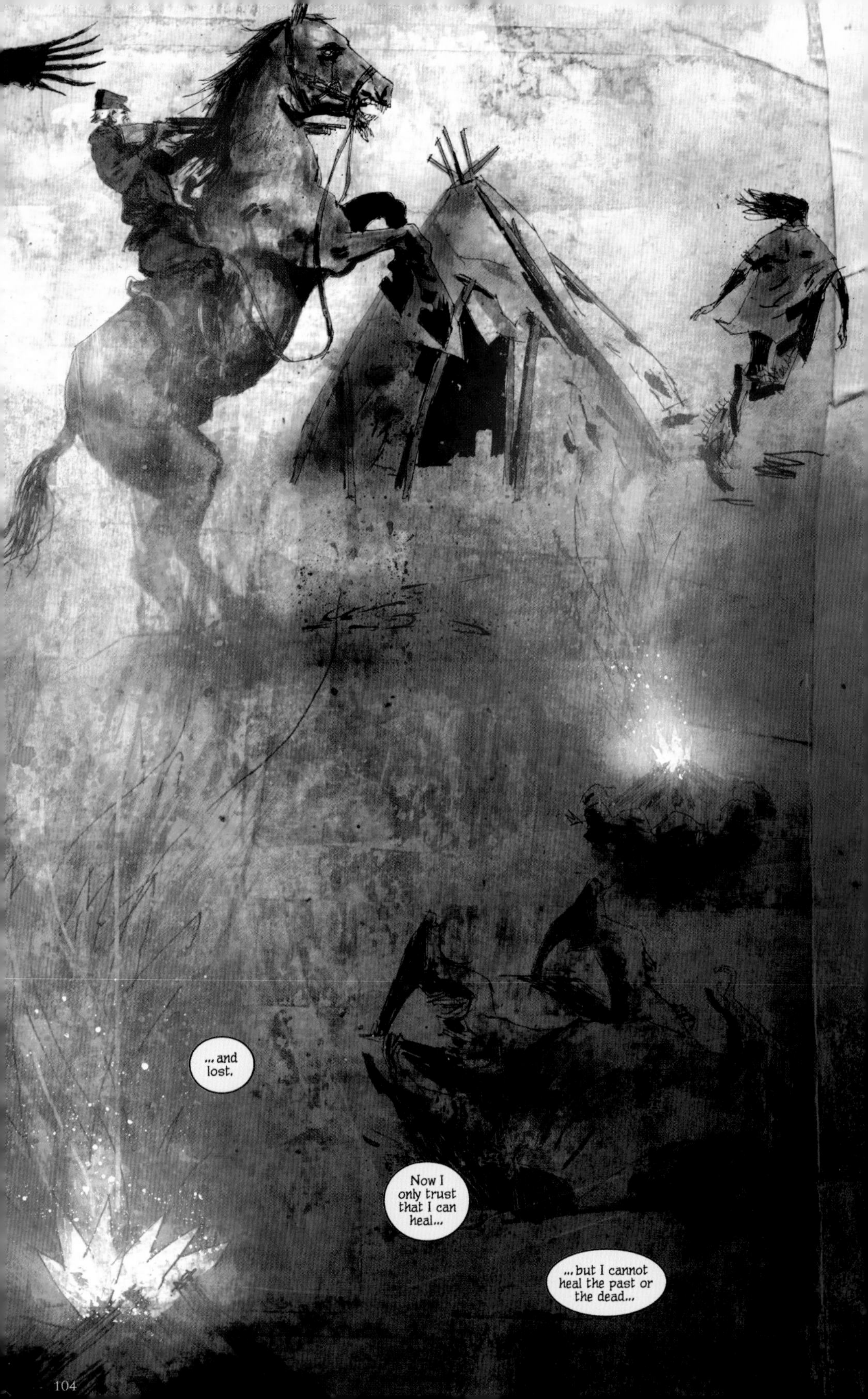
...and lost.
Now I only trust that I can heal...
...but I cannot heal the past or the dead...

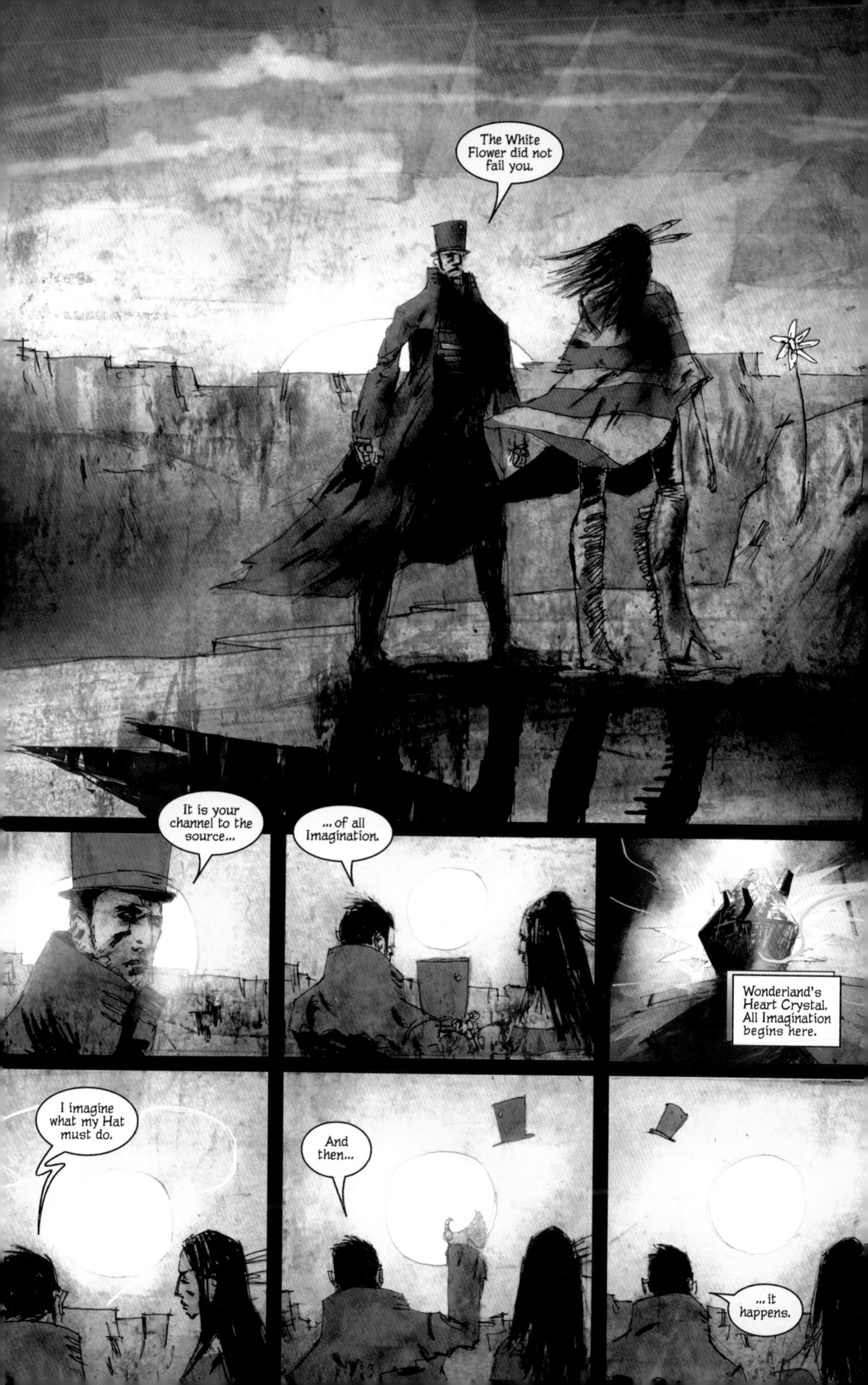
The White Flower did not fail you.
It is your channel to the source...
...of all Imagination.
Wonderland's Heart Crystal. All Imagination begins here.
I imagine what my Hat must do.
And then...
...it happens.

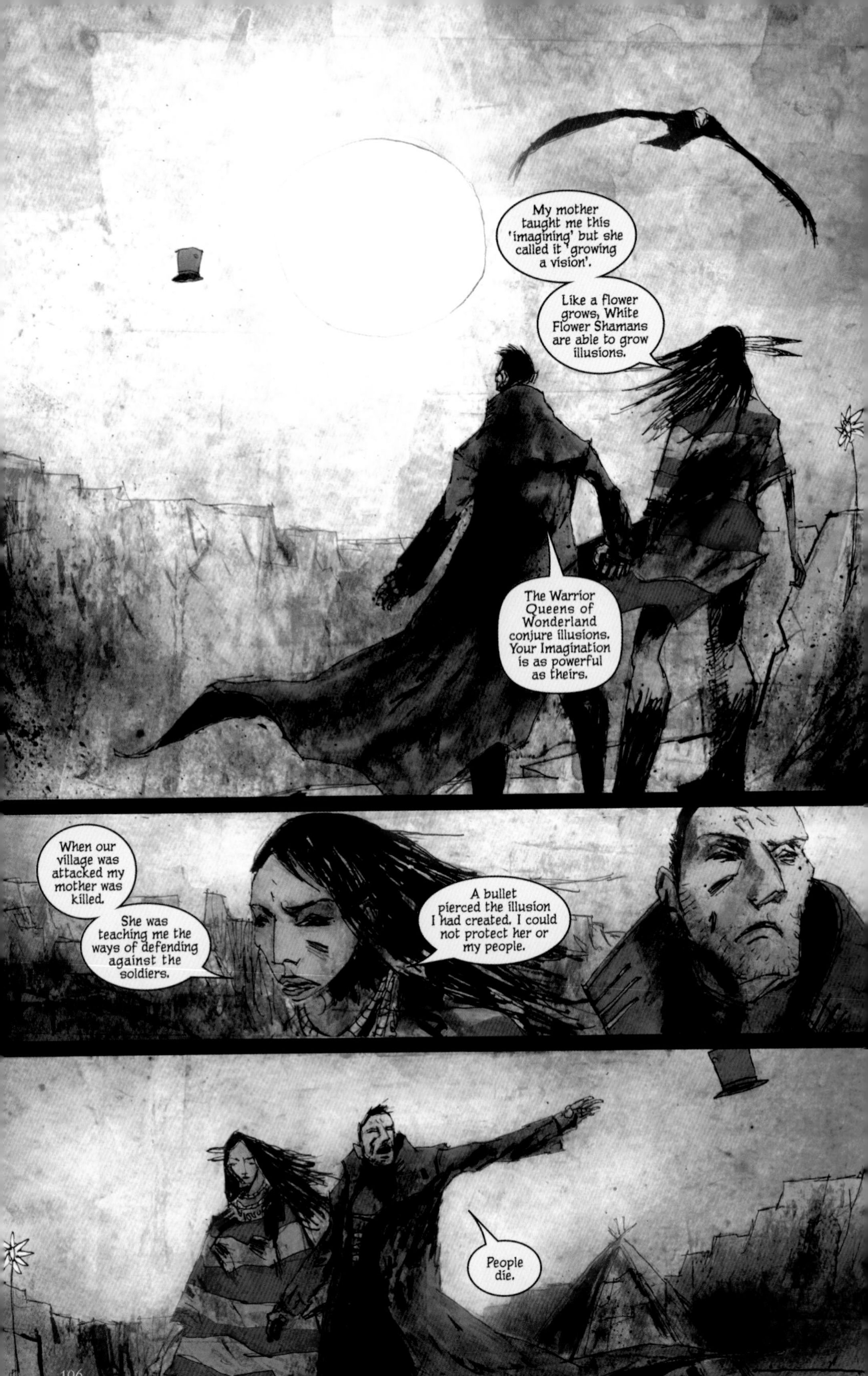
My mother taught me this 'imagining' but she called it 'growing a vision'.
Like a flower grows, White Flower Shamans are able to grow illusions.
The Warrior Queens of Wonderland conjure illusions. Your Imagination is as powerful as theirs.
When our village was attacked my mother was killed.
She was teaching me the ways of defending against the soldiers.
A bullet pierced the illusion I had created. I could not protect her or my people.
People die.

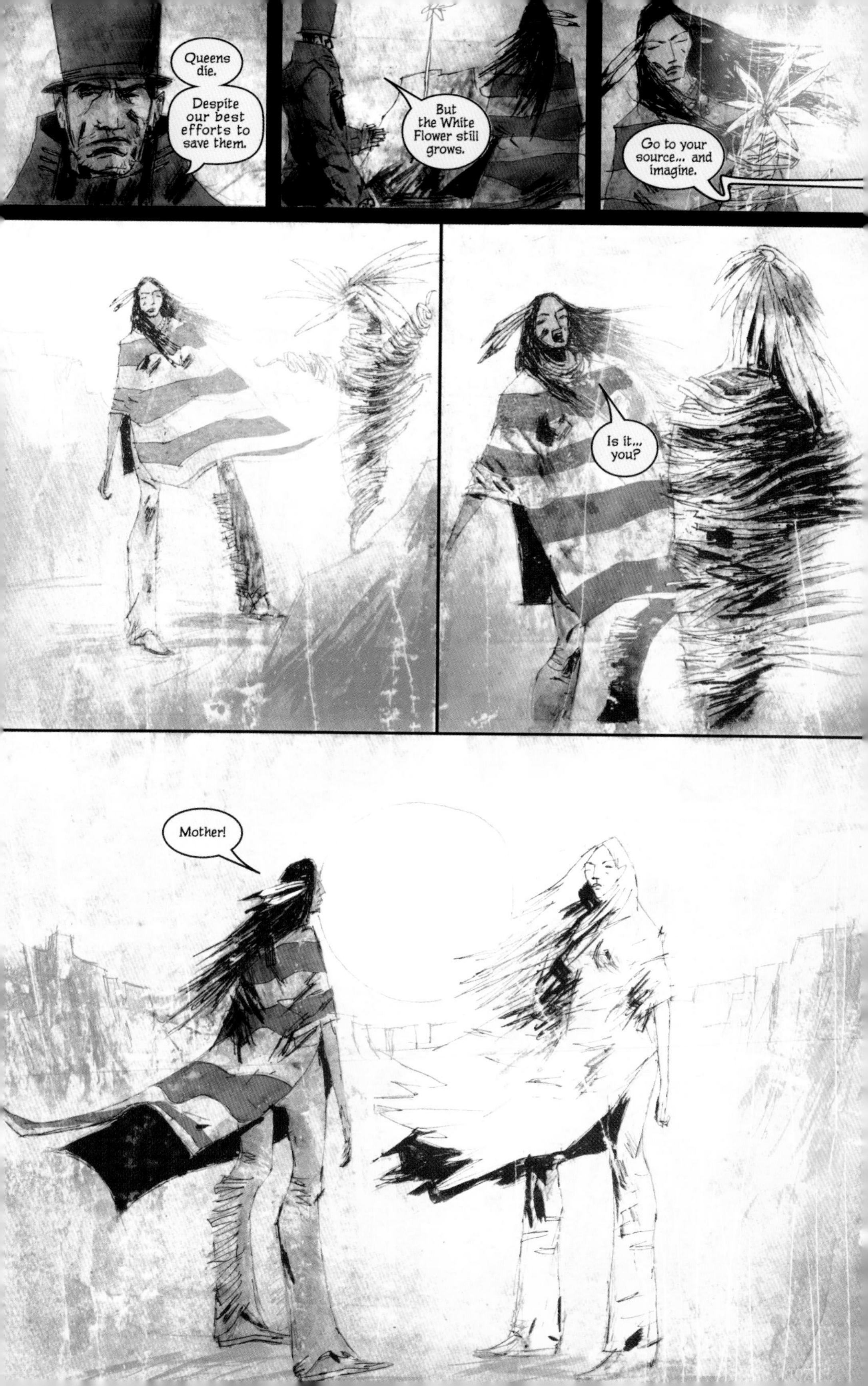
Queens die.
Despite our best efforts to save them.
But the White Flower still grows.
Go to your source... and imagine.
Is it... you?
Mother!

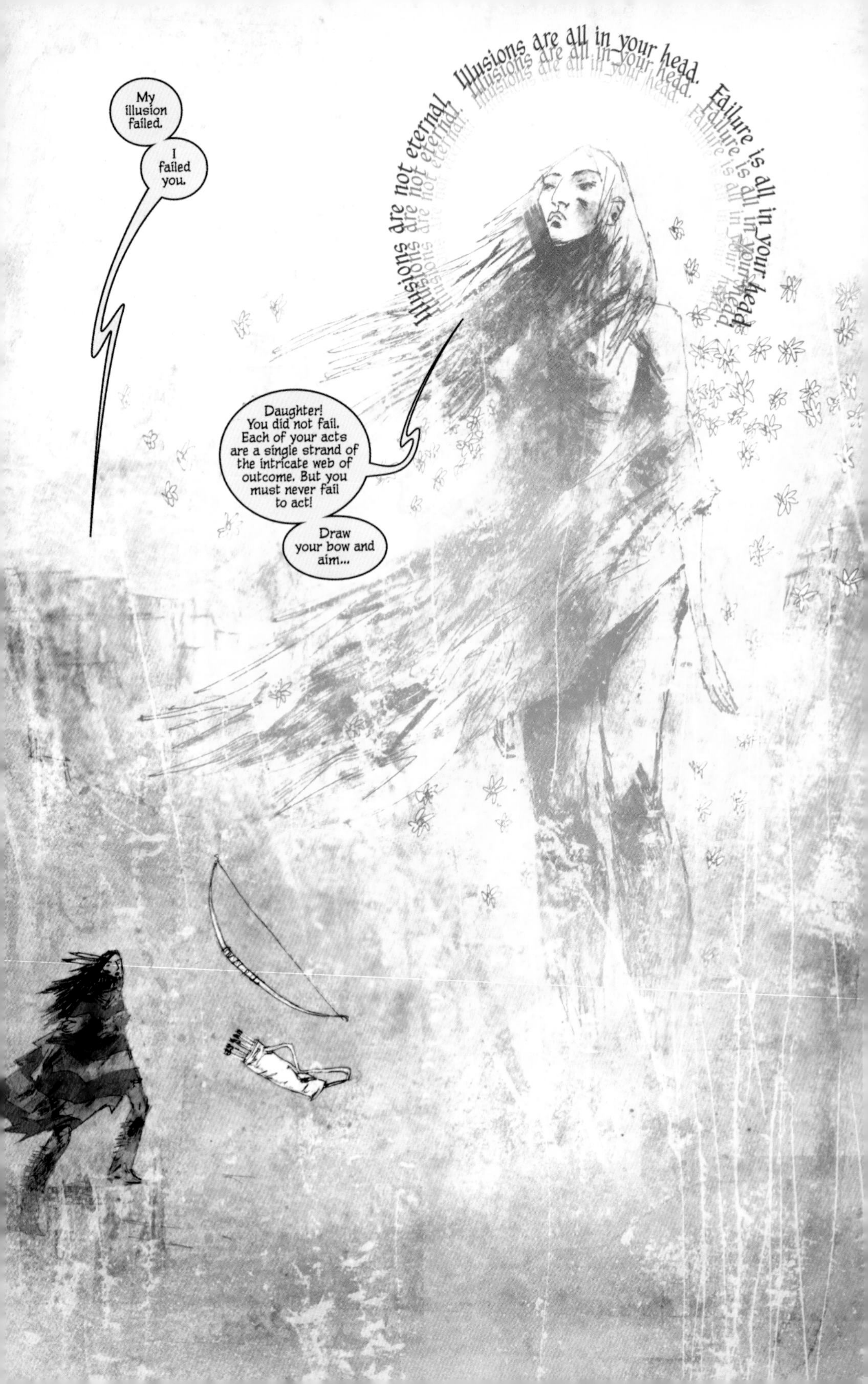

My illusion failed.
I failed you.
Illusions are not eternal. Illusions are all in your head. Failure is all in your head.
Daughter! You did not fail. Each of your acts are a single strand of the intricate web of outcome. But you must never fail to act!
Draw your bow and aim...

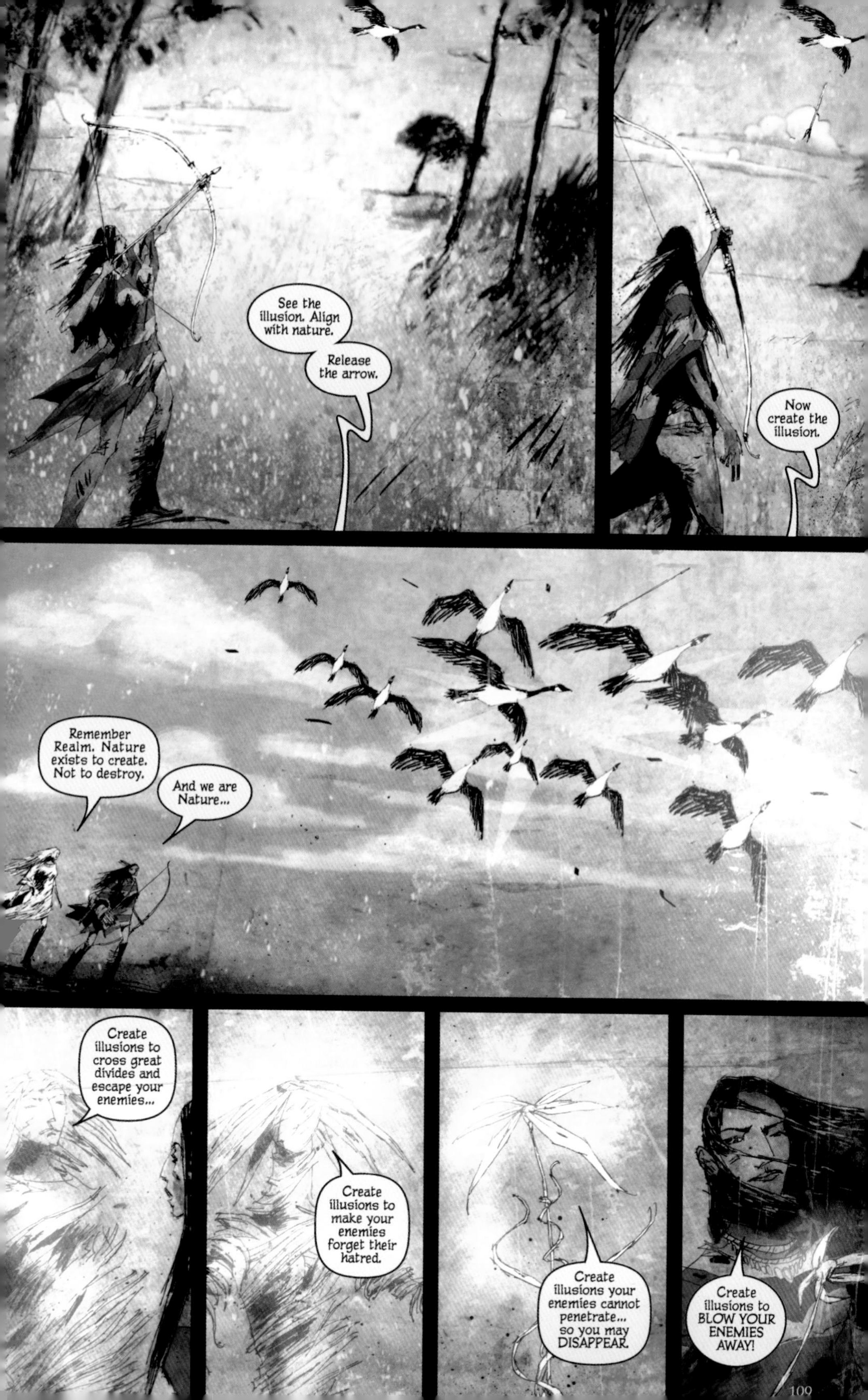
See the illusion. Align with nature.
Release the arrow.
Now create the illusion.
Remember Realm. Nature exists to create. Not to destroy.
And we are Nature...
Create illusions to cross great divides and escape your enemies...
Create illusions to make your enemies forget their hatred.
Create illusions your enemies cannot penetrate... so you may DISAPPEAR.
Create illusions to BLOW YOUR ENEMIES AWAY!

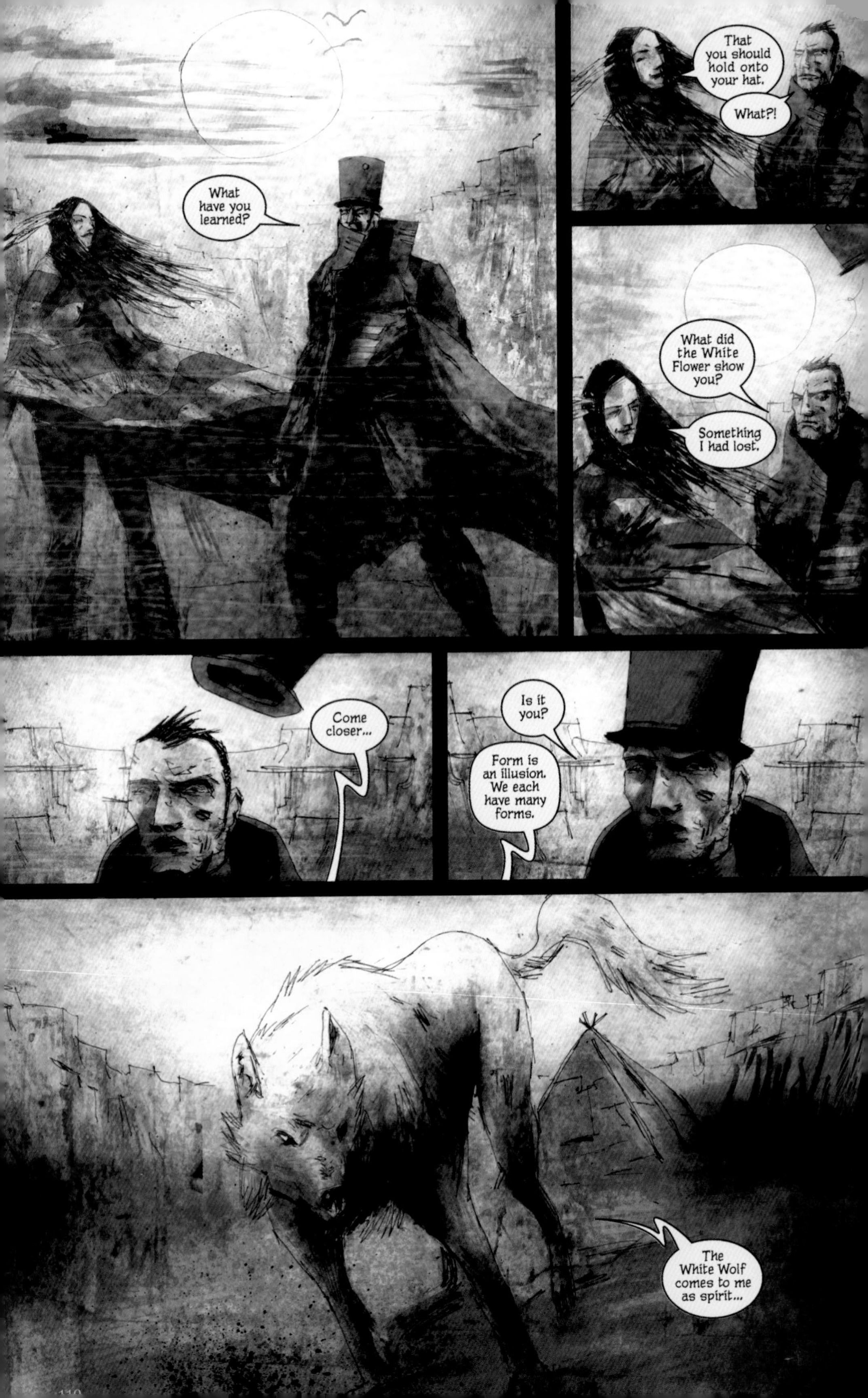
What have you learned?
That you should hold onto your hat.
What?!
What did the White Flower show you?
Something I had lost.
Come closer...
Is it you?
Form is an illusion. We each have many forms.
The White Wolf comes to me as spirit...

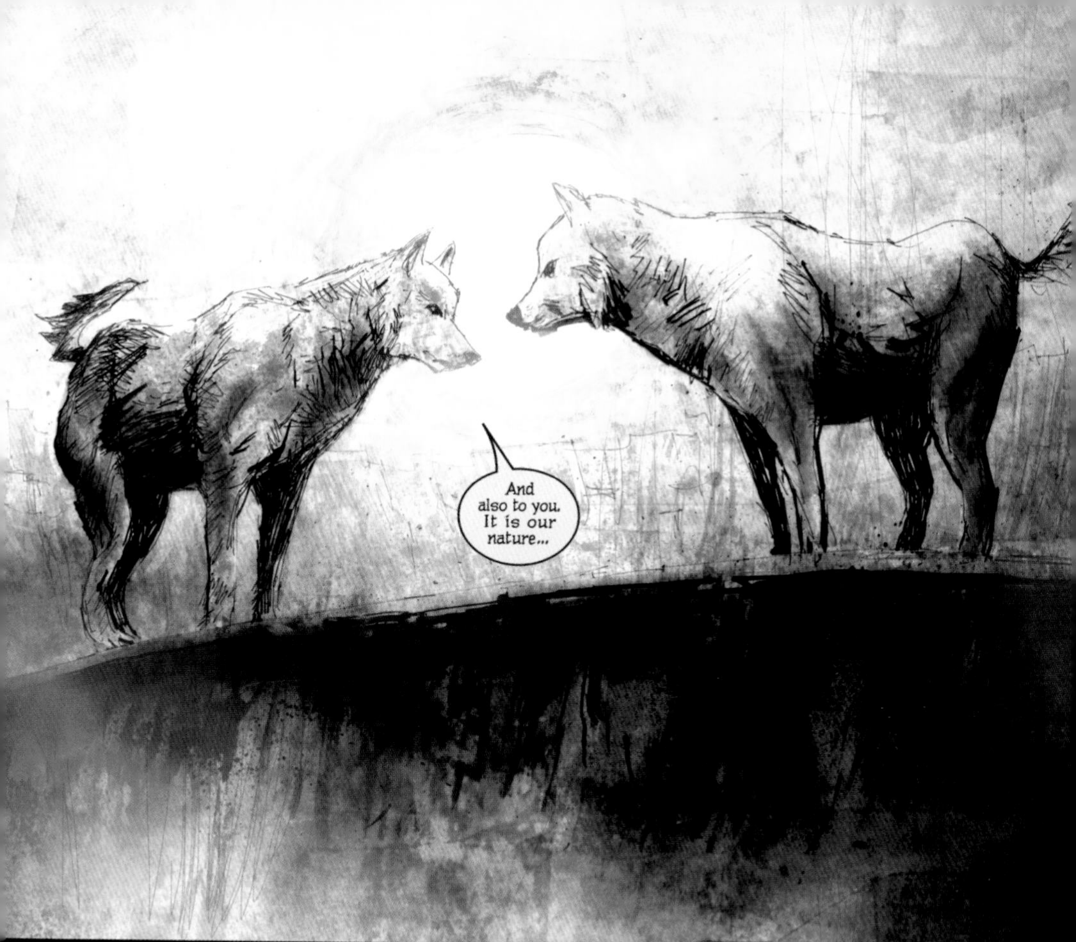
And also to you. It is our nature...

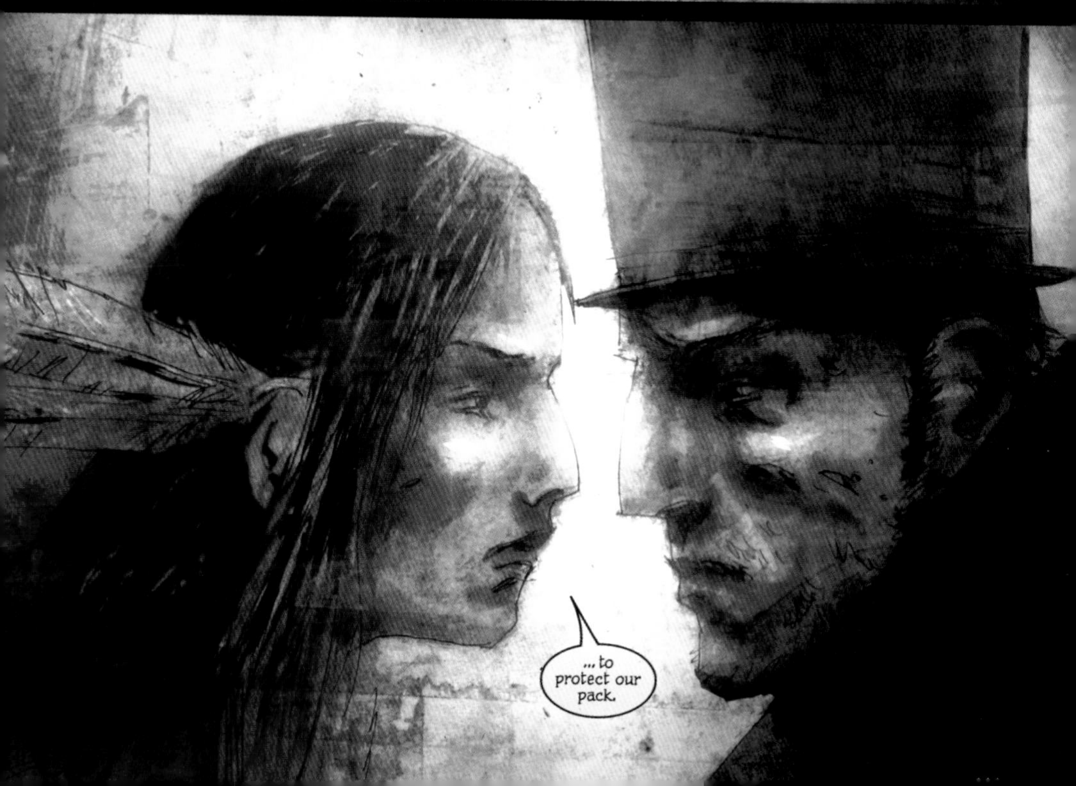
...to protect our pack.

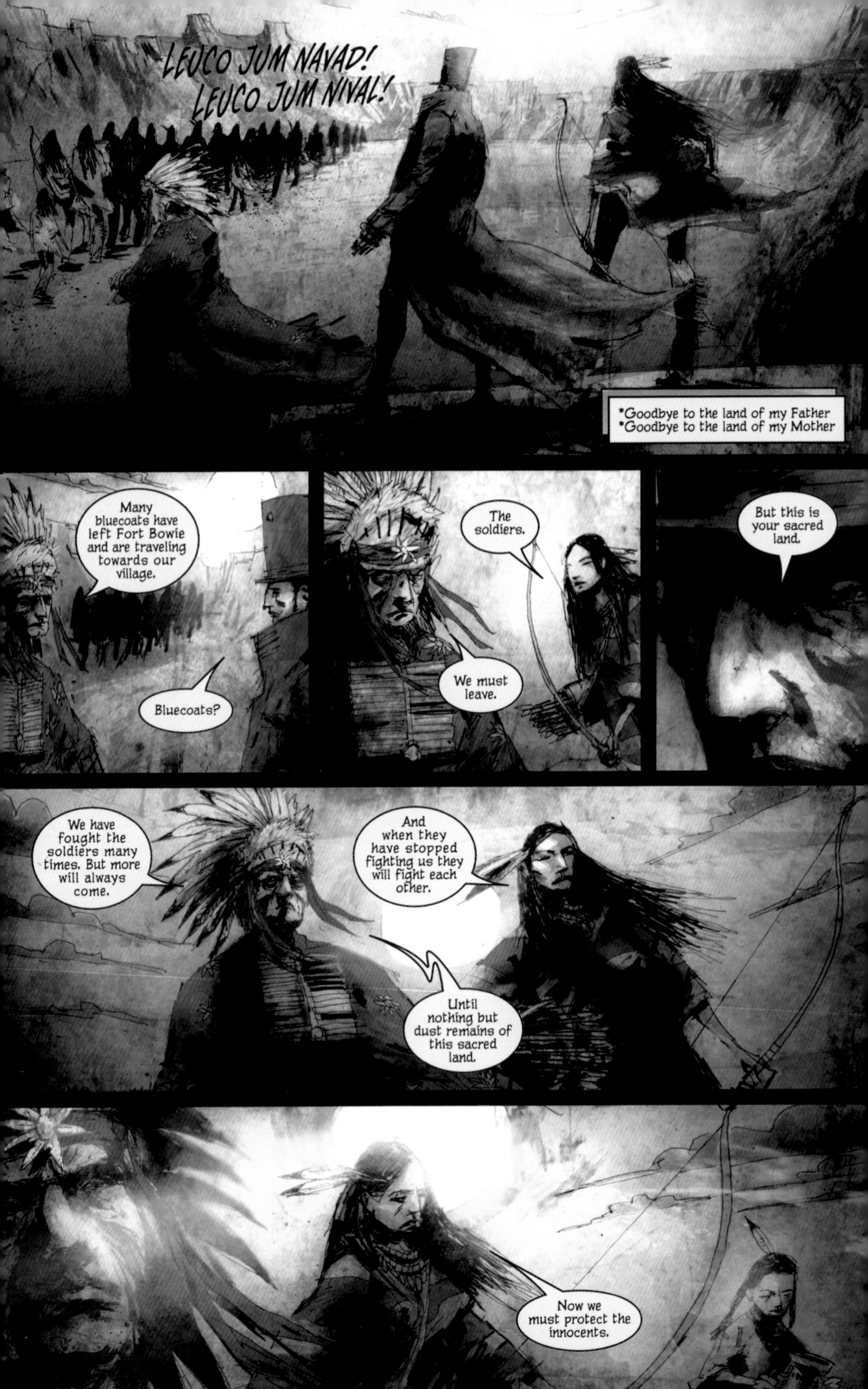
LEUCO JUM NAVAD!
LEUCO JUM NIVAL!
*Goodbye to the land of my Father
*Goodbye to the land of my Mother
Many bluecoats have left Fort Bowie and are traveling towards our village.
Bluecoats?
The soldiers.
We must leave.
But this is your sacred land.
We have fought the soldiers many times. But more will always come.
And when they have stopped fighting us they will fight each other.
Until nothing but dust remains of this sacred land.
Now we must protect the innocents.

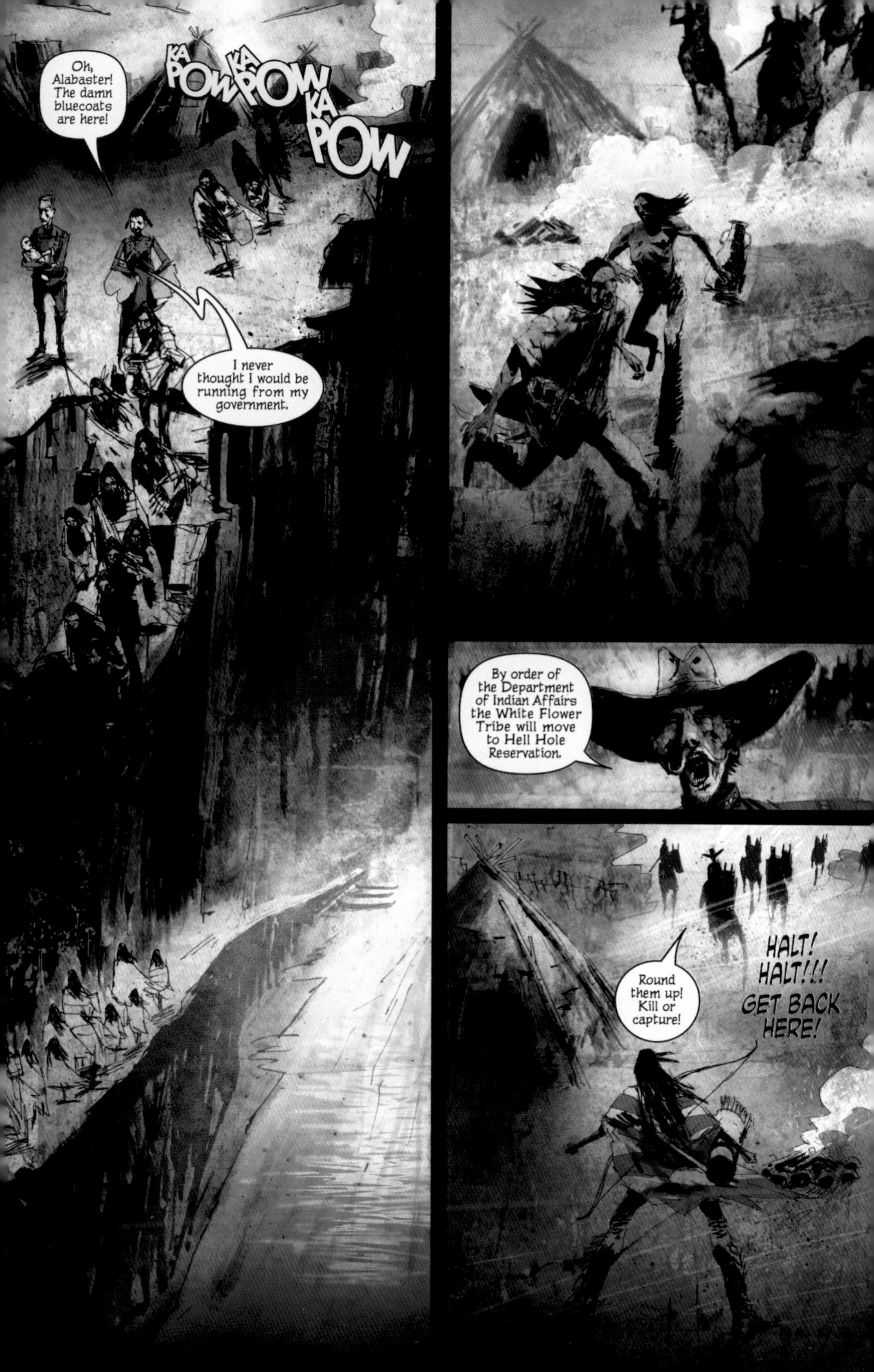
Oh, Alabaster! The damn bluecoats are here!
KA POW KA POW KA POW
I never thought I would be running from my government.
By order of the Department of Indian Affairs the White Flower Tribe will move to Hell Hole Reservation.
Round them up! Kill or capture!
HALT! HALT!!! GET BACK HERE!

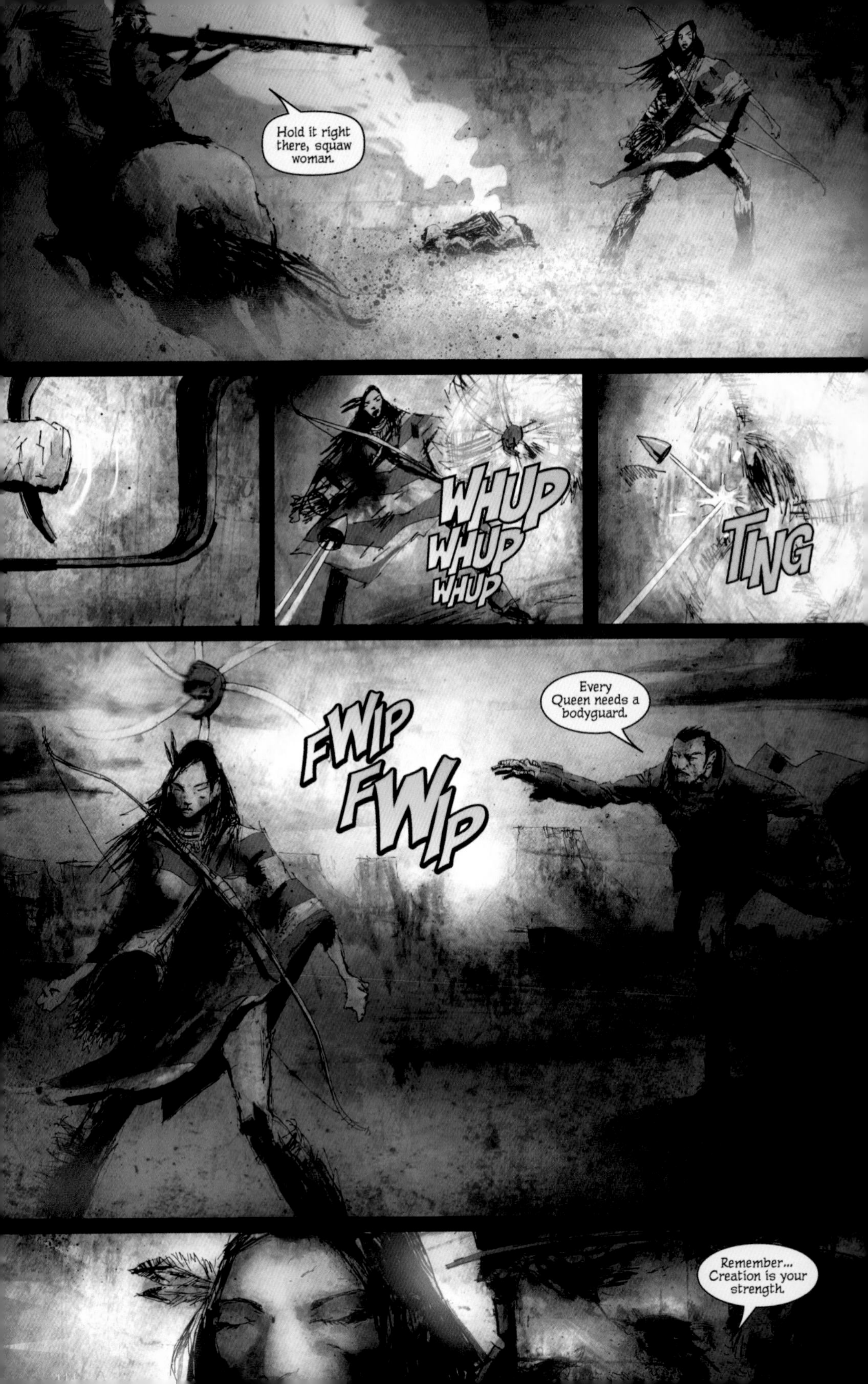
Hold it right there, squaw woman.
WHUP
WHUP
WHUP
TING
FWIP
FWIP
Every Queen needs a bodyguard.
Remember... Creation is your strength.

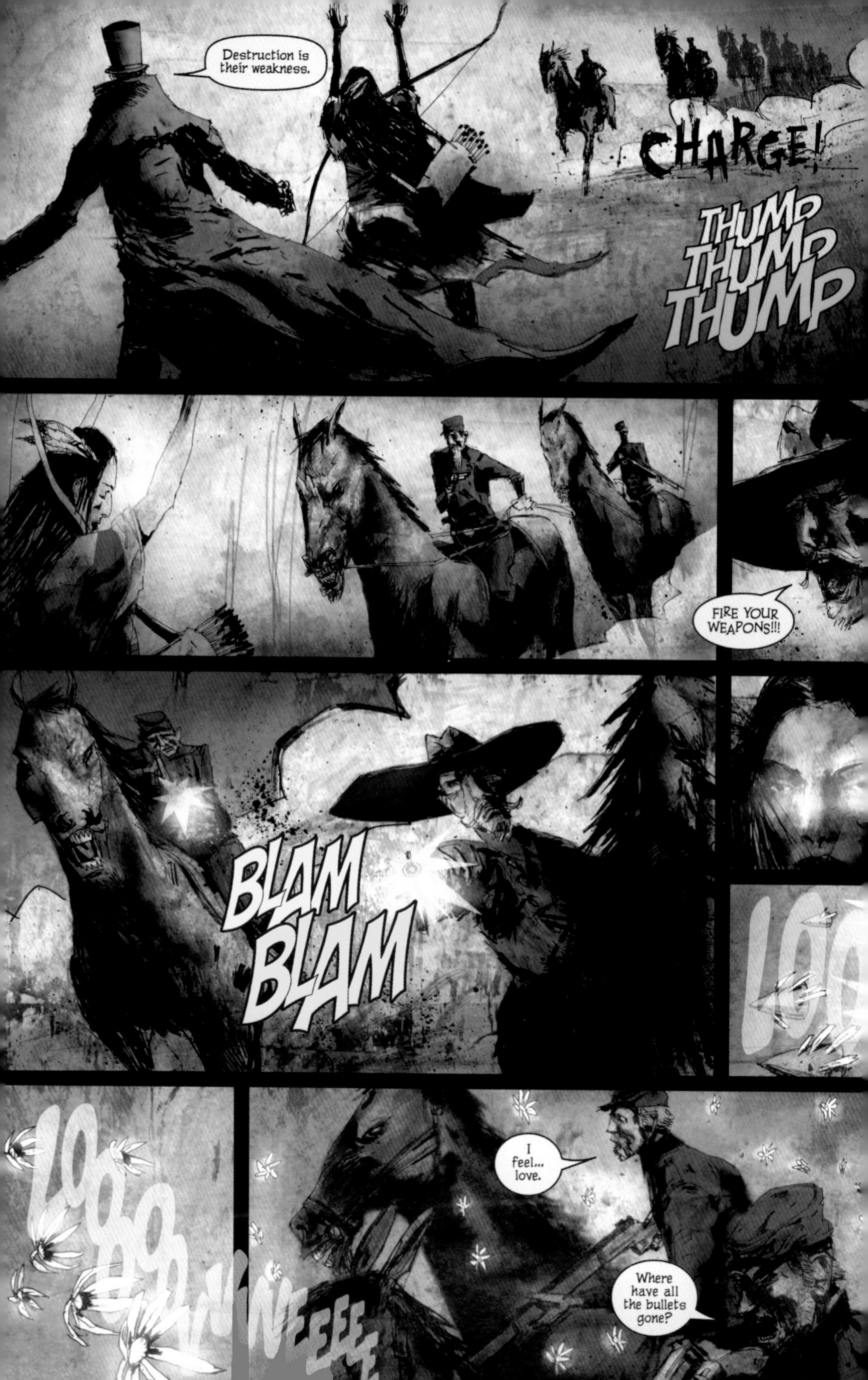
Destruction is their weakness.
CHARGE!
THUMP THUMP THUMP
FIRE YOUR WEAPONS!!!
BLAM BLAM
I feel... love.
Where have all the bullets gone?

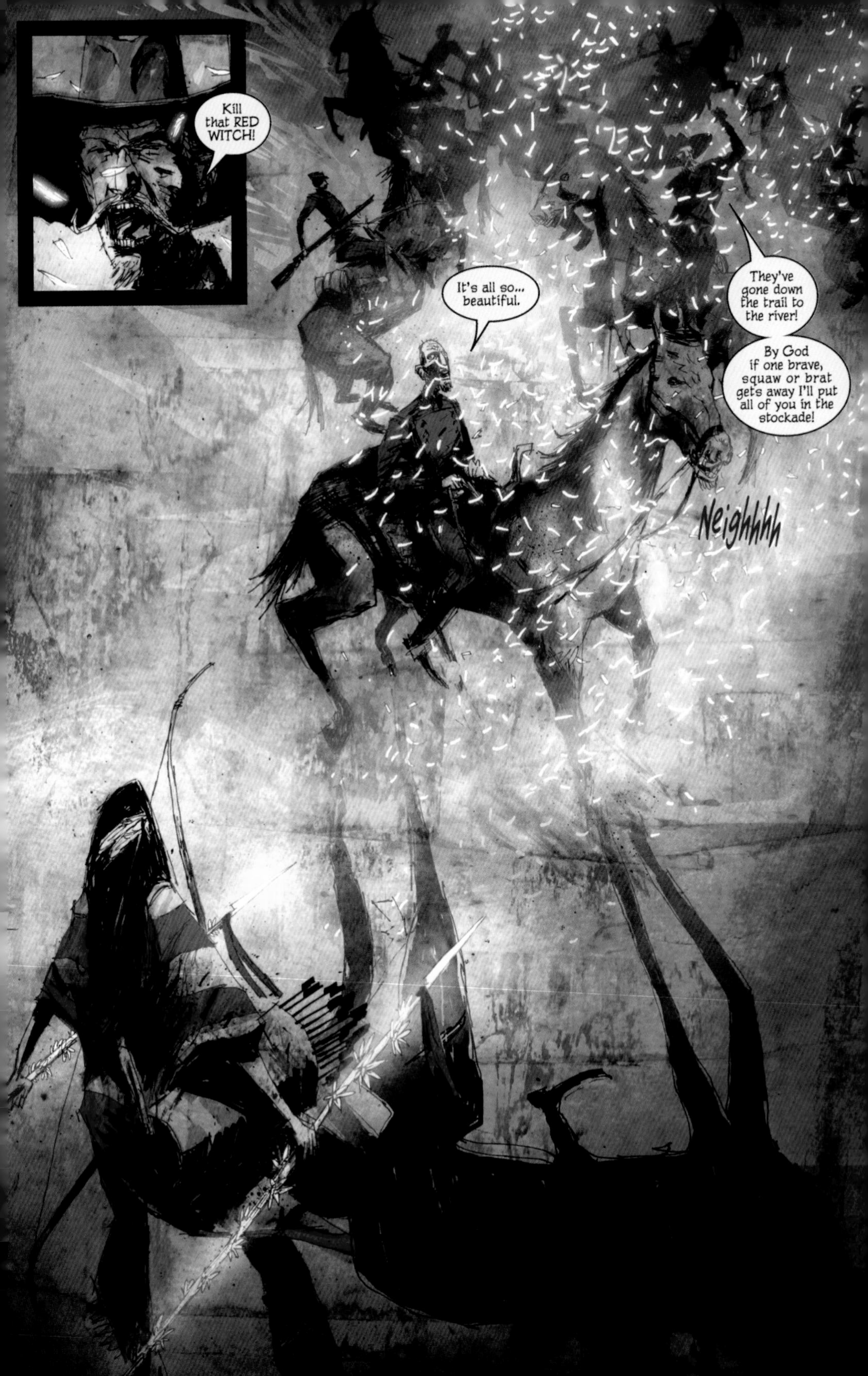
Kill that RED WITCH!
It's all so... beautiful.
They've gone down the trail to the river!
By God if one brave, squaw or brat gets away I'll put all of you in the stockade!
Neighhhh

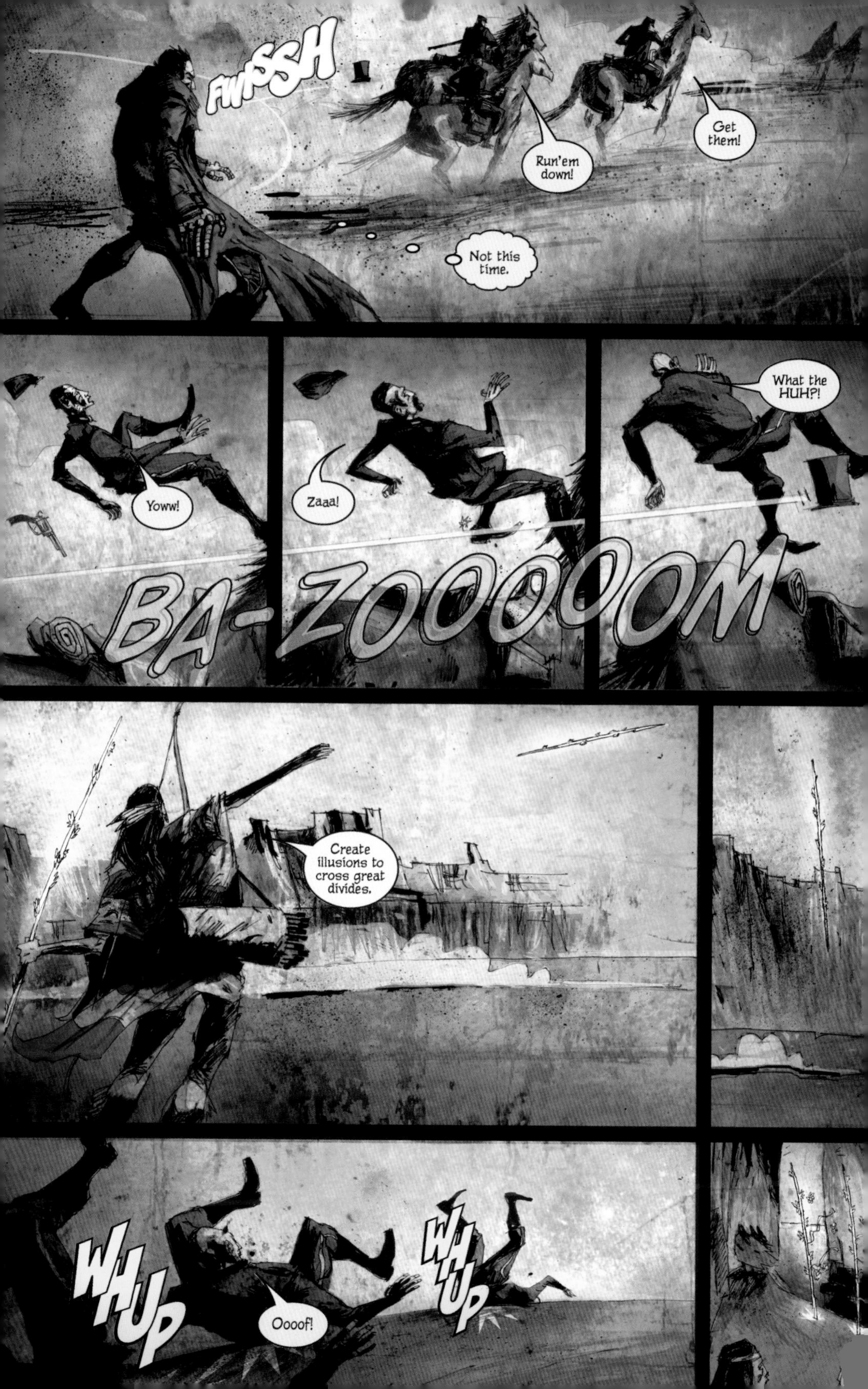
FWISSH
Run'em down!
Get them!
Not this time.
Yoww!
Zaaa!
What the HUH?!
BA-ZOOOOOOM
Create illusions to cross great divides.
WHUP
Oooof!
WHUP

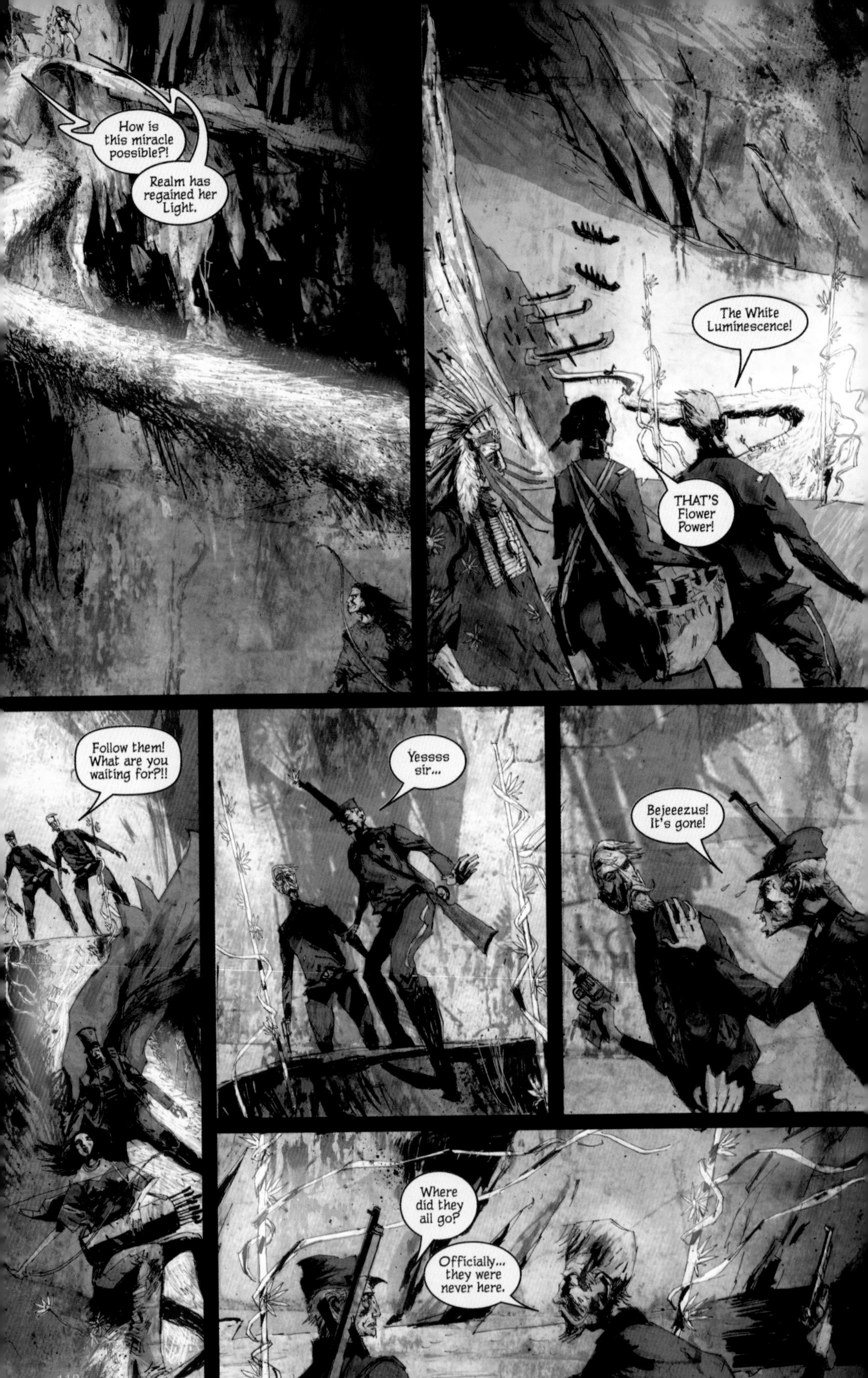
How is this miracle possible?!
Realm has regained her Light.
The White Luminescence!
THAT'S Flower Power!
Follow them! What are you waiting for?!!
Yessss sir...
Bejeeezus! It's gone!
Where did they all go?
Officially... they were never here.

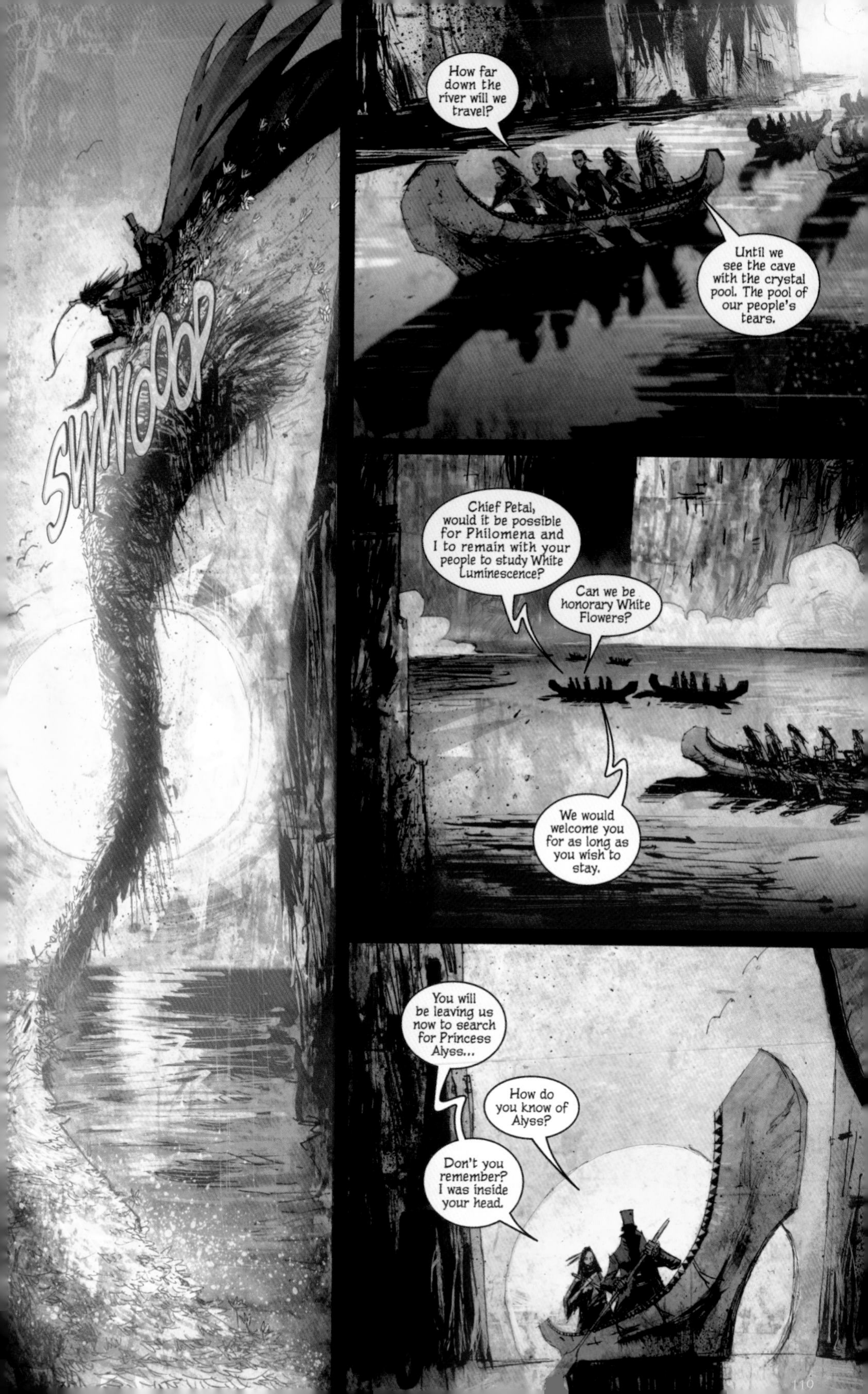
SWWOOP
How far down the river will we travel?
Until we see the cave with the crystal pool. The pool of our people's tears.
Chief Petal, would it be possible for Philomena and I to remain with your people to study White Luminescence?
Can we be honorary White Flowers?
We would welcome you for as long as you wish to stay.
You will be leaving us now to search for Princess Alyss...
How do you know of Alyss?
Don't you remember? I was inside your head.

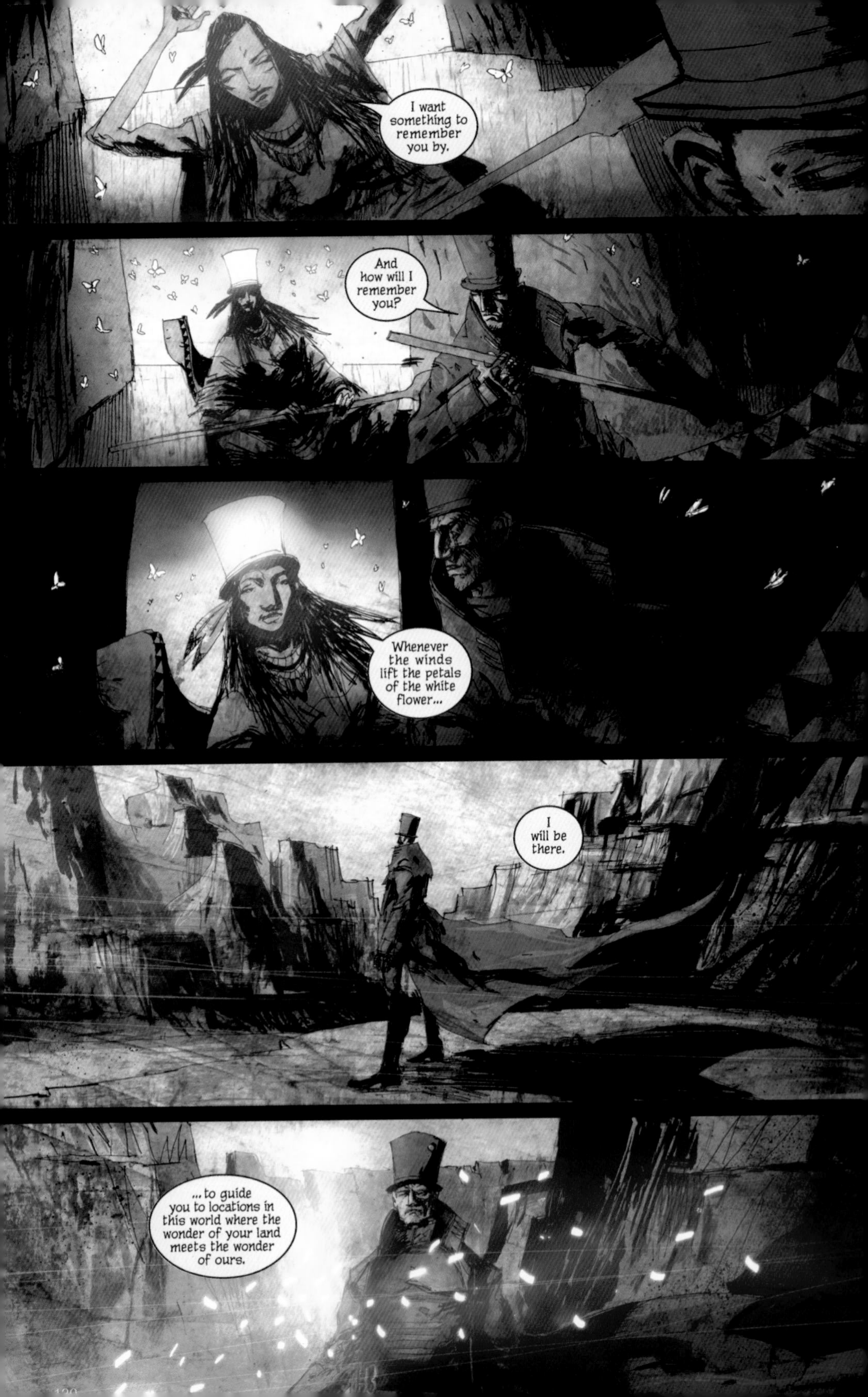
I want something to remember you by.
And how will I remember you?
Whenever the winds lift the petals of the white flower...
I will be there.
...to guide you to locations in this world where the wonder of your land meets the wonder of ours.

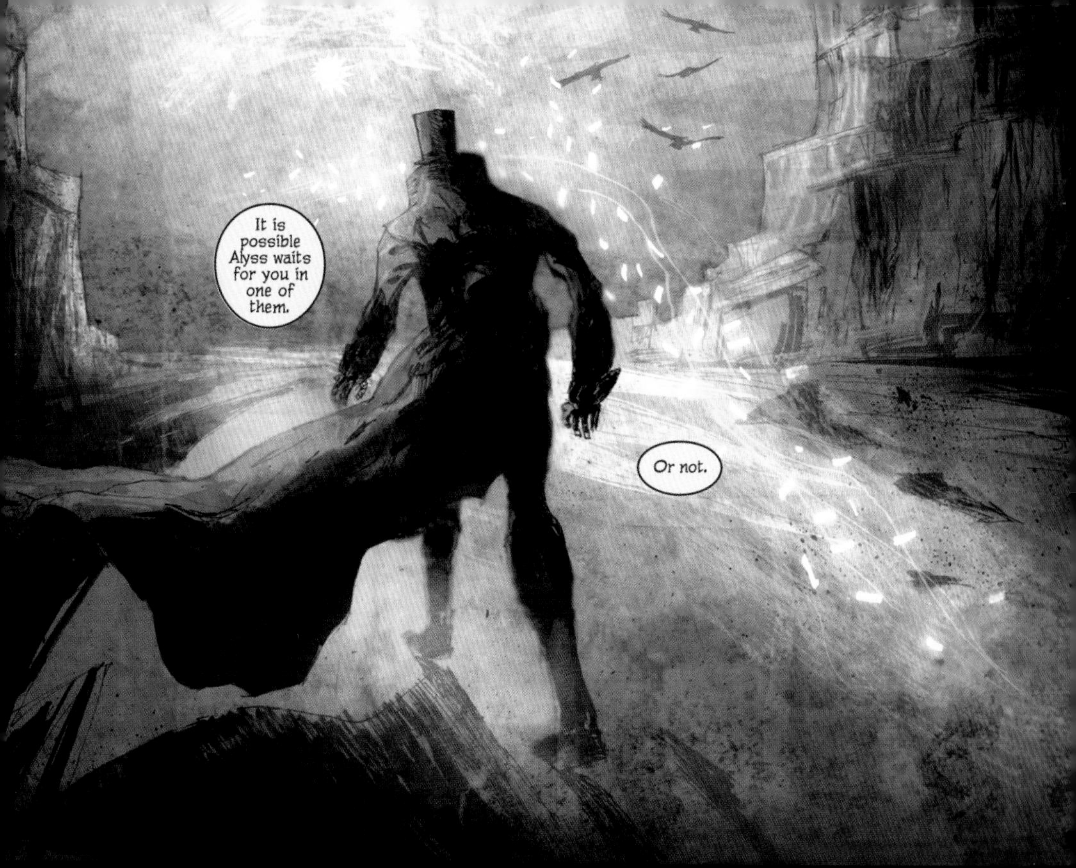
It is possible Alyss waits for you in one of them.
Or not.

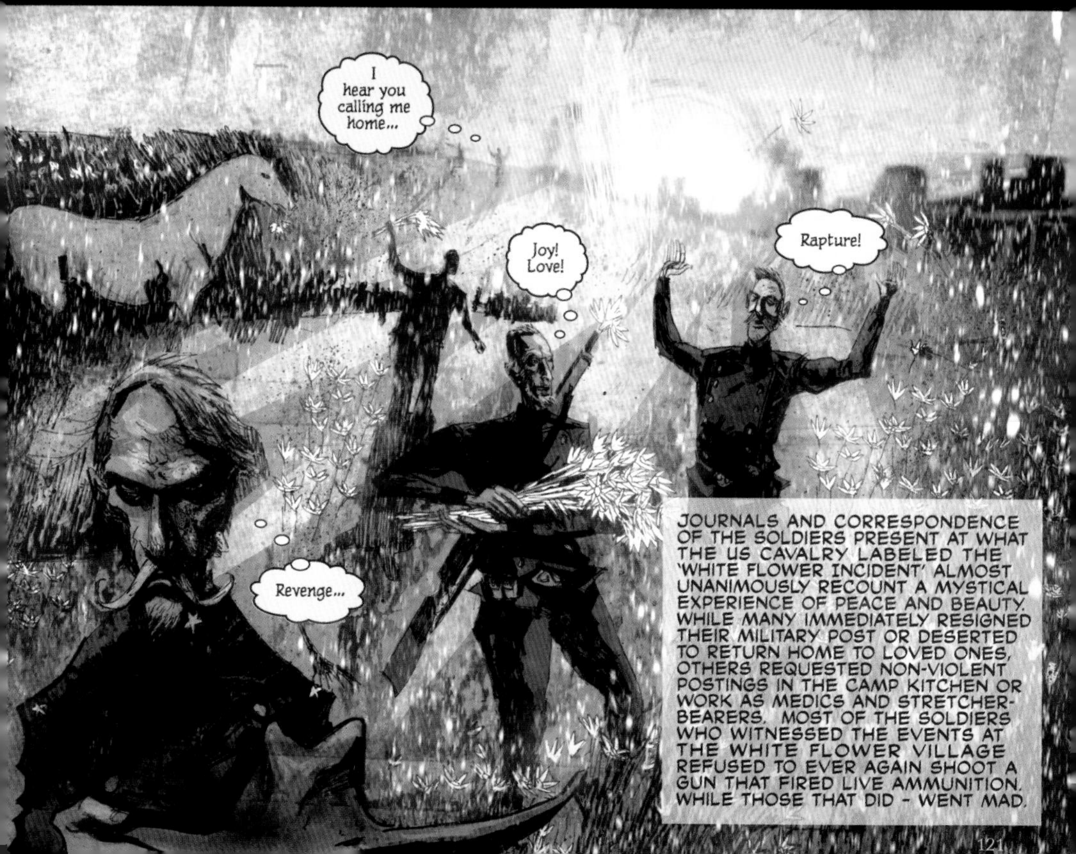
I hear you calling me home...
Joy! Love!
Rapture!
Revenge...
JOURNALS AND CORRESPONDENCE OF THE SOLDIERS PRESENT AT WHAT THE US CAVALRY LABELED THE 'WHITE FLOWER INCIDENT' ALMOST UNANIMOUSLY RECOUNT A MYSTICAL EXPERIENCE OF PEACE AND BEAUTY. WHILE MANY IMMEDIATELY RESIGNED THEIR MILITARY POST OR DESERTED TO RETURN HOME TO LOVED ONES, OTHERS REQUESTED NON-VIOLENT POSTINGS IN THE CAMP KITCHEN OR WORK AS MEDICS AND STRETCHER-BEARERS. MOST OF THE SOLDIERS WHO WITNESSED THE EVENTS AT THE WHITE FLOWER VILLAGE REFUSED TO EVER AGAIN SHOOT A GUN THAT FIRED LIVE AMMUNITION. WHILE THOSE THAT DID - WENT MAD.

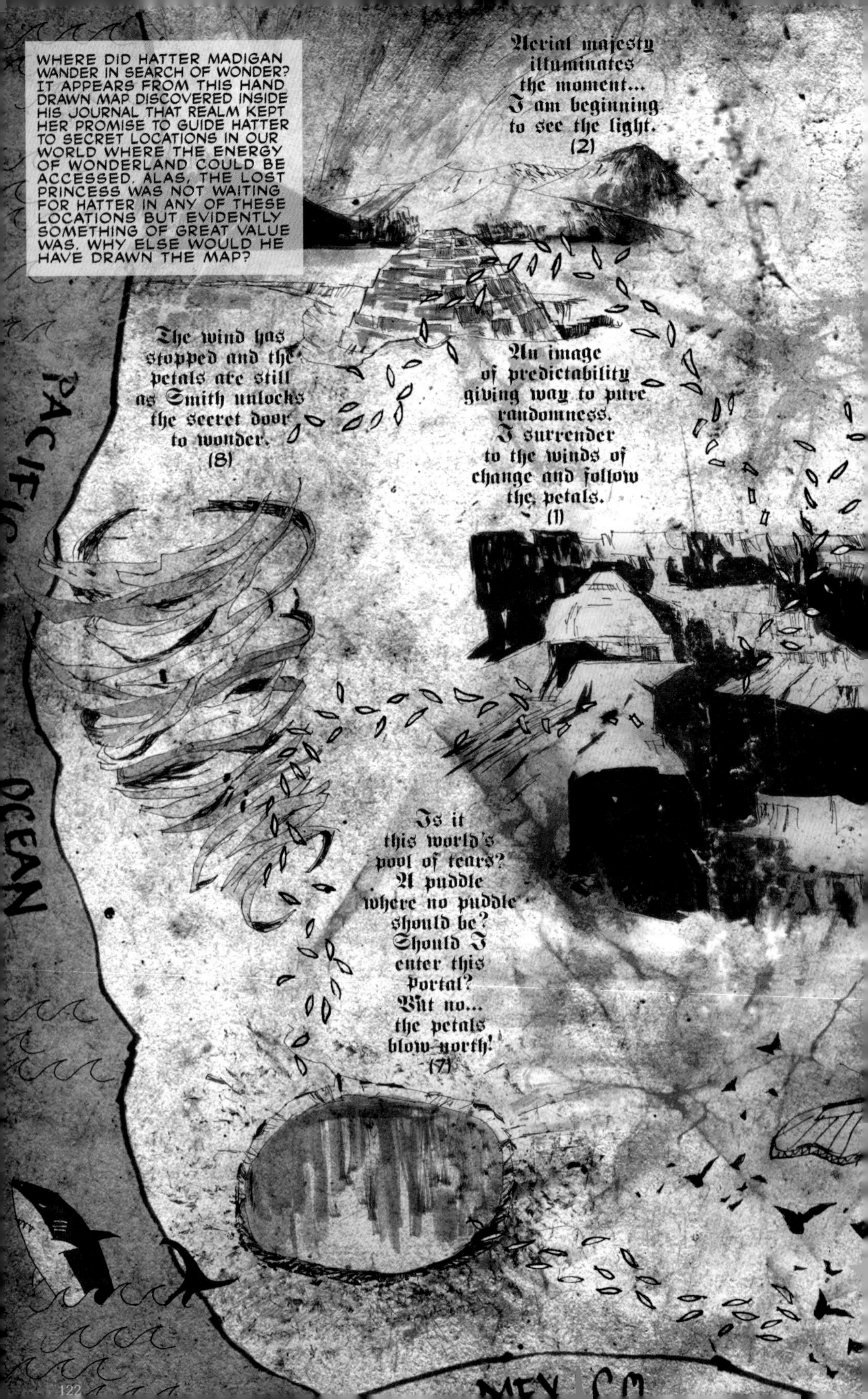

WHERE DID HATTER MADIGAN WANDER IN SEARCH OF WONDER? IT APPEARS FROM THIS HAND DRAWN MAP DISCOVERED INSIDE HIS JOURNAL THAT REALM KEPT HER PROMISE TO GUIDE HATTER TO SECRET LOCATIONS IN OUR WORLD WHERE THE ENERGY OF WONDERLAND COULD BE ACCESSED. ALAS, THE LOST PRINCESS WAS NOT WAITING FOR HATTER IN ANY OF THESE LOCATIONS BUT EVIDENTLY SOMETHING OF GREAT VALUE WAS. WHY ELSE WOULD HE HAVE DRAWN THE MAP?
Aerial majesty illuminates the moment... I am beginning to see the light. (2)
The wind has stopped and the petals are still as Smith unlocks the secret door to wonder. (8)
An image of predictability giving way to pure randomness. I surrender to the winds of change and follow the petals. (1)
PACIFIC OCEAN
Is it this world's pool of tears? A puddle where no puddle should be? Should I enter this portal? But no... the petals blow north! (7)

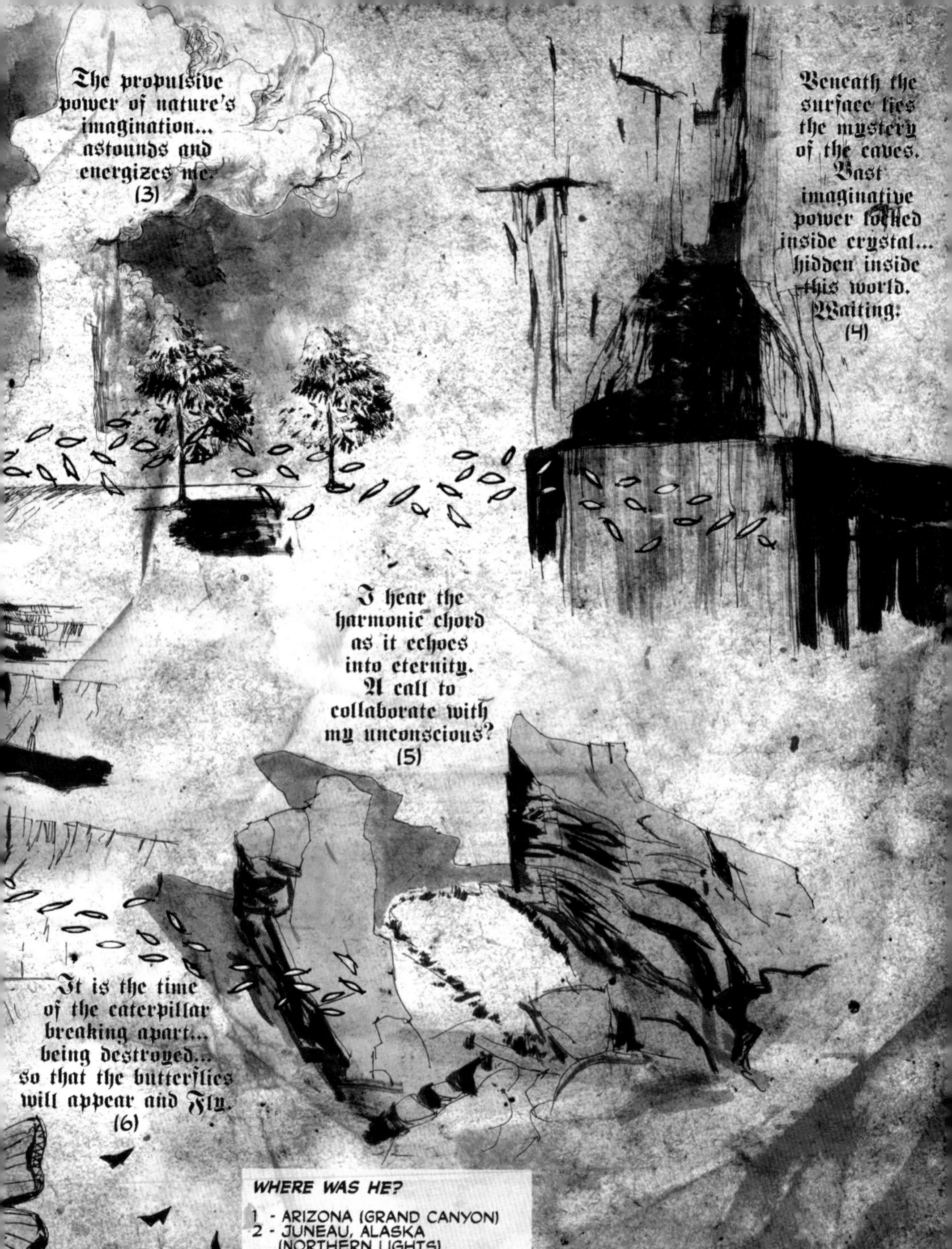

The propulsive power of nature's imagination... astounds and energizes me. (3)
Beneath the surface lies the mystery of the caves. Vast imaginative power locked inside crystal... hidden inside this world. Waiting. (4)
I hear the harmonic chord as it echoes into eternity. A call to collaborate with my unconscious? (5)
It is the time of the caterpillar breaking apart... being destroyed... so that the butterflies will appear and fly. (6)

WHERE WAS HE?

1 - ARIZONA (GRAND CANYON)
2 - JUNEAU, ALASKA (NORTHERN LIGHTS)
3 - YELLOWSTONE PARK, WYOMING (OLD FAITHFUL)
4 - DUBUQUE, IOWA (CRYSTAL LAKE CAVES)
5 - MORRISON, COLORADO (RED ROCKS AMPHITHEATER)
6 - ANGANGEO,MEXICO (MONARCH BUTTERFLY MIGRATION)
7 - SAN DIEGO, CALIFORNIA (PAVED OVER PORTAL TO WONDERLAND?)
8 - DEATH VALLEY, CALIFORNIA (ONE OF THE LOST GHOST TOWNS)

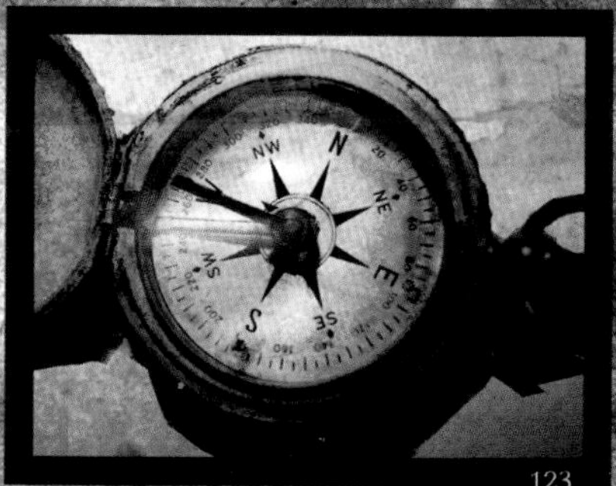

While it is true that every Queen needs a Bodyguard for protection, it is also true that every Bodyguard needs a Queen to lead. Realm shared the wonders of her world and they have brought me here to a reunion of sorts. Lost in space and time, lead only by the petals of White Luminescence, I allowed myself to wander and trust that the Glow would manifest in unforeseen ways to guide me.

Finding life in a place called Death, I open myself to further discoveries.

"A rose is a rose is a rose." —Gertrude Stein

Back Garden
to the

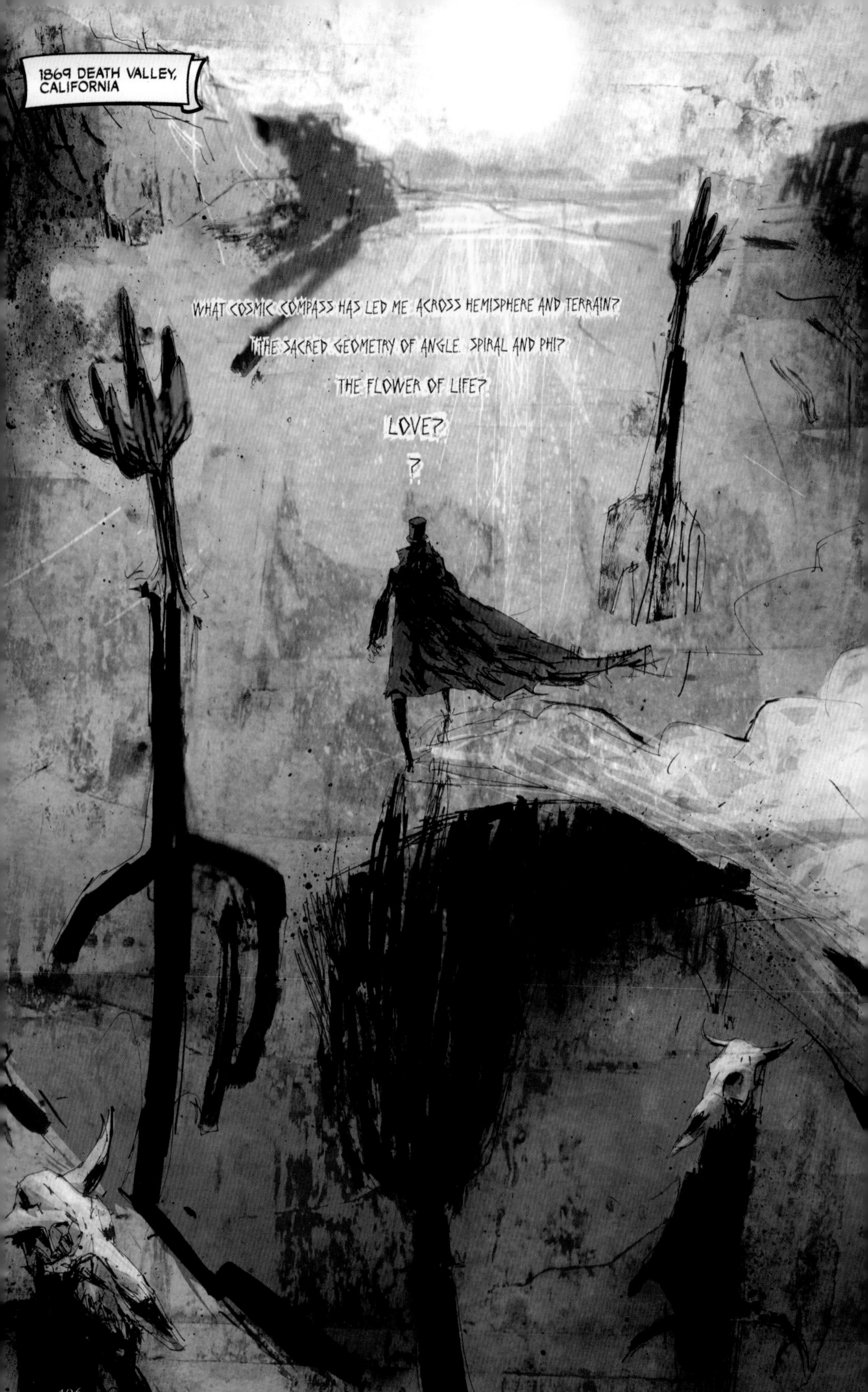
1869 DEATH VALLEY, CALIFORNIA
WHAT COSMIC COMPASS HAS LED ME ACROSS HEMISPHERE AND TERRAIN?
THE SACRED GEOMETRY OF ANGLE. SPIRAL AND PHI?
THE FLOWER OF LIFE?
LOVE?
?

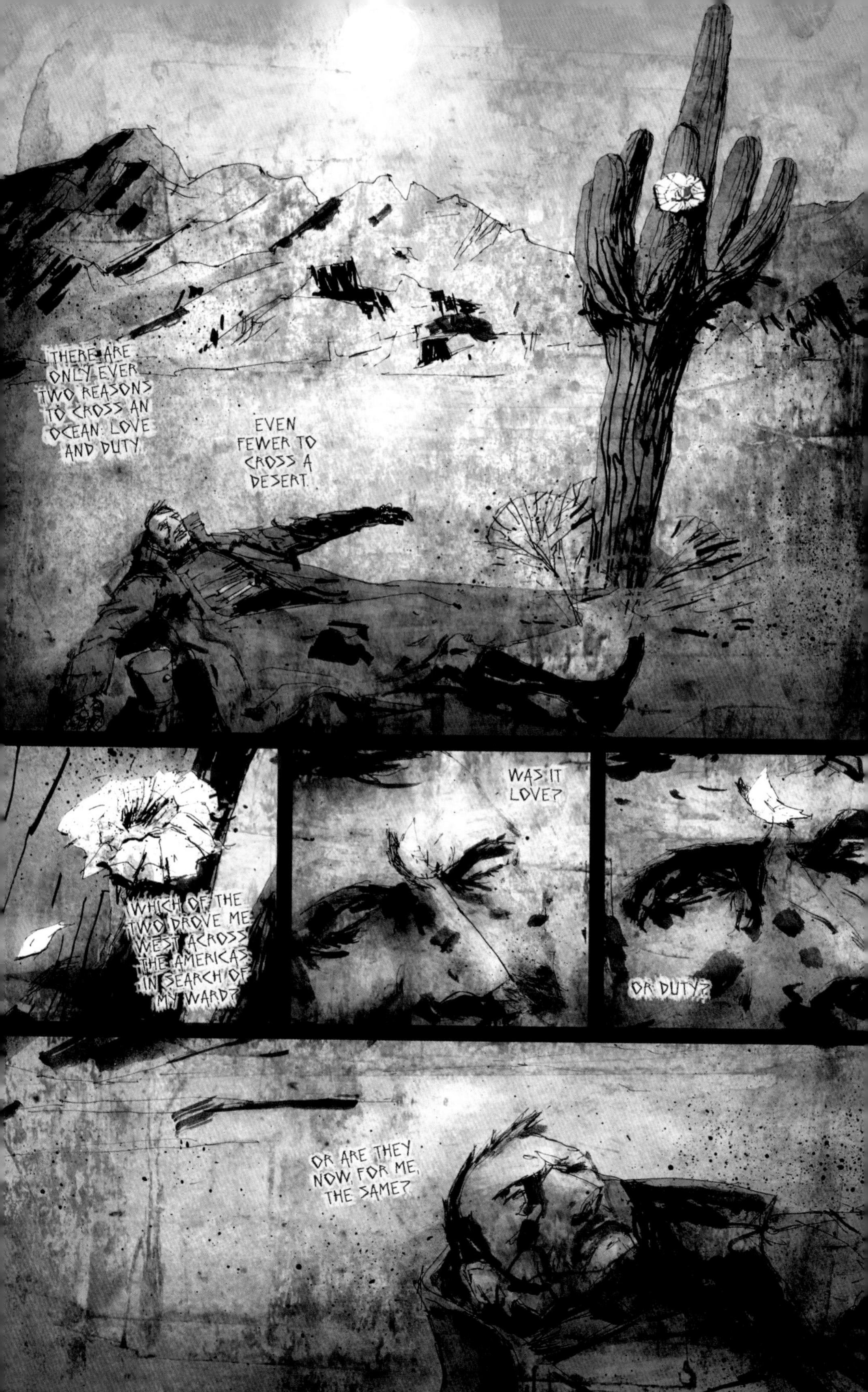
THERE ARE ONLY EVER TWO REASONS TO CROSS AN OCEAN: LOVE AND DUTY.
EVEN FEWER TO CROSS A DESERT.
WHICH OF THE TWO DROVE ME WEST ACROSS THE AMERICAS IN SEARCH OF MY WARD?
WAS IT LOVE?
OR DUTY?
OR ARE THEY NOW, FOR ME, THE SAME?

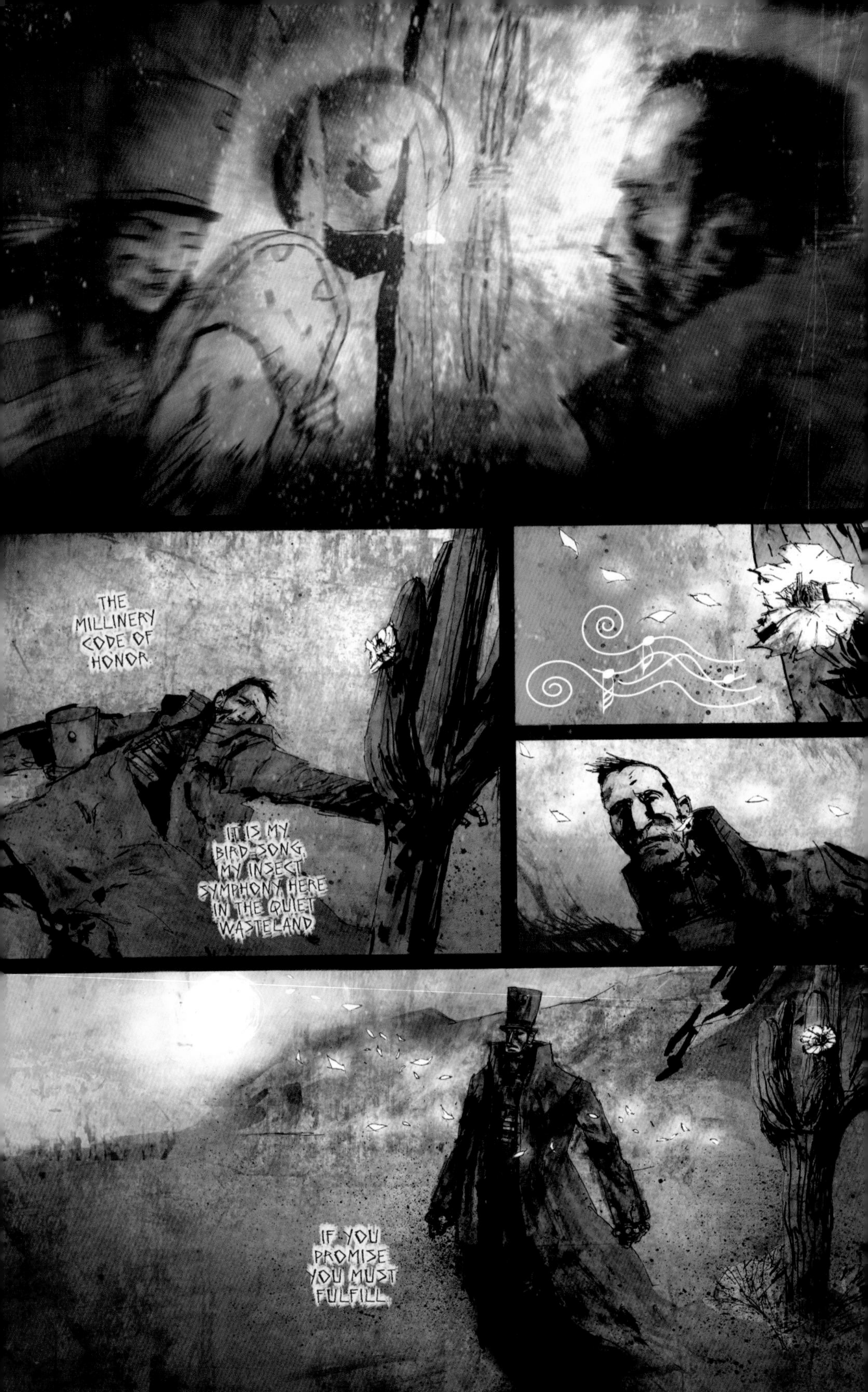
THE MILLINERY CODE OF HONOR
IT IS MY BIRD SONG, MY INSECT SYMPHONY HERE IN THE QUIET WASTELAND
IF YOU PROMISE YOU MUST FULFILL

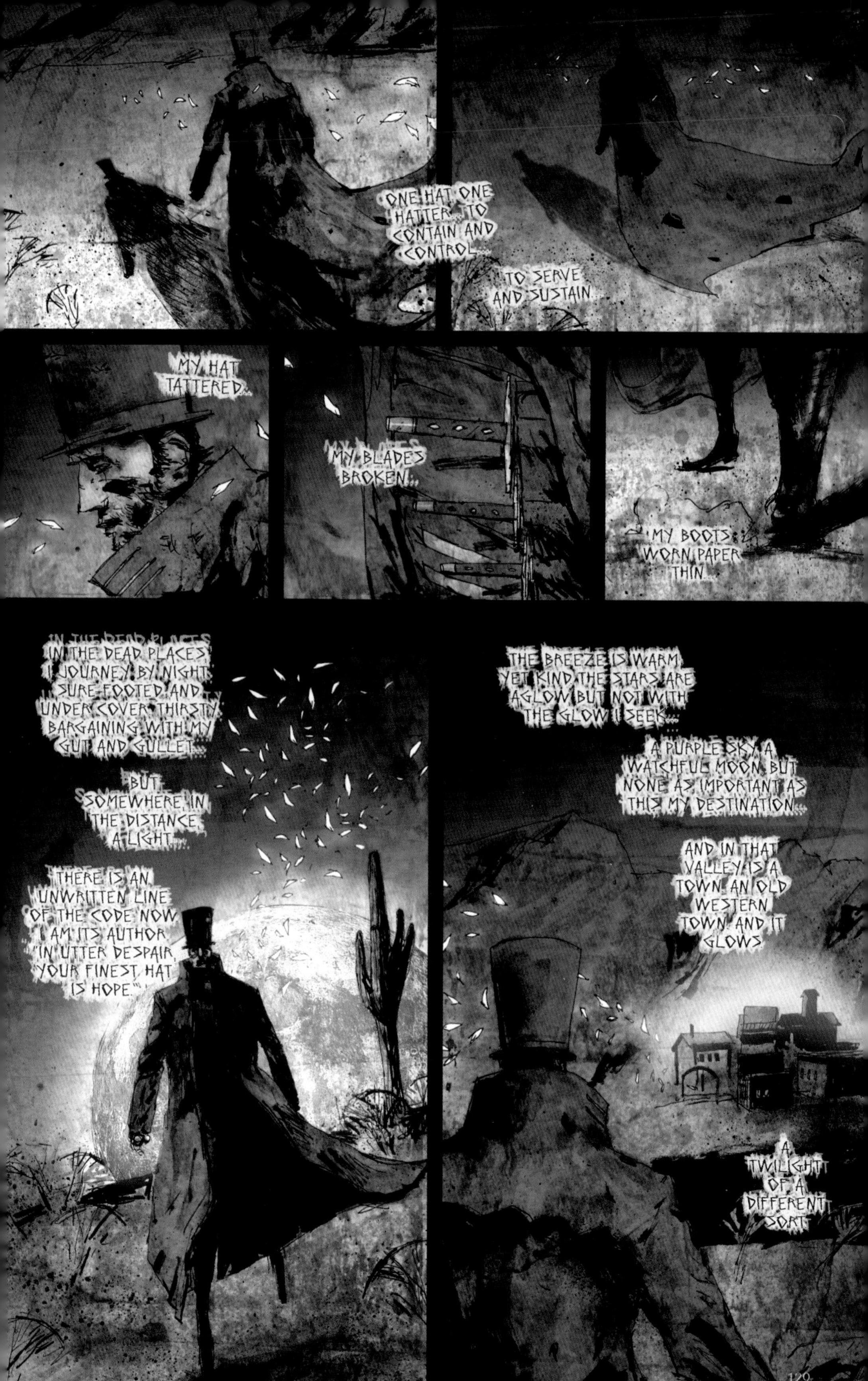
ONE HAT ONE HATTER... TO CONTAIN AND CONTROL...
TO SERVE AND SUSTAIN.
MY HAT TATTERED...
MY BLADES BROKEN...
MY BOOTS WORN PAPER THIN...
IN THE DEAD PLACES I JOURNEY BY NIGHT SURE-FOOTED AND UNDER COVER THIRSTY BARGAINING WITH MY GUT AND GULLET...
BUT SOMEWHERE, IN THE DISTANCE, A LIGHT...
THERE IS AN UNWRITTEN LINE OF THE CODE NOW I AM ITS AUTHOR "IN UTTER DESPAIR, YOUR FINEST HAT IS HOPE."
THE BREEZE IS WARM YET KIND THE STARS ARE AGLOW BUT NOT WITH THE GLOW I SEEK...
A PURPLE SKY A WATCHFUL MOON BUT NONE AS IMPORTANT AS THIS MY DESTINATION...
AND IN THAT VALLEY IS A TOWN AN OLD WESTERN TOWN AND IT GLOWS
A TWILIGHT OF A DIFFERENT SORT

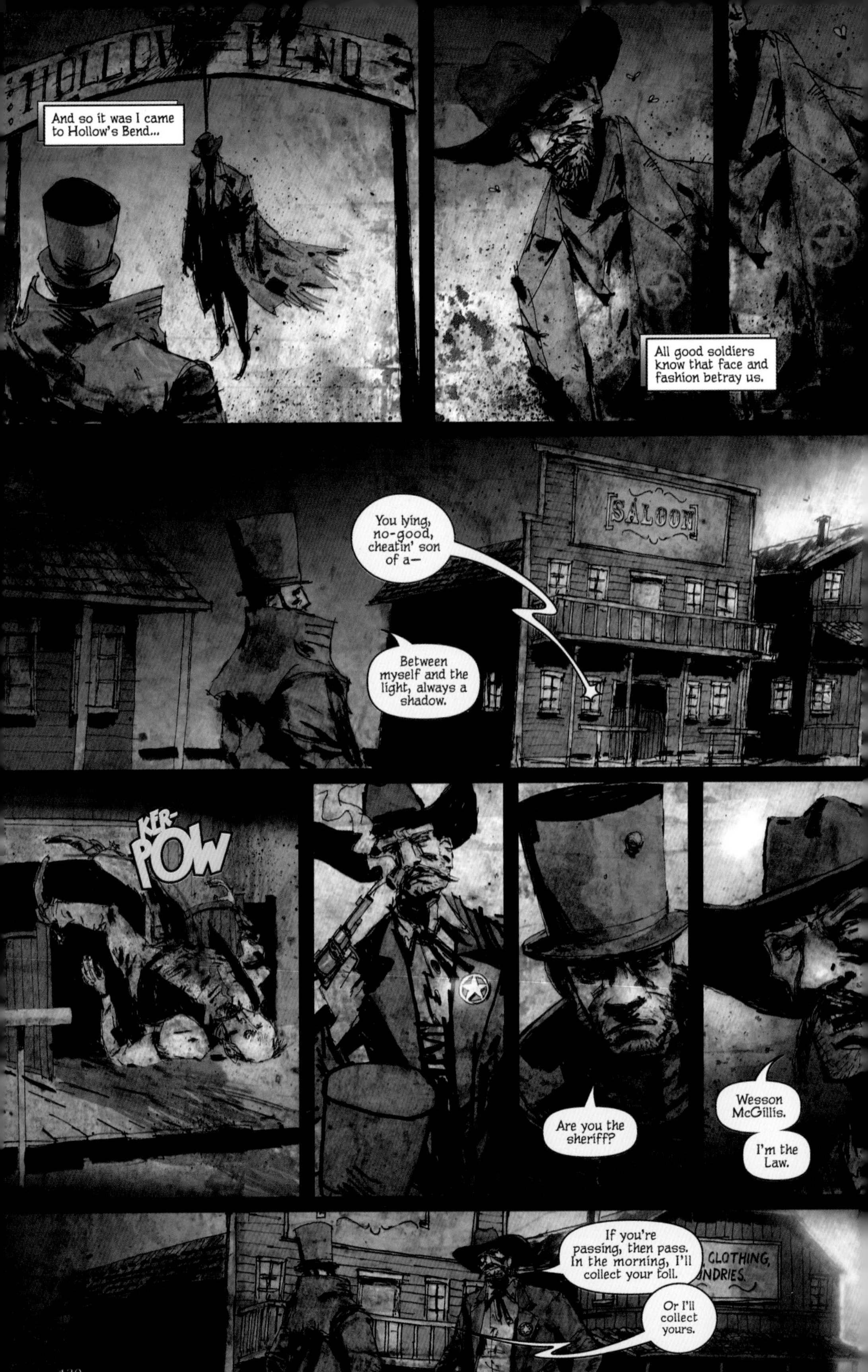
HOLLOW BEND
And so it was I came to Hollow's Bend...
All good soldiers know that face and fashion betray us.
SALOON
You lying, no-good, cheatin' son of a—
Between myself and the light, always a shadow.
KER-POW
Are you the sheriff?
Wesson McGillis.
I'm the Law.
CLOTHING,
If you're passing, then pass. In the morning, I'll collect your toll.
Or I'll collect yours.

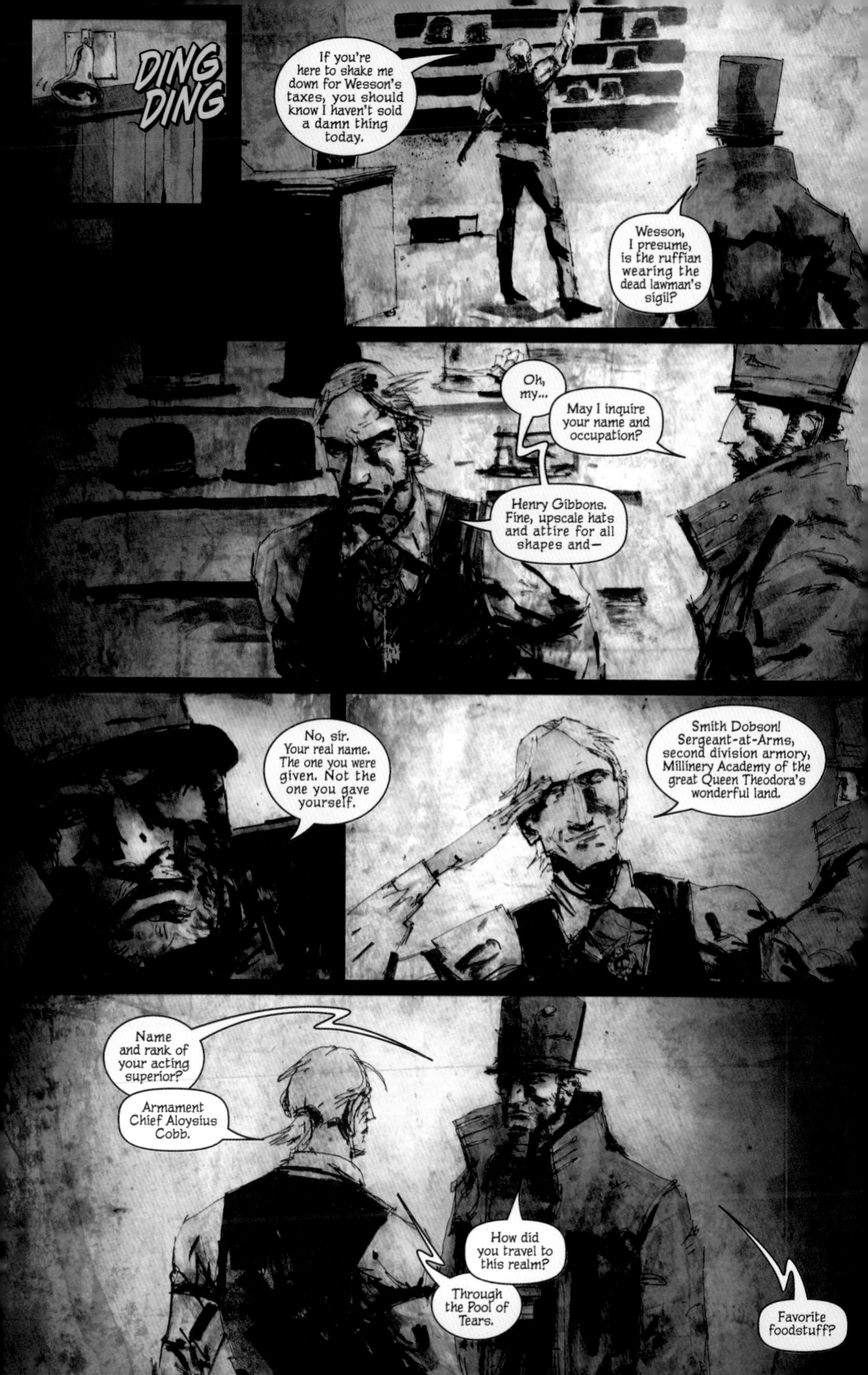
DING DING
If you're here to shake me down for Wesson's taxes, you should know I haven't sold a damn thing today.
Wesson, I presume, is the ruffian wearing the dead lawman's sigil?
Oh, my...
May I inquire your name and occupation?
Henry Gibbons. Fine, upscale hats and attire for all shapes and—
No, sir. Your real name. The one you were given. Not the one you gave yourself.
Smith Dobson! Sergeant-at-Arms, second division armory, Millinery Academy of the great Queen Theodora's wonderful land.
Name and rank of your acting superior?
Armament Chief Aloysius Cobb.
How did you travel to this realm?
Through the Pool of Tears.
Favorite foodstuff?

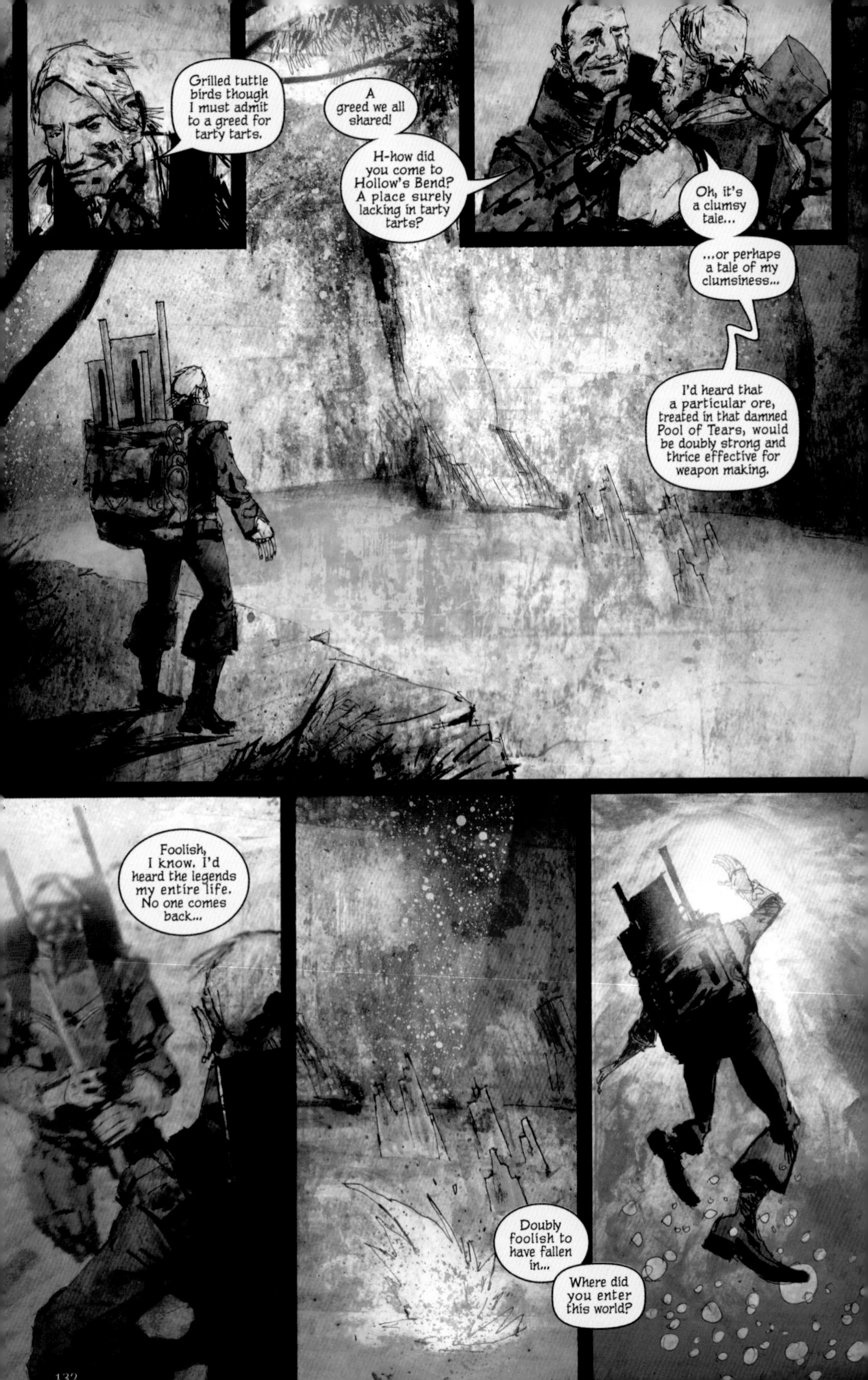
Grilled tuttle birds though I must admit to a greed for tarty tarts.
A greed we all shared!
H-how did you come to Hollow's Bend? A place surely lacking in tarty tarts?
Oh, it's a clumsy tale...
...or perhaps a tale of my clumsiness...
I'd heard that a particular ore, treated in that damned Pool of Tears, would be doubly strong and thrice effective for weapon making.
Foolish, I know. I'd heard the legends my entire life. No one comes back...
Doubly foolish to have fallen in...
Where did you enter this world?

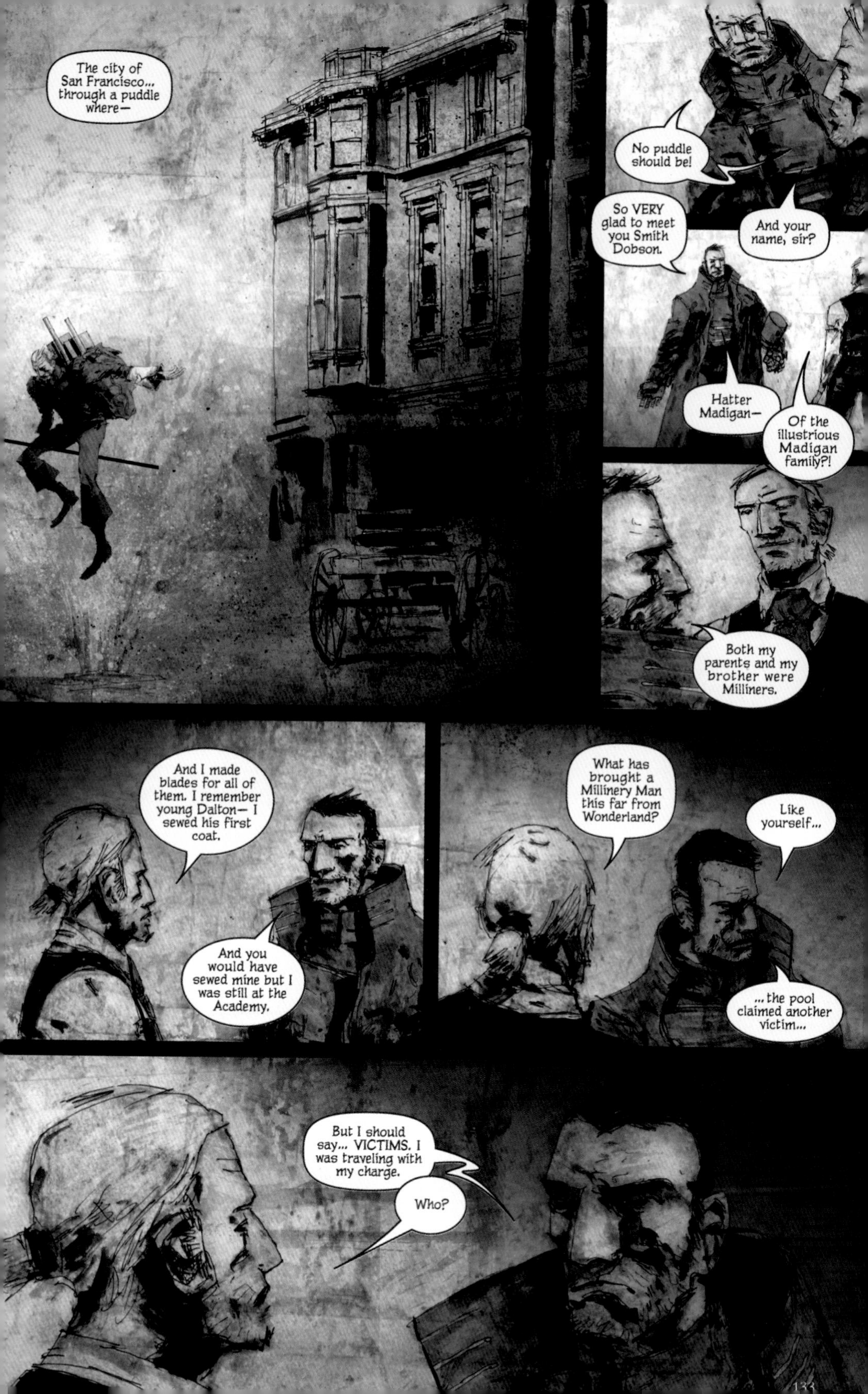
The city of San Francisco... through a puddle where—
No puddle should be!
So VERY glad to meet you Smith Dobson.
And your name, sir?
Hatter Madigan—
Of the illustrious Madigan family?!
Both my parents and my brother were Milliners.
And I made blades for all of them. I remember young Dalton— I sewed his first coat.
And you would have sewed mine but I was still at the Academy.
What has brought a Millinery Man this far from Wonderland?
Like yourself...
...the pool claimed another victim...
But I should say... VICTIMS. I was traveling with my charge.
Who?

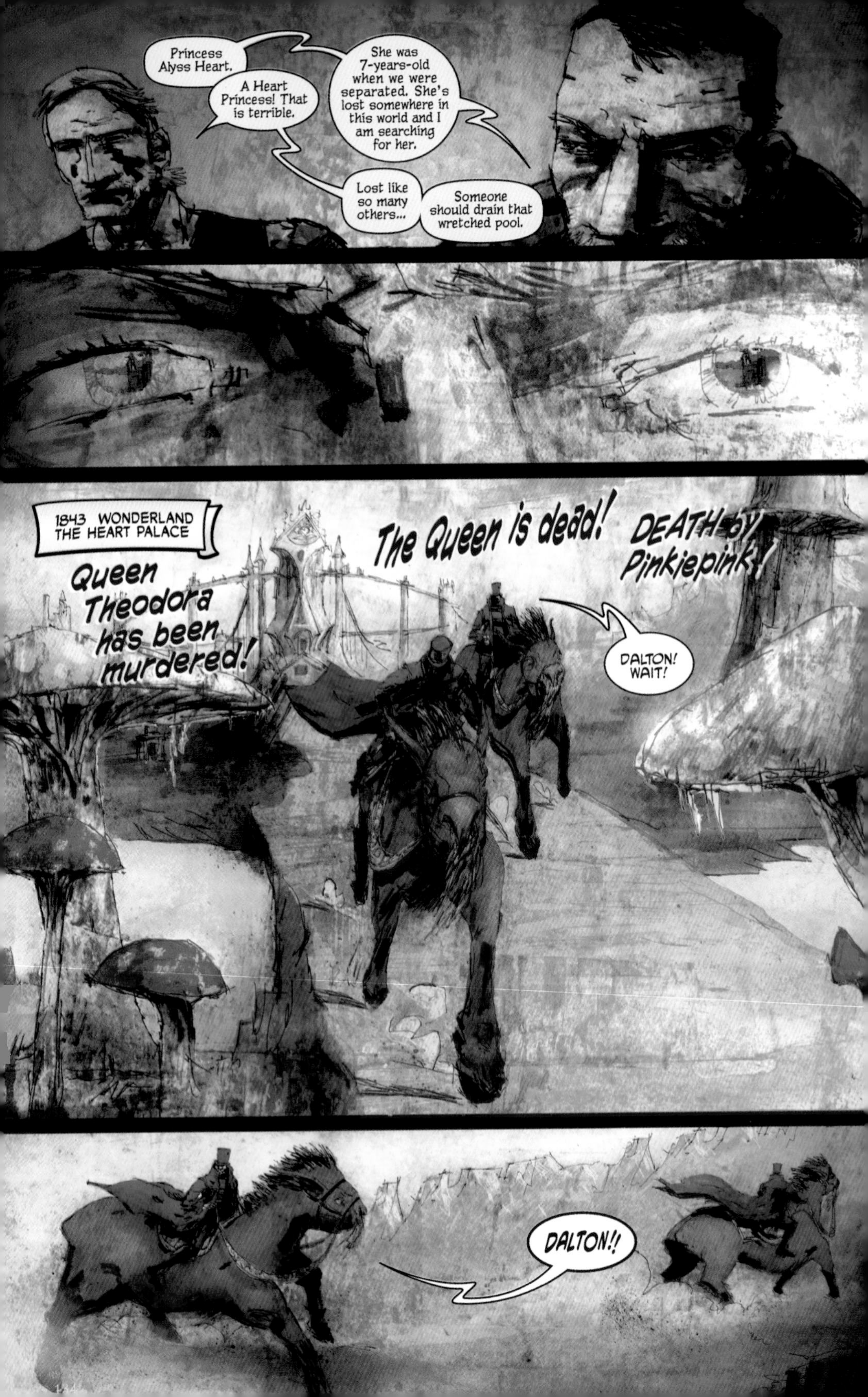
Princess Alyss Heart.
A Heart Princess! That is terrible.
She was 7-years-old when we were separated. She's lost somewhere in this world and I am searching for her.
Lost like so many others...
Someone should drain that wretched pool.
1843 WONDERLAND THE HEART PALACE
Queen Theodora has been murdered!
The Queen is dead!
DEATH by Pinkiepink!
DALTON! WAIT!
DALTON!!

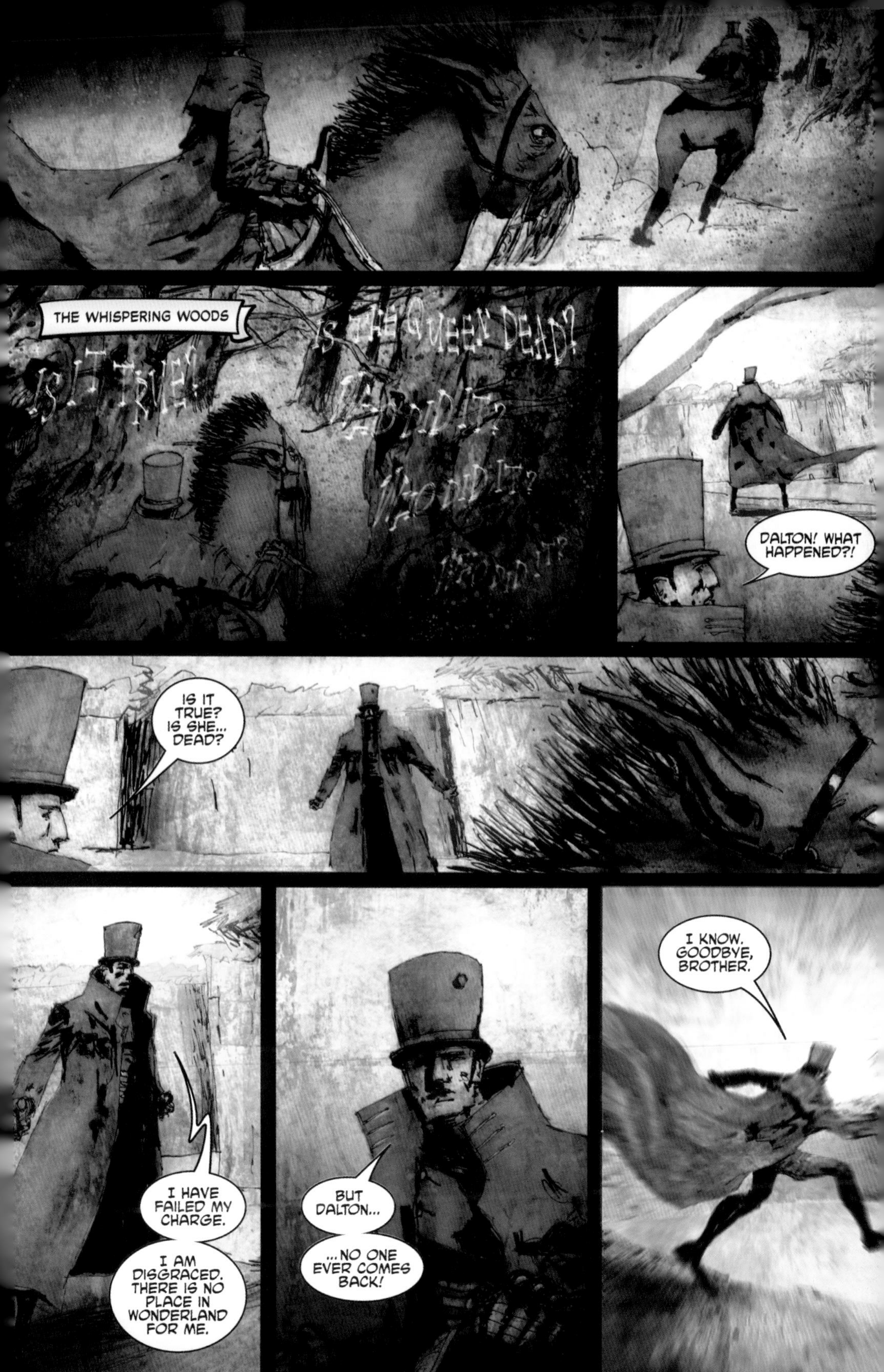

THE WHISPERING WOODS
IS IT TRUE?
IS THE QUEEN DEAD?
WHO DID IT?
DALTON! WHAT HAPPENED?!
IS IT TRUE? IS SHE... DEAD?
I HAVE FAILED MY CHARGE.
I AM DISGRACED. THERE IS NO PLACE IN WONDERLAND FOR ME.
BUT DALTON...
...NO ONE EVER COMES BACK!
I KNOW. GOODBYE, BROTHER.

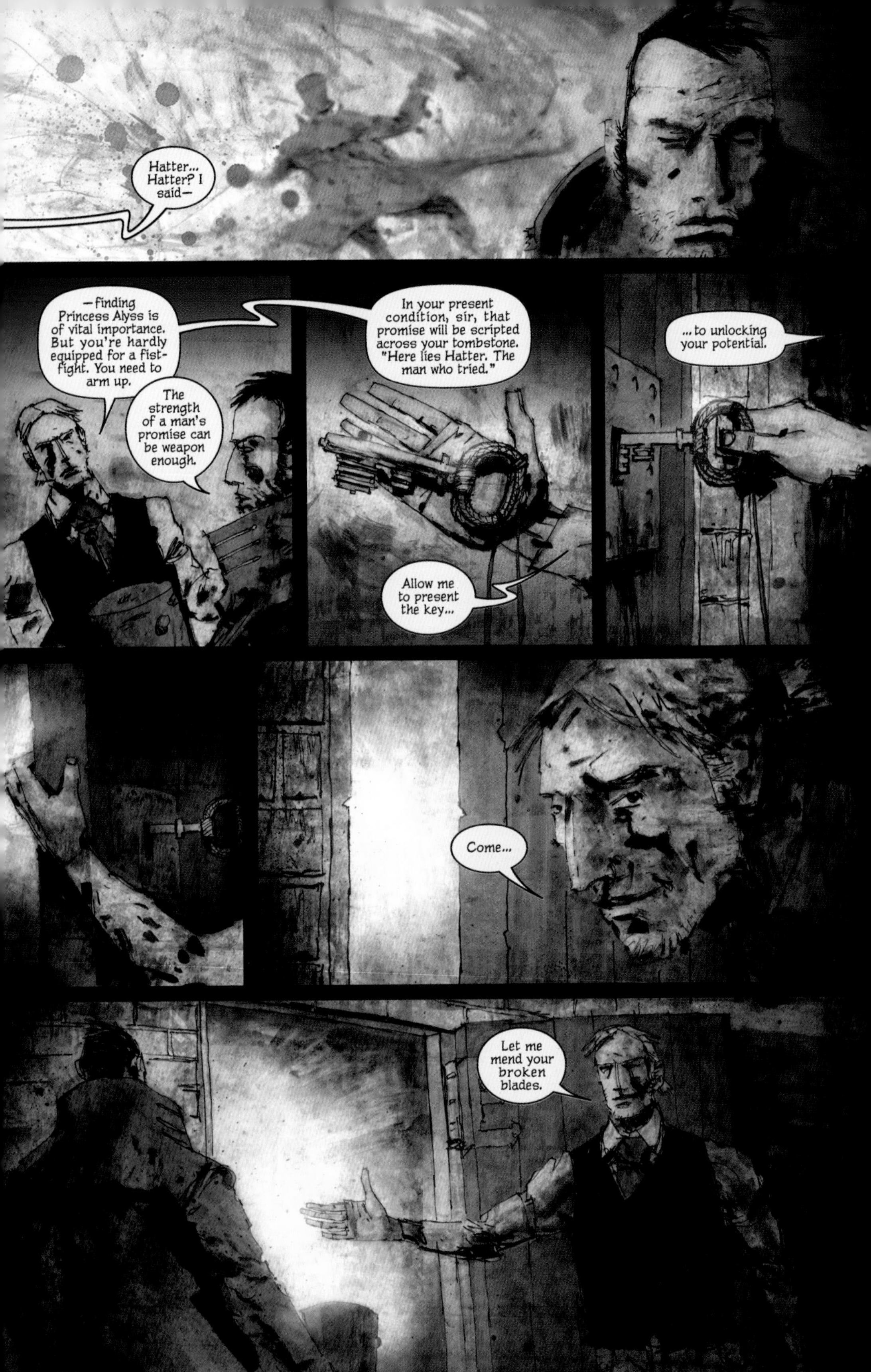

Hatter... Hatter? I said—
—finding Princess Alyss is of vital importance. But you're hardly equipped for a fist-fight. You need to arm up.
The strength of a man's promise can be weapon enough.
In your present condition, sir, that promise will be scripted across your tombstone. "Here lies Hatter. The man who tried."
Allow me to present the key...
...to unlocking your potential.
Come...
Let me mend your broken blades.

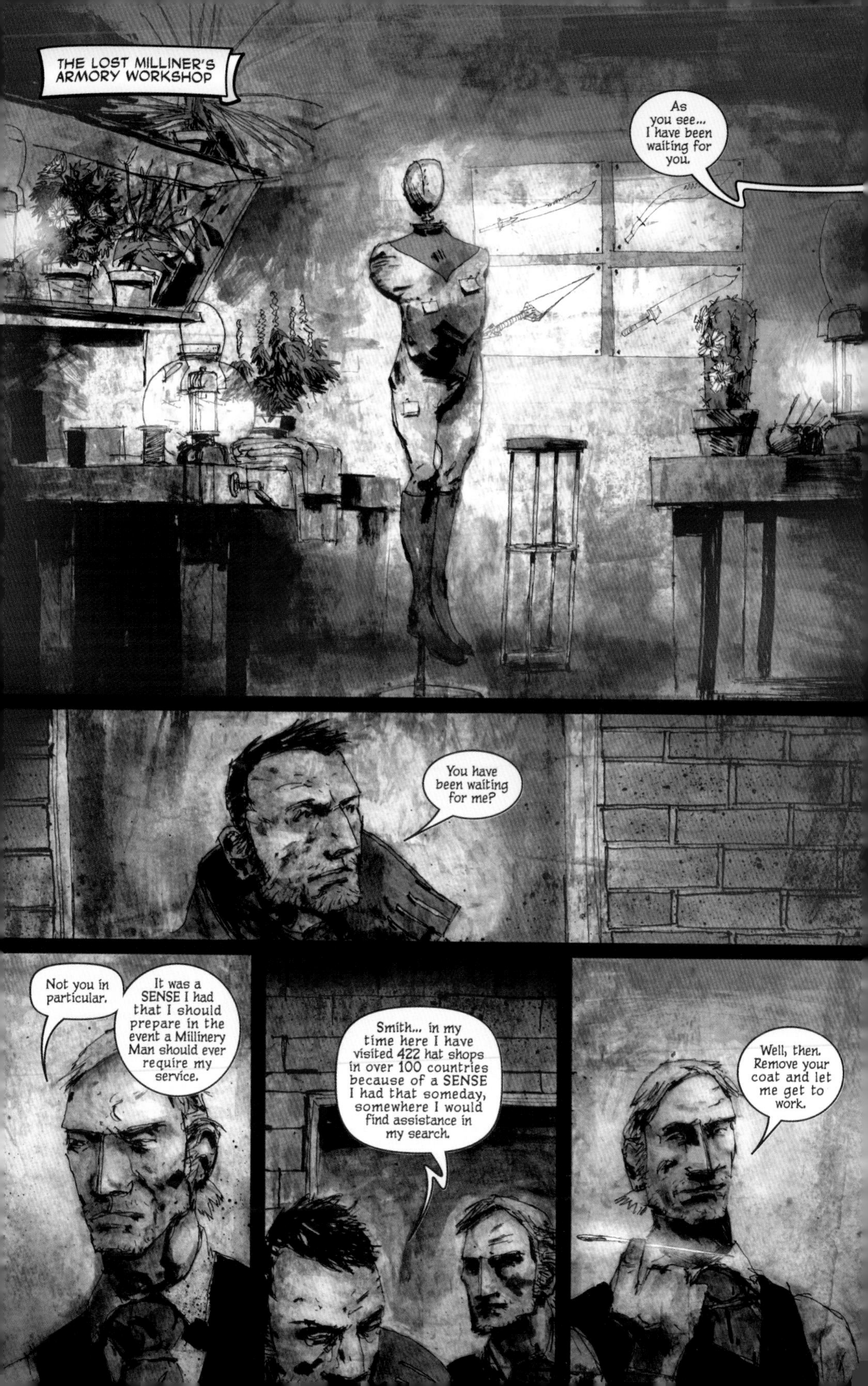
THE LOST MILLINER'S ARMORY WORKSHOP
As you see... I have been waiting for you.
You have been waiting for me?
Not you in particular.
It was a SENSE I had that I should prepare in the event a Millinery Man should ever require my service.
Smith... in my time here I have visited 422 hat shops in over 100 countries because of a SENSE I had that someday, somewhere I would find assistance in my search.
Well, then. Remove your coat and let me get to work.

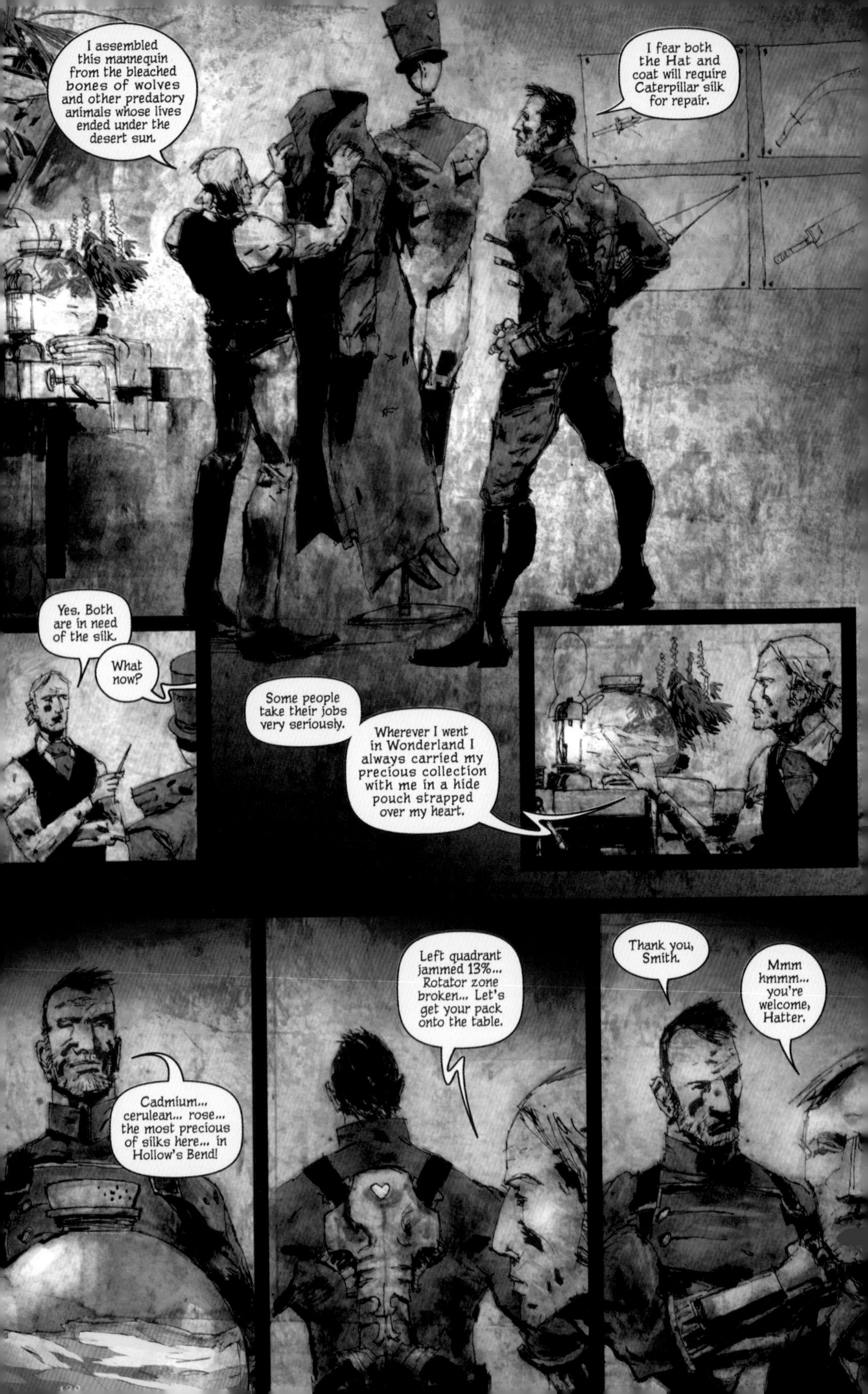

I assembled this mannequin from the bleached bones of wolves and other predatory animals whose lives ended under the desert sun.
I fear both the Hat and coat will require Caterpillar silk for repair.
Yes. Both are in need of the silk.
What now?
Some people take their jobs very seriously.
Wherever I went in Wonderland I always carried my precious collection with me in a hide pouch strapped over my heart.
Cadmium... cerulean... rose... the most precious of silks here... in Hollow's Bend!
Left quadrant jammed 13%... Rotator zone broken... Let's get your pack onto the table.
Thank you, Smith.
Mmm hmmm... you're welcome, Hatter.

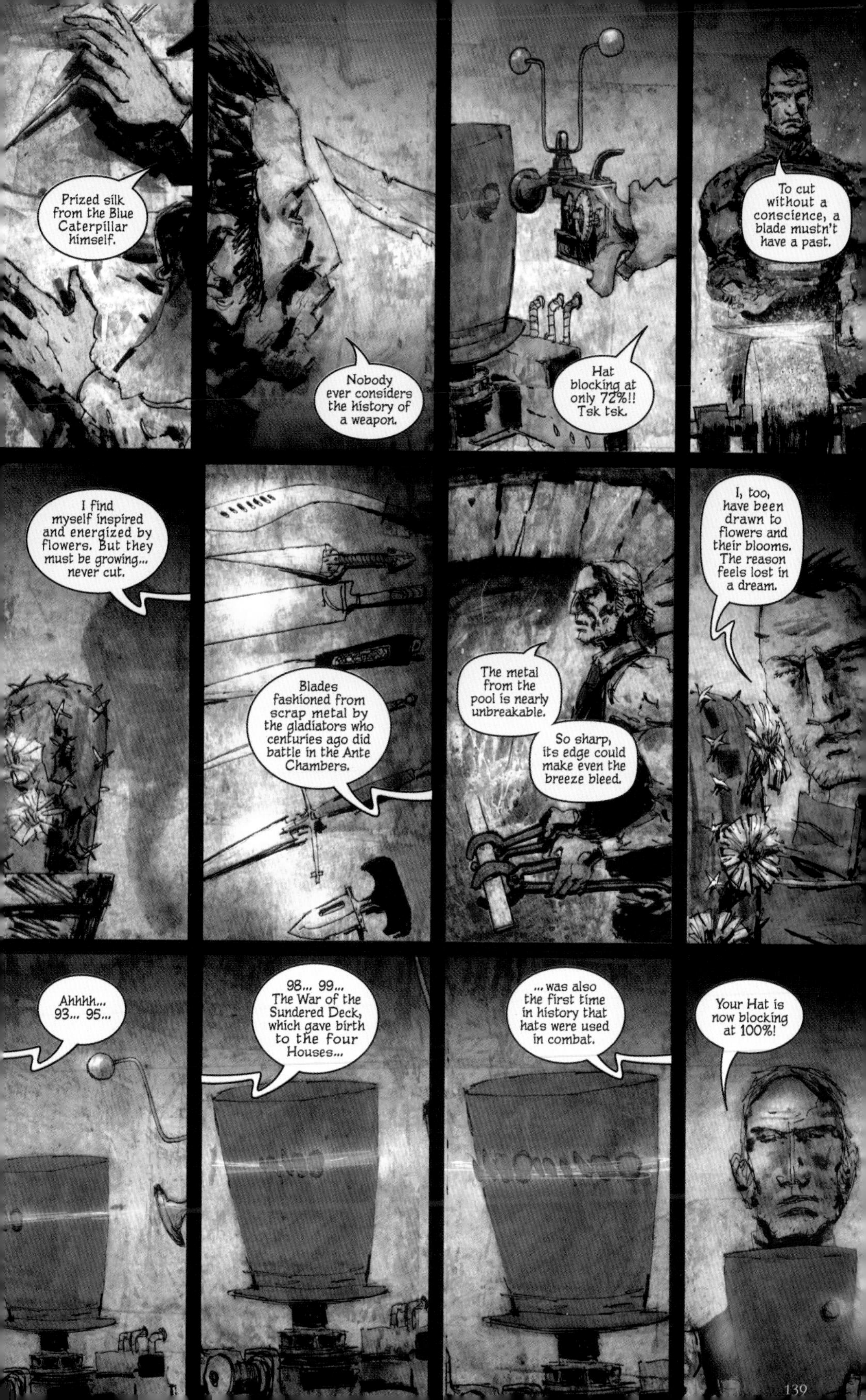
Prized silk from the Blue Caterpillar himself.
Nobody ever considers the history of a weapon.
Hat blocking at only 72%!! Tsk tsk.
To cut without a conscience, a blade mustn't have a past.
I find myself inspired and energized by flowers. But they must be growing... never cut.
Blades fashioned from scrap metal by the gladiators who centuries ago did battle in the Ante Chambers.
The metal from the pool is nearly unbreakable.
So sharp, its edge could make even the breeze bleed.
I, too, have been drawn to flowers and their blooms. The reason feels lost in a dream.
Ahhhh... 93... 95...
98... 99... The War of the Sundered Deck, which gave birth to the four Houses...
...was also the first time in history that hats were used in combat.
Your Hat is now blocking at 100%!

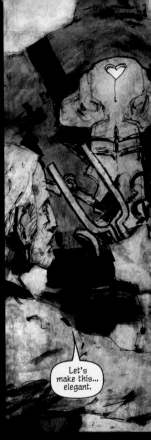

Still needs a few final adjustments.

FWIIING

As I thought... a bit of a hair trigger there.

Let's make this... elegant.

You were right before to say that Wesson was a ruffian. A month ago, he and his men murdered the sheriff and hung his corpse as a warning.

He stacked the deck. Made himself King.

He and his men have taxed and terrorized the Hollow for too long.

Happily Smith, I'll be your assassin, but why not do it yourself?

I'm a smith, not a soldier.

A man with any skill in combat doesn't pick up a sewing needle as a means of defense.

Wesson's cut throats have killed many an able gunman using their dirty tricks.

The innovations we added to your rig will counter well.

A stitch in time slays nine?

Precisely.

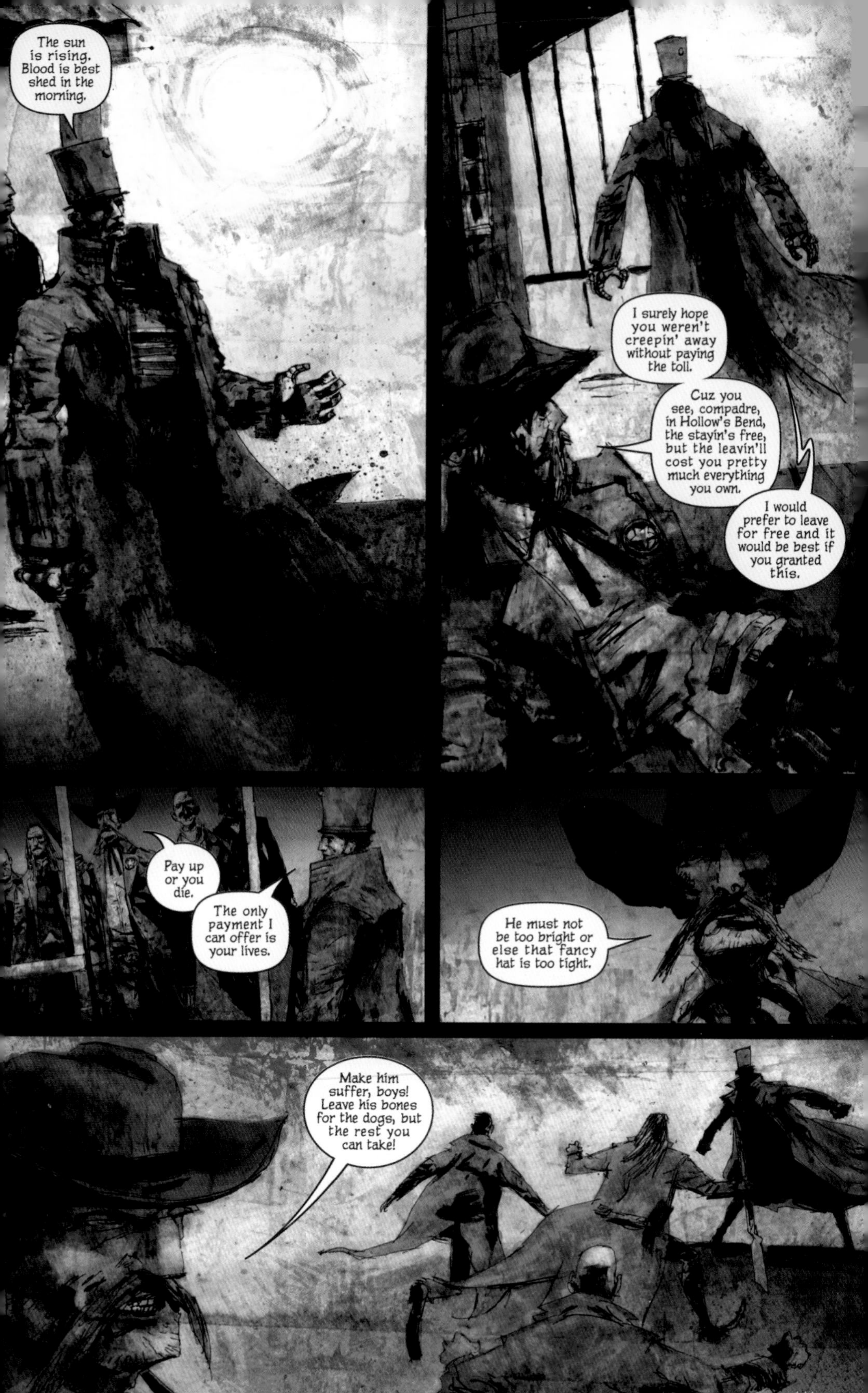
The sun is rising. Blood is best shed in the morning.
I surely hope you weren't creepin' away without paying the toll.
Cuz you see, compadre, in Hollow's Bend, the stayin's free, but the leavin'll cost you pretty much everything you own.
I would prefer to leave for free and it would be best if you granted this.
Pay up or you die.
The only payment I can offer is your lives.
He must not be too bright or else that fancy hat is too tight.
Make him suffer, boys! Leave his bones for the dogs, but the rest you can take!

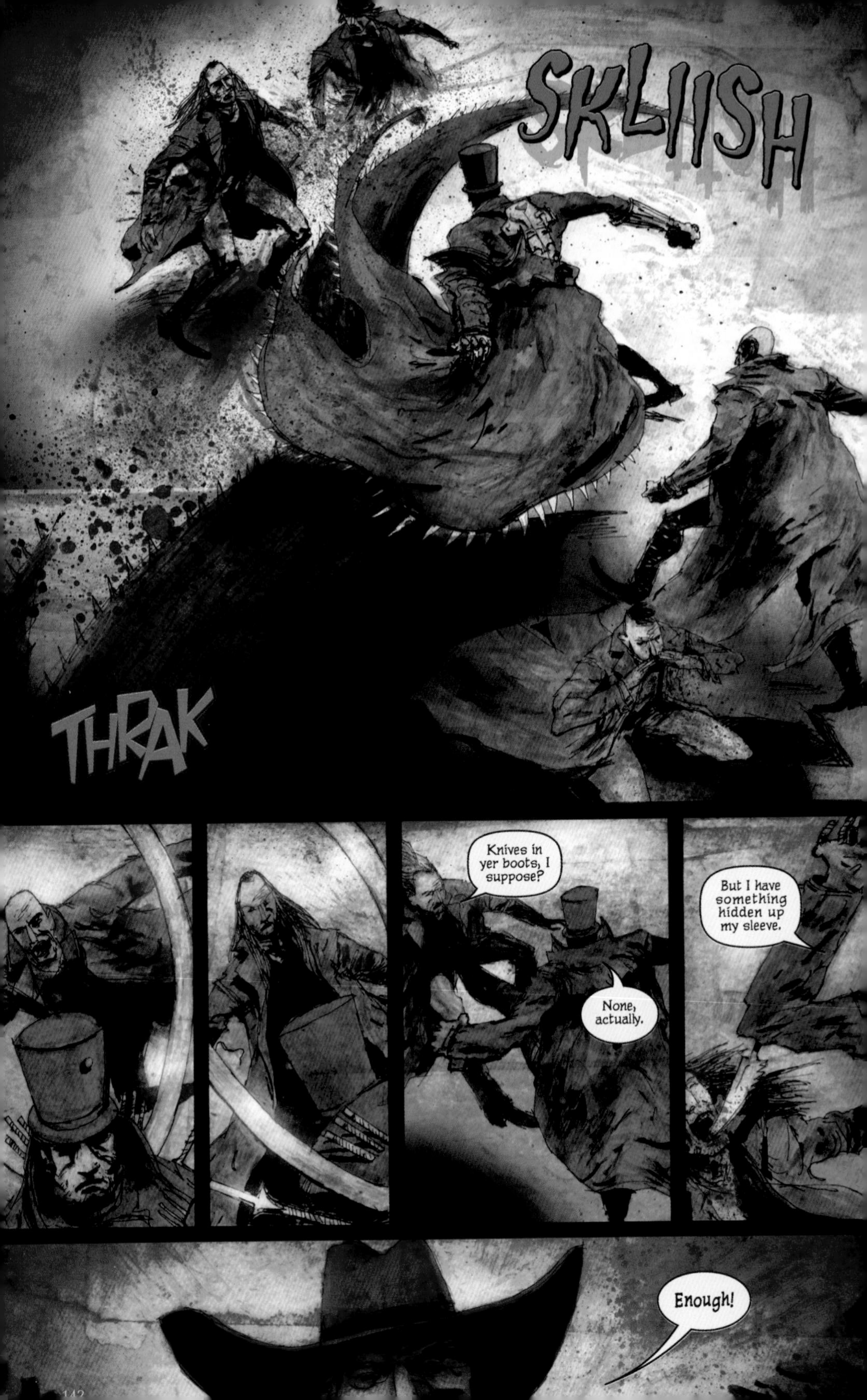
SKLIISH
THRAK
Knives in yer boots, I suppose?
None, actually.
But I have something hidden up my sleeve.
Enough!

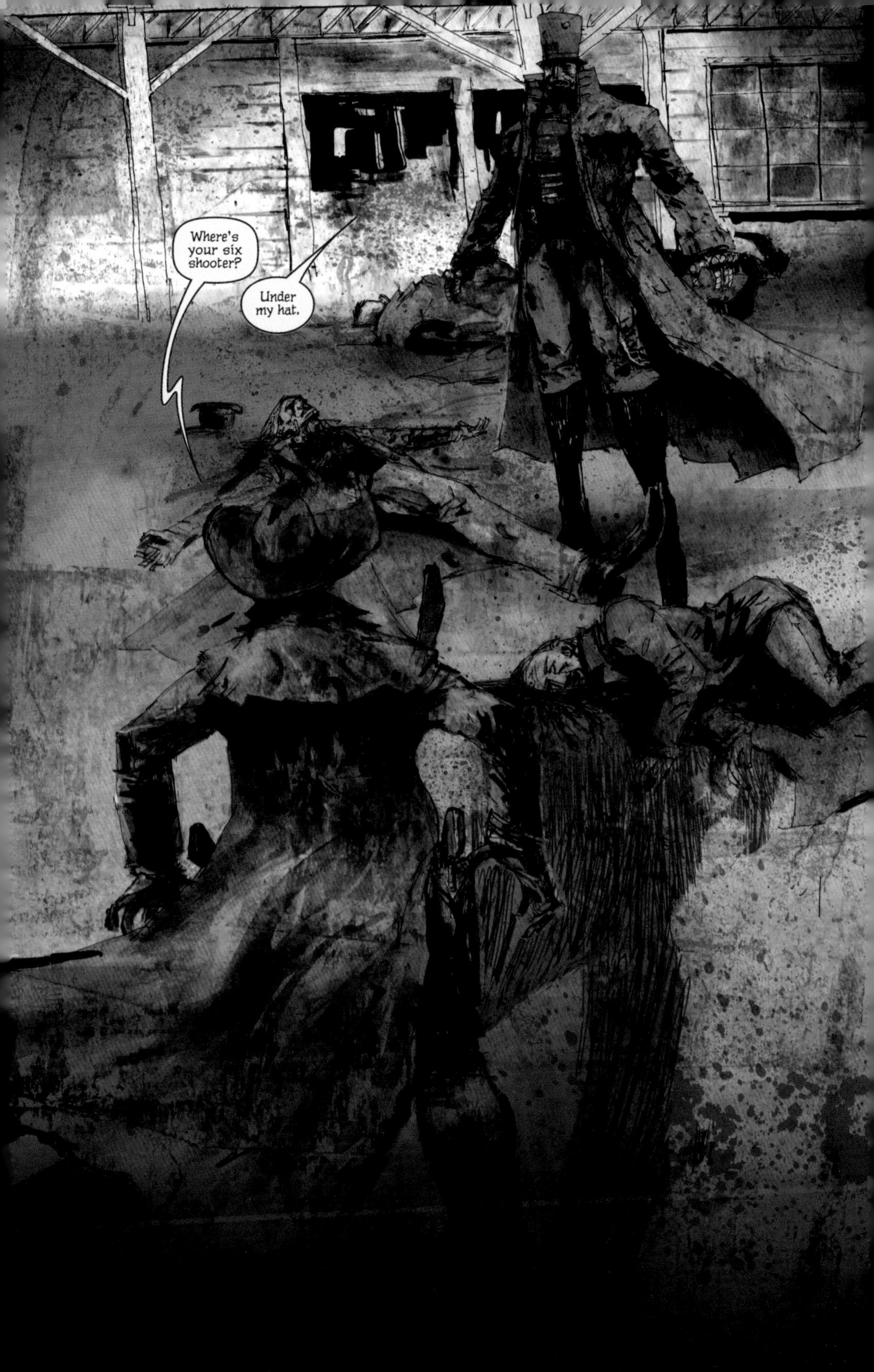
Where's your six shooter?
Under my hat.

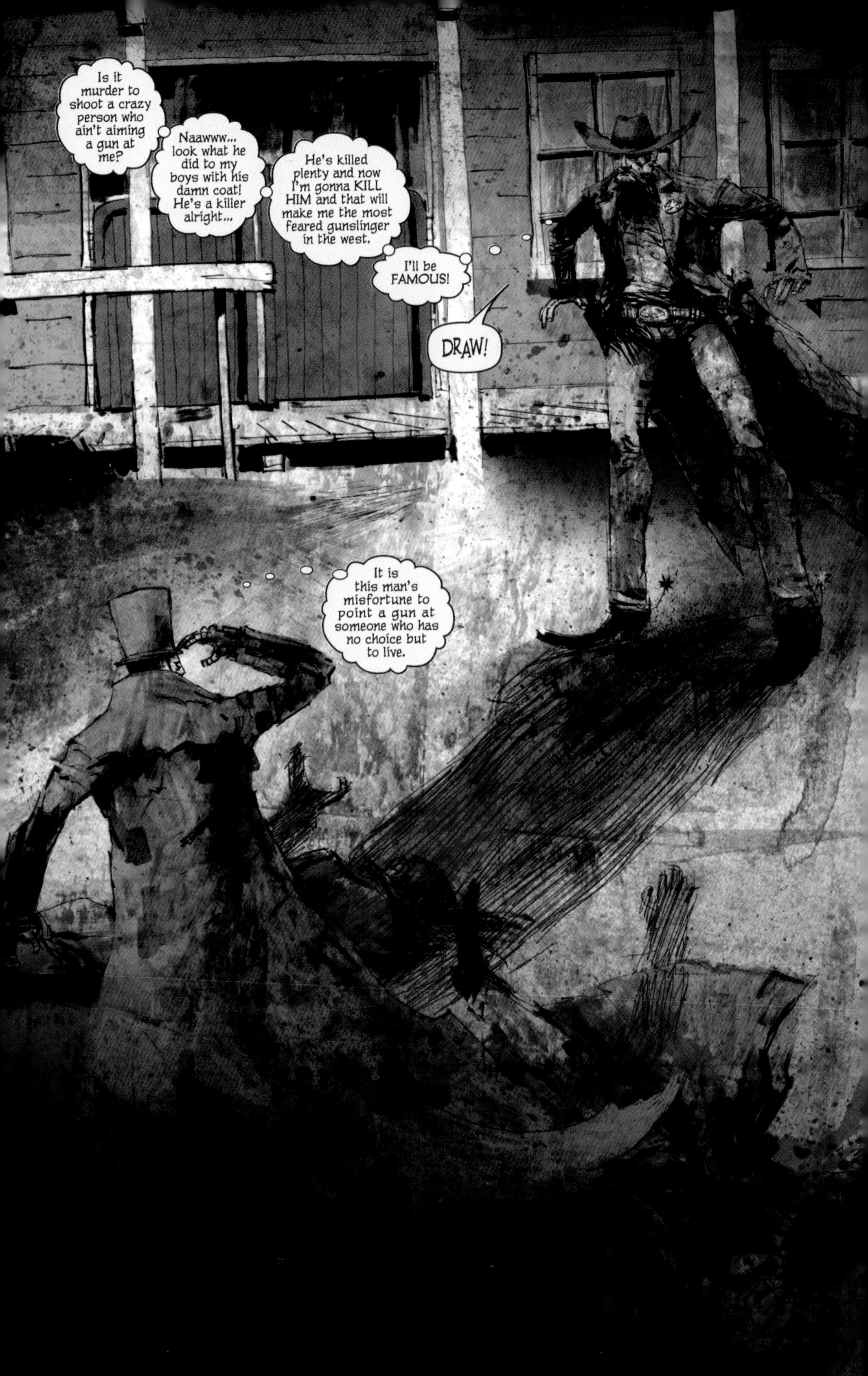
Is it murder to shoot a crazy person who ain't aiming a gun at me?
Naawww... look what he did to my boys with his damn coat! He's a killer alright...
He's killed plenty and now I'm gonna KILL HIM and that will make me the most feared gunslinger in the west.
I'll be FAMOUS!
DRAW!
It is this man's misfortune to point a gun at someone who has no choice but to live.

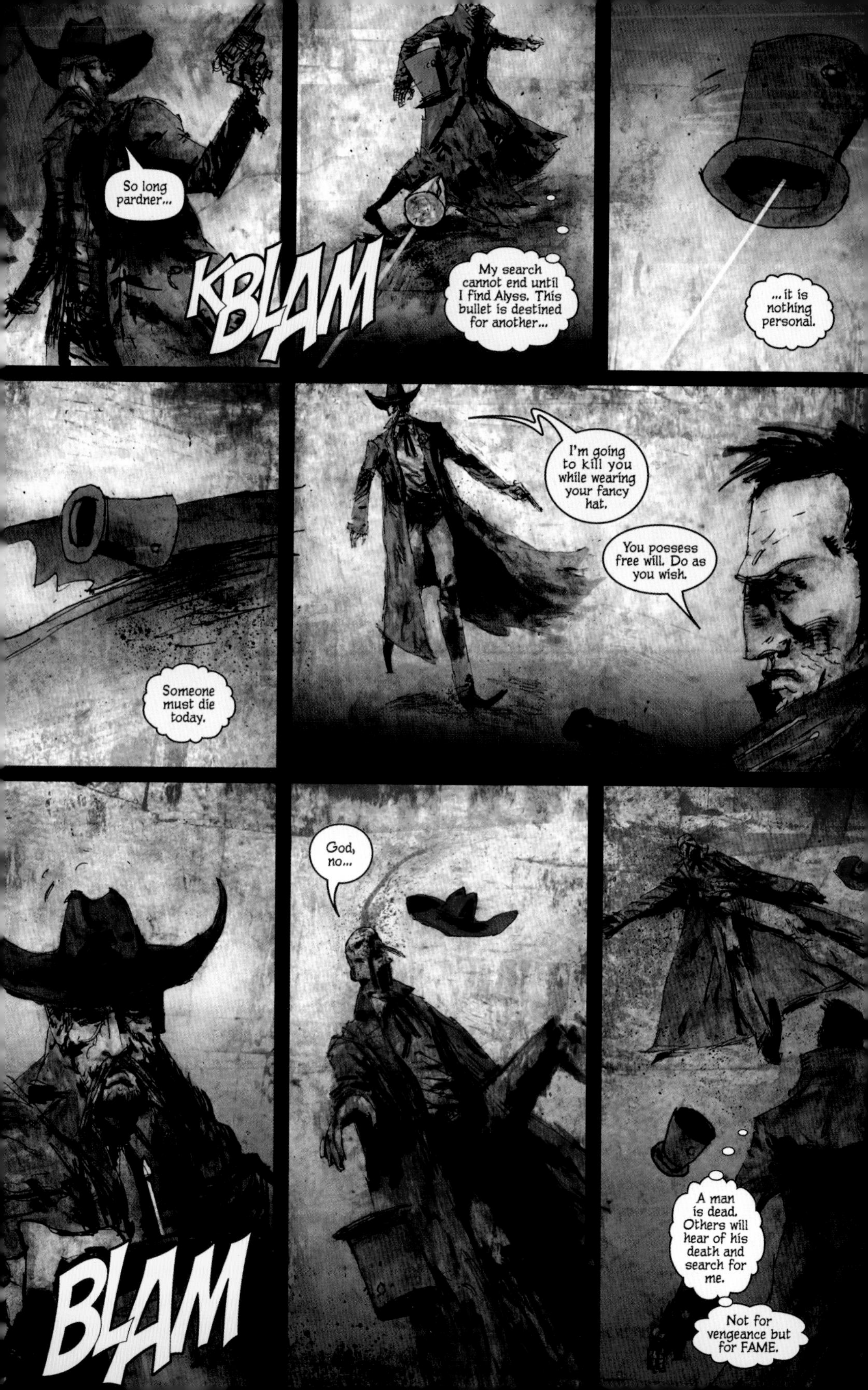
So long pardner...
KBLAM
My search cannot end until I find Alyss. This bullet is destined for another...
...it is nothing personal.
Someone must die today.
I'm going to kill you while wearing your fancy hat.
You possess free will. Do as you wish.
BLAM
God, no...
A man is dead. Others will hear of his death and search for me.
Not for vengeance but for FAME.

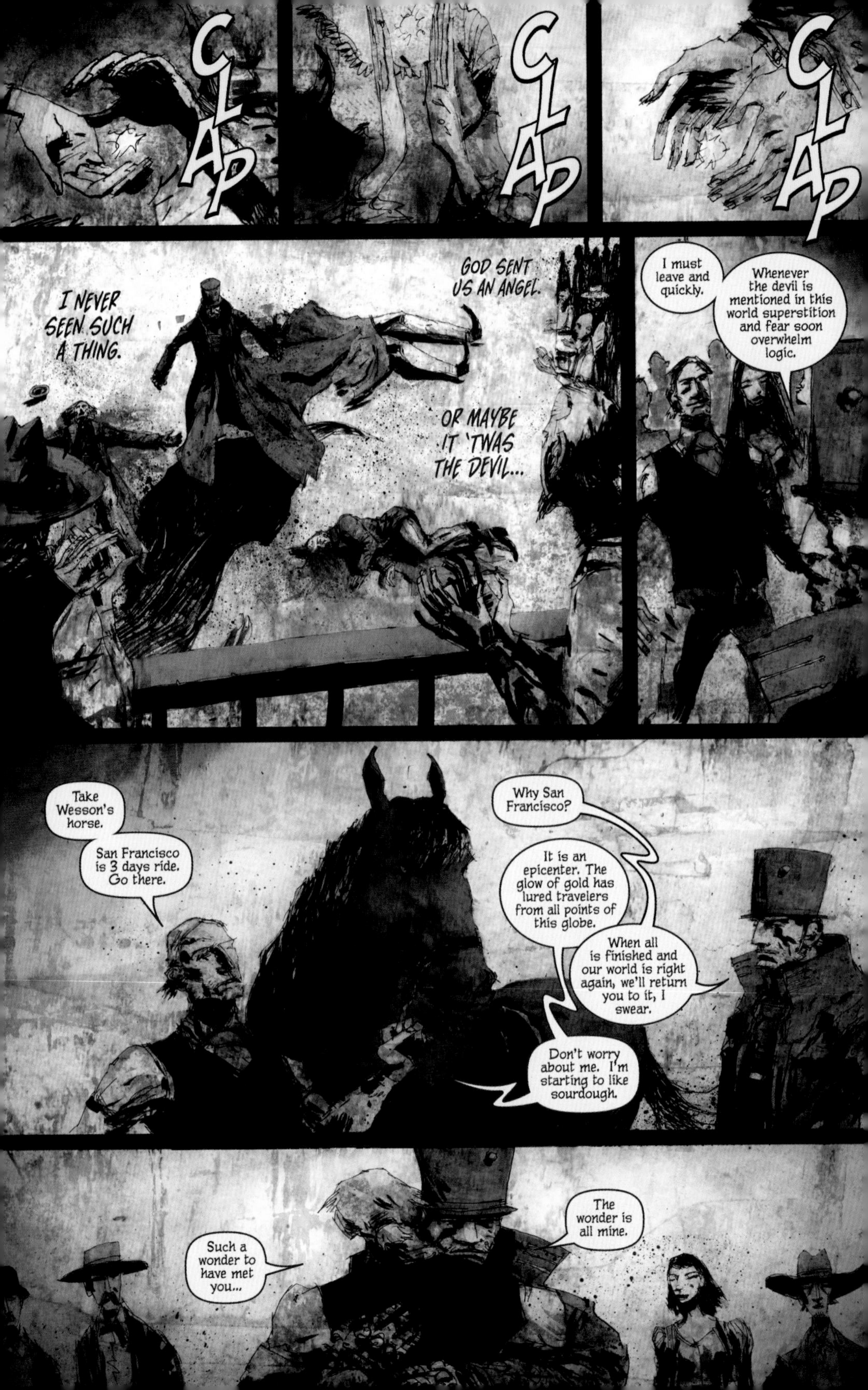
CLAP
CLAP
CLAP
I NEVER SEEN SUCH A THING.
GOD SENT US AN ANGEL.
OR MAYBE IT 'TWAS THE DEVIL...
I must leave and quickly.
Whenever the devil is mentioned in this world superstition and fear soon overwhelm logic.
Take Wesson's horse.
San Francisco is 3 days ride. Go there.
Why San Francisco?
It is an epicenter. The glow of gold has lured travelers from all points of this globe.
When all is finished and our world is right again, we'll return you to it, I swear.
Don't worry about me. I'm starting to like sourdough.
Such a wonder to have met you...
The wonder is all mine.

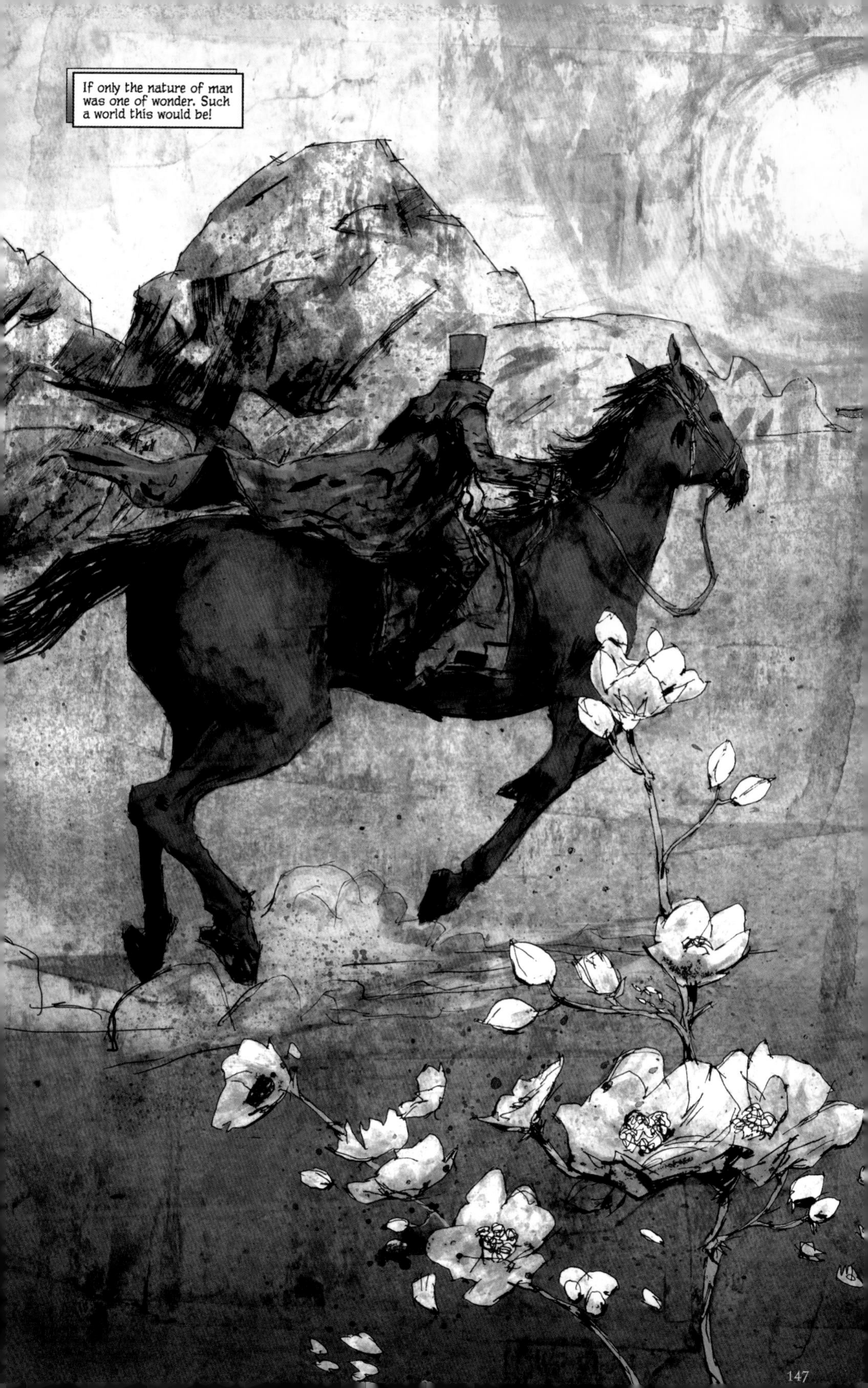
If only the nature of man was one of wonder. Such a world this would be!

"In nature there are neither rewards nor punishments"

here are consequences." –ROBERT GREEN INGERSOLL

Epilogue

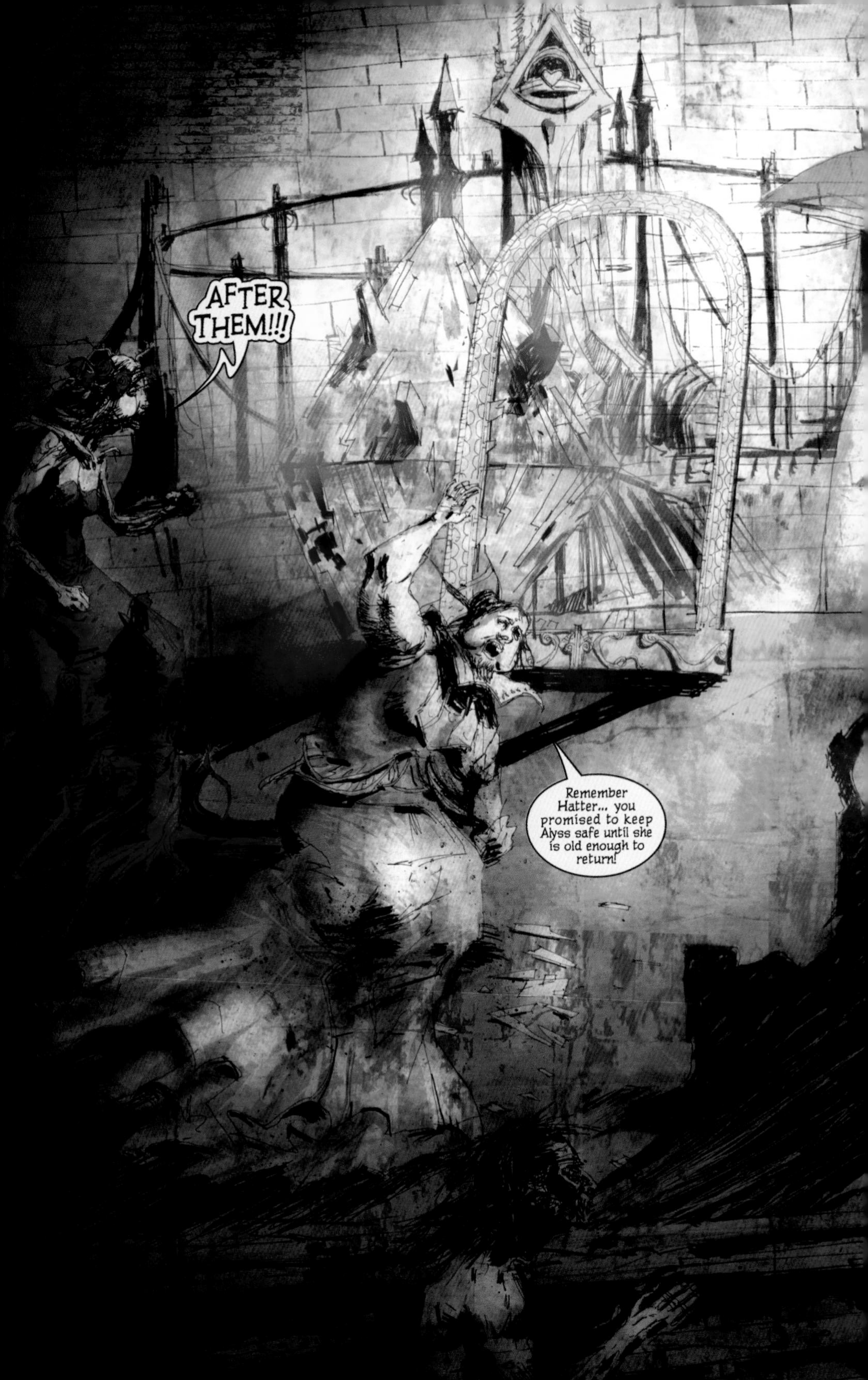
AFTER THEM!!!
Remember Hatter... you promised to keep Alyss safe until she is old enough to return!

RAWWWRRRRR!
POOL OF TEARS
ENTER AT YOUR OWN RISK
The Pool of Tears. No one comes back.
But you will... you HAVE to.
WOOO-HOOOOO!
YES YOU WILL GIRL!
YOU'LL GET BACK TO WONDERLAND!
YOU HANG IN THERE!
ALYSS WILL RETURN!
LONG LIVE ALYSS!
LONG LIVE WONDERLAND!
I believe that Alyss will return to Wonderland because she must.
But the only Wonderland we shall ever know is that which we find through Imagination... our own... and OTHERS.

HATTER M

THE
ZEN
OF
WONDER

VOLUME FOUR

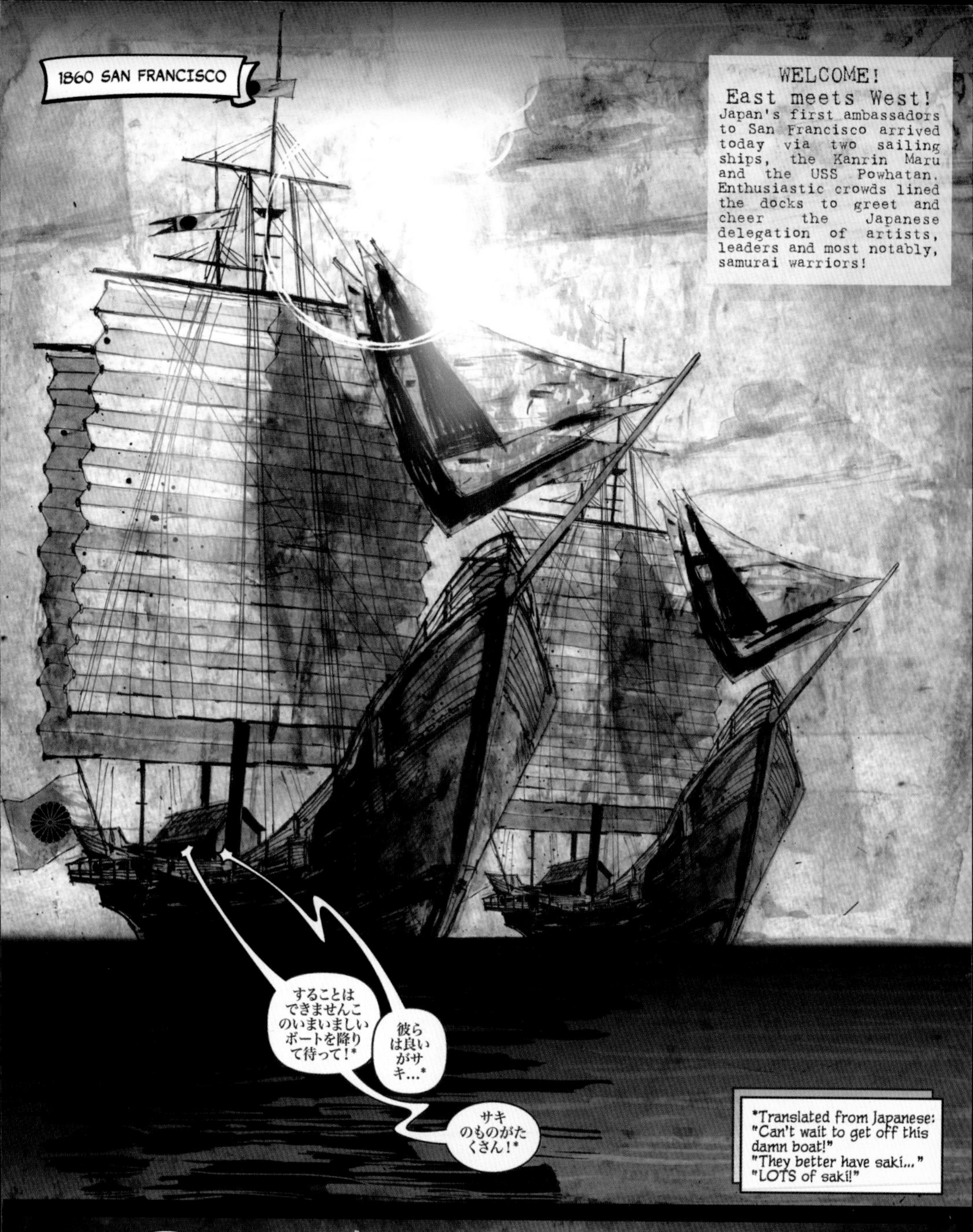
1860 SAN FRANCISCO
WELCOME!
East meets West!
Japan's first ambassadors to San Francisco arrived today via two sailing ships, the Kanrin Maru and the USS Powhatan. Enthusiastic crowds lined the docks to greet and cheer the Japanese delegation of artists, leaders and most notably, samurai warriors!
することはできませんこのいまいましいボートを降りて待って！*
彼らは良いがサキ…*
サキのものがたくさん！*
*Translated from Japanese: "Can't wait to get off this damn boat!" "They better have saki..." "LOTS of saki!"

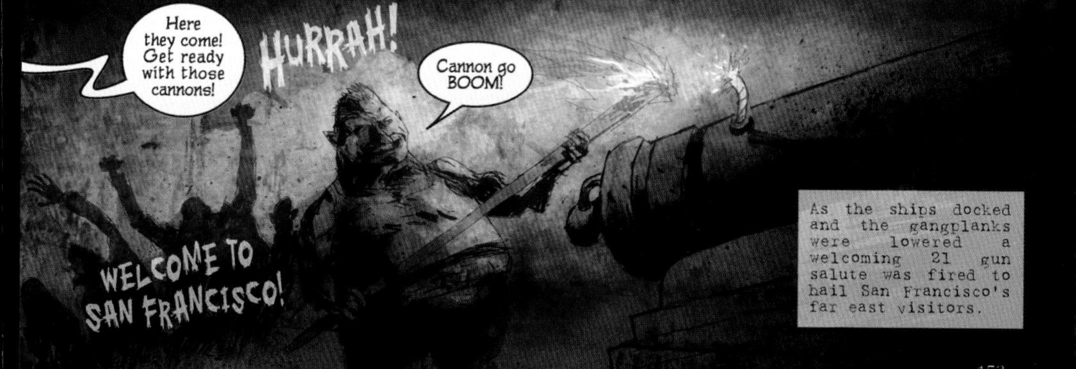
Here they come! Get ready with those cannons!
HURRAH!
Cannon go BOOM!
WELCOME TO SAN FRANCISCO!
As the ships docked and the gangplanks were lowered a welcoming 21 gun salute was fired to hail San Francisco's far east visitors.

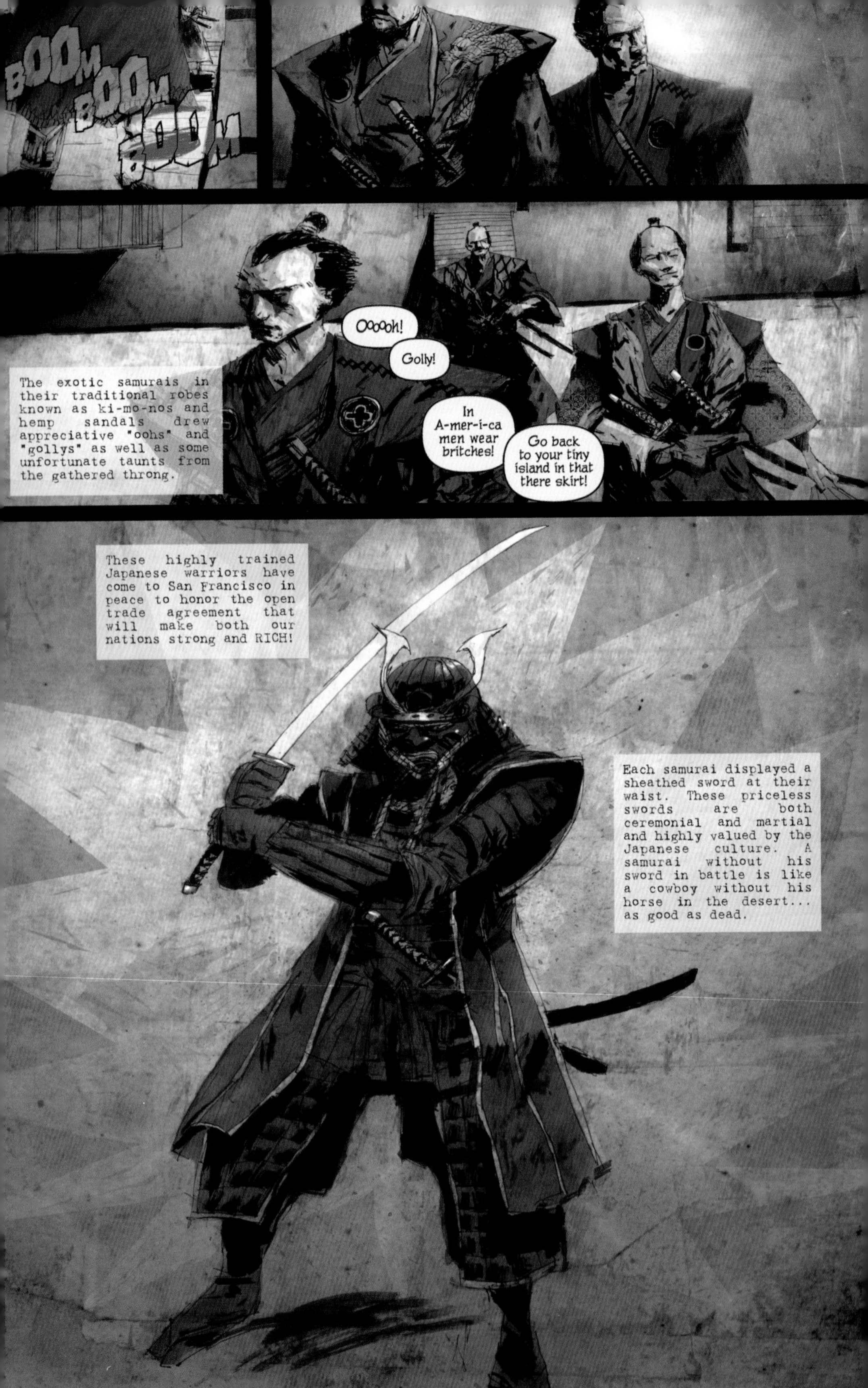
BOOM BOOM BOOM
The exotic samurais in their traditional robes known as ki-mo-nos and hemp sandals drew appreciative "oohs" and "gollys" as well as some unfortunate taunts from the gathered throng.
Ooooh!
Golly!
In A-mer-i-ca men wear britches!
Go back to your tiny island in that there skirt!
These highly trained Japanese warriors have come to San Francisco in peace to honor the open trade agreement that will make both our nations strong and RICH!
Each samurai displayed a sheathed sword at their waist. These priceless swords are both ceremonial and martial and highly valued by the Japanese culture. A samurai without his sword in battle is like a cowboy without his horse in the desert... as good as dead.

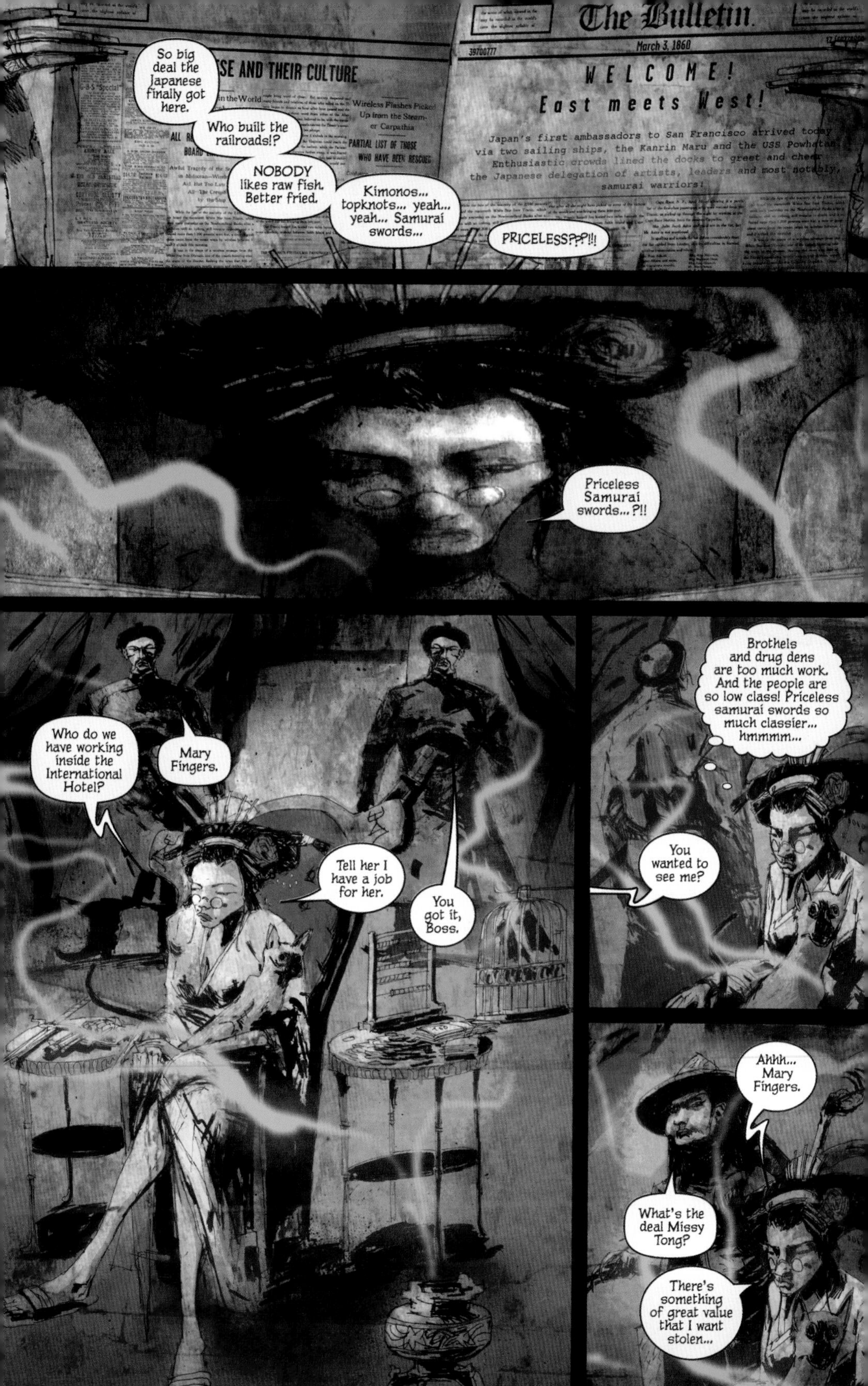
The Bulletin.
March 3, 1860
WELCOME! East meets West!
Japan's first ambassadors to San Francisco arrived today via two sailing ships, the Kanrin Maru and the USS Powhatan. Enthusiastic crowds lined the docks to greet and cheer the Japanese delegation of artists, leaders and most notably, samurai warriors!
So big deal the Japanese finally got here.
Who built the railroads!?
NOBODY likes raw fish. Better fried.
Kimonos... topknots... yeah... yeah... Samurai swords...
PRICELESS???!!!
Priceless Samurai swords...?!!
Who do we have working inside the International Hotel?
Mary Fingers.
Tell her I have a job for her.
You got it, Boss.
Brothels and drug dens are too much work. And the people are so low class! Priceless samurai swords so much classier... hmmmm...
You wanted to see me?
Ahhh... Mary Fingers.
What's the deal Missy Tong?
There's something of great value that I want stolen...

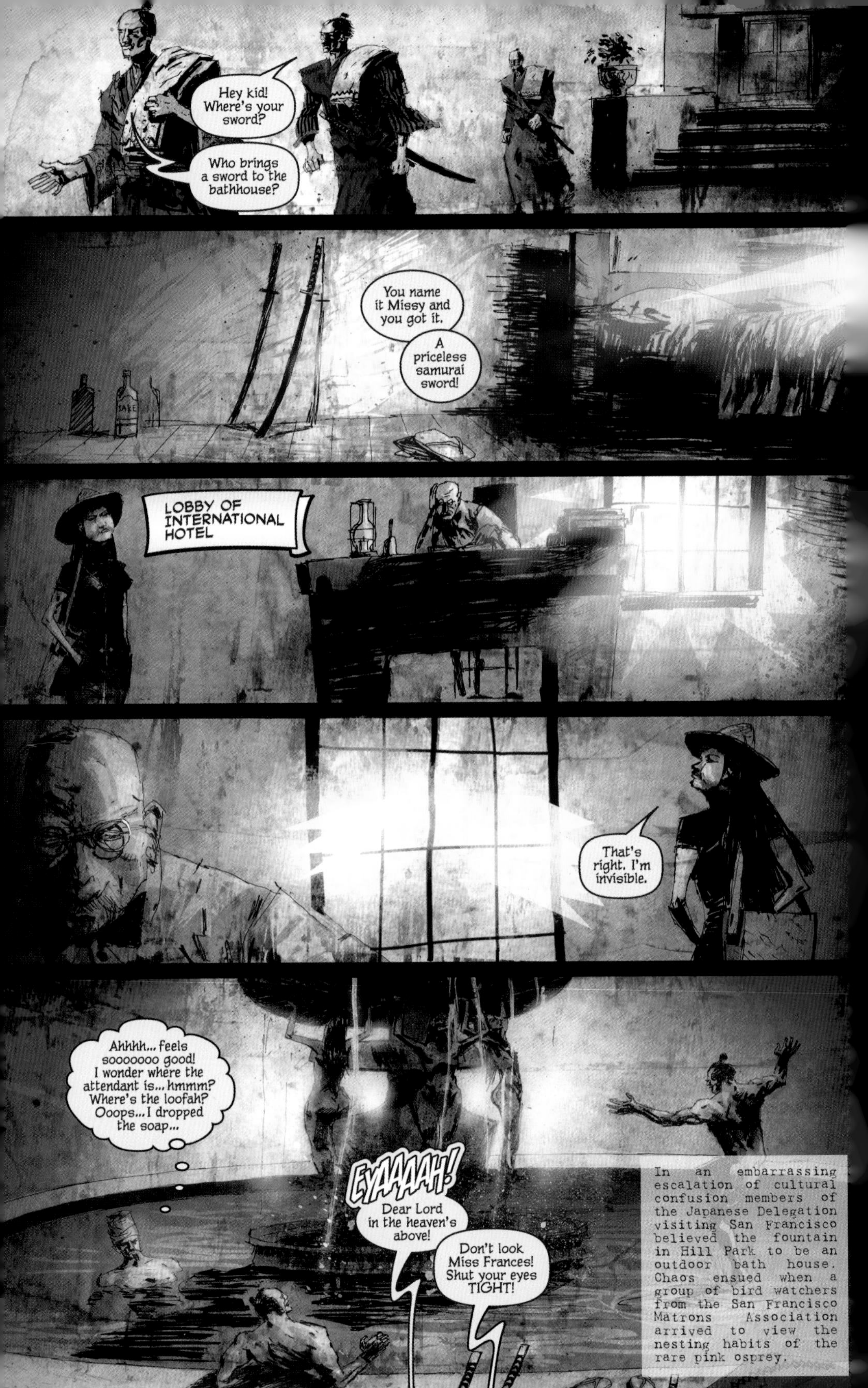
Hey kid! Where's your sword?
Who brings a sword to the bathhouse?
You name it Missy and you got it.
A priceless samurai sword!
SAKE
LOBBY OF INTERNATIONAL HOTEL
That's right. I'm invisible.
Ahhhh... feels sooooooo good! I wonder where the attendant is... hmmm? Where's the loofah? Ooops... I dropped the soap...
EYAAAAH!
Dear Lord in the heaven's above!
Don't look Miss Frances! Shut your eyes TIGHT!
In an embarrassing escalation of cultural confusion members of the Japanese Delegation visiting San Francisco believed the fountain in Hill Park to be an outdoor bath house. Chaos ensued when a group of bird watchers from the San Francisco Matrons Association arrived to view the nesting habits of the rare pink osprey.

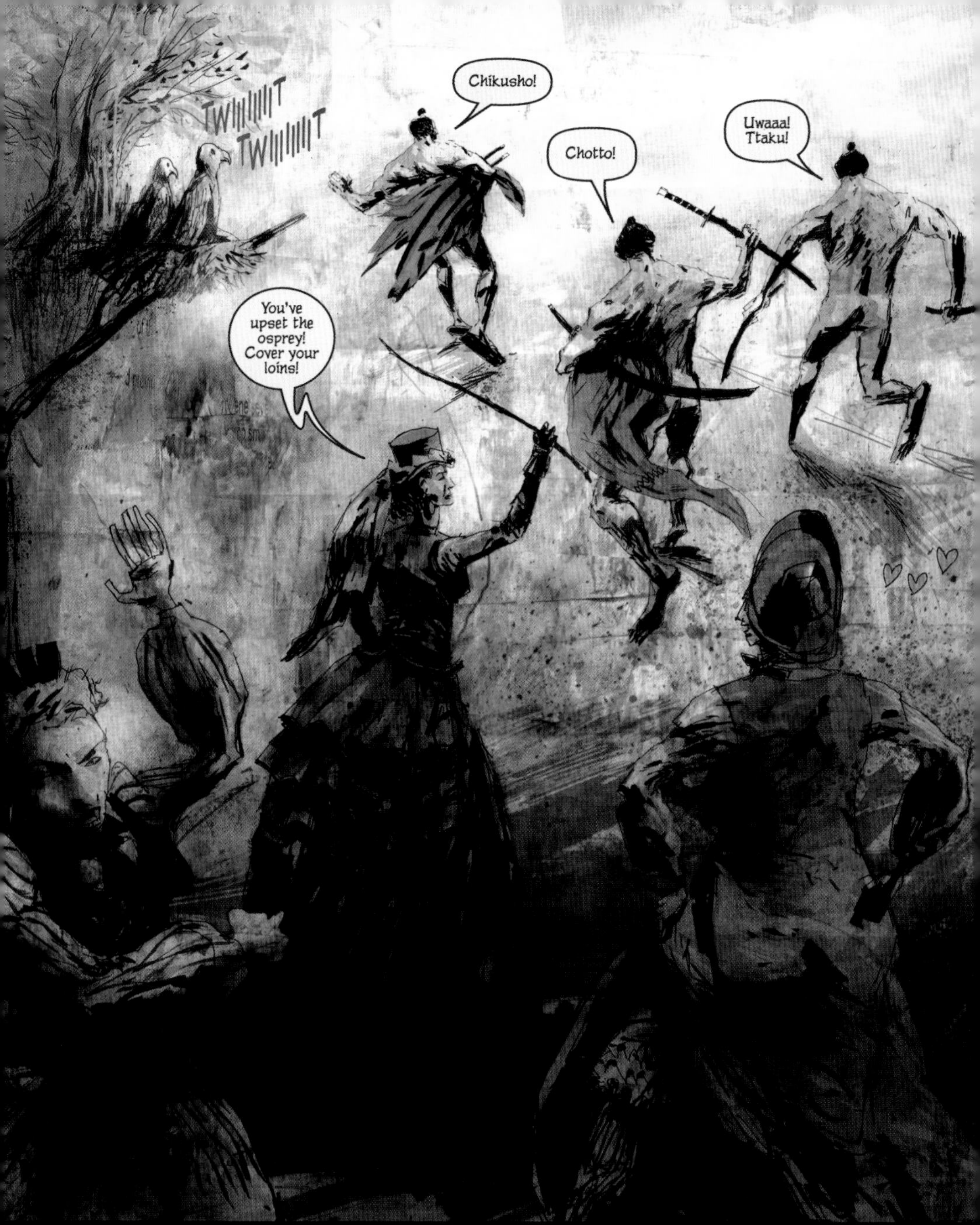
TWIIIIIIIT
TWIIIIIIIT
Chikusho!
Chotto!
Uwaaa! Ttaku!
You've upset the osprey! Cover your loins!

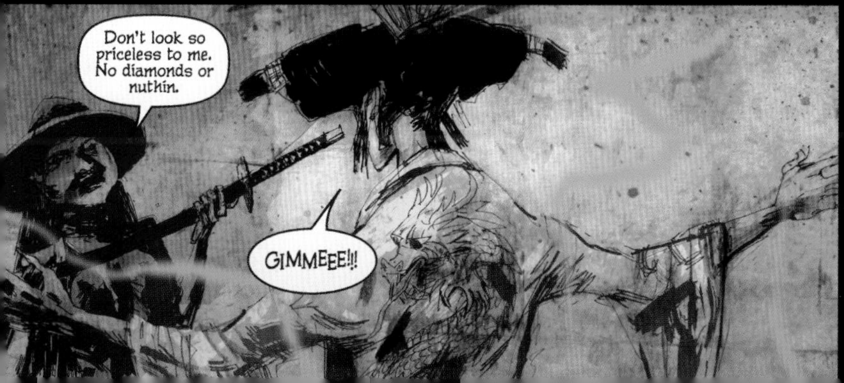
Don't look so priceless to me. No diamonds or nuthin.
GIMMEEE!!!

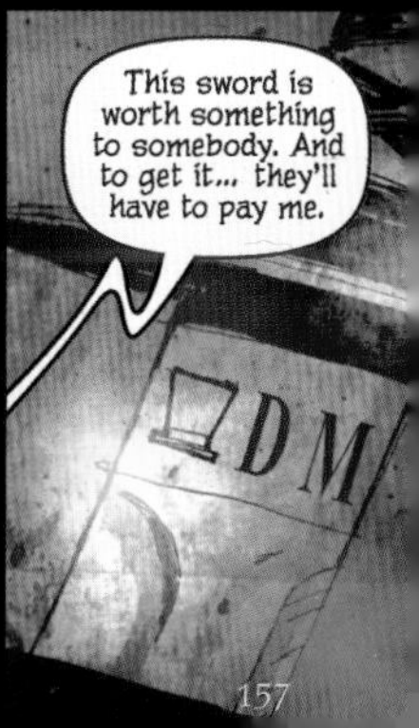
This sword is worth something to somebody. And to get it... they'll have to pay me.
DM

Illuminated

WASHINGTON D.C.
Where All the Secrets are Kept

The turmoil of the final days of the Civil War and the assassination of President Abraham Lincoln left Washington shrouded in secrecy. Nearly 150 years later our own inquisitive Colonel Barlow arrived in Washington to investigate the entries revealed in Hatter's journal for publication in this volume. In the course of his forensic research on Hatter's travels he uncovered many scintillating details, one of which still lies buried in our nation's capitol….

What was hidden inside the unfinished Washington monument?

Construction commenced in 1848, but by 1858, the government was out of money, leaving the Washington Monument to sit unfinished until 1878 when work resumed.

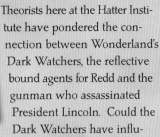

Ambitious Actor or Agent of Black Imagination?

Theorists here at the Hatter Institute have pondered the connection between Wonderland's Dark Watchers, the reflective bound agents for Redd and the gunman who assassinated President Lincoln. Could the Dark Watchers have influenced John Wilkes Boothe in his decision to kill the president? Was there a Wonderland connection? Yes and No. Evidence gathered regarding other participants in the Lincoln plot indicates that the original intent of the conspirators had been to kidnap the President. In this planned kidnapping we see the dark hand of the Watchers as their mission was to kidnap and drain Lincoln's imagination. Boothe's maniacal need for attention and a dramatic ending (actors!) evidently upset everyone's plans…including Redd's.

Deposed General Early…where did he run to?

After Dr. Obsidian Stoker hijacked his command by distributing vials of Black Imagination, General Jubal Early was spotted stealing a pair of bib overalls off a Virginia clothesline. When the Army of Northern Virginia surrendered on April 9, 1865, Early, disguised as a farmer, fled to Mexico.

What's Lincoln hiding under his hat?

In the midst of this swampy frontier capitol of wooden wheels and outhouses there was an exceptionally forward agency of avant futurists. This was Lincoln's top secret society for paranormal investigations that he named… *The Illuminated Forces.*

Forces

The Bureau of Illuminated Forces
Who were Lincoln's enlightened investigators?

ILLUMINATED FORCES

Agent's Identity Card

Name. Horatio Alabaster

Signature. *Horatio Alabaster*

By Special Order of
President Abraham Lincoln

Horatio Alabaster was Lincoln's trusted confidante. Together they shared an expanded awareness of what they termed, THE BIG IF. Lincoln authorized the establishment of the Bureau of Illuminated Forces as a top secret investigative agency for the study of paranormal and metaphysical mysteries.

ILLUMINATED FORCES

Agent's Identity Card

Name. Philomena Ark

Signature. *Philomena Ark*

By Special Order of
President Abraham Lincoln

Alabaster recruited the teenage Philomena Ark after her expulsion from the Betsy Ross finishing school for burning a flag when her unauthorized experiment with sun lasers went awry.

When Royal Bodyguard Hatter Madigan traveled to Washington D.C. in April 1865, he initially discovered the raw, unfinished capitol of a young nation in the final days of a civil war. But within hours of his arrival, the telltale Glow of Imagination led Hatter to the very center of this enigmatic paradigm of power.

The Bureau of Illuminated Forces was indeed secret. Colonel Barlow had to dig deep to uncover these images and records. But the biggest secret of all was yet to be discovered! Shall we explore further? Turn the page…

Futuristic conveyances were a passion of Alabaster and his development of vehicles for land, sea and sky rivaled Jules Verne for their audacity and ingenuity. Here is one of his early steam powered carriages.

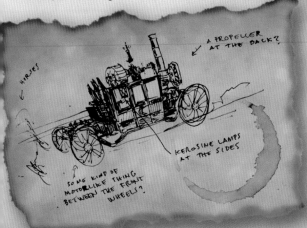

A PROPELLER AT THE BACK?

HORSES

KEROSINE LAMPS AT THE SIDES

SOME KIND OF MOTORLIKE THING BETWEEN THE FRONT WHEELS?

Steam powered rollerskates were Philomena and Alabaster's preferred mode of navigating the crowded streets of Washington D.C.

159

White

We followed Hatter and the Illuminated Forces west in search of the White Flower Tribe using a model of the compass first invented by Horatio Alabaster. The essence of this compass is its ability to direct the bearer towards the highest energy at the same time as providing geographic direction. Genius!

The Alabaster Compass – a marvel of energy and geography.

Armed with the 'Alabaster Compass' the Institutes' resident raconteur Miss Emily McGuiness went on a fact finding mission that lead her deep into the hidden history of the White Flower Tribe to answer the question: Where DID all the flowers go?

Report from the Grand Canyon

From Hatter's journal we knew that the White Flower Tribe fled their sacred lands rather than be moved to a reservation. As Chief Petal explained his tribe's ancient directive, "Should our enemies become too vast for the White Flowers to remain on the surface of this world we must go underground." UNDERGROUND? Little remains in our modern world that has not already been explored, bought and sold except that which is 'OFF LIMITS' to the public. And this is where the trail began…with a secret!

According to an article appearing in the Phoenix Gazette on April 5, 1909 the explorer G.E. Kincaid made an astounding discovery deep within the Grand Canyon of an enormous underground citadel. Briefly recounted, here is his story: "First, I would impress that the cavern is nearly inaccessible. The entrance is 1,486 feet down the sheer canyon wall. It is located on government land and no visitor will be allowed there under penalty of trespass. The story of how I found the cavern has been related, but in a paragraph: I was journeying down the Colorado River in a boat, alone, looking for minerals. Some forty two miles up the river from the El Tovar Crystal canyon, I saw on the east wall, stains in the sedimentary formation about 2,000 feet above the river bed. There was no trail to this point, but I finally reached it with great difficulty. Above a shelf, which hid it from view from the river, was the mouth of the cave. There are steps leading from this entrance some thirty yards to what was, at the time the cavern was inhabited, the level of the river. When I saw the chisel marks on the wall inside the entrance, I became interested, securing my gun and went in."

Flower Tribe

Following the navigational directives of the *Phoenix Gazette* article Miss Emily – minus gun – entered the cave described by Mr. Kincaid.

As she trekked nearly a mile underground, the long main passage lead to another mammoth chamber from which radiated scores of passageways. Several hundred rooms were discovered, reached by passageways running from the main passage, one of them having been explored are 854 feet and another 634 feet.

This message written on the wall of the cave in petalglyphics first alerted her to the hidden underground village of the White Flower Tribe.

Translated from the White Flower language:
BEWARE NEW AMERICANS!
Someday...YOU will be the Indians....

Flower Power

The spoken language of the White Flower Indians had been recorded by Hatter (an inter-realm linguist par excellence) in his journal. Working from this guide, Miss Emily was able to enlighten herself with the White Flower lexicon prior to entering the caves. The White Flower language is unique in that it is composed of the names of white flowers from around the world that are then inscribed in the flowery petal-glyphics that convey written communication. Other samples of petal graffiti found included "Flower Power!" and the story of "The Cloud that Exploded into Flames" which recounts the saga of the Illuminated Airship crashing to the ground and Hatter Madigan coming to assist Realm in restoring her Imaginative Powers.

To read more on the secret caves: www.homehighlight.org/entertainment-and-recreation/nature/the-grand-canyon-s-grand-secret.html

Stacking the Deck

One touch of nature makes the whole world kin. –William Shakespeare

Since our discovery of the first lost card linking the Wonderland cards discovered by Frank Beddor in the British Museum and the deck collected by British antiquities dealer Mr. Buffington with Hatter Madigan, royal bodyguard and artist, we have continued stacking the deck for our mutual edification. The card drawn by Hatter Madigan while incarcerated at the Lunatic Asylum for the Mad and Disillusioned depicting Wonderland's Millinery H.A.T.B.O.X. was what initially tipped us to this invaluable source material. For some unknown reason that card remained at the asylum while the others in the deck had disappeared. This naturally whetted our investigative appetite and we spent the last year circling the globe following possible leads as to where the other cards in the deck may have been… shuffled. Behold before you the most recent color art images inspired by Hatter Madigan's cards and rendered by our very own Institute artists.

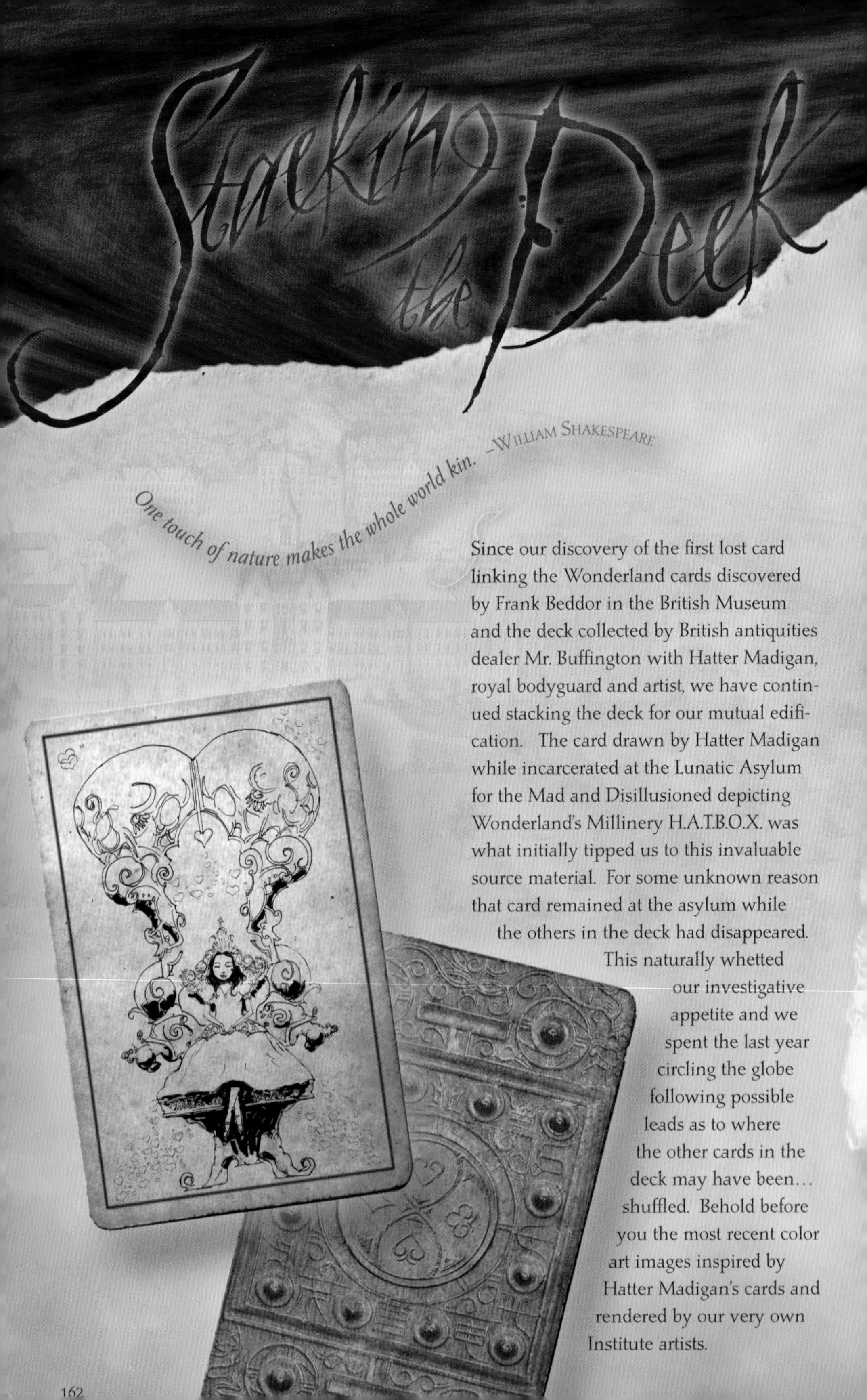

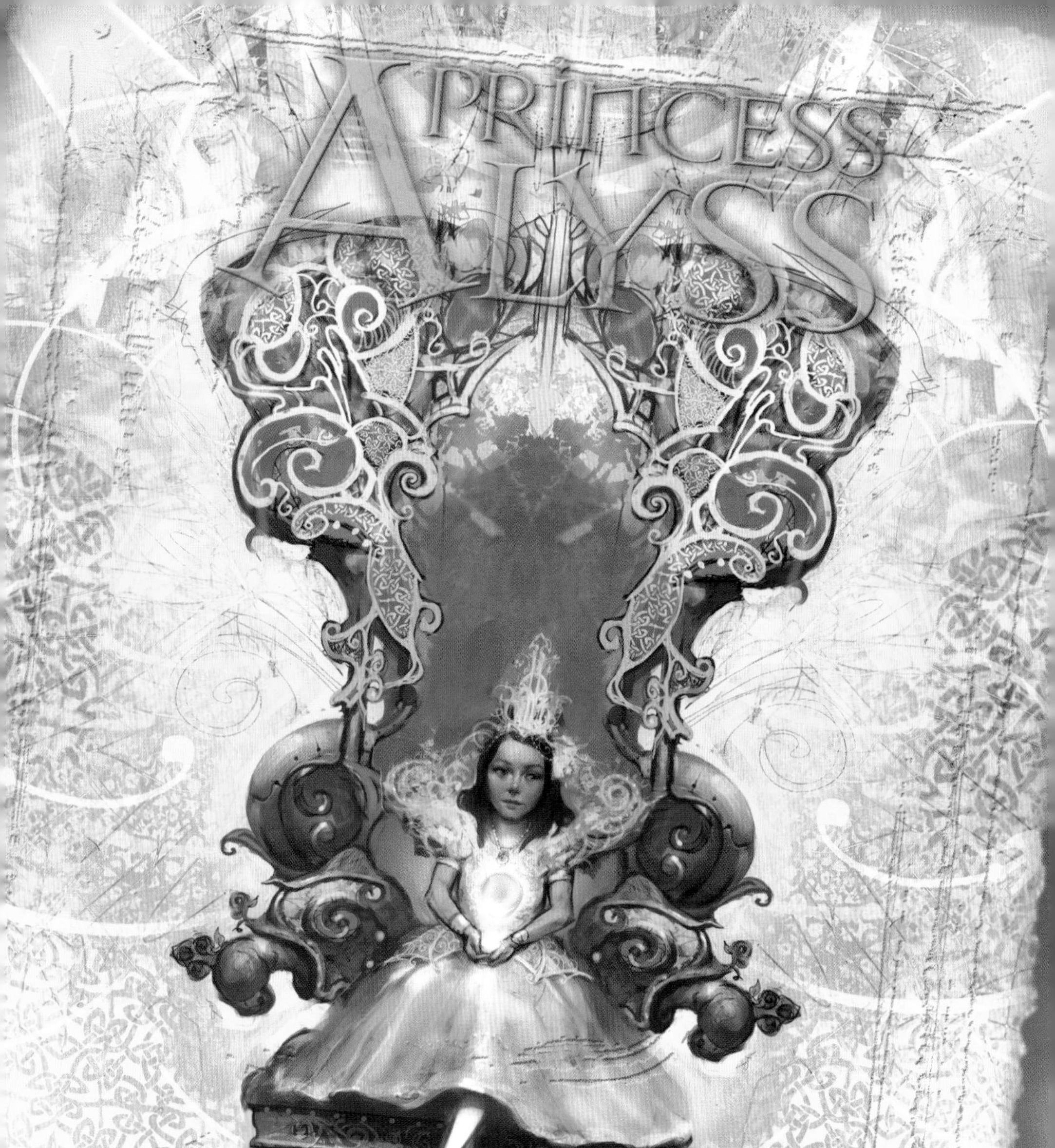
Princess
Alyss

Alyss on her mother's throne.

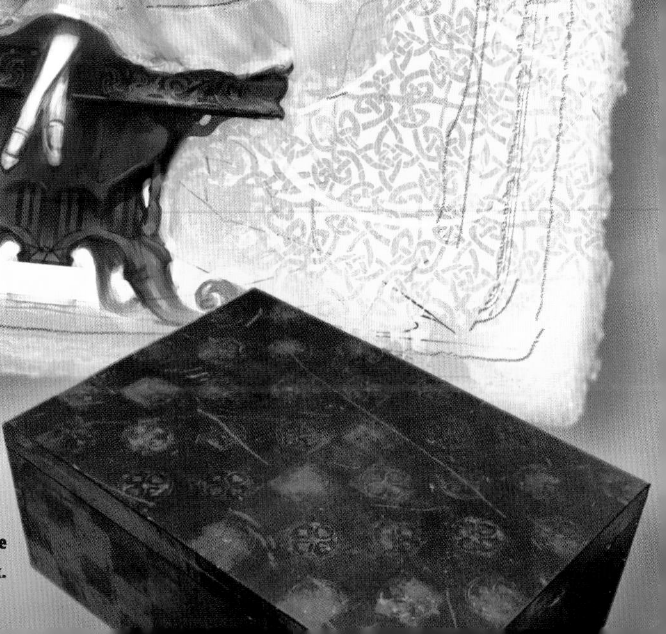

Now, after nearly 150 years, the cards can be reunited in their original box.

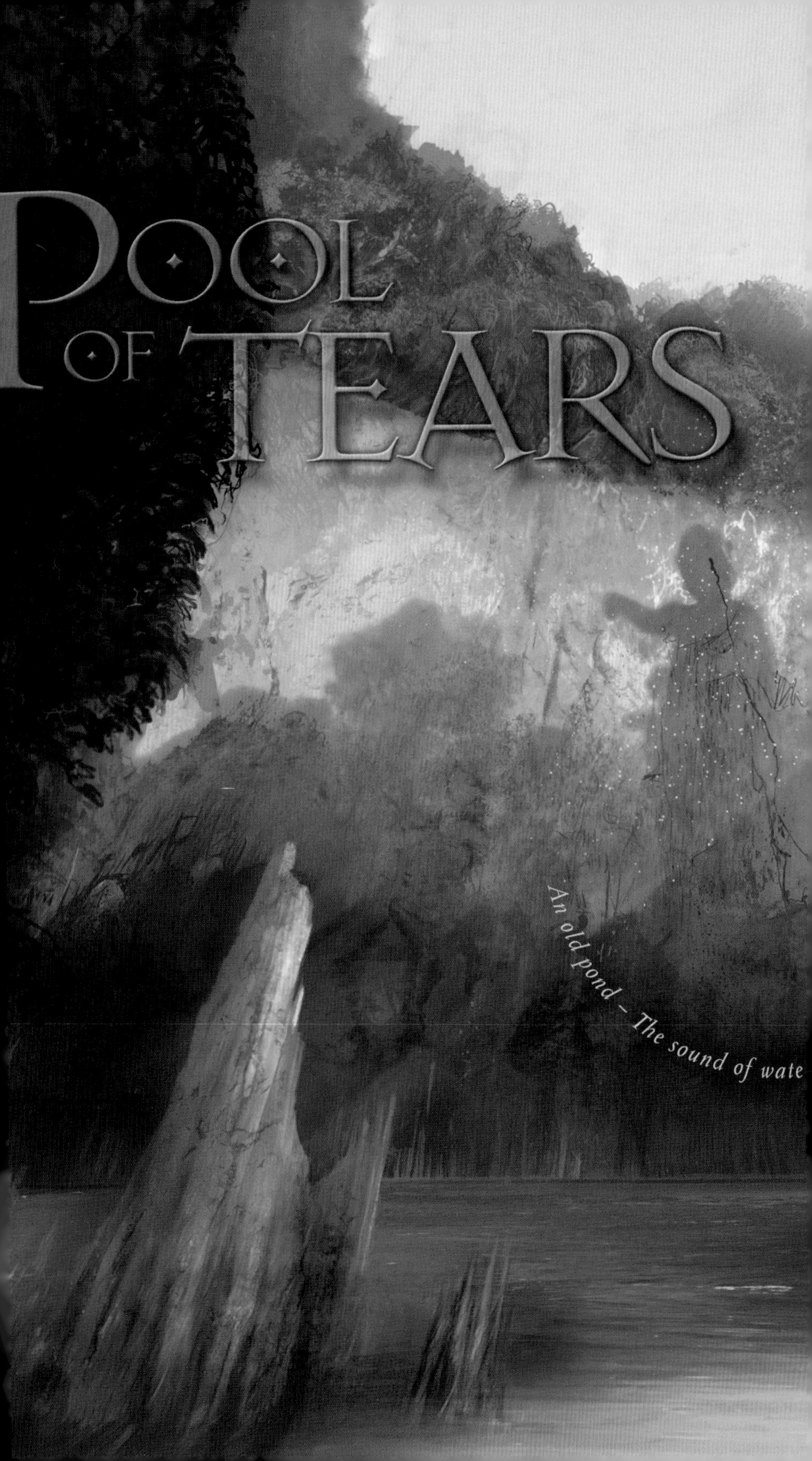
POOL OF TEARS
An old pond – The sound of wate

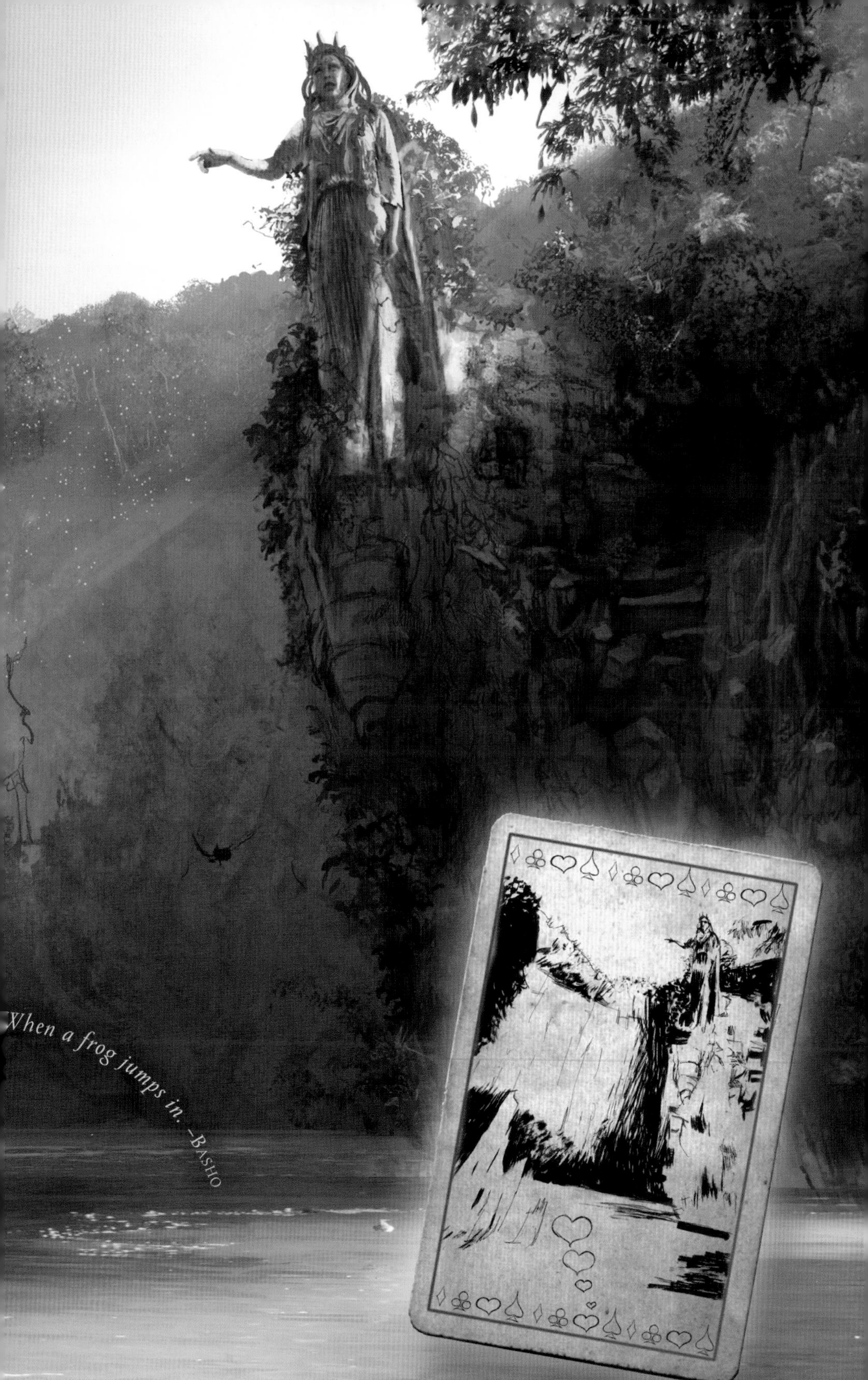

When a frog jumps in. –Basho

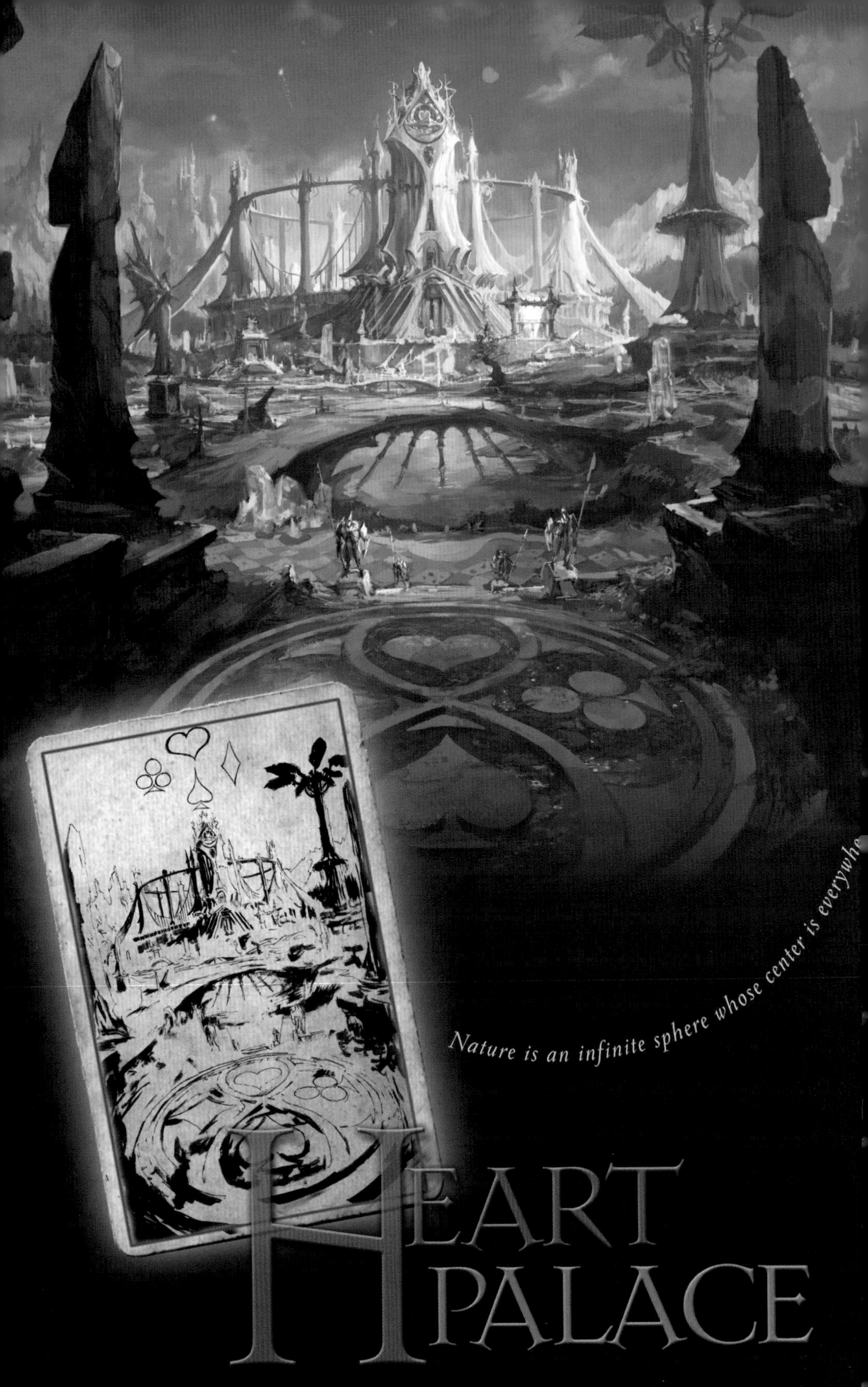

Nature is an infinite sphere whose center is everywhe

HEART PALACE

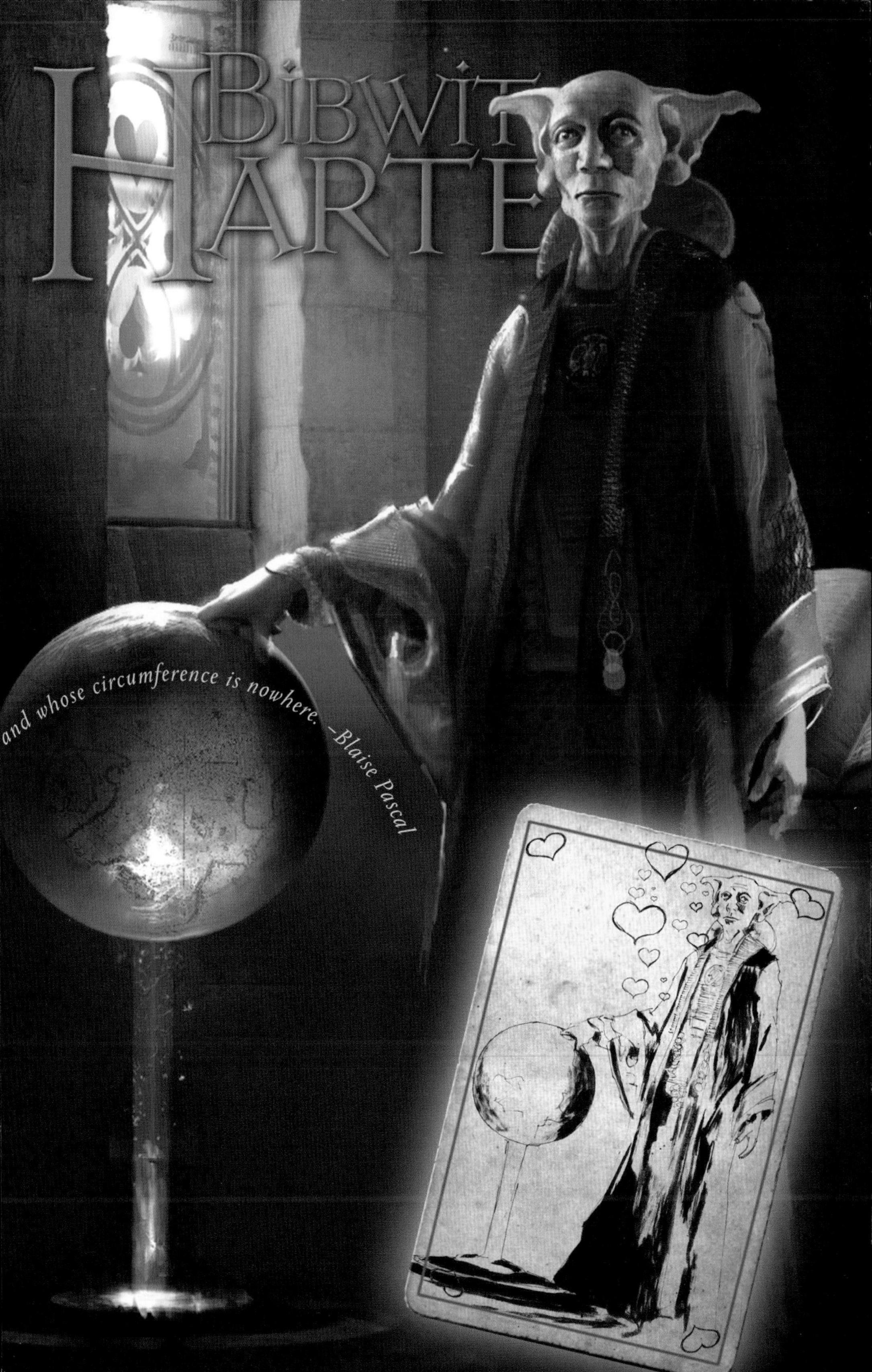
Bibwit Harte
and whose circumference is nowhere. –Blaise Pascal

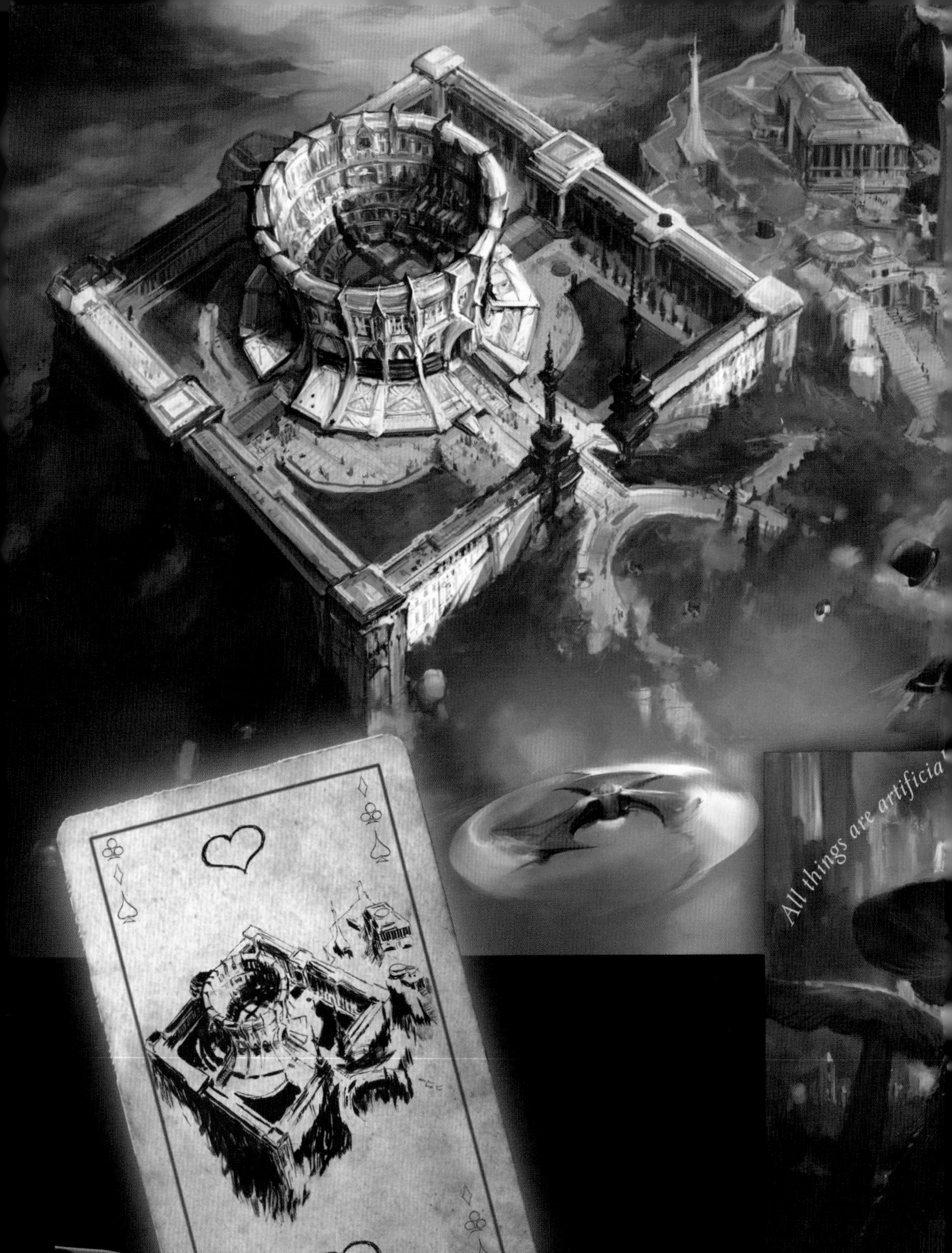
All things are artificia

The Millinery

House of Cards

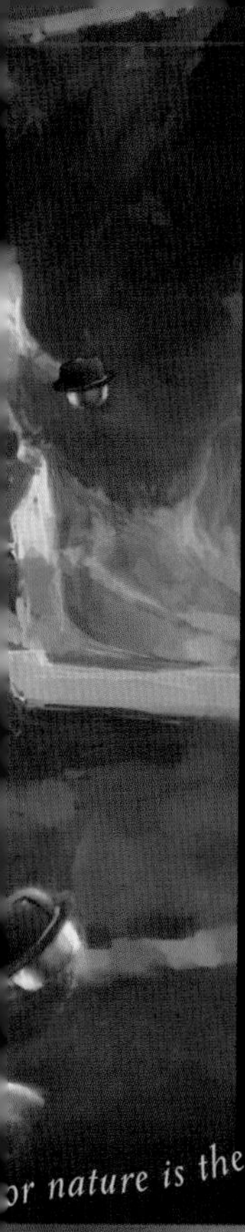

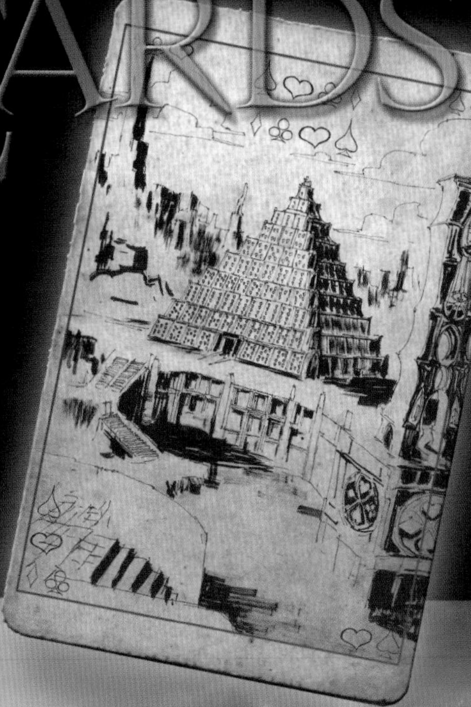

or nature is the art of God. –Thomas Browne

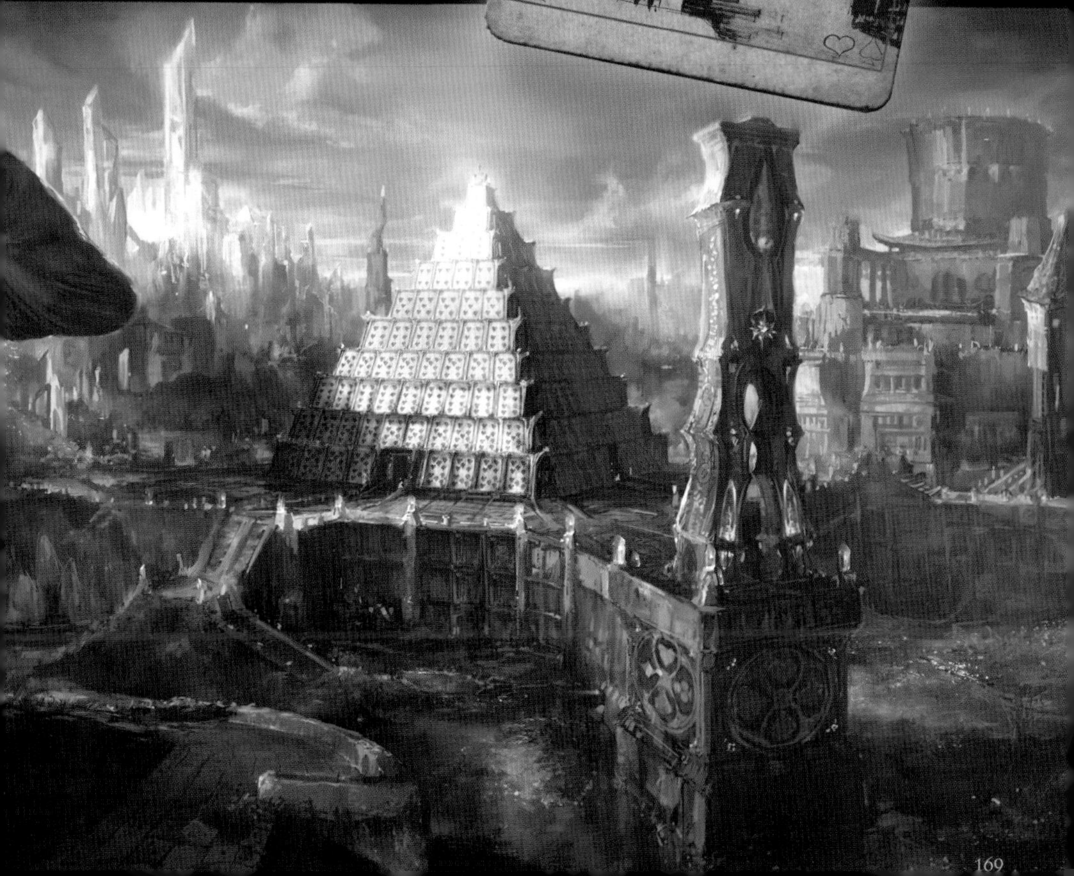

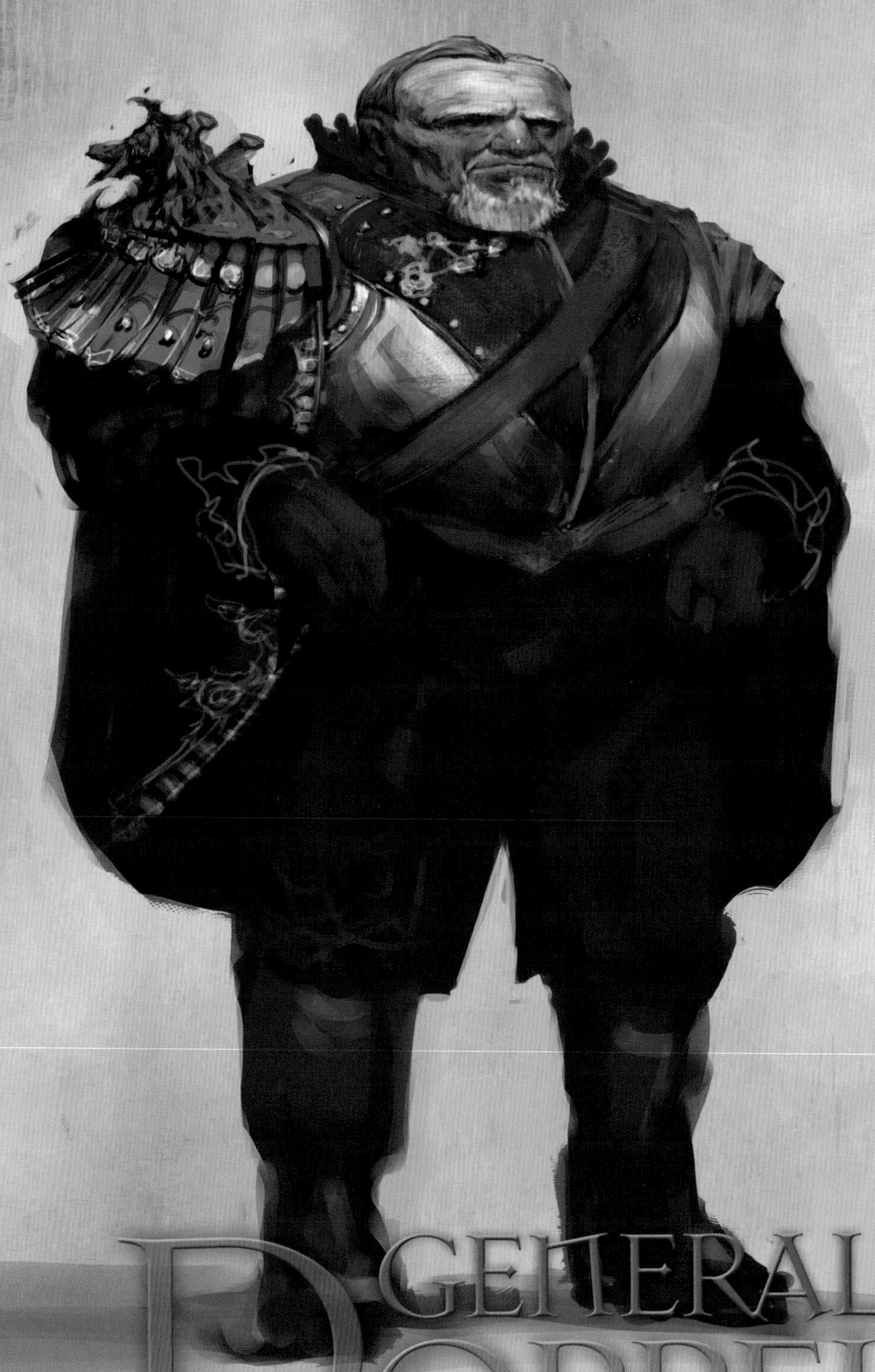

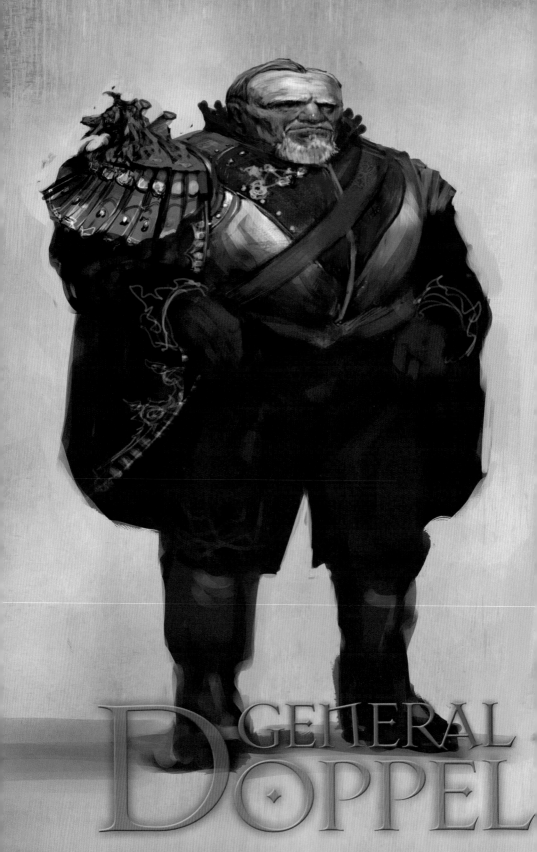

General Doppel

Nature, to be commanded, must be obeyed. —Francis Bacon

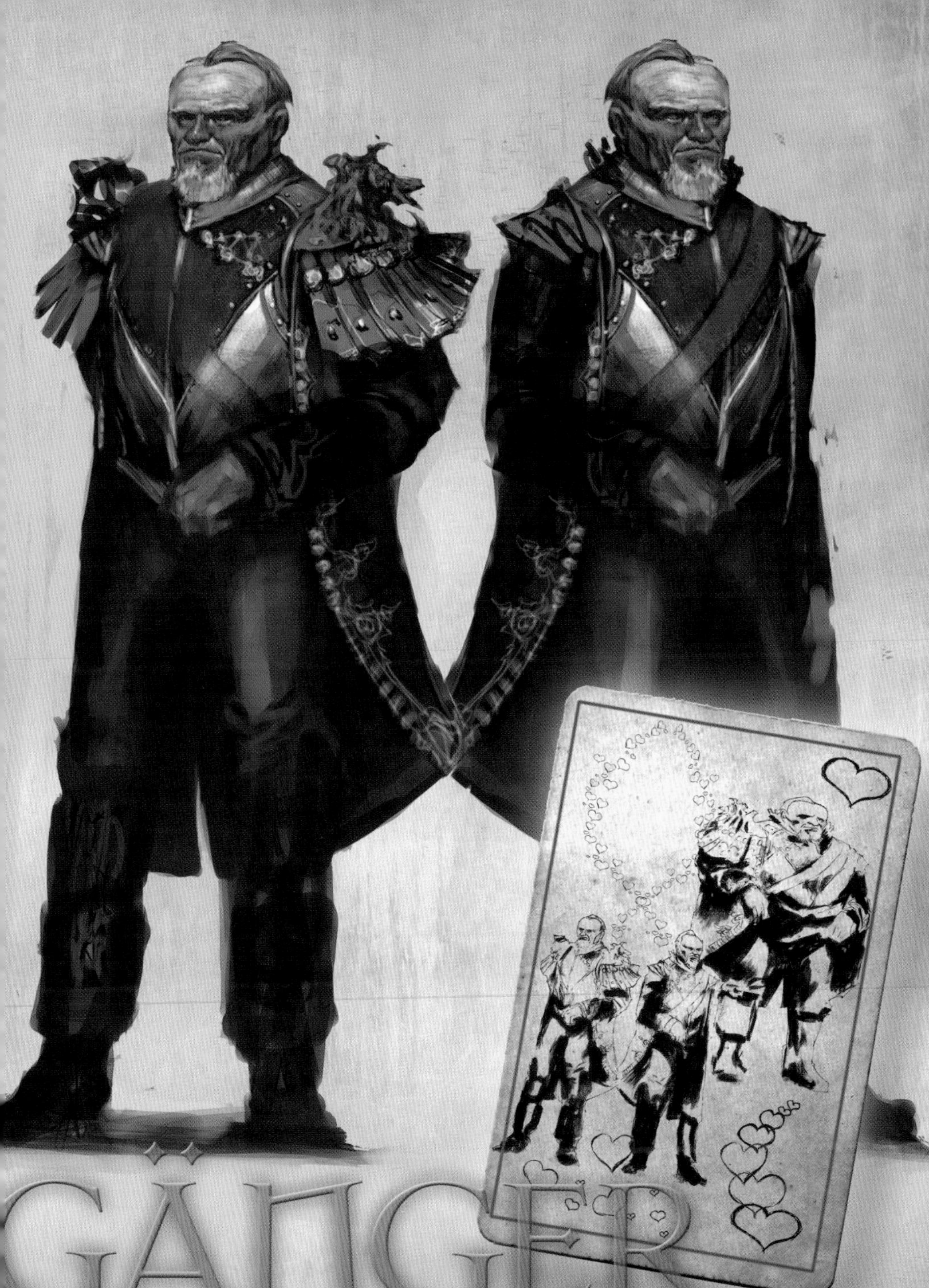

GÄNGER

Alyss in Exile

Friday before Tea

When mother ordered Hatter to take me and leave Wonderland, we fled through a looking glass that took us to the Whispering Woods. Once in the woods Hatter held me tight and ran faster than a spirit-dane. At last we came to the cliff above the Pool of Tears. It is said that no one ever comes back from the Pool of Tears, but Hatter assured me I would because I would one day return to be Queen. And then we jumped, but not soon enough, as The Cat's long claws raked out across my birthday gown and tore away a piece. He nearly got me!

But before I could scream we hit the water . . .

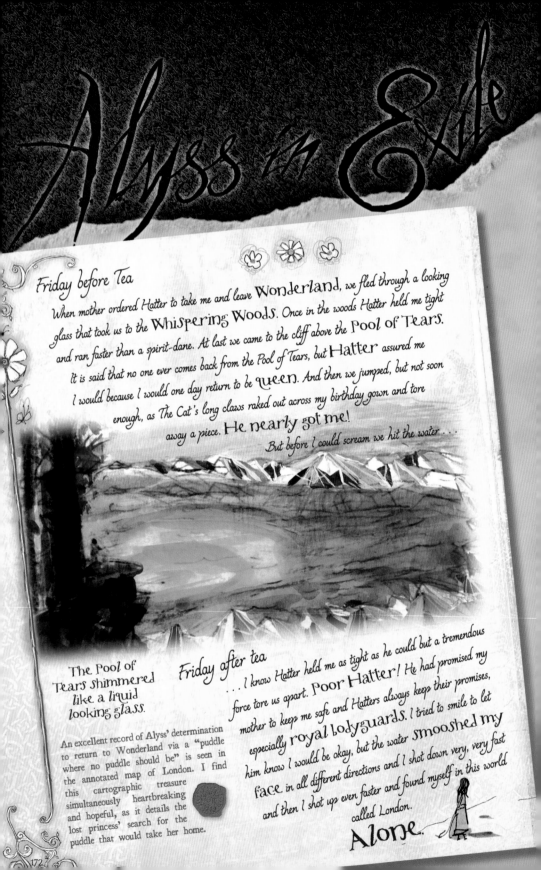

The Pool of Tears shimmered like a liquid looking glass.

An excellent record of Alyss' determination to return to Wonderland via a "puddle where no puddle should be" is seen in the annotated map of London. I find this cartographic treasure simultaneously heartbreaking and hopeful, as it details the lost princess' search for the puddle that would take her home.

Friday after tea

. . . I know Hatter held me as tight as he could but a tremendous force tore us apart. Poor Hatter! He had promised my mother to keep me safe and Hatters always keep their promises, especially royal bodyguards. I tried to smile to let him know I would be okay, but the water smooshed my face in all different directions and I shot down very, very fast and then I shot up even faster and found myself in this world called London.

Alone.

172

Sunday morning

My arrival in this world called London was sudden and frightening. I shot up and out of the puddle and found myself standing in the middle of a crowded avenue. Everything was spinning and I was cold and lost and AFRAID. Where was my mother? And where was my royal bodyguard? In desperation I began to jump in puddle after puddle searching for the way home. Then I saw a boy watching me and he was smiling and I knew I wasn't alone anymore. I was about to meet the most honorable

Quigley Gaffer.

I vow to discover the secret of puddle travel! There simply must be a way of knowing which puddle is THE PUDDLE!

"I found a puddle right in the middle of Hyde Park It didn't work!"

· MAP OF LONDON ·

Discovering and testing puddles kept me very busy since it seemed to rain every day!

I am CERTAIN that this puddle must still exist and it is up to ME to find it.

Splish!

splashh!

sploosh!

As many of our readers know, following the publication of the Looking Glass Wars, we were contacted by the British historian Dame Agnes MacKenzie. Her startling missive informed us that a trunk had been discovered in Oxford, England containing the art and journals of a young Victorian girl. Of course, the contents of this trunk had once belonged to Princess Alyss Heart of Wonderland. Since Alyss and her ordeal are at the very center of Hatter's quest we believe the insights gained from her art and journals provide valuable juxtaposition for all serious Hatter scholars. →

As thoughtful readers of Dickens will recall, orphans, urchins and estranged children were an all too common sight on the sooty streets of nineteenth-century London. It seems from Alyss' journal that she was accepted into a den of street urchins by the boy named Quigley. While Quigley was an open-hearted generous sort, the others insisted Princess Alyss pull her own weight in foraging for food and rags. Alyss' solution was, of course, to use her imagination.

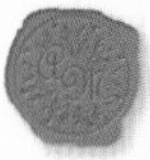

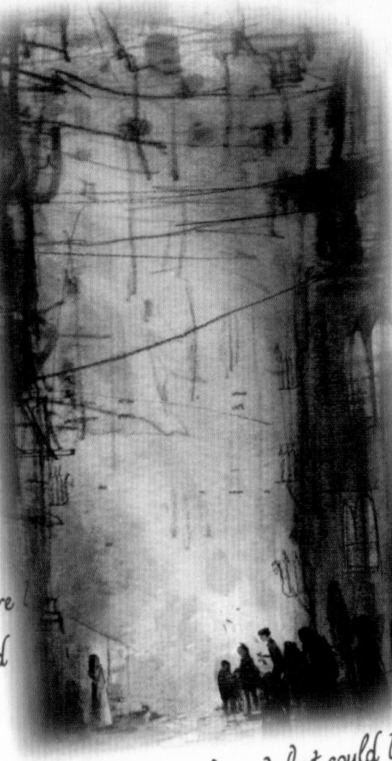

Sunday . . . raining

Quigley brought me to an alley where he and a group of other very ragged, thin children lived. Everyone was curious as to who I was and where I had come from, so I told them about Wonderland. They all loved my stories but unfortunately, they couldn't eat them. What could I do to help? As I was thinking I noticed a sad little flower in a cracked pot lying in the alley. To amuse my new friends I began to imagine the flower humming and then singing in a beautiful high-pitched voice. Quigley and the others were amazed. That's when I knew what to do!

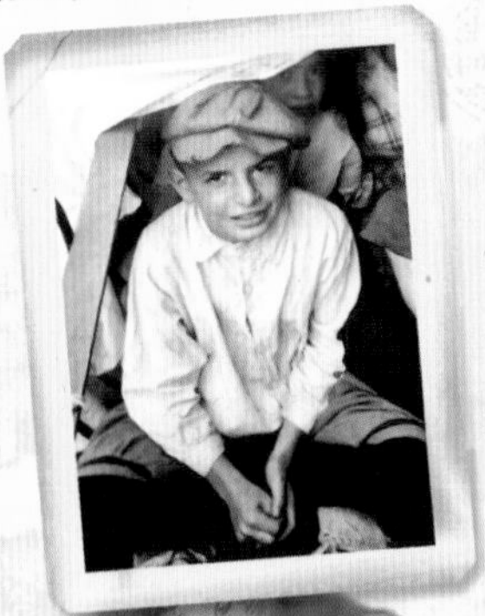

The boy in this photo reminds me of my friend Quigley.

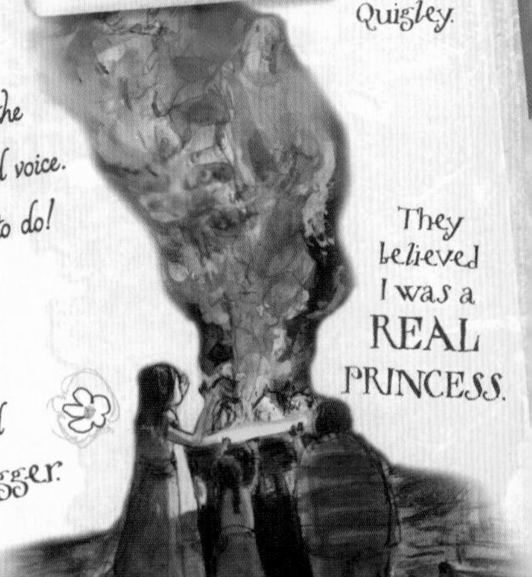

They believed I was a REAL PRINCESS.

Sunday . . . still raining

We became street performers. I would imagine the flower singing and Quigley would gather the coins tossed by those who stopped to listen. Our first show was a hit. The next show even bigger. Each day we made enough coins to feed everyone very, VERY well.

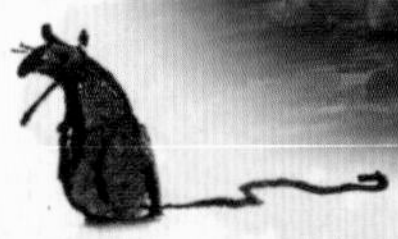

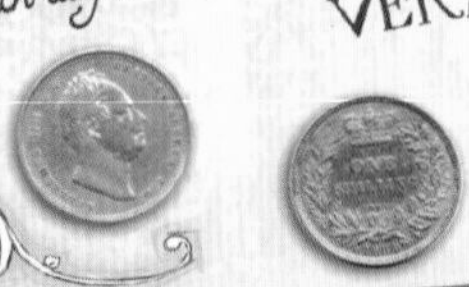

Who was this lost princess living among the uninformed and non-curious citizens of Oxford?

Once again we *creak* open Alyss's trunk to give you a look inside the heart and mind of Wonderland's most imaginative exile.

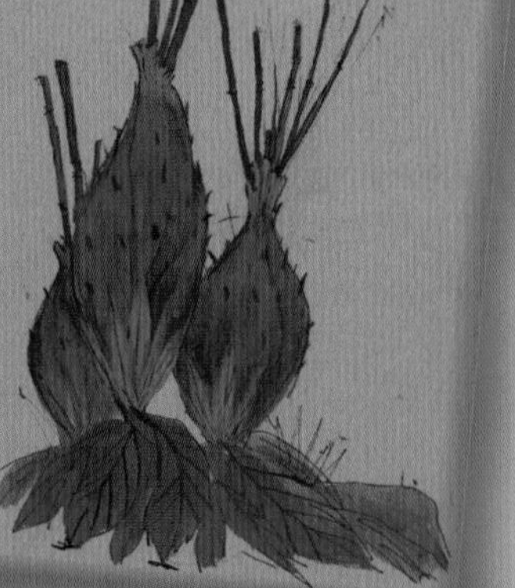

Just living is not enough... one must have sunshine, freedom, and a little flower. —Hans Christian Anderson

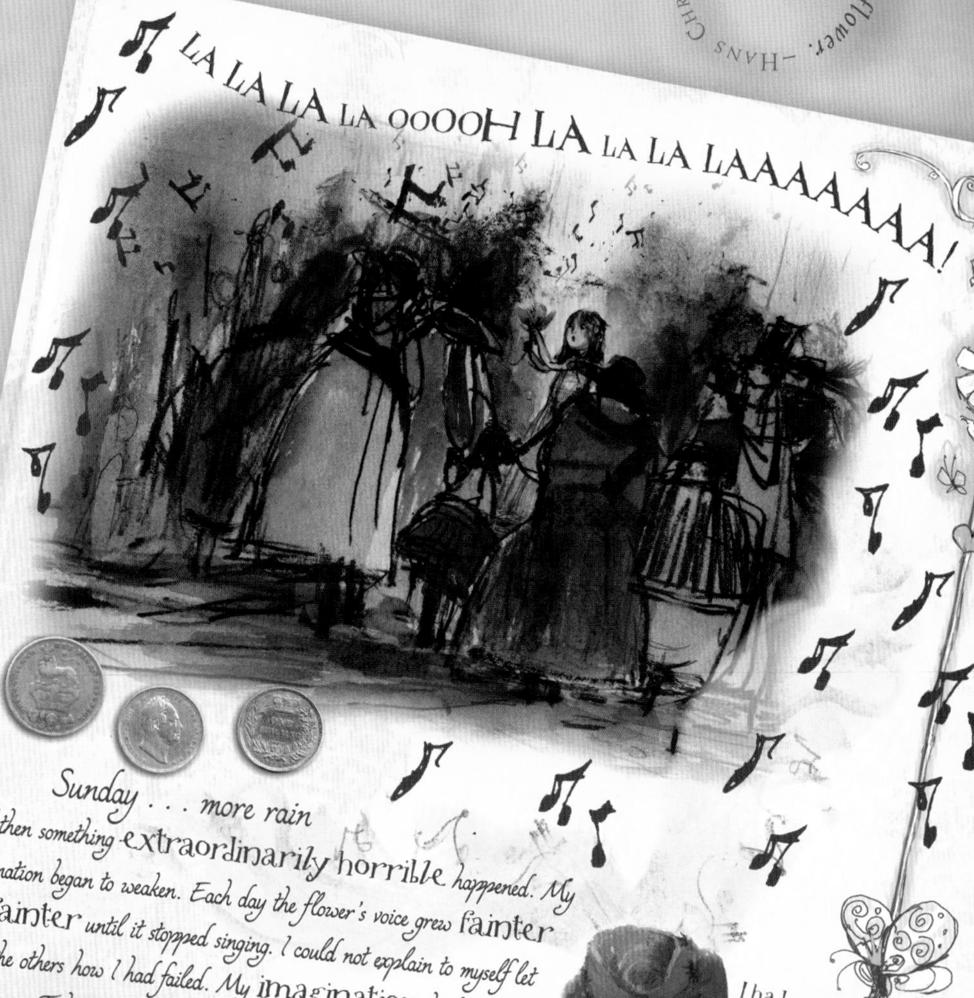

LA LA LA LA OOOOH LA LA LA LAAAAAAAA!

Sunday . . . more rain

And then something extraordinarily horrible happened. My imagination began to weaken. Each day the flower's voice grew fainter and fainter until it stopped singing. I could not explain to myself let alone the others how I had failed. My imagination had always been with me. To have it fade was like losing my last connection to Wonderland. To eat, we all had to go back to stealing food from the markets. One day we were caught by a pack of London bobbies. The other kids escaped but I was nabbed and taken to the most frightening place I had ever seen,

The Charing Cross Orphanage.

I never saw Quigley again, though I still look for him.

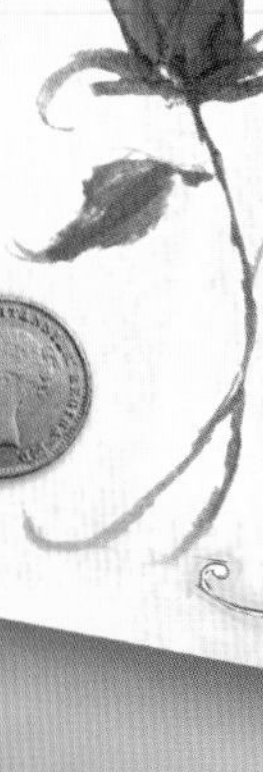

I had named the flower Tralaaa. She truly loved to sing and I will always remember the last few notes of her last song...

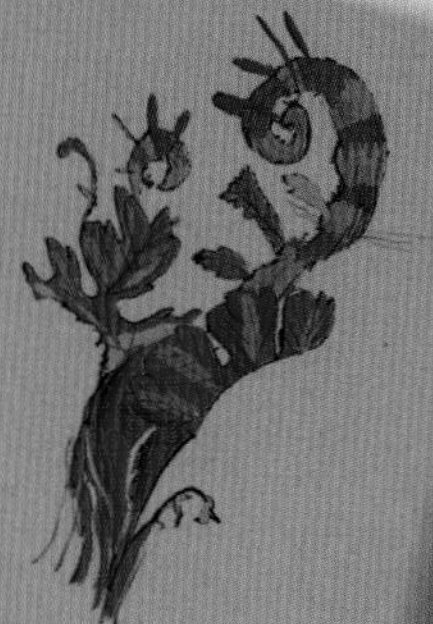

Correct handling of flowers refines the personality. –Bokuyo Takeda

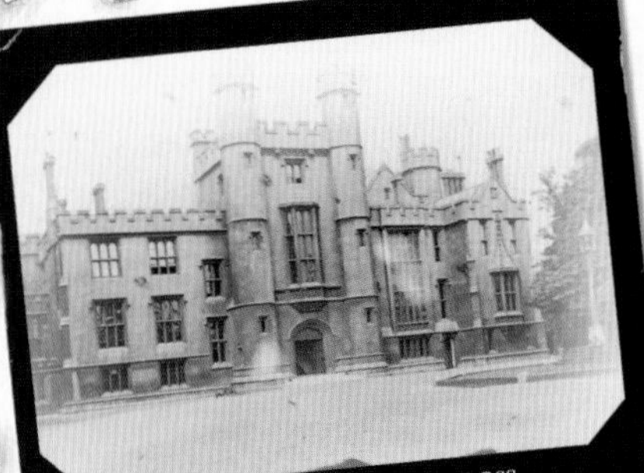

LONDON'S CHARING CROSS

Worlds collide in this document dated May 24, 1859, where a man of science, Dr. Williford, the physician at London's Charing Cross foundling hospital, unknowingly examines a princess from another realm. When asked where her family is, she insists they are in a place called "Wonderland." The doctor's keen eye noted the unusual qualities of the child, but his mind could not open to the concept of "Wonderland". Dr. Williford comments that if her oddness can be contained the wardens have high hopes for placing her in a family of good standing because "the child obviously has quite exceptional bloodlines." Indeed.

Monday sunrise

When I was delivered to the orphanage I erupted into a terrible screaming temper tantrum. **How dare they????** *This place is certainly not meant for children, it must be a* **prison** *for something exceptionally evil and nasty. But I was wrong, children were everywhere and the only things evil and nasty were the* **nasty ward mistresses** *with their stiff collars and drab skirts weighed down with bundles of heavy keys to lock the doors that keep us all from* **running away.**

CCC

Record, Charing Cross Foundling Hospital

Date of Entrance: May 24, 1859

Name of Child: Alyss Heart

Age: Seven Years

Height: 135 cm

Weight: 33 kg

Hair Color: Brown

Physical Condition: Child is healthy and has a luminous coloring. The fabric of her dress is finer than any silk and yet so strong as to repel all stains and misc. damage with the exception of one vicious gash.

History of Parents:

Name of Father: ~~Living~~, Dead

Maiden Name of Mother: ~~Living~~, Dead

Residence: Unknown

Birthplace: Unknown

Dr. Williford

Date: May 24, 1859

Remarks: Has a willful, imperious attitude and intense aversion to felines. Insists that her parents are in a place called "Wonderland." However, as long as her oddness can be contained the wardens have high hopes for placing her in a family of good standing as the child obviously has quite exceptional bloodlines.

Tuesday

I look forward to **escaping into my dreams** each night, but even this has became unbearable because my dreams now have a very **unwelcome visitor** . . .

THE CAT!

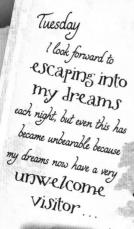

One night I decided that rather than being frightened of what was chasing me, I would imagine that I was running toward something **BEAUTIFUL**.

Each night it sneaks into my sleep and invades my dreams with its growlss hisses and hot, stinky cat breath!

here were endless doors lining he halls and I imagined I ould find my mother if I opened the **very last door**.

But when the door opened, instead of seeing her I saw all her favorite **flowers**.

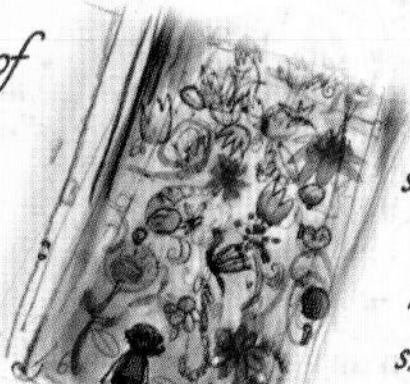

And I could smell her favorite perfume. It smells very **PINK** and **I love it**.

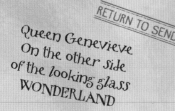

RETURN TO SENDER

Queen Genevieve
On the other side
of the looking glass
WONDERLAND

Dreams are only **night-mares** if you let them do what they wish.

Look deep into nature, and then you will understand everything better. –Albert Einstein

I hoped the rain had come from Wonderland so the PUDDLES would take me HOME.

Wednesday

I was adopted by a very dull and unimaginative family named Liddell and brought to live in their home in Christ Church, Oxford. Living in a home was very different from living in a palace, and I found it difficult to adjust, as I believe ANY princess would.

'Alice' and her sisters Edith and Lorina at Christchurch, photographed by Charles Dodgeson

Everything was so small and smelled rather of burned vegetables, while my bedchamber was just ridiculous. THE BED DIDN'T EVEN FLOAT! How could I even begin to get a perfect night's sleep???? The Liddells refuse to believe in Wonderland or that a real princess could come to their world and even though I repeatedly corrected them, they insisted on changing my name to Alice.

HOW RUDE!!!!!

Uncertain of their adopted daughter's bloodlines and wishing to make a suitable marriage (a prince perhaps???), the Liddells chose to keep her origin top secret by destroying all records of the adoption, even going so far as to forge an even going so far as to forge an "Alice Liddell" birth certificate, which modern genealogical forensics easily exposed to be false! The child was simply not born in this world.

REGISTRATION DISTRICT: Westminster ...in the County of Londo[n]

Birth in the Sub-district of Westminster

1 Name, if any	2 Sex	3 Name and surname of father	4 Name, surname and maiden surname of mother	5 Occupation of father	8 Signature, description and residence of informant	9 When registered	10 Signature of registrar
Alice	girl	Henry Liddell	Lorina Hann Reeve	Dean of Westminster School	Humphrey Ward Westminster, London, England	1852	Humph[rey] W[ard]

Hope and fear cannot alter the seasons. —Chogyam Trungpa

Adopt the pace of nature: her secret is patience. –Ralph Waldo Emerson

My unimaginative Oxford family.

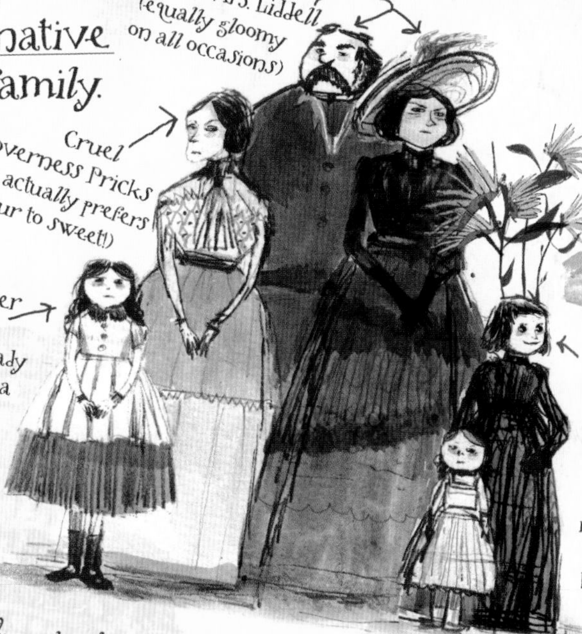

Mr and Mrs. Liddell (equally gloomy on all occasions)

Cruel Governess Pricks (she actually prefers sour to sweet!)

Proper sister Lorina (a grown-up lady in the body of a little girl)

AND ME. If it weren't for my hollizalea headdress and mini rainbow cloud I should fear becoming just like them!

Baby Edith (there may still be hope for her)

Thursday full moon!

In Wonderland I always remembered my dreams. Why am I unable to remember my **dreams** *now . . . ? Aha! I was not sleeping in a dreamgown! When I inquired of Mrs. Liddell when I would be fitted for my* **dreamgown** *she looked alarmed. I explained that in* **Wonderland** *there were special gowns in which you slept to capture your dreams. I had closets full of dreamgowns in Wonderland but requested only* **ONE** *for here. I thought I was being quite modest, but Mrs. Liddell opened her mouth very wide and shouted at me, "You must* **STOP Your incessant impossible imagining.** *Really now, I think you dream too much as it is,* **ALICE!"** *Dream Too Much??? How sad to think that anyone could ever dream* **TOO MUCH.**

I spent the rest of the day locked in my dark little dungeon of a bedroom, imagining and drawing dreamgowns . . .

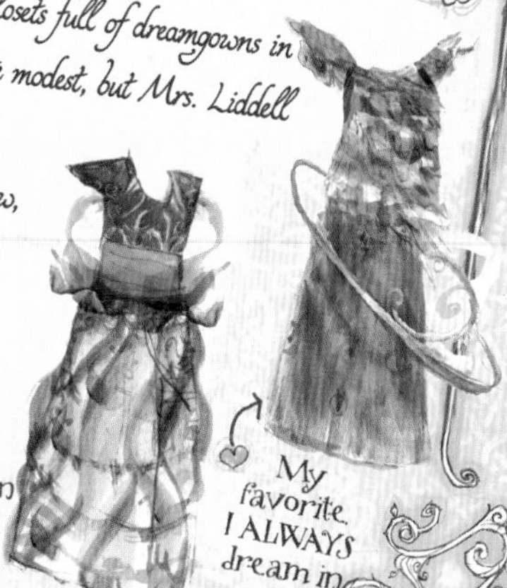

The dreams would be reflected on the gown the next morning so you wouldn't forget ANYTHING important.

My favorite. I ALWAYS dream in color.

Earth laughs in flowers. –Ralph Waldo Emerson

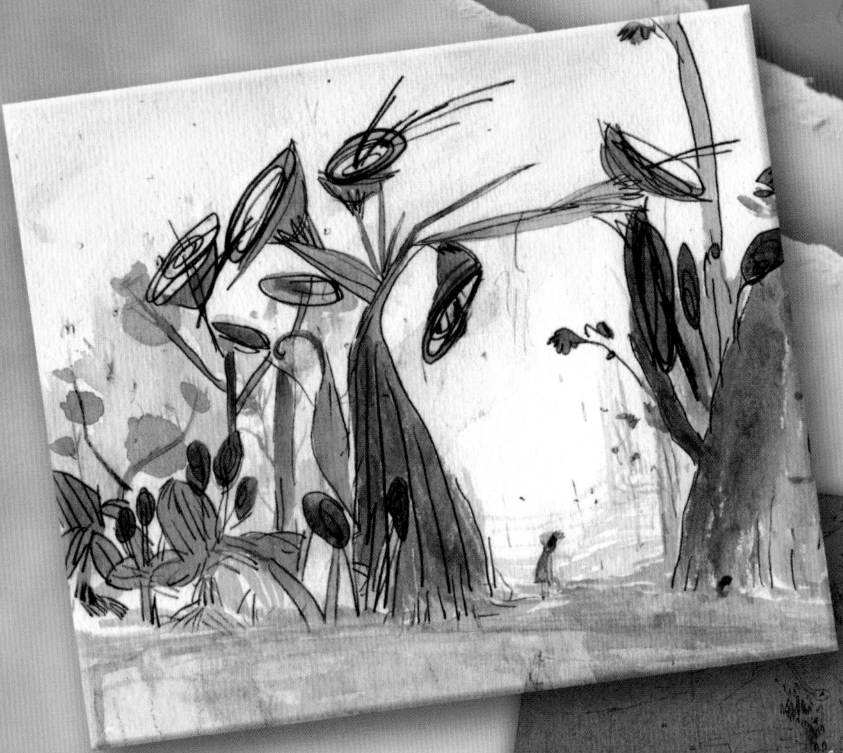

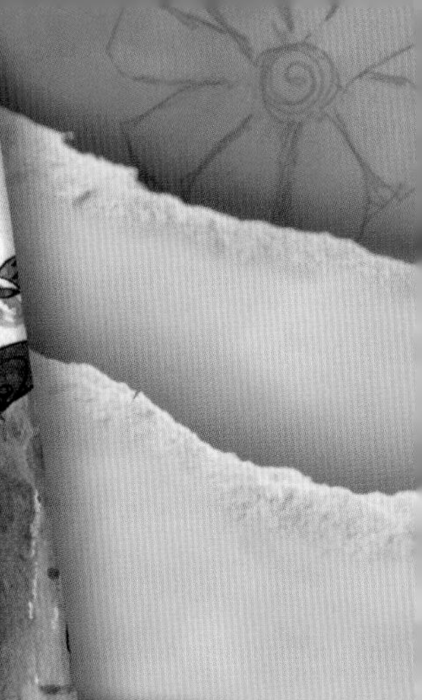

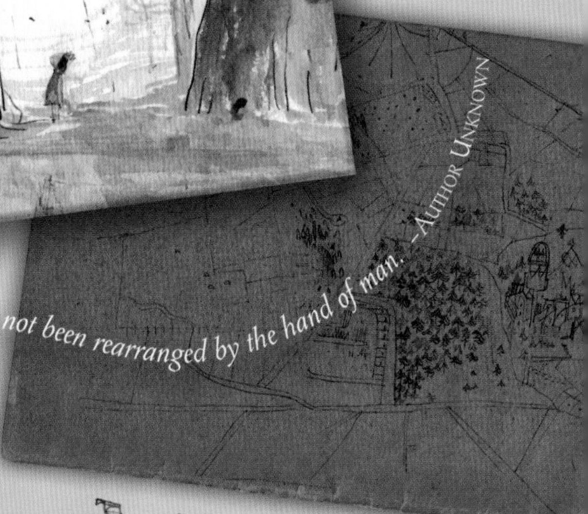

The human spirit needs places where nature has not been rearranged by the hand of man. –Author Unknown

Wonderland

by Alyss Heart

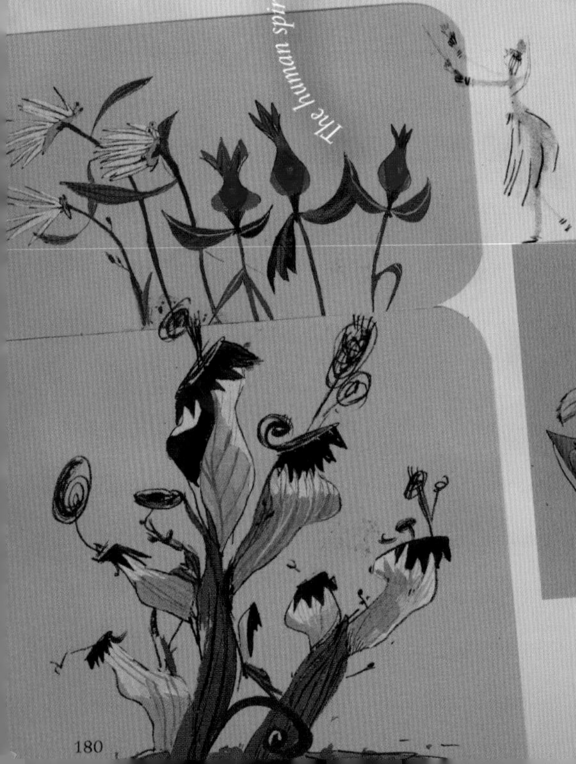

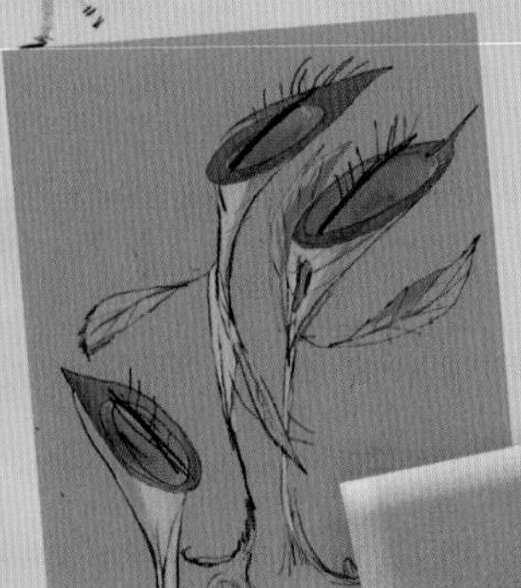

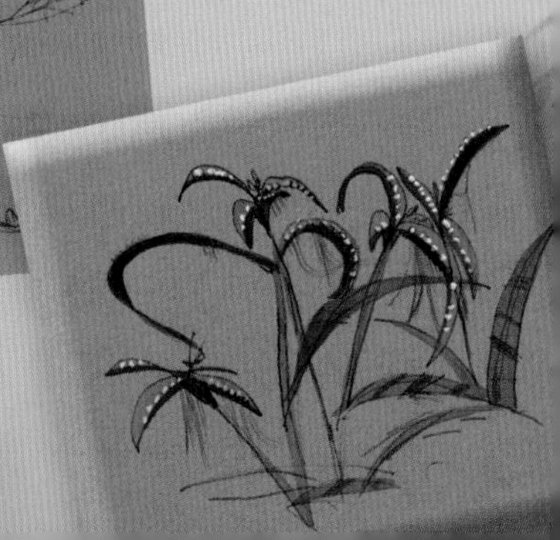

Everdear Mother,

I have been looking for you in every looking glass but I cannot find you! Please knock or call out loudly if you see me passing by the looking glass you are behind, because I am afraid I will never find you and I am so lonely for you. I miss you but I am trying to be brave and strong and remember all the ways a princess must behave to be a good queen.

I love love LOVE LOVE LOVE LOVE you you you YOU

Alyss

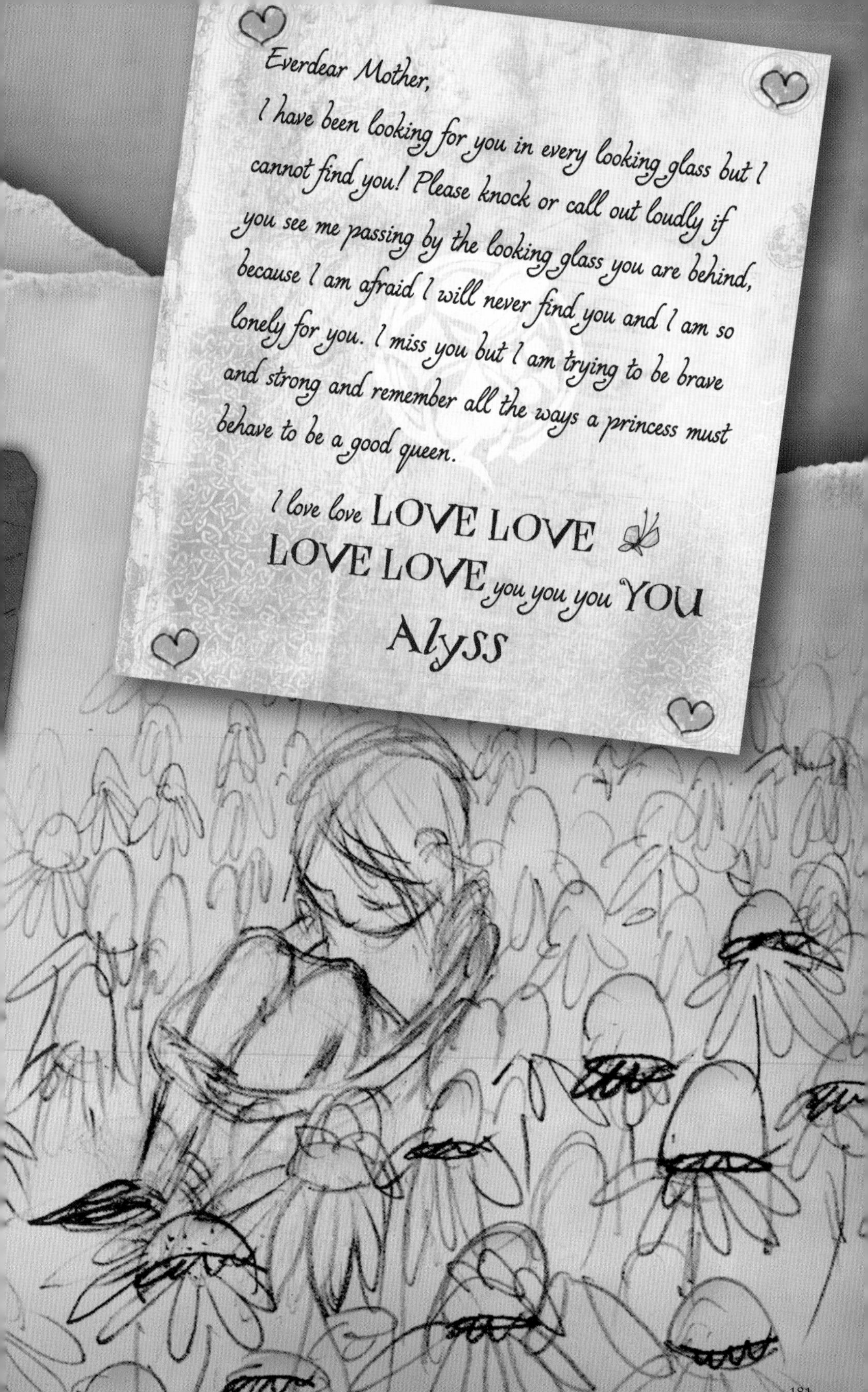

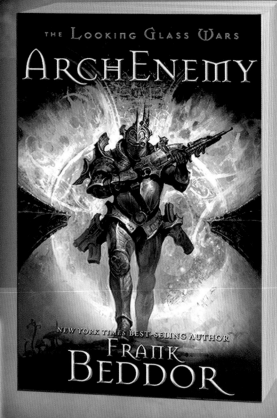

Turn the page for a special preview of

ARCHENEMY

Book Three in the Looking Glass Wars® trilogy.

PROLOGUE

Oxford, England. 1875.

Alyss of Wonderland raced up the front walk, using her imagination to unlock the door and turn the latch. Inside the house, nothing had changed. The umbrella stand and hat rack, the family pictures hanging in the hall, even the gouge in the baseboard marking where she'd thrown her ice skates one winter afternoon: Everything was exactly as it had been when she'd lived there . . . so long ago, it seemed.

"Please, what do you want?" the dean's voice reached her from the back of the house.

She sighted them in her imagination's eye: the dean and Mrs. Liddell, Edith and Lorina. Their clothes a good deal ripped, they huddled together on the drawing room sofa in fearful silence while

Ripkins—one of King Arch's bodyguards, and a deadly assassin—stood ominously before them. Ripkins: the only Boarderlander who could flex his fingertips, pushing deadly sawteeth up out of the skin in the pattern of his fingerprints.

"Please," the dean said again.

Fingerprint blades flexed, Ripkins moved his hands fast in front of him, shredding air. Mrs. Liddell flinched. The assassin took a step toward the dean, the sisters each let out a sob and—

"Hello?" Alyss called, walking directly into the room. She had imagined herself into Alice Liddell's long skirt and blouse, her hair in a tight bun. "Excuse me, I didn't know there was company."

She tried to look startled—eyes wide, mouth half open, head tilted apologetically—as she thought her double would. Wanting to catch Ripkins off guard, she pretended to be meek, cowed, and let him grab her and push her toward the Liddells.

Where he'd touched her, there was blood.

Ripkins' hands became a blur in front of him, churning air and moving in toward the dean's chest. Alyss had no choice but to expose her imaginative powers in front of the Liddells. With the slightest of movements, she conjured a deck of razor-cards and sent them cutting through the air.

Fiss! Fiss, fiss, fiss!

In a single swift motion, Ripkins spun clear and unholstered a crystal shooter, firing a retaliatory cannonade. Alyss gestured as if wiping condensation off a looking glass and the shrapnel-like bullets of wulfenite and barite crystal clattered to the floor.

The Liddells sat dumbfounded, their fear muted in the shock of seeing their adopted daughter engage in combat, producing otherworldly missiles out of the air—flat blade-edged rectangles resembling playing cards, bursts of gleaming bullets. She conjured them as fast as she defended herself against them, what with the intruder making expert use of the strange guns and knives strapped to his belt, thighs, biceps, and forearms.

"Father!"

A fistful of mind riders—ordinary-looking darts infused with poison that turned victims one upon the other in rage—rocketed toward the family.

Alyss threw out her hand and the weapons changed trajectory, shooting toward her. She annihilated them in midair with a pinch of her fingers, becoming like gravity itself, pulling whatever Ripkins hurled at the Liddells toward her until—

The wall pushed out a score of daggers. Ripkins, knocked backward by a steel playing card as big as a man, slammed against them and slumped to the floor.

Silence, except for the ticking of a grandfather clock.

"Oh!"

In the doorway stood Alyss' double, the woman she had, with utmost effort, imagined into being to take her place in this world: Alice Liddell who, with her gentleman friend, Reginald Hargreaves, stared at the dead assassin and Wonderland's queen. The dean, his wife, and his daughters looked from Alyss Heart to Alice Liddell and back again.

"I—?" the dean started.

But that was all he managed before Alyss bolted from the room and out of the house, sprinting until she was well along St. Aldate's Street. Certain the Liddells weren't following her, she walked briskly in the direction of Carfax Tower, toward the portal that would return her to Wonderland: a puddle where no puddle should be, in the middle of sun-drenched pavement behind the tower. But even from this distance she could see that something wasn't right. The portal was shrinking, its edges drying up fast. She started to run, her imagination's eye scanning the town.

"How can it be?" she breathed, because all of the portals were shrinking, the tower puddle already half its former size when she leapt for it, closing her eyes and sucking in her breath, anticipating the swift watery descent through portal waters, the reverse pull of the Pool of Tears, the—

Knees jarring, she landed on pavement. The portal had evaporated.

Alyss Heart, the rightful queen of Wonderland, was stranded on Earth.

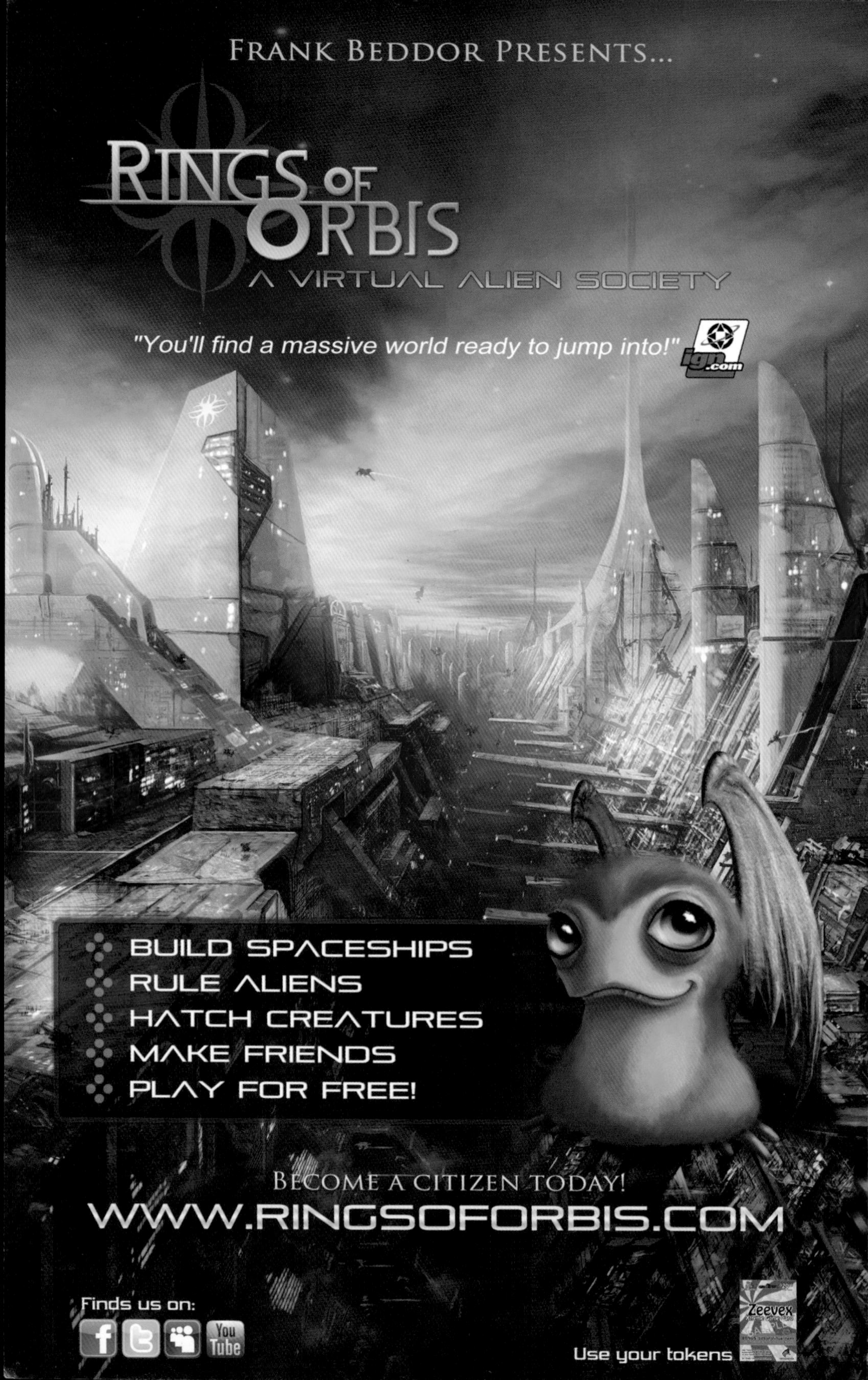

THE LOOKING GLASS
WARS
CARD GAME

Cut the Deck,
Deal Yourself in,
& Try the Game
for FREE at...

RDSOLDIERWARS.COM/LGWCARDG

roducing the first Looking Gla
game created for the iPhone..

THE
GW SLIDE
GAME

assic sliding tiles game, re-Im

lve 30 different puzzles a

ad exclusive art for your i

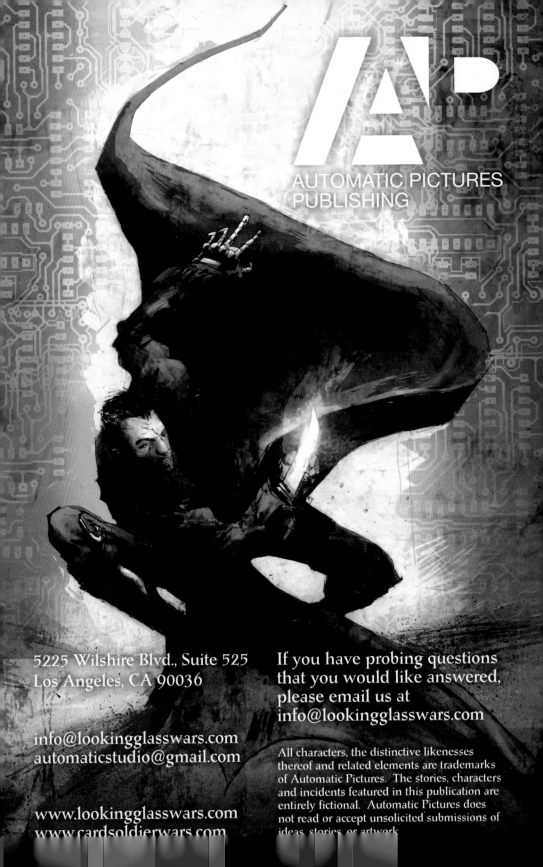

AUTOMATIC PICTURES
PUBLISHING

5225 Wilshire Blvd., Suite 525
Los Angeles, CA 90036

info@lookingglasswars.com
automaticstudio@gmail.com

www.lookingglasswars.com
www.cardsoldierwars.com

If you have probing questions
that you would like answered,
please email us at
info@lookingglasswars.com